ECKO IN THE DARK

A MIRROR WALKER NOVEL

A.C MOONEY

Hodge Publishing LLC

Conroe, Texas

info@hodgepublishing.com

ISBN/SKU:979-8-9907439-1-5

Pitch-black

Completely dark; as black as pitch.

Black

The very darkest color owing to the absence of or complete absorption of light.

Most people think that black is just a color. The darkest one, certainly… but still just a color. But not her. She knows exactly what black means. She knows the very definition of it. It is the deepest darkest color, owing to the absence of, or the complete absorption of all light. She knows that black is not really a color at all, but the absence of all color, the absence of all light. And that is where she finds herself now. In the most complete and absolute darkness, the blackest of black nights. It's a complete and utter void. ~ Ecko

Trapped on a Nightmare world and running for her life, Ecko comes to several conclusions. Oblerian is a vampire world where everything is food for something else. She's food. Whoever's in charge of the distribution of fates and destinies should be fired. Whoever wrote that prophecy about her should have every single writing utensil he owns taken away from him. Immediately and permanently.

TABLE OF CONTENTS

Scream patch
OBLERIAN
Plains
of the
Damned
Isle of
Despair
Squadron's
house

Black Forest
Bugy Forest
The Field of Screams
and Broken Dreams
Sorrow
Marshes
Dead Forest
Tangled
Woods

PROLOGUE

Run.

Run through the streets, past the shops, past the storefronts and the sidewalk merchants. Run past the strange strangers and the creepy creatures that stare after her with hate and distrust stamped upon their pinched faces. Turn her eyes away; 'see no evil'. Run past the stable with the almost (but not quite) horses, scream-neighing after her. Cover her ears and sing to drown out the sounds.

Flee! Past the butcher shop with a stink so foul wafting out of it that it causes her to gag. Cover her nose and mouth to block the stench out. Past an apothecary shop with a wooden sign that says Lekjaz the Leech, with an old fat man standing in the doorway, screaming and shaking his fist after her. "Don't you ever come back! You hear me? Don't EVER come back!"

Speed by the houses, no help for her there. Run, swift as her feet can flee, pray for wings to let her fly. Don't slow down, don't look back. Find a safe spot, a place to hide, somewhere to stop and catch her breath, to think things through.

But nowhere is safe, and everything she sees scares her. Run, run, run, run, her mind chants in time to the rhythmic percussion of her feet slapping the ground. Past crumbling, old buildings and dusty, deserted lots. Past the abandoned, broken homes that no longer have families to care for them, and never will again.

Run. Escape the alarming queerness, the alienness of this strange new world. Never mind that *she* is the alien that has crash-landed on *their* homeland. Run until the scent of salt in the wind blows into her face. Realize that the roaring in her ears is not the sound of her oxygen-starved blood as she'd first thought, but is in fact the sound of the sea, calling her, beckoning her to its shore. Follow the sound of the waves dancing over the sand and shells, all those abandoned sea creature homes.

Run ever faster, until the sands of the beach come into view. Cry out in dismay at the unwelcoming sight that greets her. She hoped for at least an illusion of safety and comfort, wished for crystal blue waters and the sun shining down to create thousands upon thousands of twinkling sparkles upon the surface. Instead, she's greeted by nighttime waters, dark and mysterious, screaming in such a loud whispery voice that there's no pretending that it's not a dangerous and deadly place.

"Come in," it whispers, crooning into her ears with its soft, gently lapping voice. "Come in and let it all go. I'll carry you away, free you from all your troubles. I'll soothe your every heartache." She turns her face away, block out the temptation, ignore the call from the depths of the sea. She drops down onto the sand instead, chest heaving, the air harshly tearing in and out of her lungs. If she doesn't catch her breath, she may as well answer that call and walk right out into the ocean. She wonders which would be worse, dying from drowning or from suffocation.

Five minutes creep by, and then ten. Finally, her heartbeat has calmed, slowed back down to a normal pace. Her breath moves in and out smoothly, steadily. Lying there looking up at an empty sky, Ecko fights to regain control over her mind, her emotions, and her own personal demons. She checks the padlocks on all the cages and boxes in her mind. The monsters trapped within are all roaring and screeching for release, rattling their chains, and heaving themselves against the walls of their prisons. It takes every bit of her strength, every ounce of determination she can muster to clear her mind and calm her heart.

Once everything and everyone has settled back down into the grudging, uneasy truce that has allowed them all to coexist thus far, the monsters go back to sleep, grumbling and snarling every step of the way. When they're finally quiet and she can think once more, the words that her father had written for her, the dream he'd had of her mother fills her mind. She wonders if she'd just run the same exact escape route that her mother had taken all those years ago, from that terrible, filthy house all the way here to the ocean.

Could this be the same spot that her mother had fallen down onto the sand? Was this where she'd opened the mirror and sent her baby girl away? Was this the very spot where her mother's mind broke, where she'd lost her will to live and had finally given up the fight? Were her own knees even now, pressing into the invisible indentions that her mother's knees had made all those years ago?

She recalls that the last thing her mother had seen was an island. The Isle of Despair, she'd called it, where the most shattered and broken lost souls go to wait out eternity. She sits up and looks out over the water, her eyes skimming over the surface until they find land. It truly is an island of despair. The very instant that her eyes find its shores, she remembers every sad thing she'd ever seen, feels every hurt she'd ever felt. Her mind replays the tragedies, reminds her heart of every single arrow of sadness that had ever pierced it.

Melancholy grips her heart tight in its clutches. It whispers hopeless nothings in her ears, promises sweet oblivion within its gentle embrace. A mournful song of sorrow sings through her very soul and threatens to swallow her up in defeat as tears course down her face. She has never felt such intense pain, such overwhelming sorrow. She can't stand it. She just wants it to stop. She wants to end it all, make all the pain finally, forever, go away. She wants to lie down and let the waves wash over her and carry her out to sea.

Intent on doing just that, she just happens to glance down and see the message written in the sand. Just three little letters, but they break the hold that the Isle of Despair had on her.

RUN.

That's all it takes to shake her out of the island's terrible, deadly clutches. Her head snaps up, searching for the messenger. She doesn't immediately see anyone else on the beach, but then her eyes pick out the faint outline of someone (or something) coming towards her from the direction of the town that she'd just fled.

She has three choices. She can sit right where she is and wait for her pursuer(s) to catch up and take her prisoner. She can walk out into the sea and let the waves take her. Or she can get up, move her butt, and fight. The images of a frantic Charlie and a distressed Susan, whom she'd unwillingly abandoned, pops into her mind and it fills her heart with determination, strengthening her resolve to find a way back home. She *must* find her way home to save her dear friends.

She also has to bring her sister back here too, back where she belongs. Or, better yet, she just needs to stop her, put her down like the rabid animal she is. She must find a way to put an end to Samara's evil. She can't do that if she gives up. So she stands up, brushes the sand from her hands and the tears from her eyes as she quickly makes her way down the beach, away from whatever it is that's decided to come after her.

The tiny, heartbroken creature lying on the shore of the Isle of Despair lifts her head up, her ears perking up for a split second. For a moment she thought, no she felt ...not recognition exactly, but *something*...some sort of connection to the girl-person across the big, salty tear-water. She watches as the girl gets up and hurries away, and whatever spark of curiosity, whatever connection she'd thought she felt goes with her. The soft little ears that hadn't been stroked in so many years droop as she lays her head back down onto delicate paws. The never-ending tears roll down her face and soak into the sand as her sighs of longing join the salted air. A puff of wind carries her breath, heavy with the scent of her sadness and longing across the expanse of the sea, right into the face of the girl that's running for her life.

The girl stops and glances back at the island for just a moment, before continuing on her journey. Unbeknownst to either of them, something had just happened. Something had been set into motion, although only time would tell the story of what was to come.

1

THIS LITTLE LIGHT OF MINE

ECKO

Listening to the steady thud of her feet pounding against the sand, Ecko's mind gets lulled into a meditative, semiconscious state of awareness. Her thoughts drift here and there, flitting about like a butterfly touching down briefly on a memory, before fluttering off to select a new memory-flower to sample. She remembers with sudden, vivid clarity, the first time she saw her father's face. She'd only been an infant, but she remembers him sitting on that bench in the park the day that they met. She'd had no idea, up until this exact moment, that her mind had somehow, miraculously retained the memory of it.

She remembers how sad and lost she'd been, crying her tiny heart out because she'd known that she was losing her mother. They had already said their goodbyes, and all that remained was for her to be handed off into the arms of a new caretaker. Her little heart felt as if it were breaking... so much fear and despair, so much pain to have to bear at such a tender young age. But then *he* lifted her up into his arms and the clouds parted, so that the moonlight shone down on his face.

The world around him had become so vivid, so *alive*, even in the darkness that surrounded them. The night was absolutely brilliant, lit up with colors that humans don't have the capacity to see, shades and hues that their limited brains cannot process. "It's ok, little one. I'm here now. I'm here." That deep, soothing voice that sounded like music, made her catch her breath and listen, and that's when her eyes met his. He smiled down at her, and in that moment... the very moment that her heart claimed his, was when her mother's spell snicked into place.

The flame-colored tufts of curls on her head muted... still vibrantly red, but the intensity and luster of it dimmed down to a color that was much more acceptable for her new environment. Her sparkling emerald eyes turned a more subtle shade of jade, and her mind hid her ability to see the extra colors in the spectrum, and then it buried all the memories of her short life that had come before that precise moment in time. She forgot her mother's face, forgot the sound of her voice. *He* became her entire world, this new father of hers.

She became, for all intents and purposes, a normal, human child. Only she wasn't normal. She would *never* be considered normal, especially not when compared to other human children. She remembers the first time that she saw things... *impossible* things in the mirror. Oh, she hadn't known at the time that they were impossible. How could she have? She'd been just a baby. It wasn't until she'd grown older that she realized no one else could see the things that she saw. But impossible or not, she *had* seen them. She can still remember the first time, that rainbow-hued world with its beautiful people and fantastical creatures.

Fast forward a few years and Ecko's still gazing into mirrors, obsessively almost. Searching, *always* searching for something, for someone, for some place. She never understood what it was that she'd been looking for, hadn't even been conscious of the fact that she *was* searching. Oh, but she had been. She'd been searching all along for all the things that she'd been missing, all the things that she'd forgotten.

She thought she'd found it when she met the girl in the mirror, the one who looked just like her... Samara. She'd lived on a very bad world and Ecko had high hopes of somehow rescuing her... until she'd gotten to know her, that is. That other girl was bad too, just as rotten as the world she lived on. She'd killed Squishy the fishy. She'd made Sigmund the teddy bear come alive and take a bite out of her. Samara had tormented her for years, breaking her things and threatening to do her and her family harm... and she'd somehow done it all from her own side of the mirror. Never once did she ever step through the looking glass to Ecko's side… alt-hough that terrifying fear had been one of her constant compan-ions in those days. Then the Bad Thing happened… the night that Samara had made the dolls come alive. The night that she'd mur-dered Ecko's entire family. The night that Ecko lost it all, lost her *everything,* her family, her home, her innocence. Even her sanity abandoned her.

Her mind hastily skips past the time spent in the psychiatric ward, those three hellish years filled with drugs and nightmares and dreams of Red Doors and a complete avoidance of all things shiny enough to show a reflection. No more mirror watching for her.

The butterfly in her mind steers clear of that area, disliking the scent wafting up off of those particular memory-flowers. It settles instead on thoughts of Charlie's beloved face, time-worn and wrinkled and filled with a light that shines bright as a star in the nighttime sky. He'd been her only light in that dark, endless night. Then Susan, the sweet, little old lady that had captured Charlie's heart and then somehow snuck into hers. Those two beautiful souls had worked so hard to help her, to keep her grounded and sane and determined to succeed, until she could get herself out of that hell-hospital. And once she was out, they'd given her a home. They'd given her a family.

It wasn't long afterwards that she'd stumbled upon a clue left behind by her father. That clue had led to another clue, and then another and another… secrets that he'd taken with him to the grave. She'd followed his breadcrumb clue-trail and eventually learned the painful truth… that Daniel Roberts was *not* her father, after all. She learned that her real father was a despicable, hateful monster and that she, herself wasn't any more human than her monster-father was.

She found that she didn't even belong on Earth at all. She discovered that the other girl, the mean one who looked like her was actually her twin sister and that the two of them had been separated by their own mother, a mother who had given her life to save her daughters from the unimaginable horror of living a life with their monster-father, the Lokskell. She discovered who she was, or at least who she was meant to be, a Wandelaar… a Mirror Walker from a world called Irredarr. She learned that she had magic locked up inside of her… a great, deep well of magic and an even greater responsibility to use it for good, to right the wrongs that had been set into motion long before her birth.

She remembers when it happened, when it all came back to her and how it felt to have all that magic unleashed and crashing through her. On her 18th birthday, the tattoo that her mother placed on her ankle had disappeared and her magic had burst free of the suppression spell that had been embedded into the ink. It had been a spell to keep her hidden, to keep her safe until she was old enough… *strong* enough, to defend herself. With the return of her magic, she could suddenly see the colors again, and oh, how she marveled and giggled with delight at the beauty that she beheld with her new eyes.

But it had been a short-lived celebration, because the magnitude of power inside of her had expanded and swelled until it all became too much for her to bear. It had overwhelmed her and in the confusion, she'd accidentally opened up a mirror to another world… a terrible, harsh and unforgiving world, her twin sister's world. And standing there on the other side, just waiting for that very thing to happen, was Samara, grinning that sinister, hateful smile.

Before she knew what was happening, her sister was rushing forward, trying to come over to *her* side of the mirror, into *Ecko's* world. The two girls struggled, one determined to come through, the other equally determined to keep her out. They were evenly matched, neither one able to overthrow the other… until Susan had walked into the room and saw what was happening. Samara had used the distraction to switch tactics, to *pull* instead of *push*. With Ecko thrown off balance, Samara had easily been able to pull her through the mirror… into her room, on her world. Then she had successfully, *gloatingly* stepped through to her sister's world, effectively switching their places.

Or course, she hadn't stopped there. Oh no. That would have been too easy… too merciful. Samara had then sent her own magic back through to shatter the one and only mirror that remained on the world that Ecko was now trapped on. Without a mirror to travel through, Samara knew that her sister would be trapped there for all time, stuck on a horrid world where monsters abound… and she would be trapped where the biggest, baddest monster of them all could, and undoubtedly *would* do all in his mighty, villainous power to hunt her down and capture her.

Ecko had already had two of the ugliest freaks imaginable try to imprison her and carry her directly to her monster-father… the Lokskell, also known as the Shadow Lord. She'd managed to escape her two hideous, would-be Ecko-nappers, but she'd taken one look at the rundown little town with its unwelcoming and downright terrifying townspeople and decided that it was *not* the place for her.

She'd immediately chosen a direction at random and then ran for her life… just as fast as she could make her legs move, in order to escape all the frightful things she was witnessing. The path she'd taken had led her straight to an ocean with miles and miles of endless beach for her to run across in her attempt to stay ahead of her pursuers.

Now she's exhausted, more tired than she's ever been in her entire life. Her body and her mind haven't had time to heal from the ordeal of being short circuited by gaining her magic too quickly or from the trauma of being thrust into this new, terrifying world. Her head still aches from the blow that the nasty creatures had dealt her too. She needs a break, desperately. So, she stops running and drops down onto the sand to rest, for just one minute.

That's all she allows herself. Whoever is tracking her hasn't made any headway in catching up to her, but they also haven't given up either. She's fairly certain that her pursuers are the foul creatures from Samara's house. Well, one of them anyway. At first it had looked like there were two pursuers, but now whenever she looks back, it appears to be only one. Hopefully the other one has given up and hasn't decided to go find reinforcements instead.

If the one that's still trailing her somehow catches up, she may still have a chance of winning in a fight. At least it would be a little more fair, one against one, and all that. Not that she plans on letting it catch up to her, or even fighting fair if it comes down to it. She's already filled her pockets with sand to blind it with, and she has the knife that she'd taken from the house. She prays that she won't have to use it, but she knows all too well what being a prisoner feels like and she wants no part of it, not ever again.

Something tells her that the time she'd spent locked up back home would seem like a picnic in the park on a nice, sunny day compared to being a prisoner here on this world. Thoughts of being kidnapped and taken to the Shadow Lord strike pure terror in her heart and she leaps back to her feet and pushes herself onward. It doesn't matter that she's tired and her muscles are sore or even that her head is pounding. It doesn't matter that she's scared and lost and completely alone with absolutely no clue where to go or what to do. What does matter is getting out of here and finding her way back home. That's *all* that matters.

She's been alternating between jogging and walking to conserve as much energy as possible, for as long as possible. But she's been at it for hours now, and she realizes that she'll have to think up a better plan. She can't walk forever; she'll eventually have to stop and rest. She'll need food and sleep. She already has to pee, but the thought of going out here, just… all out in the open, creeps her out. Just because she can't see anyone, doesn't mean that they can't see her. She needs shelter, something to hide behind, a tree, a bush, maybe even a tuft of thick, tall grass.

But there's *nothing*, nowhere to hide. This beach seems to stretch forever, an endless expanse of water on her left side and nothing but sand in every other direction, as far as her eyes can see. There's no end to it in sight either, no break in the terrain, nowhere to hide. She imagines that this must be how Sara had felt when she'd first made it into the Labyrinth, before she'd found that first opening. 'It just goes on and on and on.' Nothing but sand and water, rocks and shells, and the occasional dead fish-like creatures.

At least she *hopes* that they're dead. She has absolutely no desire to poke at them to make sure. Even on Earth, the things that occasionally crept up out of the deep blue seas had terrified her. Judging by the creatures that she'd seen today, *this* world's ocean life is infinitely more horrifying. If oceans could procreate, then this one would have to be the mother, and Earth's oceans would be its less-terrifying and nightmare-inducing babies.

The only thing that could be worse than *this* one would be the daddy ocean, and she shudders to think of the horrors that would swim in *those* waters. A couple of hours ago, she'd come across a large creature so freakishly horrifying that she'd immediately removed herself from the water's edge, just in case it had a family that would be coming around to look for it. It had been a nightmare mass of tangled tentacles, knobby ridges, and random patches of scales. It also had several mouths all over its body, and every one of those mouths were full of long, razor-sharp teeth. She didn't see any fins mixed in with the mess of fishy parts, but it had several clawed legs, like giant crab legs, and two huge pincher claws that looked large enough and strong enough to pinch her in half.

The image that immediately popped into her mind was of a Lobstrosity, the lobster/scorpion creatures from Stephen King's Dark Tower novels. Oh, not so much because of how it looked, but because of how big and bizarre it had been. As she'd walked past the dead creature (hopefully, please sweet baby Jesus, let it be dead) giving it a wide berth just in case, she couldn't help but picture it getting up and scuttling after her, murmuring its questions. Dad-a-chum? Dum-a-chum? Ded-a-chek? Did-a-chick? If that had happened, she probably would have been so terrified that she'd have turned around and run straight back to her pursuers so they could save her from the monstrosity. The sight of it, coupled with her wild imagination had shaken her up so badly that she had to keep checking over her shoulder to make sure that it didn't *really* get up and try to sneak up on her. She'd walked on for miles before she accepted that it wasn't coming after her, and then she'd returned to her regularly scheduled program of worrying about the other nightmares that *really* were following her.

'This world is *messed up*', she grumbles to herself as she trudges onwards. So far, everything she's seen here has been scary and/or downright unpleasant. Where's all the ding-dang plants? Where's all the color? Back in the town, she'd seen nothing to indicate that this world has anything of beauty to offer. The buildings and houses had all been in various states of disrepair and everything had been dim and dingy, with sort of a dusty feel, as if all the colors had been sand-scrubbed away long ago.

It's dark here too, but 'dark' isn't truly the right word to describe it. It isn't nighttime, but it certainly doesn't seem to be daytime either. When she first made it here to the ocean, she'd thought that it was early evening, twilight perhaps, but it's been hours and hours and it hasn't grown any darker, or lighter for that matter. There is no sun visible, no moon, no stars or clouds. She can't even say that 'overcast' is the correct description. There's merely a big, empty, twilight sky. Not black and not blue either, but both somehow. If she had to choose a color it would be grey, although that isn't quite right. If depression was a color, *that* would describe it perfectly.

…And what the *heck* is that noise?

There's a steady, thrumming sound coming to her from far off, a heartbeat that she can somehow *feel* deep inside of herself more than she can hear with her ears. It's oddly familiar, but she just can't seem to place it, can't remember where she'd heard/felt it before.

She almost misses the new message, had almost stepped right on it! She'd been looking out over the water, watching some sort of ocean-beast dip in and out of the waves, while murmuring a little prayer to the powers that be to keep it, whatever *it* is, out there in the water where it belongs. She'd just switched back to sand-watching, instead of sea-watching, just to add a bit of variety for her viewing pleasure, when she notices the peculiar message scratched into the sand just like the last one had been. T.U.R.N. >>>> She immediately freezes in place, with one foot lifted in the air and doing a little dance, arms pinwheeling wildly to keep her balance.

She takes a step back and slowly turns herself in a complete circle, eyes straining to see… anything other than what she'd been seeing for these past several hours. There's nothing to see, other than the great big sea, but *someone* had left that message. The real question of the day though, is it meant for her? Ok, questions, plural. Who wrote it, and how did they leave it without her seeing them? Is the messenger a friend or an enemy? Are they watching her now, somehow? And for the bonus round, the 'win the money or lose it all' question; Should she follow the directive or ignore it and continue following the shoreline?

She rubs at her forehead as she glares down at those seemingly innocent letters. She can't seem to think her way around this strange, new predicament. Her head aches mercilessly. Her legs and back are practically howling in agony from overuse, and her mouth couldn't be any drier or grittier if she'd spent the last hour licking a chalkboard.

She shrugs off her backpack, plants her butt in the sand, and glares down at those four, seemingly innocent, letters. She digs a bottle of water out and slowly, sparingly sips at it while she struggles with indecision. Her stomach rumbles, momentarily distracting her from the problem at hand with an even bigger, more important issue…food and water. How much does she have, how long will it last? She dumps everything, the whole, oversized lot of it, out of the pack so that she can take inventory: 8 bottles of water, 6 cans of sprite, a quart sized Ziploc baggie stuffed full of instant coffees and teas, 6 complete MRE's (meals ready to eat) plus 4 more packs of beef stroganoff and 4 beef stew pouches, 2 cans of Spam, 4 packages of soup mixes, 6 packs of Ramen noodles, 2 pouches of instant rice, a pouch of dehydrated eggs, a large bag of beef jerky, a tin of trail mix, a tin of saltine crackers, 2 apples and 2 oranges, 4 king sized Reese's peanut butter cups, 4 KitKats, a bag of powdered donuts, and 16 granola bars. (Don't judge! *You* try surviving years of being deprived of candy and sweets and see if you don't become a chocoholic.)

Who would have guessed that her experiences with being denied food would ever actually work in her favor? Her fear of not having enough to eat is what made her pack so much food for what was only supposed to be a 3 or 4-day (max) hiking trip. Looking down at it now, all spread out around her, it looks like so much food. A veritable feast, but she knows that it won't last long. She has enough to see her through several days, but she has no idea how long it will take to get back home. She has to make it all last for as long as possible.

With the food and water supply inventoried, Ecko quickly moves on to scrutinize the rest of her 'camping' gear. Strapped to the outside of her pack is a small tent, a sleeping bag (with an extra blanket and a 4x6 ft tarp rolled up inside of it) and her camera. Every single zipper sports some sort of keychain gear. There are 2 waterproof keyring flint match lighters, 4 different kinds of paracord survival keychains (all sporting their own survival gear items tucked inside of them) and 7, count them… *7* mini keychain flashlights because yes, she *is* terrified of the dark. Again, don't judge.

She has seen some terrifying things in her short, young life and most of them abound in the dark. She *hates* the dark and will do what she must to avoid it. The zippered pockets of her backpack are stuffed full of feminine sanitary products, and *that* had been an act of pure paranoia on her part because it isn't even close to her time of the month. But what a life saver that paranoia will be if she's still trapped here in a couple of weeks.

All that had just been the gear on the *outside* of the backpack. The inside held all the food and water, of course, 4 complete outfits (socks and undies included) then 4 extra sets of underthings because who likes wearing dirty panties? There are two pairs of thick, wool socks and 6 pairs of tiny ankle ones, also a pair of thermal underwear, a warm pair of pj's, a rain slicker and a set of warm, sturdy work gloves. Then there are 4 LifeStraw water filtration systems, 2 bottles of water purification tablets, a nifty little portable kitchen set with all the cutlery and utensils she could possibly need, a pack of foldable dishes (2 cups, 2 bowls, and 2 plates), 2 tiny folding stoves and 6 tins of canned heat to fuel them, a foldable single-serve pot and frying pan, a mini sewing kit, her toiletry bag (complete with toothbrush and paste, floss, soap, shampoo and conditioner, lotion, sunscreen, lip balm, hair brush and hair ties, and oh, thank you sweet baby Jesus, a pack of wet wipes and 2 precious rolls of toilet paper).

There's an emergency medical kit, a waterproof tin of matches, bug spray, a full sized flashlight with several extra batteries, because again, she absolutely *abhors* the dark, 2 travel sized bottles of germ-X, 100 feet of bright purple paracord, a roll of pink duct tape, a hand held, foldable shovel, a miniature bug-out bag and whatever emergency supplies *it* contains, the little case that holds her 2 bottles of required, daily medications, and 1 bottle for as-needed panic/anxiety control, a pencil pouch of random miscellaneous items (pens, pencils, paperclips and rubber bands, a sticky notepad, an odd little rubber ducky that has kitty cat ears) her cellphone and iPod and a solar powered charger to charge them both, her wallet (complete with cash, credit cards, and driver's license) a pair of sunglasses, her mother's box, and 1 Sir Didymus (which she immediately picks up and hugs to her chest.) Yeah, maybe she'd gone a tad bit overboard, gone a *wee* bit shopping happy on the sporting goods aisle. But (and there's *always* a but) as far as she's concerned, all this 'camping' gear has just been upgraded to 'survival' gear status.

She can only thank God that she'd had her backpack strapped to her back when Samara yanked her through the mirror. She shudders to think of how close she'd come to changing her mind and canceling the hiking trip. Charlie had been so upset, so worried about her going off on her own. She hates going against his wishes but she's so *very* thankful that she'd decided to do so this time. Otherwise, she would be here with no food, no water, no way to keep herself alive. Ha! The thought that her life had been saved by an act of teenage rebellion tickles her funny bone.

She can't hold back the snickers as she repacks everything back into the bag (all but her opened water bottle, a granola bar and a tiny scrap of toilet paper, because she really, *really* has to pee now.) The snickers turn into a helpless sort of giggling, but when a tiny laughter-snort escapes her, it escalates into full blown hysterics. She stuffs the last item back into her bag, snatches up the scrap of tp and runs about 15 feet back the way she'd come. Laughing throughout the entire awkward affair, she barely manages to get her jeans pulled down in time. And then she's peeing and peeing and it takes so long and her butt is just *out* there, all exposed and vulnerable.

She has a very clear mental picture of that clawed monstrosity sneaking up behind her and reaching out one of its claws to pinch her butt cheek. Dad-a-chum, Pinch-a-bum! Now she's shrieking, hysterically laughing and howling as she finishes up and buries the toilet paper (What else is she to do with it? She's not about to carry it with her, but she's no litterbug either.) She spins around to check behind her (knowing darn good and well that the creature isn't ac-tually back there preparing to pinch her bottom, but hey, you just never can tell. Stranger things can happen. Heck, stranger things *have* happened to her.) But the coast is clear, thankfully. There's nothing back there, alien sea monstrosity or otherwise.

"Teen rebellion," she blurts between her laughter-snorts. She walks back and sinks down beside her things, trying desperately to stop giggling, because she recognizes the warning signs of the on-coming breakdown. She knows that she has to take one of her 'as needed' pills in order to calm herself down, so she digs her pill case back out. Then the laughter morphs into sobs, because when she opens it… there, taped to the inside of the lid is the photo of her and Charlie that she carries with her everywhere she goes.

It's the very first one they'd ever taken together, back during that first, hopeless year in the Regal Falls psych ward. She was wearing that huge cashmere sweater that he'd given to her, just before she'd had her 'Christmas' meltdown, right before he'd gotten so mad that he'd actually broken that pervy orderly's nose. Her mental monsters are all present and accounted for in the photo too. If she looks closely enough, she can see them lurking in the depths of her eyes, hiding behind the smile that she'd plastered on her face for Charlie's sake.

She can still feel the screams that had been trapped inside, clawing at her throat, trying to rip free. She'd discarded almost every other reminder of those dark, terrible years, but not this one. *Never* this one. She'd even had several copies of it made, just in case something ever happened to this one, the original. Charlie had been her one hope, a bright, shining beacon at the top of a lighthouse, guiding her safely through the turbulent, hellish waters of her life. Even though she has thousands of better, happier photos, *this* painful, hopeful one will always be her favorite. A reminder of Hell it may be, but it's also a reminder that sometimes, even Angels will risk the hell fires to save the ones they love, even if their wings get singed and their halos melt in the process.

Big, fat tears roll down Ecko's cheeks as she lays down in the sand and buries her face against Sir Didymus. She hopes that Charlie understands why she'd decided, against his wishes, to go on that dumb hike. She hopes that he hadn't taken it as an act of rebellion, because that's not really what it was about at all. It had been more like living her life, *finally*, for herself and no one else.

She didn't want to cause Charlie worry, *never* that, but she also can't just do what everyone wants of her and nothing of what she herself wants to do.

She'd just wanted her own life, and she'd wanted Charlie to be ok with letting her live it as she saw fit. And to be perfectly honest, she'd been bored, impatient to do something, *anything* besides wait. But if she'd thought for one second that an (almost) argument between the two of them would be some of the last words they'd get to speak to one another, she would never have insisted on going her own way, even for such a small amount of time. If she'd only taken her mother's instructions seriously, been a bit more patient, waited just a little longer, she wouldn't be stuck with this terrible guilt in her heart. The thought that disappointment and worry had been the last thing she'd given him tears her up inside. Now she's bawling, she can't help it. He must be so worried about her right now. They hadn't even been able to say goodbye!

Anguished howls rip from her throat, as scalding tears of regret pour down her face. At this point there's no stopping the meltdown, so she just lets it come. She has no other choice anyway. It's too late for pills, and she's entirely too emotionally overwrought to talk herself back down. Too much had happened in too short a time period, but more than anything else, she's worried about Charlie and Susan.

Are they safe? Had Susan even been able to make him run? He wouldn't have wanted to leave the hospital, not without being 100% sure that he couldn't save her. The dear, old fool had probably stayed close by too, just in case. Had Samara found them? The track that *that* train of thought starts speeding down is not a path she can follow. It's dark, winding and twisted and fraught with danger, and the train upon it is barreling towards self-destruction.

The thoughts of what might have happened to her loved ones are just too horrifying and she cannot allow her mind to go there. She quickly hops off that thought train and boards a different one, one that's traveling down a less dangerous track with fewer, *smaller* traumatizing worries that she's better equipped to handle. But then she just shuts them all down completely. She puts an 'Out of Order' sign on every train track in her mind, so that she thinks of nothing at all while she cries it all out, releasing all the stress of the past few days.

Her new magic, her trip to the hospital and the fear of being taken and used as a lab rat, the trauma of meeting Samara face to face, and this disturbing new upheaval in her life…she lets it all out, screaming it all off her chest. After a while, the tears slow and then come to a stop altogether. She lay there, quiet and still, just staring up at the sky. She eventually settles her monsters and quiets her fears. She reminds herself that Charlie has great faith in her and that he would expect better from her right now.

She fills her heart back up with determination and hope. Yes, she's lost and alone in a harsh, seemingly unforgiving world. Yes, there are things…peopley-yet-monstery type things, and unfamiliar creatures and at least two of those people-monsters are chasing her. Yes, there's a mysterious 'message in the sand' writer that keeps trying to boss her around. And to top it all off, there may or may not be a butt pinching sea monstrosity out to get her. This is a crazy, scary world, one where she hasn't been told the rules of the game. She doesn't like it here and she wants to go home. But since she doesn't own any ruby slippers and there are no handy dandy magic beans growing on bushes and not a single Prince Charming anywhere in sight to swoop in and rescue her, she'll just have to save herself. She'll make up her *own* rules.

After a while, when she's as calm as she can possibly get, she sits back up and hugs Didymus one last time. He's all wet and soggy from her crying on him, but he doesn't mind. He's used to it. Throughout the years, his fur has soaked up thousands of her tears. "Thank you, Didymus," she whispers as she replaces him back in her bag.

She closes the medicine case back up without taking any pills. She'll take the stupid things if and when she really needs them, and not one second before. Besides, how long has it been since she'd even taken her dailies? The last time she can remember taking them was the morning of the (failed) hiking trip, the morning her magic had hit. Her *real* birthday, she reminds herself…May 18th.

Yeah, that's a strange one. She won't be able to wrap her head around *that* one any time soon. So, she's missed, at the very least, two days of meds already. She stands up and shakes the sand from her hair and clothes, then turns in a slow circle, ensuring that nothing has gotten close to her during her self-appointed time out. Her pursuer is still back there, closer, but not close enough to be an immediate threat.

She shrugs her backpack back on, picks up her water bottle and her granola bar, and glances down at the message in the sand. In the end it's pure childishness and pettiness that chooses which direction she goes. "You're not the boss of me," she mutters aloud as she steps over it and continues on the path that *she* has chosen for herself.

Grinning with pure, unashamed adolescent satisfaction, she opens her treat and stuffs the trash into her pocket. She nibbles at her snack as she walks, chewing each tidbit thoroughly to get the most out of every single bite in order to make it last longer. Eating a small amount of food slowly makes the stomach believe that it gets full faster. It's a trick she'd learned a couple of years ago, back when she'd been in the habit of hoarding food for fear of the next time it got withheld from her.

It did *not* work this time, not even close. Her stomach grumbles in protest as she washes the last bite down with her last sip of water. She absolutely *hates* being hungry. She'll make sure she eats a proper meal when she gets settled down for the night. *If* it ever gets to be night, that is. There's no telling if or when that will happen. She still has to decide how to handle *that* particular scenario, because she'll have to stop soon. She needs to refuel, eat a real meal and get some sleep.

She doesn't want to get comfortable though, just in case she has to run from...anything. She guesses that she'll have to forgo setting up her tent, even though the thought of that strikes terror in her heart. Sleeping out in the open, exposed and vulnerable, *in the dark,* is not something she's looking forward to. Logically, the tent wouldn't protect her from monsters anyway. But zipping herself up in the illusion of the tent's safety and blocking out the night with thin, canvas walls would trick her mind just enough to allow her to get some much-needed sleep.

Her stomach once again rumbles in protest, interrupting her thoughts of sleep and taking its place with daydreams of what she'll eat for dinner. Then a purely mental bell dings and the inner battle to determine who the winner will be begins. She narrows it down to two candidates, beef stew and beef stroganoff. It's a fair fight, the opponents evenly matched, but there can only be one winner and so the battle rages on and on. Intensely focused and fully invested in finding out who the victor will be, Ecko's no longer paying any attention whatsoever to her surroundings. So, it's no wonder that she goes tumbling down when her shins bang into the large boulder that's blocking her path.

"Where the heck did *that* come from," she grumbles as she sits back up and blinks the sand from her eyes and spits it from her mouth. The deafening sound of waves crashing, and a sudden feeling of claustrophobia has her scrambling back to her feet and spinning around to try and pinpoint exactly what was causing her such internal distress. Her mouth drops open in shock and her heart stutters in her chest. Trying to distract herself from her hunger and her ever-increasing fatigue had certainly become her main focus… but come on! *No way* she hadn't noticed that the whole world was changing around her!

But somehow, it *had* changed. Drastically, impossibly so. The never-ending expanse of beach that she'd grown used to having on her right side *has* ended and been replaced by a towering wall of ominous black cliffs. She estimates that there's somewhere in the vicinity of a hundred yards of sand left in front of her before the path she'd been taking dead-ends at the solid wall of rocky cliff face. The sea is still right where it's supposed to be, on her left side. But now it's *angry*, furiously hurling itself upon the cliff-face, beating itself against the jagged, black rocks in front of her.

With nowhere left to go, Ecko has no choice but to turn and go back the way she'd come, back towards her would-be kidnappers. She turns to do just that, but is once again flummoxed beyond all rational thought, because there is no beach back there either! It's gone, vanished, disappeared, evaporated into thin air, faded away, gone kaput, and every other word she can think of to explain that it's *just completely gone.* There is nothing but cliffs.

There's just about the same amount of beach left in that direction as what's now behind her. She does a 360, searching in every direction for some sort of explanation. She finds nothing. *Nothing!* No matter which way she turns, there are no answers in sight. She has somehow managed to get herself stranded on a tiny, crescent-shaped stretch of beach (about 200 yards long and 100 yards wide) completely boxed in by walls of rock on three sides and ocean on the fourth.

Before she can even try to figure out what to do, a wave comes crashing to shore and rolls up over her feet. The bottom drops out of her stomach as she realizes that the tide's coming in and will soon erase what little land remains. Will it completely swallow up her little beach? How long does she have before it's gone, claimed by the sea? In full-fledged panic mode, she runs back in the direction that she had come from, hoping against all hope that there is some sort of hidden path around the bend in the cliff. But of course not. There's just more wall, as far as she can see… and there is absolutely no beach whatsoever beyond her little bay!

While she stands there biting her lip at the impossible predicament, another wave rolls up and crashes against her ankles. Frowning down at her soaked socks and the three-inch line of moisture across the bottoms of her jeans, she realizes that she has no choice but to go up. It's either climb or swim. Easy choice when she puts it all into perspective. "Climb it is," she grumbles.

She walks back along the length of the wall, searching for the easiest route to take. There's only two ways that look even remotely passable. One leads straight to a small, round opening, an alcove or a cave about a third of the way up the wall. A cave means possible shelter for the night, but it could also mean possible monsters-in-waiting. The other path goes all the way to the top, but has three tricky spots that will be difficult, maybe even impossible to navigate. And Heaven only knows what she'll find up there at the top. What to do? What's the right choice? Where are all the bossy people telling her what to do and how to live her life when she *really* needs them? 'Come on. Come on, think! What would Charlie do?'

She turns back to check on the tide situation, to see how close the ocean had gotten in the time it had taken her to walk the length of the cliff edge. "Oh, *heck* no," she whimpers, horrified to the depths of her soul as she spins back around. Straight up to the top it is, because it's the path that's closest to her. Whatever she finds at the top can't possibly be worse than what's currently crawling out of the sea.

Bones...there is a bone person, a skeleton (man?) currently dragging itself out of the ocean. It can't stand up and walk because it's missing everything below the knees. Instead, it's lying on its chest, using its bone arms to pull itself along and it's dragging its ruined legs behind it. Its jaws constantly make the chomping motion, snapping open and closed, loudly clicking its teeth together, as if it's dreaming of chowing down on a cheeseburger. And since it seems to be staring its empty eye sockets directly at *her*, she assumes that *she's* the cheeseburger of his dreams.

'*Of course,* this world has living corpses' she thinks as she hastily begins to climb. 'Why am I surprised? Any self-respecting nightmare world just wouldn't be complete without them. Nope, wouldn't be caught dead without the animated, naked skeletons that are just *dying* to sink their teeth into something.' Her right foot slips a bit, so she blocks out thoughts of being eaten alive by a skeleton man and focuses her full attention on the utmost important problem at hand, which is successfully climbing straight up this cliff, so that she doesn't fall back down into the boney clutches of the runner-up problem.

The rocks are slippery, coated in a slimy, black, moss-type algae that makes the climb even more treacherous. Her heart pounds as she slowly and meticulously determines the safest hand and foot holds. She does not stop to look up; she doesn't want any feelings of hopelessness when she sees how far she still has left to climb. She doesn't look down either, for more than one reason. She doesn't want to know how far she'll have to fall if she takes a wrong step, but she also has no desire to see if Mr. Bonehead knows how to climb. Onward and upward she goes… slowly but surely.

"Take a breather, Ecko," she commands herself as she stops and leans against the cliff face, pressing her sweaty forehead into the cool stone for a moment. She's in serious need of a break. Her arms are trembling like Jell-O, her legs are tired and weak, not only from the strain of scaling a cliff, but also from the miles upon miles that she had traveled *before* the climb. Her breathing is too fast, and her heartbeat is thunder-loud in her ears.

She has no idea how long she's been climbing. She only knows that it feels like it's been a small eternity. At least the rocks aren't as slippery anymore. She guesses that she's reached a place high enough that the waves of the ocean never reach, because the rocks up here are fairly dry, the black algae mostly absent. There's only occasional, dried out and sickly-looking patches every so often. She wants to take a peek upwards and check her progress, because when she'd been on the ground looking up at this route, it looked like there may have been a ledge just barely big enough for her to rest upon… and it had been situated directly below what she knew would be the hardest section to climb.

She has to do it. She has to look. She *needs* to know how much further she must climb before she can rest. She takes several deep, calming breaths and murmuring a little prayer for courage and strength, she lifts her head off the wall, turns her eyes upward, and is instantly disappointed. There's a spot, about 20 feet above her, where the wall juts out several feet. It's completely blocking her view of the path above, so there's no way to determine how far she has left to go. She'd known better than to look, she really had.

"Well, break time's over," she murmurs aloud as she reaches for the next handhold. But she wasn't being careful enough. She'd assumed that there would be no more wet patches, but she was wrong. She lifts her leg for the next step up before ensuring that she's got a firm, solid hold with her hand. Her fingers slip and come away covered in muck before she can get her foot wedged firmly onto the foothold… and down she goes, slipping and sliding right back down the cliff.

Crying out, she desperately scrambles for a hold, scraping skin and tearing fingernails in the process. At last, her hand finds a solid hold and with a strength born of pure, unadulterated fear, she manages to bring her downward plunge to a halt. She does *not* take a moment to catch her breath. She does *not* wait for her heart to settle back down. She takes a single, deep breath and immediately reaches above her and starts climbing back up, *carefully* this time. If she stops now, if she lets herself think about what could have just happened, what could *still* happen, hysteria may settle in and claim her.

What could she possibly do if she has a full out panic attack while she's clinging for dear life to the side of a cliff? Nope, can't think about it. She has to clear her mind, determinedly set a new, steady pace. Carefully, cautiously, one step after another. She does a quick, mental bodycheck as she climbs to assess the damage she'd taken. Her knees and her left elbow are scraped raw, at least three fingernails had been ripped off down to the quick, and there's a cut on her forehead, right up by the hairline that's trickling blood down her face. All in all, there's nothing too terrible and it could have been so much worse.

In just a few short minutes, she makes it back up to the place she had slipped from. She sees a smear of her blood, probably from when she'd smacked her head, so she knows that this is exactly where her fall had started. She climbs past it, and eventually (finally) she makes it to the ledge that's jutting out sharply from the rest of the cliff face. She has no idea how she'll ever be able to pull herself over it, so she lays her head back against the wall. Just for a moment, just to gather her strength.

"I need you, Charlie," she whimpers as she lifts her head off the rocks and stretches an arm up over the ledge to search for something, *anything* to grab onto. But there's nothing, only empty air and smooth stone that she can't grip with her clammy fingers. Grunting with effort, she reaches further, trying to position herself up high enough so that she can see over the ledge… If she could just *see* what's up there…

A face suddenly appears, grinning down at her from above the ledge. A disgustingly, hideously, *familiar* face. The *things* that had been trailing her, the monsters from Samara's house had caught up and somehow gotten ahead of her. "Got you now, Princess," it hisses in a high, nasally voice.

So startled by the sudden appearance of the abomination, she jerks back in a purely reflexive motion, *away* from the safety of the wall. Waving her arms frantically to regain her balance doesn't do a thing to rectify her situation either. The weight of her backpack guarantees that she'll never be able to right herself. She can't even manage a scream as she falls backwards and plunges to her doom.

A pair of gnarly, filthy hands dart out and grasp her wrist at the last possible second. "Oh, no you don't! You won't escape so easily again," it crows in triumph and then snorts out a nasty, phlegmy laugh.

But Ecko doesn't hear its delighted, victorious laughter. She's passed smooth out and completely misses out on the fun of being dragged up over the ledge, tied up, and lifted the rest of the distance to the top of the cliff.

"Wake up. Oh, wake up, you filthy, lazy thing!" She comes awake instantly as the whip cracks against her leg. Her eyes shoot open and whatever the creature sees lurking in their depths convinces it to rethink repeating the action.

"Don't you hit me again. You'll be very, very sorry if you do," she says, and her voice comes out so clear, so confident, *so promising* that the creature lowers the weapon that it's holding up and takes an involuntary step back. Not that there's really anything she could have done about it if he'd decided to strike her again, not at the moment anyway. Her wrists are tightly bound together in front of her, one end of the rope held like a leash in the creature's hand.

Captured. She's been captured, and she realizes that the creature has every intention of turning her over to the Lokskell, the evil Shadow Lord… and only God knows what *that* foul man intends to do with her.

She needs a plan. She needs to escape and then find somewhere safe to hole up, somewhere quiet, so that she can search deep within herself and figure out exactly what kind of magic she possesses, as well as how to use it. What good is it if she can't even save herself from being captured? She needs a hiding place, somewhere safe to explore herself and her new abilities. For some reason, she doubts that a safe place even exists on this world.

She'll have to figure something out soon though, because there's no way she's going to stay a prisoner for long. She has no intention of going anywhere near the Lokskell. That man had given her nightmares long before she'd discovered the horrifying truth… that the vile man is actually *her father*. All she really knows is that he's spent her entire life searching for her, torturing and killing anyone that impeded that search… and that's all she *needs* to know. She does *not* want to know why he wants her or what he plans to do to her if he should ever capture her. She has no intention of finding out either. On with the plan making, so that she can get on to the escaping.

Trying to get an idea of how long she'd been unconscious and how far she'd been carried/dragged, she takes a moment to look around at her surroundings. This looks like a completely different world…again. She feels as if some sort of (cruel? merciful?) god had reached out his hand and plucked her from the treacherous edges of the cliff and dropped her down into a barren wasteland. She wonders if there'd been another of those weird location blip things... like when she'd somehow crossed over from the endless expanse of beach to the cliffs, because there's not a single trace of the ocean to be found.

It's no longer anywhere within her sight. She can no longer hear the call of the waves, nor smell the salt in the air. The terrain has once again flattened out, no longer a beach, but a sprawling expanse of plainland that stretches out as far as she can see in every direction. The words, 'The Forsaken Plains' whisper through her mind and she knows instinctively that it's what this place is called. The name fits this new terrain perfectly.

It *feels* forsaken and completely devoid of life. Just as back in the town and at the oceanside, there are no plants to be found here either, at least no living ones. Every so often there are small tufts of dried out clumps of sickly, orange colored grass, loosely clinging to the dirt around it. Even the dirt appears to be lifeless, with none of the properties of living, healthy soil. It seems nothing more than a loose, dry blanket of dust stretching for miles.

There are no bugs either, no ants, or worms, or bees, or flies even. Far off into the distance, she can see...*things*, possibly trees, standing all alone and surrounded by a void... an awful nothingness. She shivers at the feeling those 'trees' or whatever they are, evoke inside of her. She has no desire to discover just what they are either. Her intuition tells her that she needs to stay far, far away from them and insists that her mind doesn't even want to explore whatever they may be.

She's so engrossed with inspecting her new surroundings that she just about jumps out of her skin when her captor suddenly speaks up. "Then don't *make* me hit you. Get up. I'm not carrying your heavy rumpkuss, so that you can take a nap. You walk!"

She considers refusing, but quickly decides against it. She can either walk as a captive, or run as an escapee. She's too tired to run, she'll barely be able to manage a walking pace. She'll cooperate and go along for now, but once she's rested, it'll be a different story. The very moment that an opportunity to escape comes along, she's a goner.

With that decided, Ecko struggles to her feet, and Thing One (as she'd named it) yanks her forward. Thing Two is nowhere in sight, so she asks it, "Where are you taking me? What happened to your partner?" Perhaps if she got it talking, she could learn a little about this world and all the challenges that she'll be facing.

Thing One grunts, "We'll travel as long as we're able to before we have to stop and make camp. Then we'll wait for my life-mate to catch up."

That's all Thing One would disclose. No matter what questions she asks thereafter, they're all answered with grunts and hisses. She finally takes the hint and falls silent. She studies it instead, wondering just what kind of creature it is. It's hideous, that's what. A smallish male standing maybe 5 feet tall, its stature isn't overly intimidating. Although, if it could straighten its hunched back, it would easily gain at least another half a foot. Its skin is a grotesque, pukish-green color and it has patches of oily black hair upon its head, as if it's suffering from a bad case of mange.

Its deep-set, yellow eyes glare out at her from its wrinkled and heavily pocked face, and the thick, black lips do nothing to conceal the small, sharp teeth within its mouth. Large, pointy ears with tufts of black hair growing out of them jut out from the side of its head, but they don't stand upright. They look like they'd been stuck on sideways, with the sharp tips pointed towards the back of its head instead of upwards. It has a thick, long nose with huge, open nostrils (also sporting long black hairs that resemble an octopus emerging from a sea cave.) To top all those not-so-delightful attributes, it has large, clawed hands and huge, hobbit-like hairy feet. In fact, it appears to have more hair on its feet than it does on its head. The only article of clothing it's wearing is a ragged, pieced-together pair of pants that she will forever be grateful for. The hairy, filthy butt crack that she's been forced to follow behind for the past hour or so is more than she *ever* wants to see of its body.

"Stop." Thing One's sudden command out of nowhere doesn't even startle her. She's much too tired to be bothered with feelings of fear, or any other emotions for that matter. Her legs have turned to jelly, her back aches from the strain of carrying her heavy backpack for so long, and her stomach is so empty that she firmly believes that it's trying to devour itself.

"This is as far as we go. We'll camp here." he grunts. "If you behave, I will remove your bonds. Will you behave?"

She tiredly nods her head as he unties her. She's too exhausted to try anything, too tired to even speak it out loud, but she mentally mumbles, 'Thank you, sweet baby Jesus." She briefly rubs at her scraped, raw wrists before she shrugs off her pack and sinks to the ground. Thing One hisses sharply and stumbles back a step. "You can remove your body parts? How? How do you do this?"

Ecko stares blankly at him, mentally listening to the sound of crickets chirping in her head. She's got nothing. She doesn't understand what the heck he could possibly mean by that absurd, random question.

"Hu?" is all she manages to say before he points down at her backpack and responds sharply. *"That* was a part of you just moments ago, and you took it off and now it is no longer a part of you. How? Can you take off your arms, or your feet? What about your head? Surely you can't take your head off. Can you?"

Um...yeah. She's still hearing those crickets. "Are you dumb?" She can't stop them. The words just pop out of her mouth, before she can even think about trying to reign them in. She cringes as she watches Thing One's face flush with anger. It changes from his normal, puke-green color to a deeper shade, a sickly, army green. It's actually a bit (grossly) fascinating to watch.

Fearing that he'll strike out at her in anger, she hastily explains. "It's not a *part* of me. It's a bag, a pouch, to carry my things in. Like the one you have there, hanging from your belt… uh, from the rope tied around your waist. Mine's just bigger, that's all," she tells him as she snickers, on the inside, of course. She points at his own much smaller sack. He frowns as he looks from his bag to hers.

Seemingly disgusted with the whole conversation, he opens his bag and takes out a couple of furry, mutated rat-like creatures and tosses one down in the dirt in front of her. "Eat," he commands just before he crunches into his own. Putrid, black fluid dribbles down his chin as he repeats, "Eat!"

'Yeah. Not in this lifetime' Ecko thinks as she almost gags with revulsion. "Umm, no thanks. You can keep it. I brought my own," she says as she scoots away from the disgusting meal he'd provided. She struggles to open her bag with hands that are numb from being bound so tightly together for so long, but finally she manages it.

He watches curiously, and also with a healthy amount of fear, as she takes out a bottle of water, an apple, and another granola bar. As hungry as she is, she's even more exhausted and in desperate need of sleep. She'll eat her meager meal and then she's going to sleep… for twelve hours straight if she's allowed to. But somehow, she doesn't really believe that will happen. 'Hopefully it takes Thing Two a good long while to get here', she muses as she takes a healthy bite of the fruit.

Her captor had said that they were stopping to make camp and to wait for his mate to catch up, but he shows no signs of setting up a campsite. He has no way to set up a shelter, no way to make a fire. Not that she's complaining about the shelter situation. She hasn't got the slightest desire to crawl into a tent with him.

She finishes her apple in record time and has just opened her granola bar when whatever god in charge of this world decides that daytime is over and is now time for the occupants of his domain to go to sleep, immediately…this very instant. How has she come to this conclusion? Because right then, the powers that be click the lights off… with no warning whatsoever. As dimly lit as this world had been throughout the day, at least there had been *some* sort of light source, even if she hadn't been able to figure out where that light was originating from. Now, that small bit of light has just been removed and the world is suddenly plunged into absolute darkness…the blackest of black.

Most people think that black is just a color. The darkest one, certainly… but still just a color. But not her. She knows *exactly* what black means. She knows the very definition of it. It is the deepest darkest color, owing to the absence of, or the complete absorption of all light. She knows that black is not really a color at all, but the *absence* of all color, the *absence* of all light. And *that* is where she finds herself now. In the most complete and absolute darkness, the blackest of black nights. It's a complete and utter void.

She cries out sharply as a debilitating fear instantly fills her heart and her mind. She drops her food into the dirt and frantically fumbles at her bag for one of her flashlight keychains. It was a smart move on her part, to have them dangling on the outside of her bag, because within seconds, she has a thin, bright ray of hope shining outwards, holding the night at bay and preventing the darkness from swallowing her up into its depths forever. Her sigh of relief is almost as loud as Thing One's resounding screech of fear.

"Aaarrrggg! What dark magic is this? Don't you point it at me!" he shouts in total panic. "How do you conjure fire? How do you hold it within your hands and yet it does not burn you? Oh, you surely *are* a witch! I didn't believe when the Shadow Lord's other bratling child warned that you would curse us. I should have listened. I should have kept you bound up tight! I should have gagged you!"

Thing One punches himself in the side of the head repeatedly, as he mutters fearfully to himself, cursing himself for being such a fool. But after several minutes of her just staring at him in fascinated shock (and not attempting to cast a spell on him) he finally quiets. Who knows, maybe he's waiting to be turned into a toad. Since she doesn't quite know how to do that, she asks him what had just happened instead. How had it gone from daytime to nighttime so…*quickly* wasn't the right word…. instantly. How had it gone so *instantly* from daytime to nighttime? But he doesn't understand what she's asking. Her words are apparently as unfamiliar to him as the instantaneous day-to-night process was to her.

"What is this date-time that you speak of. What is night-time?" he asks her.

So, she tries again. "Well, you know, one minute we could see each other, could see the world around us and now we can't. Daytime we can see, and night is dark so we can't see each other anymore."

He snorts at her. "There is only the Pale and the Pitch, no date-time, no night-time. Are you dumb?" He sneers it at her with his whiny, nasally voice in such a way that she immediately knows he's still salty from when she'd said the same thing to him earlier. Just for that, she's not explaining what a flashlight is. Let the nasty little creature think she can melt him into a stinking puddle of green puke. Without another word, she unrolls her sleeping bag, climbs as far inside of it as she can get, and zips it up around her. With her little light shining brightly inside of her sleeping bag/make-shift tent, Ecko closes her eyes and promptly falls into sweet, blessed slumber.

2

SHE'S HERE!

The Lokskell

His eyes rove over his beauties, his lovely, dancing ladies. He admires each of them, one at a time… but only briefly, before moving on to the next. Time after time, his gaze returns to her…*always* her. All the others move to the beat of the music for him, because they must. Because he demands that it be so. *She* dances because she feels the beat inside of her. It is the only thing she has left in there other than screams.

Even now, some distant part of her mind recalls the sound of music. Perhaps it sparks memories of joy, and her body must celebrate it. It bewilders him that no amount of pain administered has ever made her stop dancing. Nothing he has ever done to her has managed to drown out the beat or silence the music in her heart. And he desires her for it. Above all else, *she* is the one that he wants to turn his attentions to…always. Whether it's his lust that he gives to her or his anger, it matters little to him. It only matters that *she* is the one he always wants to bestow them upon.

45

That's what perplexes him. He doesn't understand why he craves her so. Perhaps he wants to hear her music, feel her joy...and that enrages him. She shouldn't feel anything more than horror after all this time, after all he's done to her. But also because... joy is not meant for the likes of him. That emotion is for small, simple beings... weaklings. He forces his eyes to his next option, and although lovely in her own right, he finds his attention wanting to stray back to *her* once more...and it *infuriates* him.

At some point during this ritual, the current female companion selection process, he becomes aware of the man standing off to the side, patiently waiting in the shadows for his presence to be acknowledged. He hadn't knocked, hadn't asked for permission to enter. He's *never* knocked, and he is the only one that's lived to do it more than once. But he knows better than to disrupt any of the *activities* that may be taking place in this room when the doors are shut. So, he'd entered the room on silent feet, just as he's always done, and he stands quietly, waiting for the horrors to end, or for the Master to notice and acknowledge him... whichever may come first.

He knows well not to interrupt or try in any way to rush the Shadow Lord while he's busy with his ladies, no matter what happens or how gruesome things may get. He keeps his eyes firmly fixed on the far wall, never once letting them stray. The women are all beautiful, tragic things, but he can do nothing for them. They are not his to save; they are not his to avenge.

So, he waits quietly while the Shadow Lord, the Lokskell, as many call him, studies his ladies... watching them dancing in their silks and satins, their jewels and lace. They twirl and dip and spin around and around for him, until he finally chooses his pleasure for the evening. He gestures her forward, a tiny, petite blonde, and she shows no outwardly signs of emotion as she approaches. Without a word, she lowers herself to her knees at his feet and bows her head to wait for his commands.

"You may go," he dismisses the rest with a careless wave of his hand. The others all turn and silently file out of the room, closely followed by the guards waiting in the hall. His men will escort them back to their cells and ensure that they remain there until he calls upon them again. Only when the room is cleared does he acknowledge the man's presence. "Speak, Agnit Haldore. What news do you bring?"

The man, whose name literally translates to *infinite spirits* doesn't speak; he never does. Not in the typical sense anyway. But that's not to say that he can't communicate. He just does so in a more unique manner than most. Although the Lokskell knows what's to come next, he watches intently anyway.... just as he always does, just in case he can one day learn to replicate the man's magic or even steal it for his own. Not that he really *needs* the man's abilities. They're not much different from some of his own. He just *wants* them, as he wants them *all*.

Agnit Haldore reaches up, grasps his own face in his hands, and then he *pulls*. His hands are somehow able to latch onto his own spirit and he begins to draw it out, tugging it forward until it rips free of his body... but just his head. He *has* the ability to peel it completely free of his body, but that's not what he chooses to do this time. There have been only a handful of times that he's actually removed his entire spirit. Total removal leaves his body unanimated and completely vulnerable. Typically, he'll just rip his soul in half, letting one half out to do his bidding, keeping the other half locked inside to animate and protect his body. But in this instance, he has no need to go even that far with it. He needs only pull his spirit out just enough to free his head… the mouthpiece. The identical, but incorporeal spirit head floats out beside his real, tangible head, making him appear to be a two headed aberration. It never ceases to amuse the Lokskell to see the self-appointed manservant/castle-overseer/spy/messenger/errand boy stand before him with two heads.

"She has betrayed you, M'lord," the spirit head immediately reports, simply and to the point. The Shadow Lord frowns as yet again, he wonders where this odd man had come from. The two of them have been trapped in this castle together for hundreds of years, and still he knows next to nothing about him. In the beginning, he'd felt an intense distrust for the man, just as he did for everyone. But Agnit Haldore had long ago proven himself not only loyal, but also incredibly useful. He'd once asked the man why his spirit could speak when he, himself could not.

The man's body had merely shrugged, while his spirit claimed that his physical self had been born without a voice.... as if that explained anything. It was odd. Normally it's the living that makes so much racket, with the spirits tending to be silent, watchful things. But despite the oddities and his initial distrust of the man, the Lokskell had decided to let him live, for he has always disliked unsolved mysteries and enigmas. He wants to know *everything*, and it's not often that he cannot learn the how's and the why's of any given situation.

After all this time, he still hasn't figured this man out, but the mystery no longer plagues him as it once had. They've been acquaintances and peaceful roommates for so long now that his need to know has all but vanished, turned into nothing more than a passing query that's quickly forgotten in the face of more important issues, like the present one at hand.

"What do you mean?" he asks now, his voice calm but oh, so deadly.

Agnit Haldore, as always, refuses to look him in the eye, focusing on his left ear instead. "She is gone, Sire."

His brow furrows and his voice deepens threateningly. "Gone? Gone where?"

The man shrugs his physical shoulders, while his spirit mouth simply replies, "I do not know."

He stares at that ghost-like apparition and wishes (not for the first time) that he could find a way to rip it out himself and torture it. "Surely you followed her. *You* were charged with watching her, after all. Surely you did not fail me in this?"

Agnit Haldore straightens his shoulders and stands just a little bit taller as he explains, "Where your daughter went, I could not follow."

The Lokskell feels the anger creeping in. He knows that he needs a distraction, and so he turns his attention to the woman kneeling at his feet. He reaches out and gently strokes her face. "Get up. Remove your blouse for me. Slowly," he commands. As he watches her trembling fingers lower and undo each button, he resumes the conversation. "Tell me, where could my daughter have possibly gone that a spirit could not follow?"

The man's eyes stay fixed to his master's ear as if his very life depended upon it, not straying so much as a millimeter while he relates what he'd witnessed. "Samara went through the mirror, Sire… to another world. She broke the looking glass behind her to ensure that none could follow in her footsteps. I'm sorry, but she is gone. I could do nothing to stop her in my spirit form."

The Lokskell's breath comes faster and his blood heats, as much in anger at his daughter as from the little flashes of smooth, womanly skin that he's getting tantalizing glimpses of. The woman opens the last pearl button, but instead of removing the garment, she clutches it against herself with both hands. Already angry, this tiny act of defiance has him suddenly, out of control, *furious.*

Moving fast as a snake, the Lokskell reaches out and strikes her hard across the face, knocking her to the floor. "Did I tell you to stop?" Eyes full of tears, she shakes her head as she quickly gets back up and pulls the blouse open, shrugs it off her shoulders, and lets it fall to the floor. Then she stands there, miserably waiting for whatever would come next. He takes a deep breath to calm himself and continues to watch her even as he speaks to the man. "Give me the details. Tell me everything that transpired."

Agnit Haldore clears his throat. "There's not much to tell, M'lord. She was watching the mirror, just like you ordered her to, when her reflection suddenly changed. She looked quite different inside the glass and I realized that it was that Other girl. The one that you've been searching for. Suddenly, the glass began to glow with a bright blue light, and it seemed to melt and become fluid. Next thing I know, Samara reached inside that liquid and yanked her right through the mirror. Then she stepped in and took the Other's place. The mirror started to…"

But here, the Lokskell interrupts him. "Wait. You say my daughter pulled the reflection girl through the glass and then she went into it? You're certain that is what transpired?" Suddenly excited, he reaches out and strokes his fingers over the woman's breast, thrilling at how her nipple puckers at his touch, at how her body responds, even though her mind is unwilling.

"Yes, M'lord. They struggled fiercely. Your daughter was trying with all her strength to push her way in, and the reflection girl was fighting just as hard to keep her out…to keep her on her own side of the mirror. But when Samara suddenly pulled instead of pushed, the Other girl was caught off guard. She was thrown off balance and your daughter yanked her right in. That's when Samara stepped through, turned, and told your hobglins to seize the imposter and bring her to you. Then she shattered the glass into a thousand tiny fragments that could never be pieced back together. Forgive me, Sire, but I…"

But the Shadow Lord impatiently waves his apologies aside. "Ecko is there? On Oblerian? Taking Samara's place? Now? *Right now?* Why was I not *immediately* informed that my other daughter had resurfaced?" He rages on before the man can get a word in edgewise. "Where is she now, my Ecko? Tell me that the hobglins were smart enough to listen. Tell me that they followed Samara's instructions and are even now on their way to the castle with my long lost daughter!"

But Agnit Haldore cannot tell him that, for he does not know. "I don't know where she is, M'lord. My instructions were to watch Samara. That is what I did. When I could no longer do as you commanded, I terminated the wandering half of my spirit and came straight to you, so that I could relay all that I'd witnessed. I cannot even begin to hazard a guess as to where the reflection girl… this *Ecko* is now."

The terrified woman trembles violently and whimpers in fear as the Lokskell's eyes light upon her with a terrible, unholy gleam. "But the hobglins were still there with her when you left? Tell me!"

The man's head bobs as his spirit head answers. "Yes, M'lord. Samara's magic not only shattered the mirror, but the force of it also threw them all back against the wall. The three of them were unconscious upon the floor of the hovel when I discontinued the other half of my spirit."

The Lokskell crooks his finger at the softly crying woman. "Go back at once," he orders as he reaches out to grasp the woman's hips in his hands and drag her closer. "Go back and find out if those two imbeciles are still there, or if they're actually following Samara's orders. Find out if…oh, forget it! I'll do it myself." He closes his eyes and mentally tracks down his Night Shades, the ones that are there on Samara's world… on Oblerian.

It takes only a matter of seconds and they immediately scatter, each one with its own set of instructions on what to do and where to search for his dear, beloved new daughter. When he opens his eyes, he grins wickedly at the woman, reveling at the feel of her body trembling beneath his fingers. He bunches the silk of her skirt in his hands and cruelly rips it off of her. He knows just what to do while he waits for more news.

"Leave, Agnit Haldore," he orders, but he never looks away from the woman's shivering, naked form as he adds, "Or stay and watch, if it pleases you. I've never minded an audience." He laughs at how absurd the man looks when he turns and flees without even taking the time to realign his spirit within his body.

3

HOBGLINS

Ecko

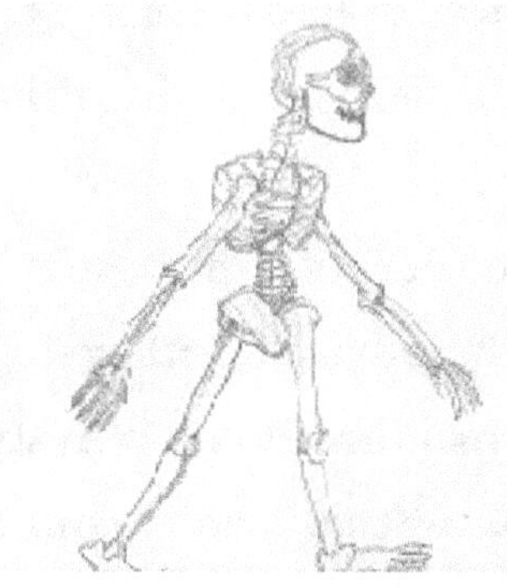

Ecko dreams that she's still walking along yesterday's empty, end-less beach. She's singing, belting out the lyrics to Fear (one of her favorite Blue October songs) and trying her best to keep her spirits up through the hopelessness of her situation. She's dancing, badly but enthusiastically, as she walks along, spinning and jumping about, fist up in the air when she spots it, still far off into the dis-tance. The song dies upon her lips as dread washes over her, just like the waves lapping at the shore. Her fist raised up above her head in a show of defiant victory over her own fear slowly drops back down to her side.

All manner of dark, depressing feelings overtakes her then, because even though there are miles and miles yet between them, her heart immediately recognizes what her eyes can't even clearly make out yet. The Red Door stands upright, unaided and unsupported by walls or even a frame. It's just there, uncannily supporting itself, waiting for her to come up with a magical key to unlock it. All her life she's dreamed of this door, terrible, disturbing dreams that have haunted even her waking hours.

She's spent countless dream-time hours trying to get through it, wasted innumerable sleepless nights thinking about it… devising plans on how she could unlock it, contemplating where it would lead, and wondering who the sobbing, grief-stricken woman that could be heard on the other side may be. What secrets lay beyond its time-worn threshold? Why did it plague her so, and where, for the love of all that's holy, could she find the key that would give her the answers that she so desperately needs? Surely, she would know peace, *finally*, once and for all if it would just open up to her and reveal all the unknowns within.

It beckons her closer now, taunting her to solve the riddle just as it always has. But something's different this time. She feels it as she walks along, her entire consciousness focused on that crimson rectangle of disappointment and despair. A tingle, a spark down in the depths of her core suddenly flares to life, and it grows and spreads as she approaches until there's a sizzle of electricity flowing through her. *Something* is waking up inside of her, pulsing and flexing, testing the limitations of her mind, her body.

Her eyes refuse to look away as her feet carry her unwilling body ever nearer until she's close enough to reach out and press her palms against the vermillion surface, trace the crevices in the wood with her fingertips. She stands before it with tears in her eyes and despair in her heart, hopeless and keyless as always, certain that it will still refuse to open up for her, but also knowing that it won't stop her from trying. She *always* tries. She doesn't really have a choice in the matter. It's become a reflex, a habit, a desperate, automatic reaction. She always fails… and she forever tries again, every single time that it makes its appearance in her dreams.

Now, as her hand reaches out to grasp the knob, that strange blue energy that she'd felt only once before shoots from her fingers, straight into the keyhole. It engulfs the knob and then flows over the entire surface of the door, covering it with a shimmering blue blanket of pure energy. Reaching into the mesmerizing beauty of the energy field, she feels it come back to her, tickling over her skin, flowing back inside of her.

Taking a deep, steadying breath, she hesitantly tests the knob. Dream Ecko begins to sob as it easily, *magically* turns in her hand. The Red Door is *unlocked*. The key was her magic and it had been inside her all along. She just hadn't known it, hadn't understood.

She freezes up for a moment, suddenly terrified of what she'll finally find on the other side, but then she slowly pushes it open. A dazzling white light shines out, momentarily obscuring her view. She shields her eyes, squinting to try and see past the glare to what's hidden beyond it. There's a silhouette of a woman standing there, a shadow figure made featureless by the intensity of the surrounding light. She can't see who it is. But she *must* see! She just has to know! Finally, once and for all, she must learn the truth of the Red Door, learn who the mystery woman is. She must know why this woman has haunted her for her entire life.

She takes a step forward. She tries to lift her foot over the threshold, tries to step into the light. A resounding scream, a shriek of pain and unimaginable suffering rings out and strikes pure anguish straight into her heart. Her very soul instantly begins to weep as the door slams shut in her face. There are no words to describe the sorrow, the hopelessness that she feels in this moment, dream though it may be.

Somehow, Ecko had connected with her, just before the way was shut. That poor woman...all her emotions, everything she'd felt had slammed right into her. The weight of it, the utter wretchedness of it drives her to her knees. Her head bows in sorrow as the Red Door disappears back to wherever doors go when they don't lead to anywhere. She remains there on her knees in the sand for a long, long time. To have been so close, *it had been right there within her grasp*, and then to have it snatched away so suddenly, so cruelly...it is the very epitome of failure and defeat and despondency, and it leaves her feeling broken and shattered inside… just like shards of a shattered mirror.

Her dreams changed then, as dreams so often do. The rest of her sleep hours are just as disturbing, a chaotic blend of reality, memory, supposition, and fear. She dreams of Charlie, lost in the snow somewhere, calling and calling for her, like Auntie Em had cried out for Dorothy in The Wizard of Oz. She dreams of a strangely handsome (even if he *was* blue) man with horns and claws. She dreams of shadows chasing her, of Bone-men and bodiless wings flying at her, and all manner of strange, unnatural things. And she dreams of her mother, the woman that had loved her enough to give up her own life so that she'd be safe.

Her body jerks and twitches spasmodically, until she's suddenly jolted from her dreams by a disturbance outside of her makeshift tent. Even though her body desperately cries out for more sleep, it's actually a relief to awaken and leave all those uncertainties and fears back in Dreamland. All that's left to remind her of her most recent night terrors is a lingering sense of dread and a desperate urgency.

She cracks her dry-as-sandpaper eyes open and pokes her head out to see if morning has come yet, and to see if anything had changed while she'd been asleep. Night, or Pitch as Thing Two had called it, has passed. And while there is no sunshine, it's at least bright enough to see the world around her. Visibility, believe it or not, actually turns out to be a most unfortunate thing though. At least in this particular moment of time, because the missing member of their little group has caught up and is now making her way towards them.

She looks very similar to her mate, but she's the taller of the two. Her skin is a lighter puke-green, as if there's more stomach acid mixed into her vomit coloring than his, and it dilutes her own putrid skin tone. Her eyes are orange and have a cruel, malicious glint in them. Her large, pointy ears stick straight up on either side of her head and her nose is thin and sharp, the tip of it curved downward like a hook. Just like her mate's, her top half is also bare, her orange-nippled breasts sagging down her belly like empty, deflated balloons. She looks positively lethal, *poisonous.*

Apparently, Thing One and Thing Two are *very* happy to see one another again, because they immediately fall into one another's arms and carry out some sort of nasty, puke worthy reunion. They grasp each other by the shoulders, close their eyes and press their foreheads together, which isn't the bad part. That part is actually sort of sweet, even if they *are* hideous to look at. It's what comes *next* that turns her stomach and forces her to crawl back into the relative safety of her sleeping bag-tent.

They lift their heads, look deeply into one another's eyes, just like human lovers tend to do. But then ...oh. Oh, it's so bad. So nasty. They sniff at each other, like dogs do, and then their six-inch, slimy green and black mottled tongues come out to play. They lick all over one another's faces, grunting and snarling, teeth snapping, bodies grinding into each other. Then, and this is the *really* horrible part...they're tearing at each other's pants, and they fall down, right there in the dirt to do the dirty. They don't seem to remember, or even care, that she's there.

She wishes with all her might that she *wasn't* there. She gags, and not knowing what else to do, retreats into her sleeping bag to wait it out. She has just enough time to wonder why the heck she didn't make a run for it, while they were distracted, before the two creatures both let out a loud pig-grunt and then fall silent. Thankfully the whole 'Welcome back, Dear. So glad to see you' mating ritual had only lasted three minutes from start to finish, but they're three traumatizing minutes that Ecko wishes she could scrub from her mind… with bleach and a brillo pad. She prays that she never has to witness revolting creature love, ever again.

She waits until she's sure that they're done and not about to go for round two. Then she waits even longer. She wants to allow them plenty of time to get properly redressed, not that she's sure they even took the time to completely discard their pants in the first place, but better safe than sorry. She figures the coast is clear and it's safe to come out when they start speaking...about her apparently.

She slowly, cautiously pokes her head out, keeping her eyes averted from the last place she'd seen them. "See?" Thing One screeches in his nasally voice. "It's made itself into a cocoon! Is it supposed to do that? Wait, look! It is emerging!"

Thing Two has yet to say much of anything, but she isn't silent. Oh, no. Apparently, she's a mouth breather. A very loud mouthbreather. She seems to be the leader of the pair, smart, cautious, vicious, and much, much more dangerous than her mate. She narrows her eyes and hisses at her as Thing One rambles on. "I do not think it has transformed. It is still just as repulsive to look upon. Perhaps it has emerged prematurely?"

Ecko's mouth drops open as he plunges into a lengthy, one-sided discussion, describing all of yesterday's events. "*I'm* the repulsive one?" she mumbles as she goes about the business of partially setting up her tent, Thing Two watching all the while. With that completed, she digs in her backpack for her empty water bottle and then she cuts the top of it off with her Swiss army knife.

She desperately needs to do her morning business and she absolutely refuses to do it in front of them. Seeing as how there's no shelter anywhere, in any direction, a trip inside the tent with her fancy, new chamber pot will have to suffice. She ignores Thing One's continuous whisperings as she zips herself into the privacy of her tent and quickly takes care of her business. But the moment she comes back out of the tent to carry it away and empty it, she gets bombarded with questions and ridicule over her 'bashfulness'.

"Why have you collected it? Is it useful? Why did you not just release your waste from your body right down into the dirt if you are just going to dump it there anyway?" On and on with the questions. They want an explanation for every single move she makes. Why is she wiping her hands? What is a wet-wipe? What kind of beast did the food she was eating come from?" She finally gives up and ignores them as she eats one of the oranges and a Reese's peanut butter cup.

They don't seem to notice that she's stopped responding to their interrogation anyway. But Thing Two never once takes her eyes off her. The shrewd female watches every detail as she peels the orange, separates it into sections, and then opens the candy wrapper to reveal all four circles of deliciousness. Sending up a silent little prayer of thanks to the Heavens, she digs into her breakfast. She can't hold back her sighs of pleasure as she snarfs it down in record time. When all that remains is one last chocolate cup and one wedge of the fruit, Thing Two decides that Ecko has had enough to eat and that she needs to share. She marches over and snatches the last of the food up and greedily stuffs it into her own mouth.

"Hey!" Two very indignant, affronted voices ring out simultaneously. Ecko, because that was *her* breakfast, darn it, and Thing One because his mate hadn't shared it with him. They both watch as the selfish female chews once, twice before a look of disgust washes over her face.

"Uuuggh," she grunts as she spits the mangled, partially chewed mess to the ground, bringing a look of pure panic to Thing One's face. He pulls out a long knife, so long that it's almost a machete, from a sheath at his waist. He points it at her and shouts, "You dare to poison my mate? You foul, wretched creature, you will pay with your lifeblood!" Then that dumb, psychotic male runs straight at her as if he wants to skewer her like an Ecko-kabob. Would have too, if Thing Two hadn't stepped in and stopped him, because *she's* certainly too shocked to even try to defend herself.

"Idiot!" Two yells and lands a swift, powerful blow to the side of One's head. He falls to the ground, howling and holding onto his head as if to ensure that his brains don't leak out.

"Have you lost your reason? It was foul upon my tongue, 'tis all. It wasn't poison. I live still, but should you have harmed her, *both* of our lives would be forfeit. The Lokskell would make us suffer greatly and he would dispose of us only when he grew tired of torturing us. And *then* who would care for our young hobglinets back at home? Certainly not your fat mother. She's already eaten three of them! I did not go through the pain of birthing them just to help your mother's girth grow larger. She may *not* devour any more of my younglings. Get up! Stop that mewling, you infernal weakling."

As he scrambles to obey his missus, she turns her hateful eyes back on Ecko. "You. Get up and be ready to travel in a thrice. Do not make me repeat myself. I can make you hurt without leaving a single mark on that revolting, pale skin of yours."

Ecko jumps up and scrambles to obey the missus too. Thing One is dangerous, because he's dumb. Two is dangerous because she's smart, and inherently mean spirited, as well. Yes, the female is the one that needs watching. It would be a mistake to ever think her the softer, weaker sex.

They set out in a brisk, no-nonsense speed-walk. They each have their own jobs to maintain. As the leader of the group, Thing Two sets the pace. Thing One, at the back of the line enforces it. Ecko, sandwiched between the two of them, works on coming up with a plan on how she can ditch her unpleasant kidnappers, while she tries to keep up with Two and avoid being prodded in the back by One. There is nowhere to run to, nowhere to hide, so if she can't manage to take them both down simultaneously there's just no way she can manage an escape. She won't be able to fight them off, not even just one of them. Remembering last night's dream, she searches deep inside herself for that blue electric energy. She stares down at her hands for so long, willing the magic to appear, that Thing Two demands to know why she's looking at them.

She's certain that she feels a tingle in her fingertips, but then again, maybe it's all in her head. Wishful thinking, and all that. Regardless, a tiny, useless tingle wouldn't help her anyway. She briefly thinks about trying to sneak off during the night, but there's just no feasible way. Even if she manages to sneak away, which is very unlikely, they would see the light from her flashlight for miles and miles. They'd easily be able to follow. She doesn't even entertain the thought of trying to make a go of it without a light either.

Even if she were brave enough (and she is *not)* the darkness is too dark, too black, too absolute. It had been overwhelmingly, debilitatingly terrifying just sitting still upon the ground last night with it surrounding her. Even though there is absolutely *nothing* to trip over or run into, she can't just walk blindly out in the Pitch. With no light, no landmarks, no *anything,* she would probably get turned around, and with her luck, would wander back to camp to be recaptured. Escaping will have to wait, at least until a better opportunity comes along, one with at least a small chance of success.

The trio travels for hours and hours in a replay of yesterday's endless march along the beach. Only the scenery and the company seem to have changed. Ecko misses the Ocean. She was alone, but not a captive. She was running from her pursuers, but she could sit and rest every so often. Shoot, even the sea creatures, in all their frightening strangeness were preferable to these two. What she wouldn't give to have her grabby, butt-pinching monstrosity back... and at least the view had sometimes been interesting.

The world around her now is just one huge expanse of dreariness and yawn inspiring boredom. There's not much conversation amongst them either as they march onward towards her doom. For the most part, it consists of grunts and occasional hisses, but she does manage to discover what her captor's real names are. Thing One is called Blaxx and his witchy wife's name is Urza. Fitting, but she likes them better as One and Two.

Ecko feels hope for the first time in what seems like forever when she finally spots something, far off in the distance. She keeps her eyes locked on it as she tries to figure out what it could possibly be, as they draw closer. This whole situation reminds her of her dream, and she hopes with all her might that it's not the Red Door up ahead of them now. But then she *knows* that it's not. It can't be, because she would feel it if it were.

Another hour passes before they're close enough to determine what it is, not that seeing it clearly actually explains what it is. It appears to be some sort of plant or tree, but it's so *very* strange. It's obviously vegetation of *some* kind, but it looks just like a telephone pole rising high up in the air. Its diameter, from the bottom and most of the way up, remains consistent, the same size as a standard utility pole. About ¾ of the way up, it begins to taper off, thinning until the tip of it is no more than the width of her arm and ending in a pointed tip.

There are no branches, no limbs or twigs, nor any leaves, but at the point where it starts tapering off, it has long, thin vines that stretch up even higher into the air. And they're *moving*, slowly blowing about, just like balloons floating on a breeze, although there *is* no breeze. The base of the tree/plant has a massive mound of roots that are only partially buried under the ground. The visible part of the root system, the part that's exposed above ground, is a nasty snarl of somehow menacing roots and rhizomes.

The group is getting close now, only 200 yards remain between them and the alien tree. She's so focused on trying to figure it out that she fails to notice their leader has stopped walking, causing her to slam right into her. Urza spins around and growls at her.

"Sorry!" Ecko exclaims as she backs away, with her hands held up placatingly.

Urza narrows her mean, poison eyes on her captive and snarls, "I'm starving. We missed Firstmeal because of you. But it's almost time for the Foul-Kries to migrate. We will wait here until they fly. If we are lucky, we'll get to eat Middlinmeal."

Ecko hastily turns away when Urza fumbles with her pants, lowers them, and then squats to the ground to relieve herself. Unfortunately, she turns herself towards Blaxx, and he's doing the same. She slaps her hands over her eyes and ignores their laughter. Ugghh, no thanks. Green yangs and green dongs are NOT something she ever wishes to see again.

After a few long, uncomfortable moments, they finish up and Urza says, "Drop your waste. Sit. Rest. We will not remain here long, and we won't be stopping again until the Pitch is upon us."

So, she takes ten large steps forward until she can no longer smell the overpowering stench of their pee, before she drops down onto the dirt with a tired sigh. Her body is so sore and she's fairly starving too. She needs water, and she needs to eat a proper meal or twelve. She's contemplating setting up her little stove to heat up the beef stew that she was supposed to have eaten for dinner last night, but was too exhausted to fool with, when she hears what sounds like a loud, screaming wind.

Try to imagine what a roaring tornado that has sucked up a thousand screeching banshees sounds like and *that* would come close to what she's hearing now. And it's getting closer with every passing second. Her eyes grow wide, and her heart accelerates to the point that it's causing actual physical pain.

"Here they come!" Blaxx shouts over the shrieking as he raises his hands to plug his ears with his fingers.

Urza gets right up in her face as she mimics her mate. She plugs her pointed ears with her fingers as she yells, "Are you dumb, girl? Protect your ears!"

Protect her ears? Ecko wants to protect her entire *Ecko*, not just her ears. But it's too late to run and there's nowhere to hide, so she reaches up and shoves her fingers into her ears too. She turns her eyes back to the sky just as the first huge, winged creature flies into sight. It's leading a whole flock of the vile beasts, and they're carrying that screaming whirlwind sound with them.

The flock is still several miles away, but the closer they come, the louder their cries get. The reason behind their name becomes perfectly clear as soon as that first one soars over them. When Urza had called them Foul-Kries earlier, she'd assumed that meant f-o-w-l, but it *has* to be f-o-u-l, because that's just what the *thing* flapping above her is. Everything about it is foul. Its screeching cries make her feel dirty, nasty all over, as if she'd been dipped into a tub of supernatural, liquid negativity. And it *looks* like what would happen if an ugly pterodactyl made love to its vulture-cousin and produced a disfigured, inbred baby of doom.

She wants to drive her fingers further into her ears, all the way into her skull, if need be, and close her eyes forever… anything to block out what this terrible thing is making her feel. And this is just *one* of them, the first one, the leader or a scout perhaps. There are literally *thousands* of the abominations approaching, no more than sixty seconds behind it, blacking out the already dull light in the sky.

"Stop looking, you stupid shite! Do you wish for death?" She just barely hears the words over the screams, before Urza slams into her back and tackles her to the ground. Ecko refuses to pull her fingers out of her ears long enough to make even the slightest attempt at breaking her fall. She just lets herself crash, face down into the dirt as she repositions her finger plugs more securely and slams her eyes tightly shut. The crushing weight of Urza sitting upon her back, holding her down, doesn't faze her in the least. She doesn't even care that she can't draw in a full breath. She just wants it to end… Just please, *please* make it stop.

The shrieks grow louder and louder as the flock reaches them, contaminating them with an awful soul-sickness. It is the most dreadful thing she's ever experienced, surpassing even her sickest days of drug withdrawals, and it goes on forever, drawing every ounce of good, pleasant feelings out of her. She doesn't realize that she's crying (though it wouldn't surprise her either) until the revolting things have passed them by, taking their cries with them. Finally, an eternity later, the heavy heifer gets up off her back, so she cautiously unplugs her ears as she sits up to scrub the muddy trails of tears and dirt off her face.

"Idiot," Urza snaps as she takes the whip from the belt around her waist. Ecko cringes back, certain that she's about to get struck, but that's not Thing Two's intention at all. Urza turns and sprints towards the tree/plant, shouting for Blaxx to 'get his stupid arse over here and help her.' Ecko keeps her butt planted in the dirt, mouth dropped open in shock and morbid fascination as she watches the scene(s) taking place before her.

The alien tree has apparently used those floating vines at its top as a trap, a snare to catch its prey. It has one of those horrific bird-things wrapped up tight with its vine 'feelers', just like a spider wraps its meal up with strands of silky webs. The Foul-Kry is struggling, desperately trying to break free, but even as she watches, more and more of the feeler vines move in and wrap themselves around it, further securing their hold on it.

Ecko briefly wonders why it isn't screaming its repulsive head off, but then she sees that the feelers have wrapped themselves around its beak to silence it... Perfect, just *perfect*. A *smart* carnivorous tree/plant... *thing.* And yes, she is *very* certain that it's a meat eater. It didn't send out a trap and catch its prey just for sport, or to take a trophy back home to hang upon the walls. No, that plant is about to have lunch. The only question is, how will it accomplish it?

Urza and Blaxx have skidded to a stop, a cautious ten feet away from it. They're both slightly crouched into fighting stances, both brandishing weapons. They move in as a team, obviously comfortable with fighting together. Blaxx, with his machete in his hand, is staring at the root system, down at the base of the tree. His wife, holding her whip at the ready, is watching what's now going on up in the air. The very tip top of the tree trunk begins to slowly roll in upon itself, coiling itself downwards towards the base, as if it's a giant party horn, one of those party favors that you always see at children's birthday parties, those things that you blow into and make the paper tube unroll, and then suck the air back out to make it coil back in on itself.

'*Maybe it's a proboscis*', Ecko thinks to herself. That's just what it looks like, a long, stretched out and fully extended butterfly tongue that is now rolling back up, slowly curling itself back towards its body (in this case it's rolling itself towards the ground) The whole thing just rolls up, curls in on itself, and it lowers the struggling bird-creature right along with it.

Urza and Blaxx step in closer, weapons raised and ready, watching closely, waiting for the plant to bring it within their reach. But a sudden screech from the sky has them all jerking their eyes upwards, all of them *with* eyes, of course. The plant stays steady, right on course, focused only on getting its food to the ground. It doesn't seem to care one tiny bit that a very large, very angry Foul-Kry has just swooped in to save its Foul-mate.

The shrieking is horrific, and Ecko is quick to slam her fingers back into her ears. But Urza and Blaxx don't have that luxury.

They can plug their ears and avert their eyes, but then they wouldn't be able to fight the newcomer off. It lunges at them continuously, razor sharp claws and beak snapping at them.

Urza cracks her whip, striking it over and over again. Blaxx stands ready to help, but the bird creature never comes within reach of his shorter weapon. And while his wife fights for their lives, he makes a terrible and deadly mistake. He's turned his back on the tree/plant.

A single, stealthy root has unraveled itself from the root mass, and is now slithering through the dirt towards him. It wraps itself around his ankle and yanks him down before he even realizes what's happening. He yells out and, unfortunately, drops his machete as he crashes to the ground. He immediately starts scrabbling, clawing against the dirt to find a handhold, as he slowly gets dragged backwards towards the tree.

Urza, distracted by the danger that her mate has found himself in, gets slashed across the chest by one of the bird creature's massive claws. The force behind the blow knocks her to the ground and the Foul-Kry, anticipating its victory, swoops in for the kill.

Meanwhile, lunch is being served back at the alien tree's house of horrors. It's finally finished rolling itself down into a coil, and now the feeler vines are lowering the bird creature the last two feet, dangling it directly above the snarl of roots. Blaxx screams for his wife to help him as that one sneaky-snakey root continues to reel him in, but she can't help him. She's much too busy dealing with her own inevitable demise.

But God help her, Ecko actually feels bad for Blaxx. Not in a creepy, Stockholm syndrome sort of way, but in a 'Oh, my God, he's about to get eaten alive' kind of way, because now *all* the roots in the snarl are beginning to slither around.

They move aside, rearranging themselves until a giant, gaping maw is revealed. The 'mouth' opens wide as the feelers lower the captive bird creature straight down into its obscene gullet. It's almost like room service. Or, better yet, it's like peasant servants, hand-feeding grapes to their masters, only much, much messier.

When the Foul-Kry appetizer is shoved halfway into the maw, the feelers release it and retreat... And the bird begins to scream. Thankfully, not for long, though. The next few minutes are filled with the horrific sounds of crunching and squishing, and then a huge spray of blood squirts up out of the plant's mouth-hole like an erupting geyser, spraying all over the coiled trunk. And also all over poor, stupid Blaxx. The feelers immediately swim/float through the air, making a beeline straight for the gruesome carnage.

They dip down and plunge themselves into the mess and start the cleanup process. Apparently, nothing gets wasted, because the feelers are sucking up the blood, as if they're straws, complete with disturbingly loud, slurping sounds. The blood that has splattered on Blaxx must be acidic because it immediately eats through his pants, and every bit of skin that it touches is bubbling up, smoke curling up off of it. Of course, Blaxx is now adding his own howls of misery to the screeching of the remaining Foul-Kry that's still trying to skewer Urza with its claws.

Ecko is pretty sure that this is the end of the line for Thing One and Thing Two, but Urza displays her craftiness and resilience, proving beyond a doubt that she has a fierce desire to continue being a mouth breather.

At the last second, before the bird-creature can impale her upon its massive dagger-claws, Urza rolls, suddenly and swiftly, right over to her mate's discarded weapon. She snatches it and thrusts it upwards, just as the creature gets within her reach. The death cries of a Foul-Kry are something that she'll never be able to put into words, and never, ever wants to hear again.

The horrid thing crashes to the ground as it shrieks in such a deafening volume that it makes her feel as if her very soul is shriveling up inside of her. *That's* how terrible and disturbing it is. Even the unfortunate Blaxx is momentarily more concerned with blocking out the noise than he is about the horror of being eaten alive by a plant. He throws his hands up over his ears, completely abandoning his fight to escape, as he continues to get dragged along to his unwilling (and one sided) lunch date.

Even after the Foul-Kry falls silent and still, Blaxx (and Ecko) are both too shaken by the trauma they've just been put through to do anything more than sit there and wallow in their own respective miseries. Urza, not so much.

She immediately leaps back up to her feet and strides over to the plant, the machete clutched in her hand, to rescue her mate. With a scream of pure rage, she slashes the sneaky-snakey root in half. Then she bends down and grasps her man by what little bit of hair he has on his head and drags him back to safety. With a snarl of disgust, she deposits him next to Ecko and then drops down to tend to her wounds. Not only does she have a deep gash across her chest, but there's also blood leaking from her eyes and her ears. Apparently, the Foul-Kries can cause some serious internal damage without ever having to get near its victims. Given enough time, they can literally just scream you to death.

"Get up off your lazy arse, butcher this beast, and prepare the Middlinmeal. Do it not, and you will not get to eat any. You have sat there like a lump, whilst we almost lost our lives to feed you. Such a lazy, ungrateful thing, is you." Urza must not be on her deathbed, because she still retains the ability to complain and threaten.

"And you!" she snaps at Blaxx. "Shut up that yowling! Help the chit with our meal."

But Ecko's already shaking her head and scooting backwards on her butt, removing herself from Urza's reach, out of striking distance.

"I am *not* eating that. It's foul! And I haven't got the first clue how to butcher anything, especially not *that* something. Besides, you didn't do all this to feed me. You know I have my own food. You did it for *you*." She stubbornly sits right there, just waiting to see which one would win, Urza's rage or her smart, sensible reasoning. Would she risk garnering the Shadow Lord's retribution by doing her bodily harm, or would she swallow all that bitter anger and unpalatable pride?

Thing Two is deviously smart, and after a moment of snarling and spitting, she gets up and walks over to take her anger out on her mate. He's busy doing as she'd commanded, first draining the Foul-Kry's acid blood, then skinning and chopping up the carcass… the jet-black carcass. Apparently Foul-Krys are all dark meat, *very* dark.

Urza slaps Blaxx soundly right against the side of his head, and when that doesn't satisfy her need to vent and abuse, she balls up her fist and proceeds to pummel him senseless. After about the fourth punch, he decides he's had enough, and he reaches up and plants his own fist in her belly. Suddenly, there are fists and elbows and feet flying everywhere. They're having an all-out war, a brutal fight for dominance. There's grunts and groans and pig squeals, and then, just as suddenly as the fight began, their anger turns into lust.

Ecko jumps up, grabs her backpack, and hits the road, figuratively speaking, because there *is* no road, not even a trail. She makes sure to walk far out of the Roly-Poly Meaty-Eaty tree's reach. Her captors are too busy to notice her departure, but she's sure that they'll catch up, just as soon as they're done being pigs.

An hour or so later, they do. She hadn't gone far, and it wasn't an escape attempt. She was merely removing herself away from the filth so that she could tend to her needs and eat her own meal in peace. She's set up her little cook stove and she's munching on trail mix while she waits for the beef stew to heat up. It smells just like heaven and she's seriously considering slurping it up cold.

Urza and Blaxx walk up to her campsite, and they must find the aroma appealing too, because they sniff and snuff and snort while trying to breathe it all in. They're not even mad that she'd gone off on her own. They must have also come to the same conclusions that she had. They knew that she couldn't really get very far, not in this terrain. They could easily track her no matter which direction she decided to go.

She shrugs to herself and ignores them as she puts out the flame on her canned fuel and gets right down to filling her very empty and equally disgruntled belly. It is absolute, heavenly divine bliss. Not even Urza watching every detail can distract her from the seriousness of the business at hand. At the moment, all she cares about is quieting the raging, snarling monster that her stomach has become.

Blaxx busies himself with opening up the large pouch that he'd apparently made from the Foul-Kry's leathery skin to carry all the meat in. Since his mate had done the hard work by killing the beast, he'd been in charge of carrying out the menial tasks. He'd drained its toxic blood, skinned it, deboned most of it and chopped the rest up into manageable proportions. Then he'd fashioned a lunch bag out of the beast's own skin to carry it all in. Now he's piling up tufts of dried grass, the severed root from the Roly-Poly tree, and what appears to be some kind of dried buffalo chips. When it's all set up to his satisfaction, he turns to her and holds out his disgusting, cow poop, buffalo chip hand.

"Give me your FireFairy, so that I may start a fire and heat my lady's Middlinmeal too. Mine died two Pitches past. I always forget to feed the nasty little blighters."

Ecko stares at that outstretched hand as if it carries the plague upon it...which is *very* likely. "FireFairy?" she asks. "What's a FireFairy? I don't have...whatever it is that you want."

He grunts and then rudely kicks dirt at her. "You know very well what I'm asking for! You give it to me now, or I'll make you sorry to be amongst the living!" So, in retaliation, she takes out her lighter and jabs it towards him, while striking the flint in his face. He scrambles back so fast that he trips over his own feet and tumbles backwards.

"Aahhieee!" he screeches as he hits the ground and rolls away.

"How?" Urza demands, simply and rudely to the point.

Ecko merely raises an eyebrow and smirks at her. "Magic," is all she says, because knowledge and Earthly technologies are the only real advantages she has over her kidnappers. The more 'magical' she appears, the less willing they'll be to do her harm. With this thought, an idea, the very beginnings of a plan, takes root in her mind and begins to grow. When the time is right, she just might be able to get away from these two, and quite easily.

She enjoys one of her precious KitKats for dessert, while Thing One and Two eat their cold, uncooked meal. Blaxx gripes the entire time, complaining that he hates it cold. Urza doesn't seem to mind in the least. Maybe she's just starving and doesn't care how she fills her belly, but it really seems like she's enjoying her food just the way it is, straight off the dead carcass.

"Yes Smeagol, give it to us raw and wriggling," Ecko mumbles below her breath as she averts her eyes in pure self-preservation.

She can't afford to throw up her own meal. The sight of those two revolting creatures scarfing down chunks of stringy, black meat is more than she can bear.

They've been back at it, steadily marching onwards for a couple of hours, when Ecko points to a figure up ahead and informs them, "Someone's out there, heading this way." Blaxx and Urza have nothing to say to that. They don't appear to be concerned and they don't alter their course or even slow down. After a while, when they're close enough to see who, or what it is, she stops dead in her tracks and refuses to get any closer to it. *It* doesn't care in the least and continues to close in on them.

"We need to run… like right about now would be the perfect time," she insists as she starts to turn away and do just that. Urza reaches out and grabs her arm to prevent her from fleeing.

"What is your problem? Why do you wish to run from the man-bones? They are dumb things, harmless and not to be feared. They merely wander about, nothing more. It will pass us right by."

But Ecko doesn't believe *that* for a ding dang second. There is no way that something so frightening is friendly. But Thing One and Two just stand there (forcing her to stand between them) watching as it approaches. Urza begins to frown when it gets about twenty feet away and shows no sign of going around them. And now it's chomping at them, gnashing its teeth together with a sort of grunting, grinding sound. It lifts its bone arms up and clutches its fingers in the universal 'give me' signal… and it's heading straight for *her*.

"Uh, guys? I really, *really* don't want to get eaten today. Can we please run now?" She tries to jerk free of Thing Two's hold, but it feels like she has a fist of iron gripping her tight. But worry, at last, factors into the equation as Urza finally realizes that all is not well. She steps in front of Ecko, placing herself directly into the biting zone.

But the boney-man isn't after *her*. It's snapping its teeth and snarling, but it doesn't try to bite her or harm her in any way. It merely tries to walk through her to get to Ecko. Only God knows what it will do to her if it gets past her kidnapper/tormentor/protector.

In the end, Urza is forced to 'put it down' in order to make it stop trying to get at her prisoner. She uses the machete knife to cut all of its limbs off, and even when it's lying in a bone heap at their feet, it *still* chomps its teeth at Ecko.

Blaxx scratches at one of the bald patches on his head. "Why'd it do that Urza? What'd it want?" he asks. She has no answers for him, but she too, is curious as to why it wanted the girl so badly, and also what it would have done if she'd let it do...whatever it had been intent on doing.

"Would it have eaten her?" Urza wonders aloud. She grunts at her own confusion and rudely prods her prisoner to get her walking again. She marches onward and keeps her mouth shut, listening intently as One and Two debate.

"It looked like it wanted to eat her. Perhaps she tastes good?" Blaxx offers. Urza scoffs at that. "You know that bone-men don't eat. They tread dirt. 'Tis all that they do, all they have *ever* done.

Besides, had it eaten her, where would it have put her? It has no belly to fill! Perhaps…. perhaps the Lokskell has taken command of them with his Night Shades. Perhaps he sent them to retrieve the girl. If that is so, we will eventually have a problem. There are scores and scores of bone-men walking about, and more crawl from the Dead Sea every Pale."

"If they have all been instructed to come after her, we will soon be swarmed by the bone walkers and we *will* lose her to them. We can fight off a few of them, but if we run into a hoard, we will not succeed in this mission. We must make haste and get her to the Black Forest before that can happen." With that, Urza steps up her speed walking to jogging.

Ecko groans at the increase in their pace. She'd already been struggling with how fast they were traveling. "What *are* they? Where do they come from?" She asks as she tries to ignore the burning in her legs and the cramp in her side.

Blaxx actually answers her questions for a change. "They are the cursed dead, but no one knows how or why they were cursed. No one knows where they come from. All that is known is that they come up out of the Sea to endlessly wander about our land."

Encouraged, because she'd actually gotten an answer out of him, Ecko decides to keep pressing her luck and ask more questions. "Why do we have to hurry to the Forest? Will we be safe there?"

"Safe?" Blaxx snorts out a nasally laugh. "Nowhere is safe, you dumb twit. But at least there are places to hide, trees to climb in the Black Forest…Bone-men can't climb." Now it's her turn to laugh with an unlady-like snort. "Yeah, just like bone-men are harmless and do nothing but walk around looking pretty."

They have nothing to say to that, but Urza *does* look as though the thought had already crossed her mind that the bone walker's mannerisms had been drastically altered, and that she is, even now, working on a plan of action to take if such a thing does occur in the not-so-distant future. They all fall silent as they each contemplate what exactly could be happening with the bone walkers. Ecko really only has two concerns. Why do they want her, and how the heck would she be able to escape a hoard of them?

For the next two hours or so, the trio alternates between their two speeds, the fast walk and the even faster jog, until a line of trees (hopefully not the Roly-Poly Meaty-Eaty kind) appears on the horizon. Urza calls a halt to their progression and instructs them to get the campsite set up. "This is as close as we go for now. We will wait out the Pitch here, and then make our move just before the Pale arrives. Get moving. Eat. Tend to whatever needs you may have and then make your Pitch-nest."

Ecko, still staring out at that line of trees in the distance, doesn't move until Urza steps up beside her to have a look too. "Is that the Black Forest?" she asks with a tremble in her voice.

"No," Urza grunts with a shake of her head. "That is a Scream Patch. The Black Forest lies just beyond."

Then Ecko shivers and asks the dumbest question in the history of dumb questions. "Is it dangerous?" she whispers, and Urza looks down and meets her eyes.

"Very much so," she assures her before turning away to get ready for food and sleep. Ecko sighs heavily and does the same. She quickly sets up her tent, which is thankfully one of those pop-up ones that basically assembles itself. She's busy setting up her stove when the Pitch is upon them, just as suddenly as it had been yesterday. Blaxx and Urza laugh uproariously when she cries out in fear at the sudden darkness. Thankfully, she already has her lighter in her hand. She quickly strikes the flint and uses the tiny bit of light that it provides to locate one of her flashlights.

"Eeecckk!" the two Things shriek as they shield their eyes from the bright light. "What is it? Kill it immediately!" Urza commands. Ecko turns it away, but she refuses to turn it off.

She holds onto it the entire time that she cooks her meal and also while she eats. When she's full and can keep her eyes open no longer, she crawls inside her tent to lie down. She falls asleep listening to them whisper back and forth about her 'magic.' They wonder what powers she has and why she hasn't tried to free herself with her magic, why she hasn't cursed them yet. She'll show them some 'magic' just as soon as they make it to the Black Forest. Human technology seems as alien and magical to them as walking bone-men, meat-eating trees, and geographical blips that seem to teleport hapless travelers to random locations is to her. She'll use their belief that she's some sort of magical witch to her advantage.

It's time for her to leave this little group, before they get her any closer to the Shadow man. The words of Dylan Thomas float through her mind, just as sleep comes to claim her. *'Do not go gentle into that good night, Old age should burn and rave at close of* day. *Rage, rage against the dying of the light.*' Ecko has no intention of going quietly into the night. She'll not be taken to her father, meek as a lamb to slaughter. She *will* rage against the dying of the Light… and she'll bring her flashlights with her.

She sleeps the sleep of the innocent, where there are thankfully no dreams to haunt her, no Red Doors to taunt her. When she wakes and opens her eyes to find that the world is still in Pitch, with her tent still shrouded in darkness, she has to wonder what it was that had woken her from such a sound, blissful sleep.

She lay oh, so silent and still inside her bedroll, listening for the sounds of … anything. But all she can hear is the whistling of Urza's nose and Blaxx's enthusiastic, gusting snores. All is well (as well as can be expected) and she settles back in to try to get some more sleep. It's no use though. She's awake now, and so is her mind.

There's no shutting her thoughts up long enough to fall back into slumber. She breathes a heartfelt sigh of disappointment and gives up on sleep. As quietly as she can manage it, she unzips her tent and crawls out. A startled yelp escapes her lips when the beam of her light illuminates a pair of glittering eyes staring back at her. Her heart stutters in her chest, before she realizes that it's just one of the Things. Urza's awake, sitting up and watching her, although how she can see *to* watch her is a mystery. The Pitch is the ultimate blackness, completely devoid of light.

Urza stands up and kicks her husband sharply in the ribs. He sucks in a huge, loud snort and jumps up. "Huh? What? I weren't humping your litter-sister! I swear you are the only she-hobglin for me!"

Urza grunts in disgust, cuffs him upside the head, and turns her back to them. "If you two want to eat Firstmeal, now is the time to do it. The Pale is approaching, and we need to be at that Scream Patch before it arrives. Eat. Get your things packed up and be ready to run on my mark. Move!"

She snaps out her orders like a deranged drill sergeant, and Ecko hurries to obey. The last thing she wants is to be forced to leave her tent behind, and she knows without a doubt that's just what'll happen if she's not ready in time. But she has to know if she'd heard Blaxx right. "Wait!" she calls out as she begins folding her tent back up. "Did I hear your husband say hobglin? What's a hobglin?"

Thing One snorts out a snicker as he slices two large hunks of foul-meat off the bird carcass that he'd toted around all of yesterday. Urza glares at her as she accepts a piece of stinking, black meat, but surprisingly, she answers the inquiry.

"*We* are hobglins, you dumb shite, Blaxx and I. You don't know anything do you? How have you survived all this time? You are dumber and more helpless than a hobglinet." Then she turns away with one last snort at the stupidity of her captive as she quickly consumes her portion of the Foul-meat.

Ecko stares after her. She can't believe it. She's been calling goblins hobglins all her life. It had started when she was young and couldn't say the word goblin correctly. She'd tried and tried, but it would never come out right. It always came out as hobglin instead.

Her dad had thought it was cute, so he'd started calling them hobglins too, and the name just sort of stuck with them. The two of them had fought off many a hobglin in her young years. They'd been her most favorite monsters to fight. A single tear rolls down her cheek as she whispers, "Oh, Dad. I miss you." What she wouldn't give to have her father here now to help her fight the all too real hobglins.

She manages to get her things packed and ready to go within minutes, so sits down to eat her last apple while she waits. She's also stuffed a granola bar into her pocket, just in case she has to eat lunch on the run. She silently stares out into the black void around her, missing her dad, missing Charlie, missing Earth. She wonders what Charlie's doing right now and she prays that he's ok. Is it Pitch there? She quickly corrects her own mental blunder. *Night.* Is it *night* there?

But then her thoughts jump to Samara. What is her twin up to? Where is she? Who is she hurting? She knows without a doubt that her sister is out there hurting people, on *her* home world. And just like that, Ecko starts getting *angry*, absolutely *furious*, and the monster named Rage that lives in her head comes a-calling, knocking at the walls of his cage with his promises to help her, if she will just *let him out!* But she's still too afraid of him, afraid of what he'll make her feel, of what he'll make her do. She's afraid of the monster he'll turn *her* into, and so she turns away from him once again and ignores his demands. Because, what if, just what *if* she lets him out and he takes over, twisting her into something like Samara, or worse?

Something strange happens then, something completely unexpected. Rage speaks to her from inside his prison…calmly, eloquently, convincingly.

"You must become a monster to stop a monster. You will have to grow your very own set of claws. I can help you. You have a deep well of magic at your disposal, abilities that you have yet to access and cannot even fathom. And you never will if you do not embrace us. We are not the demons that you perceive us to be. We are you, nothing more."

And now she is more terrified of her own mind than she's ever been before.

"Maybe this will help convince you. Perhaps it will push you to do what must be done."

Suddenly, the darkness, the Pitch that she's been staring into disappears, replaced with an image, a vision of her twin. It's as if her thoughts of Samara have opened up some sort of mind-link between them, allowing her to see her sister, to watch her from afar. It's almost as if there's a mirror in her *mind* and she can use it to see exactly what her twisted twin is doing.

And she'd been right. Samara is up to no good, causing chaos, destroying things, and hurting people everywhere she goes.

4

GET WELL SOON

Samara
(Ecko's vision)

Completely unaware that she's being spied upon, Samara strolls into a bargain store, the kind that boasts that every item inside costs only .99 cents. Shopping, the very picture of normality, a routine activity that most humans carry out at least once a week. Samara isn't there to *buy* anything. She's there to learn. Sure, she'll take whatever she wants, and if she can cause an uproar while doing so, well, that's even better. She'll consider it a bonus. But her main goal right now is to learn as much as possible, to assimilate, infiltrate the human's ways. Knowledge is power, and she craves it.

On a world far, far away, Ecko anxiously 'watches' as Samara stops right inside the doorway to look around before making her way down the closest aisle. There's a bored young man listlessly pushing a broom across the floor, but he stands up straighter and smooths his hair down at the first sight of her. The frumpy, older woman at the checkout register is less impressed, and she rolls her eyes, because this is the first bit of interest that the young man has shown in the six hours that he's worked of his current, eight-hour shift.

Samara slowly walks down the personal hygiene aisle, confusion clearly expressed on her face. She picks up boxes of soap, tubes of deodorant, and bottles of shampoo. She turns them this way and that way, inspecting them closely, trying to figure out what they do. She even tries shaking them. Frustrated by her lack of understanding, she calls the man over to help her.

"You. Come here." He smiles charmingly, *hopefully* at her as he approaches. "What is this? Is it ale? It does not look like ale. Is it for drinking?" she asks as she thrusts the bottle of shampoo towards him.

Confused by her questions, he nervously rubs the back of his neck. "Uuhhh, you don't know what shampoo is? Are you from another country or something?" When she stares blankly up at him, he hurries to explain that it's for washing hair.

"How?" she demands to know.

He turns the bottle over and mumbles, "Well, it's pretty easy. It tells what to do right here on the back. When you're in the shower, (and he swallows hard at the thought of this beautiful woman...naked and dripping wet in the shower) you put a bit of this in your hair and you scrub it all around. Then, when you rinse it out, your hair is clean."

Samara takes the bottle from him and shakes it again. "How do I get it out?"

The man shows her how to work the cap and she spends the next minute clicking it open and closed, open and closed. She turns her attention back to the large selection of bottles on the shelves and demands to know why there are so many and how to choose which one to use. He explains some of the differences and the benefits of their diversity, but then he smiles sheepishly at her.

"Honestly, I don't even look at any of that stuff. I just buy the ones that smell good to me. I like this one," he says and takes a green bottle off the shelf. He holds it under her nose and squeezes gently to send a puff of the scent out. Her eyes widen in pleasure, and she selects one for herself. She opens it and lifts it up to sniff it, but she doesn't know not to squeeze too hard. She squirts a big blob of conditioner all over her face. She yelps and tosses the bottle to the floor, causing the man to laugh.

But he doesn't laugh long.

The look she gives him makes his heart stutter, and not in a good way either. Shivering with sudden unease, feeling as if cold, clammy fingers are creeping down his spine, he clears his throat and hurries to placate her. "Calm down, girl. It's ok. Here…"

He opens up a package of wet wipes. "Let's get you cleaned up." With hands that tremble from being so close to her, he wipes the mess from her face, while she stands still and blinks up at him. When he's finished and her face is clean once more, he clears his throat and steps back. "Here, try again, but this time don't squeeze so hard."

She repeats the process and manages to smell it without squirting it straight up her nose. Her eyes light back up, and this time when his heart stutters, it has nothing to do with fear. Funny how warning bells and danger signs can be ignored and so quickly forgotten in the face of beautiful things. Beauty oftentimes is a clear indication of danger. The world is full of such things. Beauty does *not* negate danger, but that is a lesson that men have never learned. Case at hand, the young man's breathing speeds up as his heart pumps with excitement at her obvious pleasure.

Samara proceeds to smell every single bottle of shampoo, conditioner, and lotion on that shelf. Once she's sniffed her way down the aisle to the dental section, she turns to her companion and asks what the tiny brushes are for. After he explains toothbrushes and toothpaste, she demands a demonstration. Knowing that he'll have to buy the items at the end of his shift, he shrugs and does what she asks of him. The things a man will do to impress a woman...

He walks her to the restrooms, and propping the door open with a garbage can, shows her what to do. "Don't swallow it!" he yells. But it's too late. "You're supposed to spit it out. Like this." He spits his into the sink and then rinses his new toothbrush.

"That's ok," he continues. "It won't hurt, just this once..."

But Samara is starring in fascination at the water flowing out of the faucet and swirling down the drain. The poor guy has to spend the next ten minutes explaining sinks and pipes and water cleaning facilities. He eventually manages to lead her away from the restrooms, and they walk back through the store. As fate would have it, her attention lands on the shelf that contains the contraceptive items. *Of course,* she must know what condoms are for and how they work.

The young man's face is blood-red, and he stutters heavily while he tries to (respectfully) explain. She's obviously very frustrated with his answers, or lack thereof, so she snatches a box and thrusts it against his chest. "Show me" she demands, and he immediately gets all choked up and goes into a coughing fit. She waits patiently while he thumps on his own chest to try and get his breathing back under control.

When he's finally able to suck in a full breath, she asks what his problem is. "You are embarrassed. Why? I know that you find me attractive. You cannot lie and say that you don't wish to mate with me. I can feel your desire for me. So, what's the problem? Is it *her*?" She points to the cashier who's been watching the whole fascinating scene unfold. The older woman scowls angrily when Samara continues. "Is the old hag your mate then? Is this why you won't lay with me, why you won't show me how these con-dums work?"

Suddenly, the man's choking again.

"What is *wrong* with you?" she snaps. "Maybe it's best if we *don't* mate. I don't want to catch whatever sick you have. Come along." She grabs him by the hand and pulls him along with her to the next aisle, out of the register lady's line of sight.

"I'm starving. Where can I find food?" Samara asks as her stomach grumbles loud enough for him to hear it too. The young man, wanting to redeem himself (and recover the possibility of teaching her *all* about condoms... but later, and in private!) is quick to lead her to the food section. He opens a bag of chips, hands it to her and tells her that the BBQ flavored ones are his favorite. She peers in at the chips suspiciously. "This does *not* look like food," she snaps.

But it *smells* like food, sort of, so she reaches in, takes one, and slowly, cautiously puts it into her mouth. She crunches into it and a look of such wonder comes over her face that the man is humbled by how beautiful, how *angelic* she looks.

And then...and then…faster than his brain can even process what's happening, she becomes a snarling, rabid beast, right before his eyes! She reaches into the bag and grabs a handful of those fried ovals of deliciousness and shoves them into her mouth. She barely chews before she swallows and crams another handful in. Then she's tearing into packages and eating the contents of everything she can put her hands on, as fast as she can! She moves from the chips to the crackers, then on to the nuts and raisins and fruit snacks. She's snarling, actually *growling* like a wild animal that hasn't eaten in days. The young man's eyes just about bug out of his head as he fearfully backs himself as far up against the shelves as he can get.

It's only when Samara gets to the Little Debbie snack cakes that he snaps to the fact that he has a serious problem. After tasting that very first artificially sweetened treat, she reaches out and swipes every single box of snack cakes off the shelves. Then she sinks down to the floor amongst her prepackaged feast and digs in…literally. The young man watches in shock, and also a fair amount of disgust and morbid fascination, as she devours more food (in mere minutes, mind you) than anyone he'd ever seen take down at one sitting before.

Eventually, she stuffs the last brownie with sprinkles into her mouth, lets out a loud, rumbling burp, and then flops backwards to lay down right in the middle of the mess. And what a mess it is! The young man looks up and down the aisle at the shredded boxes, the discarded plastic wrappers, the crumbs and spilled food. "Holy crap!" he gasps. "Cleanup on aisle four!" But then he groans when it clicks that cleaning up aisle four is *his* job.

"Ah *man!*" He angrily kicks a half empty can of cashews and watches as the rest of them pour out and go skidding across the floor. Samara sits up and grins a sticky, sugar-high smile up at him. He feels himself softening at the look she's giving him, but then she ruins it. She spots a blob of icing on the floor beside her, leans over, and then licks it right up off the dirty tile that's had thousands of funky shoes tracked over it. He slaps a hand to his mouth as he feels his stomach roll with nausea.

"Thirsty," she says. "Get me something to drink. I must wash all this down."

He reaches into the drink cooler and gets her a Cherry Coke. He's entirely too shocked by it all at this point to even think about telling her no.

"Oh. *Oh!* This puts bubbles in my nose!" She burps loudly then and adds, "In my belly too. Mm, this is *good.* Earth food is delicious. No wonder there are so many fatties here!"

Samara looks down at herself and grimaces. "Ugh, I am sticky. I will need to go with you to your home and use your water-pourer. I will use soap and shampoo. And I will clean my teeth. And then you will show me how the con-dums work!"

Ecko fearfully sucks in a breath as she watches them, holding it in her lungs because the young man is shaking his head, telling Samara no. He tells her that he can't leave yet and then tries to explain that he has to clean the mess she'd just made first. It's his job.

But all Samara hears is him saying 'no' to something that she wants. She's done with *no.* Her eyes go black as her Shadows come out to play. They pour from her hands like foul, inky smoke and head straight for him. They flow *into* him… in through his nose and mouth, and he instantly stops backing away from her. She commands only the bare minimum of her Shadows to take hold of him, just what's needed to get the job done. Using her Shadow magic still takes a lot of concentration, and it leeches energy from her. She has no desire to wear herself out, thus making herself vulnerable. But *this,* this is so very easy, effortless almost and she hardly feels the strain at all as she commands him to take her to the place that he lives.

David, her Shadows whisper to her through the mental connection. *His name is David.*

"Well, David," she says, "Take me to your home. Now." David immediately steps over the mess and heads towards the doors. "Don't forget to grab the con-dums," she calls to his back.

As they make their way to the doors at the front of the store, she sees something strange. *Everything* on Earth is strange, but these are even more so. There are *things* in the corner, back behind the register lady (who's staring at them with her mouth wide open in disbelief.) Round things that are trying to fly away but have a rope tied to them, holding them captive. Some have faces, some have those strange marks that her new man-friend David had said were *written words.* She walks over to study them more closely. They must have given up all hope of freedom, because they do not struggle anymore at all. They listlessly move about, occasionally bumping into one another.

They're so strange, so *alien* to her that she just can't figure them out on her own, so she uses her Shadows to rummage around in David's head for answers. She learns that these things are called balloons and they are not living creatures at all. She has her Shadows rifle through David's head, reading every bit of information, accessing every memory he has of these... absurdities.

She 'sees' what the messages written on them say, what they are meant for. There seems to be balloons for most every occasion... Birthdays and Best Wishes, Congratulations and It's a boy/It's a girl designed exclusively for disgusting, mewling infants. She 'sees' a memory of David as a child, crying over one of these Happy

Birthday balloons when it bursts open and explodes. Oh, she has *got* to try that! She yanks one down, one that says Welcome! on it. She grasps it in her hands and gives it a squeeze. Then she squeals and laughs like a child at the loud pop it makes when it bursts.

"Hey!" register lady angrily calls out. "You'll have to pay for that, ya know."

Samara ignores her and pops another one, and then two more in quick succession.

"You stop that right now! You can't just come in here and do whatever you want!"

Samara slowly opens her fingers and releases the balloon that she was just about to kill, and it gratefully floats back up to the ceiling to live out the remainder of its life, happily and unmolested, amongst its balloon-mates. She picks up a spool of pink balloon ribbon and begins to unroll it, wrapping it loosely around her hands.

"*Can't?* What do you mean, I *can't*? I just did," Samara croons as she walks towards her. Not yet realizing the danger that she's currently facing, the woman harrumphs at her. "Well, you *have* to pay. David, tell her! If you don't pay, if you try to run, I'll call the cops. You don't want that kind of trouble," she insists as she crosses her arms over her chest.

"No, you're right. I don't want *that*. Here, let me make it right," Samara murmurs.

"That's what I thought," the woman fires back in a smug, satisfied voice. She turns away to get the balloon pricing chart to see how much to charge, and Samara steps right into her little cashier bubble that only employees are allowed in. She opens her mouth to make a fuss about it, but Samara shuts her up when she wraps all that pretty, pink ribbon around her neck and pulls it tight. When register lady finally stops twitching, she lets go and steps back, making room for the lifeless body to slump to the floor. Then she walks back over to the balloons and makes her selection, as her Shadows force David to bend down and smooth the hair back from the woman's face and straighten her name tag. *Deborah*, her Shadows tell her. The old hag's name is… *was* Deborah.

"Well, Deborah," she chirps as she ties the balloon that says GET WELL SOON onto the dead woman's wrist. "I sure do hope you feel better real soon."

Ecko cries out at the brutality of it, at the needless death of an innocent woman. Desperation claws at her mind, even as misery fills her heart. That woman's blood is on *her* hands, her death is all *her* fault. She's the one that's responsible for her twin being there. Every life that Samara takes is more blood added to *Ecko's* hands. She must hurry and find a way to fix this, for pretty soon she'll be absolutely *drenched* in the blood of innocents.

"I'm coming, Samara. I *will* find a way back home and I *will* stop you." Ecko urgently whispers this vow and somehow, even though entire worlds separate the two of them, Samara hears it. Somehow, she feels the promise of it resonating deep within her. She can suddenly *feel* her sister's eyes upon her, and she knows that Ecko has somehow found a way to spy on her. Her head snaps up and she grins at the mirror in the corner of the storefront. "You can try, sweet Ecko. And oh, how I hope that you do." Then she steps out of the store, dragging the mindless young man named David behind her.

5

WHERE IS SHE?

K r i s p i n

"Where is she? Where *is* she?" Over and over, Krispin snarls this question into the empty rooms in his Samara-less house. His rage is equal to that of the Lokskell's, immense, savage, and infinite.

He's pacing the floor, punching his fists through the walls, clawing deep gouges into the wooden floors. He's destroyed everything that he owns in a fit of sheer madness. It all lies in ruins, littered upon the floors of his broken home… everything but the items that they'd acquired during their time together. *Those* he had gently, lovingly placed into their playroom. He'd set them up as a shrine, a place where he can go to worship his love until he has her back in his arms, back in his bed where she belongs.

"Where is she? Where is she? Who took her?" he growls as he paces and punches, punches and paces. He'd made a terrible, unforgivable mistake in assuming that he'd known exactly where she would run when he watched her flee from her father's men. He thought that she'd head straight to their safe place, straight to the secret, old room under the ground. They'd come across it years ago, when they were just younglings.

101

They'd been running from her guards at one time or another, and when they'd gotten close to it, *something* down there had called out to the darkness within Samara. She'd followed the call, had been unable to resist it. It had led her straight to a strange metal door hidden under a thick layer of dirt. There were…. *things* down there. Twisted, unspeakable things, and his girl had taken one look around and had fallen in love with its ambience and macabre decor.

They'd had to leave the hatch-door open in order to illuminate the dark depths as they'd explored every bit of wickedness that room contained. So caught up in her morbid fascination, *she* never noticed the amorphous creature that crept to the opening and silently slipped out into the night. But Krispin had, and the creature *knew* that he'd seen it. It had held a single hazy, smoke-finger up to where it's lips should have been, somehow winked at him despite not having eyes to do so, and then quickly disappeared.

Later, after they'd explored the room and all it had to offer, Samara had deemed the place their new secret hideaway. She declared that *this* was where they would always meet if they ever had to split up and run separate ways.

So, when he saw her escape her guards, when he'd watched her run from her home, he automatically assumed that she would head straight there. It was her safe place… and he just *knew* that he could beat her there. And he couldn't wait to surprise her.

When he arrived, he'd quickly climbed down into the darkness and blended himself into the shadows around him. He'd waited there for her, his body hot and hard, eager with the anticipation of what he would do to her when he had her in his arms again. His little tease-tart was going to pay so deliciously for the things she'd said about him, for the lies she'd told her father. Oh yes, she would have no pleasure-screams left in her throat by the time he got done with her.

To distract himself while he waited for her to arrive, Krispin had lifted the braided lock of hair from his pocket, hair the color of flames and soft as spiddersilk. The long, vibrantly crimson rope was such a shocking contrast against the muted blues and greys of his own skin, and he adored it. He always had. Those wild red curls of hers was what had first attracted his attention, all those many years ago. He'd loved *her* from the first time he'd ever set eyes on her.

Hiding there in the darkness, twisting the length of hair around his fingers, rubbing it over his lips, he couldn't help but think back to the day he'd stolen it from her. She'd fallen asleep with her head on his chest, and he was stroking all that silky-soft hair back from her face so that he could watch her…to see if he could get glimpses of her dreams. She was always so *hard* in her waking state, forever hiding behind her rage. He loved her anger, he truly did. It was such a powerful, magnificent thing to behold. But she couldn't hold onto all that fury while she was asleep. She was soft then, sweet. Vulnerable even, although he would never, *ever* say that to her. He valued his own balls too much to risk what she would do to them if he ever did so.

He loved her, more than his own life, and he wanted her to love him back. Nevermind that if she ever loved anyone other than herself it would probably change her, fundamentally change who she was on the inside.

As he'd been running his fingers through that untamable mane of hair, he'd gotten the idea to take a lock of it for himself, to have something that he could hold onto when she wasn't there in his arms. Without even thinking about what the price that such an action would cost him, he'd quickly snipped it from the back of her head where he hoped it would go unnoticed. But she'd noticed right away. She'd felt him take it, and she'd been pissed, just as he knew she would be.

Oh, but she'd loved it too. She'd loved the sentiment behind it, though she'd never admit it. He could always tell when her heart felt something, *anything*, by how bad she bloodied him. The amount of blood he shed was always a clear indicator of how angry she was. Feelings of affection, (dare he say love?) feelings of attachment or commitment have *always* angered her above all else. Oh yes, she'd secretly loved the fact that he'd taken her hair, that he'd wanted something of hers to hold onto during his sleep hours. But she'd hated that she loved it, and so she hid behind all that anger of hers. She'd punished him for making her feel something other than rage and lust. She'd punished him for hours upon hours for his tiny, sentimental indiscretion.

But… she hadn't demanded that he give it back. Once his punishment was done, she'd allowed him to keep the lock of hair, and it became his most prized possession.

Krispin hid there in the shadows for over an hour, thinking about the past with that braided strand of hair pressed to his lips, but she never came. He'd waited for her, and she never came to their hideout. And by the time he realized that she wasn't coming at all, it'd been too late to find her. She'd disappeared, vanished and no one could tell him where his dark angel had flown off to.

The last one to see her had been old Lekjaz. He said that she'd run right past him, as if all the spooks of the BelowNeath, the Underworlds, were chasing after her. And that, just a few minutes after she'd zoomed by, two hobglins had gone running past him too.

The information had done nothing to help Krispin, as he'd already known about the hobglins. He'd seen them leave her house and chase after her with his own eyes. He'd had no doubt that his lover would outrun them, though. Samara could run swift as the wind, and hobglins are notoriously slow. And yet, she'd never made it to their secret place. It made no sense.

With no other leads, Krispin had then climbed to the top of the tallest structure left standing in town, an old, crumbling tower from a time long gone. He'd looked everywhere, searched every direction, straining his eyes to see as far out as possible. The longer he'd searched, the more he'd begun to feel like she'd never made it out of town at all. He didn't believe that she could have passed beyond his sight. It was highly unlikely, as his vision is most excellent. His eyes can see for miles upon miles, even in Pitch. If she were out there, if she was still free and hadn't been captured, she would *still* be running and he would see her out there now, either walking along the sands of the Dead Sea, or in the openness of the Forbidden Plaines.

Or she would have run straight to the hideout. And since she hadn't gone *there*, and she wasn't anywhere within his sight, that meant she was still here in town somewhere. She *had* to be. Fury filled him at the thought that someone had dared to take her and had hidden her away from him. Or… and his cold, reptilian blood had begun to boil in his veins at the thought, she'd found herself someone new.

Maybe she'd already replaced him with a new lover. Perhaps she'd run straight to this new man's bed, even as he, Krispin was frantically searching for her. She had thought him dead, after all. It was a logical assumption that she would look to another male if he were no longer there to satisfy her voracious needs.

He'd howled as his head had nearly exploded from the pressure of his rage, as thoughts of her lying with another besieged him. He'd gone tearing through the town, kicking open doors, searching in closets and under beds. He'd knocked over furniture, searched in every cubby hole and every crawl space. He'd scoured every inch of every single home and mercantile in the entire town. He'd slaughtered everyone that tried to stop him or get in his way, which was only three people, because they all *knew* better than to get in his way. He'd even gone back to check the secret room one last time, just in case she'd shown up after he'd left.

But she still hadn't been there. She hadn't been *anywhere*. His lover was gone, lost to him. He'd thrown back his head and howled out his rage and anguish, his utter desolation. He'd gone a little crazy then, and somehow had ended up back in his home, with no memory of how he'd gotten here.

A low, continuous growl rumbles from his throat as he glares at the useless, meaningless mess around him. He kicks the door right off its hinges as he storms out. He's decided to go over to Storver's to get rip roaring drunk. He does not like liquor. He loathes the feeling of having his senses dulled, of being vulnerable and out of control. But he's desperate to cool his blood down, untie the knot in his belly, and ease the pain in his broken heart, even if it's only for a short while. Drinking himself into sweet oblivion sounds just about perfect to him right now.

It watches intently as the blue one destroys everything in his path. It watches him howl his anguish from the rooftops. It understands the rage. It feels it too. Were all of its carefully laid plans for naught? Where did the flame-haired female go? How had she vanished so completely that she'd left no trace behind? Will she return? It needs answers, and so it trails behind this Krispin, following his every move. The blue man had been the woman's mate and he's obsessed with getting her back. Surely when she returns, if she returns, this creature will know of it and will waste no time in reclaiming her. And then it won't waste any more time either. It will make its own move... and claim them both.

6

WELL CLARICE, HAVE THE LAMBS STOPPED SCREAMING?

E c k o

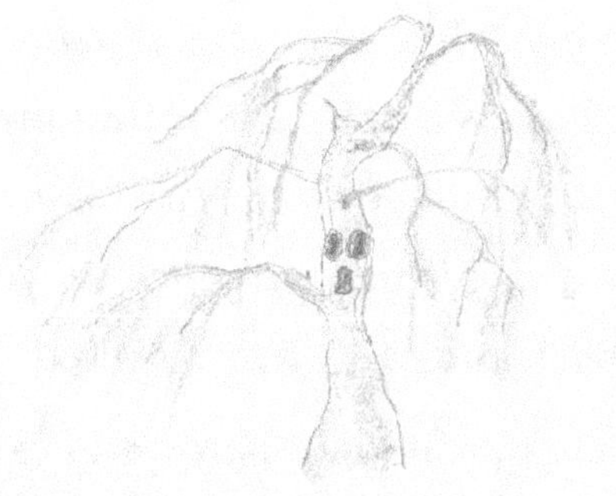

A sudden, sharp jab to the middle of her back jolts Ecko back into the here and now. She blinks up at Urza in confusion while her mind adjusts itself, jerking her out of her vision of Samara's life and back to this reality.

"What in all of the BelowNeath are you staring at? I said get up! 'Tis time to make our move, *now*, whilst the trees are in their deepest slumber stage. If we wait much longer, they will wake while we are amongst them," Urza scolds.

Ecko's abruptly yanked to her feet as she's fumbling with her flashlight.

"Are you dumb? You cannot bring that fire torch amongst the trees. Put it away." Urza gives her an impatient shake before shoving her backwards.

She clutches her flashlight, holding onto it for dear life. "What do you mean 'put it away'? I can't see in the dark! I'll never make it through without it."

Blaxx snorts. "I told you so. She is blind during the Pitch. Completely blind and as helpless as a newly dropped hobglinet. Useless as man tits."

Urza scowls at her while she tries to come up with the best course of action. "This is a problem," she snaps. "She cannot go floundering about, bumping into the trees. Nor can she shine that beacon and give us away. When we get close, you will just have to lift her onto your back and carry her. Now let's go!"

With that, she clamps her hand around Ecko's wrist, and then they're running as if the hounds of hell are after them.

"He doesn't… have… to carry…me," she puffs and pants from the exertion of running. She does *not* want to be carried. The last thing she wants to do is get close enough to smell the overwhelming stench of them. "You can lead me through. I'll hold onto you. Just like you're holding onto me now. I'll follow your every move. I won't let go."

"We shall see," Urza grunts back. She is 100% focused on the run and they're closing in on the Scream Patch faster than Ecko had thought they would.

"Turn it away from them, you infernal idjit! Do you *wish* them to wake and eat us?"

Ecko hastily points the beam of light to the ground and watches where her feet land until their great leader brings them to a stop.

"Put the torch out now and if you do not wish to be carried, you do exactly as I say. Hold onto my shoulder and do *not* let go. We will be moving slowly, quietly, so it should not be too difficult to hold on and follow behind, even for you. Try not to make any sound as we pass. Do not talk. Do not even breathe loudly. Do not walk heavily. Step slowly and lightly upon the ground. The trembling of the dirt from our footsteps can just as easily awaken them as our voices will. If anything should happen, if I am forced to speak out, you will follow my instructions immediately. Do it not and you will die a most horrible death. Do you understand?"

She doesn't wait for a reply, but snatches Ecko's hand and slaps it onto her shoulder. "Silence now. And remember to tread lightly."

And then they're all moving forward, sneaking and creeping along on their tiptoes like Scooby Doo and Shaggy trying to avoid monsters.

When the trio is perhaps fifteen minutes into their carefully creeping trek, Ecko starts wondering if they'll ever make it out of the Scream Patch. She also can't help but wonder why it's *called* a Scream Patch. So far, it's been nothing but a silence patch. She hasn't found a single clue as to how this place got its name, and she hopes to keep it that way, because this place (and the whole situation) is absolutely dreadful. Her eyes can't even make out the hobglin in front of her, much less anything else that may be prowling about in the depths of the Pitch around them.

But she can *feel* them out there, lurking just beyond her vision. She can feel their life forces, and she knows without a doubt that they're living, sentient beings. She can also sense the alienness, the *wrongness* of them. They're hostile, malevolent beings and she grows more and more anxious the longer she's amongst them, surrounded by them. It may be silent as a graveyard outside, but her mind refuses to take the hint. It just won't shut up and let her be.

It *never* shuts up. And right now, she's wondering which is worse... Seeing the terrifying thing or being completely blind and *imagining* the terrifying thing? She doesn't know the answer to that for sure, but she suspects that the answer is her imagination. Her mind can be a horrific place where even *she* refuses to dwell sometimes.

Then again, whatever these things are that surround them now... maybe they *are* better left unseen. They make her skin crawl, as if there are *things* wriggling and squirming all over her. But then, with a shudder of revulsion, she realizes that things *are* crawling on her, skittering across her arm, sliding across her back, and slithering across her cheeks.

She wants to scream so badly. Never has she wanted anything more, but she raises her fist to her mouth (the hand that's still holding onto the flashlight like it's a lifeline even though it's turned off) and bites down on her knuckles, *hard* to hold the screams inside. This is another old trick she'd learned years ago, just another way to keep all her emotions (monsters?) locked inside so that they didn't spill out and make her hurt anyone.

She clamps her other hand down tight onto Urza's shoulder and gives it a desperate shake to alert her to the fact that all is *not* right in their world. Urza stops for a moment and Ecko senses the movements as the hobglin turns her head to look back at her. She must have seen something alarming, something *terrifying*, because she suddenly shouts out, "They're awake! Run for it!" Then, that inconsiderate jerk takes off without any other warning.

And wouldn't you just guess it? Unprepared and startled out of her wits by the sudden shout, (after such a long, thorough silence) she loses her grip on Thing Two's shoulder. She's left behind and alone in mere seconds, and more and more *things* come out to touch her, crawl on her. Terror and indecision hold her frozen in place as panic consumes her. Should she try to sneak out, blind and alone? Or should she turn the flashlight on, so she can see and then make a run for it?

"Run, you dumb shites! Blaxx, move your flabby, floppy arse!" Urza shouts from way up ahead. Apparently Ecko hadn't been the only one to freeze up. Blaxx is still behind her, and he shoves into her now as he rushes to catch up to his mate.

"Run, girl!" he screeches, passing her up as she stumbles forward. "The time for stealth has passed! They know we're here."

That's all the encouragement she needs. She clicks the flashlight on, just as something reaches out, slithering over her face and clutching at her hair. She immediately takes off, legs pumping faster than they've ever moved before.

"It's got me!" she yelps as the bad thing snatches at her hair. She cries out in fear and pain and then, like the big dummy that Urza keeps calling her, she turns her head and shines her light to see what it is that's just yanked a patch of her hair out.

Because she's focused on the 'monsters' off to the left, she's not looking at the one directly in front of them, blocking their way forward. She doesn't realize that Blaxx has stopped in his tracks to stare up at it, and she slams right into his backside, sending them both sprawling belly-down into the dirt. He picks himself up with nothing but a grunt, and *that's* when she knows for sure that they're in serious trouble. A hobglin without anything derisive to say, especially when he's been knocked down is definitely something she should be worried about. In this case, it's a clear indicator that he's more terrified than he is inclined to be nasty to her.

Their tumble has landed them in a small clearing surrounded by a circle of the alien trees. She gets up off the ground and takes up a position beside Thing One (Thing Two is nowhere in sight, most likely long gone) She raises her flashlight up and aims the beam at the tree directly in front of them. It's huge, *massive*, and it's just *wrong*, somehow. She stares up at it, apprehension and dread washing over her, fear clinging to her like a second skin.

It looks for all the world like a giant, distant cousin of Earth's weeping willows. A wintertime weeping willow, bare and leafless, but the bark on this one is all wrong. It's very dark colored, sort of a greenish, greyish color, and it's covered in large, lumpy warts. It looks sick, diseased, and she wants nothing more than to tiptoe a wide berth around it and then forget she'd ever come across it.

There's a good fifteen feet between them and the tree, but it's *reaching*, stretching its branches towards them. And the branches nearest to them are moving, swaying in the air, much like those feeler vines on the Roly-Poly Meaty-Eaty tree. What she'd thought were bugs (and worms and snakes and all manner of slimy, slithery things) crawling across her skin were actually the branches of these trees that surround them. She shines her light on those thin, naked branches, her eyes tracing them all the way back up to the trunk…and that's when she realizes how very, *very* wrong she'd been.

She wishes she could turn back time, go back to the moment she'd decided that *seeing* the bad thing would be better than remaining blind and dumb, go back to depending upon her imagination to come up with its own description of current predicaments. *Nothing* her mind could conjure up would ever come close to this.

She doesn't realize that she's shaking her head and slowly backing away, until Blaxx grabs her arm to keep her beside him. "No. No, no, no, no, no," she repeats over and over again. Because, unbelievably, her light has come to rest upon a face, a man's panic-stricken face, embedded right into the tree trunk. His skin is reddened and peeling from exposure and his bushy, black caterpillar eyebrows are raised up high on his forehead, frozen there in a perpetual state of terror. Her heart stops beating in her chest and crawls up into her throat to block her airways as the beam of her flashlight glints off of his fear-filled eyes. Her blood runs cold when the man's mouth opens wide, and the first petrifying scream rends the air.

His cry is quickly followed by another, a woman's voice this time, ringing out from somewhere above him. Ecko jerks the light up higher and it reveals the woman that's just added her cries to his. She could *almost* pass for human, with her pale, soft-looking skin and her ruby red lips, lips that are opened wide to let the screams out. But her eyes are reptilian, mustard-yellow and mottled with thin brown lines and those lizardy, vertical-slit pupils. And of course, those eyes are focused directly on *her* with her bright light beacon. That light starts to dance and bounce around, because her hand is suddenly trembling so hard. She frantically moves the light up and down the tree, illuminating face after face after face.

They awaken the very instant that the light touches them. Their eyes snap open, and when they see her, they immediately open their mouths and add their own cries to the ones already ringing out. She realizes that it's not just people that are trapped inside the trees. There are faces of all types of creatures, alien, humanoid, and bestial. There also seems to be several skeletal faces thrown into the mix. Apparently, some of the bone people got caught up in…. whatever this is. There's even a Foul-Kry up towards the top of the trunk, and it's adding its own dreadful voice to the mix.

But it's the face of a little white lamb with its itty-bitty pink nose that convinces her to stop looking at all the individual faces, to stop trying to identify all the many different kinds of living creatures. It's just a tiny baby and it's bleating so sadly, so desperately that she feels like her heart will surely break if she doesn't escape the sound of it. Its cries seem to fill her mind and drown out all the other screams, until it feels as if the lamb has surely moved in and taken up residence right there inside her head. She can't stand it; she *has* to go to it. She just *has* to help the poor, sweet thing.

She doesn't realize that she's walking towards it, until Blaxx grabs her arm and yanks her back. "Do not follow the cries. Do not answer the call. You cannot help them, not any of them. They are naught but bait now, kept alive only to lure more victims in," he tells her.

As if all that's not bad enough, the branches have come *more* alive now. They've woken from their previously lethargic state and are now writhing and slashing all about in the air, just beyond their reach of the two petrified onlookers.

Blaxx grabs her shoulders and gives her a jarring shake. "Put out your fire torch! You're waking them all!"

But it's too late for that. If their presence and her light hadn't already accomplished it, the alarm seems to have already gone out, and it's a bell that cannot be unrung. There's no way to stop it, no way to take it back. The cries are being taken up and passed along from tree to tree, to the very furthest reaches of the Scream Patch. All around them, the screams are ringing out, one after another, and together they're making the most discordant and inharmonious sounds. It's like the most disturbing mind jarring, soul shattering, cacophonous song ever sung.

Even in her terror, her recalcitrant mind still has a mind of its own, with the ability to bring up random tidbits of knowledge/memories that she's gathered throughout her life. And right now, it's reminding her of her favorite books, the Fever series by Karen Marie Moning. The story is all about the Fae world, filled with all manner of strange creatures and preternatural beings. In these stories, there's a thing called the Song of Making. It does exactly what it sounds like it would do.

When sung, it creates life from nothing. It's a thing of great and terrible power, and only the Fae queen can sing it. Ecko imagines that the terrible sounds she's hearing now is the Song of *Unmaking*. It's what would come about if the faerie queen stood in front of a mirror and sang her Song of Making into it. In the mirror world, it would be reversed, sung backwards… and it would do the exact opposite. It would unmake things, undo them, break them down to such a molecular level that they blink out of existence entirely, like they had never even been created in the first place.

Yes, *this* is just what a Song of Unmaking would sound like, made up from the screams of thousands of trapped souls, the cries of the forever damned. It's a sound that's inherently distressing, more agonizing than can ever be put into mere words. It's torturous to listen to and it strikes terror deep within her heart. All she wants to do is escape the horror of it, *right now*.

She whirls around, shining her light upon this tree and that one, illuminating the hundreds of faces trapped within the tree trunks. In her panic, she never once considers extinguishing her flashlight. There's not a single thing on this world, or any other, for that matter, that's powerful enough to make her switch that light off and return her to the blindness of the Pitch. She will *never* be without a light, not *ever* again.

"You fool! We're dead because of you. You've brought doom upon us!" Blaxx wails.

Ok, now that's just not fair. Their situation may not have become so dire so quickly had she not turned her flashlight on, but the light is *not* what started it all. Yes, it seems to have been what awakened the faces, but those branches had already been awake and aware of her presence among them. They'd been all over her. Touching her.

Not that it matters *why* the faces woke up and started screaming, belting out their misery and howling out their pain. It only matters that they're awake *now*, and that they've woken up every one of their friends in the Scream Patch.

How unfortunate that she now knows exactly how the Scream Patch had gotten its name. She longs for the return of the silence patch. The shrieks from the Foul-Kry's were nothing compared to the screams surrounding them now. Those had been horrific, yes, but they were purely a defense mechanism, specifically meant to scare away any and all threats. These, on the other hand, are the painful outcries of the terrified, the screams of the lost, the forgotten, and the damned. The Foul-Kries could cause the blood to flow from every one of your orifices, but these Screaming Willows, singing their torturous version of the Song of Unmaking, could very well make your *soul* bleed.

The song doesn't seem to affect Blaxx nearly as much as it's getting to her. He grunts as he drops his Foul-Kry 'lunchbox' and plops down in the dirt. Her mouth drops open in disbelief when he lays down, one arm cushioning the back of his head and the other thrown up over his eyes, all while the deafening scream-song plays on repeat...on and on and on for all eternity.

"Umm, what are you doing?" she cries out in disbelief. "This is definitely not the time or place for a nap! We need to figure out how we're going to get out of here."

Blaxx doesn't say anything at all, but merely lets out a little snort of dismissal instead.

"I'm serious! I am *not* going to sit here and wait for…. whatever it is those things want to do to us. I have no idea what that may be, but I'm not doing it. Do you hear me? I mean, come on, really, what *is* this anyway? What did those trees *do* to those poor...creatures? How did they get those faces, those living, breathing, *screaming* faces in there? Are there people walking around out here with no faces? Walking all about with blank empty spots at the front of their heads where their faces used to be? Nope, uh-uh. Not me. Not today, Satan. My face will *not* be the next one implanted onto those trees. I wouldn't look good up there anyway, my coloring would clash with all that grey-green…." Her frantic, nonsensical babbling trails off when the irritated hobglin glares up at her and snarls, "Would you shut up yer blither-blathering? Look up, stupid one! The Pale is upon us. 'Tis too late to do anything now. Without the darkness, the trees can see us. They will not allow us to pass." And then he throws the arm back over his eyes, just as the world around them suddenly goes from nighttime to day, illuminating the world with the dull, muted light of the Pale.

"Finally! Oh, this is wonderful!" she cries out with heartfelt relief. She's smiling such a beautiful smile that when he looks back at her, he shudders at the hideousness of it.

"Uugh, wipe that disgusting smile from your face, you imbecile. What have you got to be happy about, you strange, feeble-minded twit?"

She laughs as she turns her flashlight off and stuffs it in her pocket. "The Pale has come, and we can finally see!"

He grunts and reminds her that *he* had no trouble seeing through the Pitch.

"Well, now I can see too. And now that we can *both* see, we can work together to choose the best path, the one that will get us safely through the Scream Patch. We're going to make it out of here!"

She suddenly realizes that she's having to fairly shout to be heard above the deafening cacophony of screams around them. "Umm, does it seem like they're getting louder?" she yells above the noise. Glancing around at the trees, she notices that every single face is turned towards her, every pair of eyes is trained solely upon her. She gulps and drops down to the ground beside Blaxx.

"Hey, is it just me, or are they screaming louder? And are they staring at me or is that just my just imagination too?" With sudden inspiration, she reaches into her bag, takes her earbuds out and shoves them into her ears, just to block some of the noise out. That helps, but not nearly enough.

She glances at Blaxx and finds him staring at her as if she has suddenly grown another head. "Why are you putting vines into your ears? What are they for? Is it magic?" She ignores his questions and repeats her own. He sits up and sighs heavily, condescendingly, before answering. "Yes, they're getting louder and yes, they *are* staring at us. *We* are the only reason that they're even awake. They *should* be asleep right now. They usually go into their deep sleep just before the Pale arrives. They do not like the light. They don't move or even make a sound at this hour, unless they sense food nearby. And if you haven't figured it out yet, *we're* food! Now shut up and go to sleep, or just shut up and let *me* sleep!"

She stammers and splutters at the absurdity of it. "Sleep? Sleep? Why would I go to sleep? How *could* I go to sleep? How can *you?* There's no way we can possibly sleep through all this noise!" she shouts as she raises her hands to cover her earbud-plugged ears. They just aren't cutting it. She'll have to turn some music on and blast it on high volume to drown them out.

Blaxx laughs. "Clearly, you've never been to a hobglin mound. Relax, girl. We'll just wait them out. We'll take our rest here throughout the Pale, until the Pitch returns. Of course, we'll also have to wait out most of the Pitch too… until they go back to sleep again. See? You just got to think things through without panick-ing."

She can't believe how stupid this creature is. Truly. "That's it? *That's* your plan?"

When he grins smugly up at her, she just about loses it. "You want to sit here and do nothing for twenty-three hours? Because that's how long the Pale lasts. I know. I timed it. Twenty-three hours for the Pale and thirteen for Pitch. I can't stay here and lis-ten to those screams for *thirty-six freaking hours*. I just can't."

Blaxx frowns because clearly, he hasn't considered just how long they'll be sitting there if they go with his plan. "That *is* a long time," he reluctantly agrees. "I don't think even *I* can sleep that long. Hmm, there must be something we can do to pass the time. If you were a hobglin, we could rut the Pale away, but you're too ugly to mate with. Not even the mighty Kurinrak, king of all hob-glins would lie with you, and he humps anything that moves. And besides, Urza would murder us both anyway. Oh, I know! You can teach me some of your magic! Yes! I'll be the envy of the mound, if I could do some of your tricks. Teach me, wench."

Ecko gags and then gags a second time. She quickly sends up a 'Thank you, sweet baby Jesus for making me too ugly to mate with', before she turns her iPod on. She desperately needs some sort of divine intervention, but since that doesn't seem to be forth-coming, she'll settle on some musical inspiration.

She blasts her eardrums with her all-time favorite band, Blue October. She sings along, belting out the lyrics to several songs, until she feels her whole mentality shifting. Normally, music is her only saving grace. It's what helps her get through each day, but she hasn't had the opportunity to listen to a single song the entire time she's been stuck on this nasty world. (The ones that play in her head don't count.) She hadn't even turned her iPod on, mostly because she's had to be on such high guard the whole time.

She's had to listen so carefully for anything that might want to harm her, which, so far, has been *every single thing* that she's encountered. Even the vegetation here wants to eat her. Shoot, she hadn't even been safe from dead sea monstrosities. But another reason for the music silence (torture!) was battery conservation. She's not quite sure if the dim light of the Pale will charge her solar-powered charger.

But she has the music playing now and oh, how she's missed her Blue inspiration! She breathes deep, feeling so much better on the inside... in her heart, in her mind. The Pale looks just the slightest bit brighter. Her situation seems just a tiny bit less intimidating.... until she glances over at the trees and sees all those open mouths. She may not be able to hear them with her ears, but she can still hear the sounds of their tortured screams echoing through her mind.

'Just one more song', she negotiates with herself. Just one more and then she'll figure out what to do, how to get herself out of the mess she's in. She figures that she might as well get as much enjoyment out of it as she possibly can. She accesses her saved videos and pulls up the song 'Fear'. *This* is her theme song, her mantra, and there'd been a time when she'd sit for hours with it playing on repeat, watching it over and over and over again. She'd tell herself that if that beautiful singer with his wounded, tortured soul could find inner peace after all he'd been through, then so could she. It had gotten her through some dark, dark times.

She watches it any time she needs an extra little boost of goodness and positivity. Whatever she's lacking, whatever seems to be missing in her life, this song provides a small dose of it. Hope? Sure, we've got your hope right here. Peace? All she has to do is close her eyes and listen. Understanding, forgiveness, self-love? It's all right there in the words of the song, in the struggle-stamps, the tattoos that decorate his skin that tell the story of the fights that he's won, and the fights that he's lost. It's in the ghosts that haunt him, the ones that shine out of his eyes for all who care to take a closer look.

And finally, it's there in his newfound, well deserved inner peace, the truce between himself and his demons. It's the absolute conviction in his voice, his vows to get back up and do better tomorrow. He tells himself to believe in himself and then get back up again. It's a song of pure inspiration and motivation, a balm to her wounded soul. All she has to do is believe in herself and keep getting back up whenever her ridiculously bizarre life knocks her down.

That's exactly what she intends to do. Now that she's bolstered her spirits a bit, she turns the music off and puts the player away. The terrible cacophony of screaming, which is inconceivably louder and harder to endure now, fills her mind and immediately begins to wear on her. Maybe some food, some sugar will help. Food *always* makes her feel happy, at least for a little while.

She reaches into her pocket for her squished granola bar and takes that first blissful bite. It's while she's enthusiastically chewing said bite that it occurs to her that they may be sitting here, being mentally tortured for hours on end for no good reason at all. She groans in disgust, turns to her idiot companion and starts a very important debate.

"Why are we waiting here again? What *exactly* are we waiting for?"

Blaxx watches her eat and quickly decides that food is a *great* idea. He takes out his own snack and bites a huge mouthful of jet-black Foulmeat off what appears to be a leg bone. She scoots away from him, adding a couple more feet between them when he answers her with his mouth full, his lips spitting and spraying foul chunks everywhere.

"We are waiting for their next sleep cycle to come around. Since you riled them up right before their last one, we will have to wait throughout the whole Pale and most of the Pitch too. We should be able to sneak away fairly easily at that time. As long as you don't be an idjit and light your fire stick again. You *have* to show me how to do that magic."

"I'm confused," she confesses. "Didn't you say that they're only *really* awake and active when they see food?"

He snorts and rolls his eyes. "Yes, Dummy."

"And didn't you say that *we're* food?"

He heaves an impatient sigh… "Yessss, you twice-damned Dummy. We're food."

"And they can see us over here, right? They can *clearly* see us, sitting here on the ground?"

"How stupid *is* you? They have eyes, do they not? Lots of them. Of course, they can see us. We're the only reason that they're awake at this hour."

"But if they're awake and watching us now, won't they *still* be watching us in the morning… when it's their beddie-bye sleepy time?"

He scratches his head. "Yes, but when the new Pale comes around again, they will go to sleep. That is what they do. That is how it is done."

She nods agreeably, even though she does *not* agree with his faulty logic. "Ok. There's just one last minor detail that I think you're forgetting. *Why* will they go to sleep? Will they suddenly forget about us once their next sleep time arrives? Surely, they will *still* be able to see us through the Pitch, the same way that you and Urza can see through it. Surely, they're going to continue staring at us, drooling over all this tasty, scrumptious see-food…food that they can clearly *see*, all throughout the Pale and then all through the Pitch. They're going to watch every move we make and they're going to *continue* to scream about us sitting here all the way up until the time comes for them to go back to sleep. Right? Are you with me so far? My question is, *why* will they go to sleep, if we are still sitting here looking like dinner?"

She throws her hands out to point out the faces watching them. "They're not just going to suddenly decide that they're no longer hungry, or that we no longer look like a pair of tasty nutritious and delicious chicken dinners! Surely, they won't think to themselves, 'Oh, it's sleep time now! Let's just forget about eating and go to sleep and pray to our face-stealing, scream-gods that another meal is dumb enough to come wondering around when it's actually time for us to be awake again!" She sucks in a deep breath, chest heaving and heart pounding from the oxygen deprivation that her impassioned speech had brought on.

"My point is, they're not *going* to go back to sleep at their next sleep cycle, because they'll keep watching us the whole time we're here. It's not like we can hide from them and make them think we've left, or make them forget about us. I don't know exactly how these Scream Willows work, but if *I* were a face-thieving, people-eating tree, stuck in the ground and unable to go anywhere to get myself some food, I would snatch up every single fast-food meal that came my way. I wouldn't let them pass by, just so I could go back to sleep. I would do my sleeping *after* I ate my meal!"

Then that idiot, who likes to claim that other, *smarter* people are the dumb one's, blinks once. He glances over at the Scream Willows that are still staring at them and still steadily howling. He looks back at her. Blink. Blink, blink. He turns his head… looks at all the trees throughout the Scream Patch. Turns back and stares at her. Silently, with the dusty, unused wheels in his mind creaking as they slowly, reluctantly begin to turn. Then… "We're dead. They will *never* go to sleep with us sitting here amongst them as we are. You've doomed us both."

Ding, ding, ding! *Finally,* she's gotten him to see that they're in real trouble here and that they can't just wait it out until it's

Scream Willow beddie-bye sleepy time. And while forcing him onto the same page that she's on *should* have been a positive step forward on the path of finally moving in the right direction, it is *not*. She hasn't improved her lot in the slightest. She'd thought that they would be able to work together, come up with some sort of plan. She was wrong. All she'd managed to accomplish is to thoroughly freak out the imbecile in their midst.

Blaxx proceeds to have a full out panic attack, complete with jumping to his feet and running circles around her. He's adding his own hysterical screams into the mix, tearing at his patches of hair and then throwing his hands up in the air, waving them like he just don't care...she can't help herself. As frustrated as she is, as scary as this entire situation is, she laughs as she reaches for her camera. She intends on showing Thing One exactly how ridiculous he looks, just as soon as he calms down enough to look at the photos. She snaps several before he gets tripped up over his own feet and goes sprawling on the ground right in front of her.

He just lays there, staring down at the dirt for a moment, and then he throws his head back and starts crying. He's dramatically wailing, rolling about in the dust and he sounds *exactly* like Smeagol had sounded when Sam and Frodo put the elf rope around his neck in The Lord of the Rings. It would have been funny, it *should* have been. But he's riling up the rest of the screamers, the *real* screamers, the ones that actually have a reason to scream.

There's a new, frantic pitch to their cries and they've become so loud that it feels like blades slicing through her mind. She knows instinctively that she can't take this new pitch at this decibel for long. She covers her ears with her hands as she stretches her foot out and nudges him to get his attention. "Blaxx! Stop that! You're hurting them. Can't you feel it? Can you not hear it?"

He shuts up and stops acting like a dramatically dying cockroach long enough to call her an idjit again. "The halfwit says I'm hurting them. *I'm* hurting *them*! Them!" He sits up and dirt cascades off his body in a miniature dust storm. "They're about to eat us for FirstMeal and you're worried that I'm hurting them? You truly are as dumb as you look." Then he's muttering to himself, cursing her and calling her every derogatory name he can come up with.

"Blaxx!" she yells to snap him out of it. "Look. Check out the pictures I took of you while you were getting in your morning cardio." Honestly, she just wants to distract him, to get him to stop freaking out so that they can get on with the 'working together to rescue themselves' part of the day. But that's not *exactly* what happens.

She holds up her camera, so that the screen is turned towards him. "Look at this one here. It was perfect timing! I've caught you with your tongue hanging out, your eyes all bugging out…. uummm just like they are right now …*what*?"

And then that stupid hobglin is back on his feet, pointing at her and shouting, "Witch! Black magic! *Soul stealer!* You've stolen my soul and trapped it in your magic soul box!"

He's shaking his head back and forth, shouting at the top of his lungs about soul suckers and magic and spells. She turns the camera off and lays it on the ground. Then she holds her hands up in a calming, placating manner to show him that they're empty. "It's ok, Blaxx. Calm down. I can explain. It's not magic. I am not a witch, and I didn't steal your soul. I don't even know if that's possible, much less how to do it."

But he's not listening, or perhaps he's not hearing her words over the uproar around them. So, she stands up and slowly walks towards him, one hand still held up in an attempt to appease him. His eyes grow wide and he quickly backs away from her, still frantically shaking his head in terror.

She frowns and stops advancing on him. "Look, come back over here. Let's talk about this. Stop backing up! Look behind you, Blaxx!" She shouts that last part, because he's backed himself up, almost within the reach of those feeler branches...*and they know it too.*

They've become highly agitated, snapping themselves back and forth through the air, stretching as far as they can reach. The very tips are actually behaving like a hand that's opening and closing, beckoning in the 'come here, gimme gimme' gesture.

"Look Blaxx. Just stop and listen. I'll prove it. I'll aim the camera back at me and take a picture of myself. Why would I do that if I'm stealing souls?" She picks the camera up off the ground and turns it towards herself. But she's seriously underestimated his superstition and his terror. He immediately spins around and takes off running to escape the monster that he now believes her to be.

And in his haste to get away from *her*, he runs straight into the deadly embrace of the real monster.

"Well, that wasn't the plan at *all*," Ecko whispers to herself in horrified disbelief. Her legs refuse to support her weight any longer and she drops back to the ground, unable to tear her eyes away from the visual horror of a tree that consumes living creatures for breakfast.

The instant that those feeler branches grab a hold of him, they drag him up into the air where more and more branches can reach in and get a grip on him too. They wrap all around him, some even slithering up inside his pants to wrap around parts unseen. They wind around and around him, until he resembles a bobbin, a living spool that holds thin, vine-like tree branches instead of thread. Every inch of him gets wrapped up, all but his head. The branches stop winding just below his chin.

All those lumps in the bark that she'd thought were warts, aren't warts at all. They're actually mouths, disguised as boils and warts and growths. Round, sucker-like mouths, hundreds of them *on each branch*, latch onto him. Blaxx is screaming out for Urza, begging his wife to come and save him as all those mouths start sucking him dry, slurping *him* up into *them* as if he's some kind of grotesque, hobglin smoothie.

But that's not even the worst of it. Oh no, things around here *always* get worse. A large knot, high up on the trunk that has, until now, gone unnoticed amongst the screaming faces, opens itself up and produces a single white branch. But it's so strange, so *alien*, that 'branch' isn't quite the right word for it. It's more rootlike in appearance, perhaps closer to a taproot than a branch. It has no bark, as if an old man had taken a sharp knife and skinned it so that he could whittle cute little animal figurines from it.

It appears strangely smooth and elastic, slimy even when compared to the warty, lumpy mouths on the rest of the tree's branches. It emerges right out of that knot, slithering down, stretching itself to reach the terrified hobglin. When it's positioned directly above him, it plunges the rest of the way down in a sudden, lightning-fast jabbing motion, straight into the top of his head and burrowing itself in deep.

Blaxx's eyes grow wide, and he stops crying for his mate long enough to turn his startled gaze upon her. "You've doomed me. Oh, you nasty, *nasty* witch. You've killed me." And then he's screaming again, but his words are all gone now. All he has left is screams of pain and terror, as the root begins sucking him up too, much faster than the little mouths are managing to. It *is* the taproot, and it sucks up and absorbs all the hobglin nutrients into itself to transport back to the tree, and oh, dear God, she can't make herself turn away.

As the meal flows through it, it begins to swell up, becoming fleshy and bulgy until it very much resembles an umbilical cord. It sucks all of Blaxx's insides up, until there's nothing left inside him. He appears to be deflating, just like a balloon that's slowly losing all of its air. He crumples in on himself until he resembles Sigmund the stuffed teddy bear, after her dad had de-fluffed it (before he'd dismembered it and burned it to ashes.) Poor Blaxx suddenly looks for all the world just like the teddy bear's empty pelt, after it had lost all its stuffing. And then... unbelievably, his outsides start getting sucked in too.

It begins at his deflated feet, the furthest point from the umbilical root. Ecko's mind replays the scene from the Wizard of Oz where the Wicked Witch of the East's legs shrivel up and get sucked under Dorothy's house after the ruby slippers disappear from her feet. Blaxx's feet get pulled right up into his empty legs, causing the branches that are wrapped around them to lose their grip and fall away.

With nothing else to latch onto, they return back to where they belong, higher up in the air and closer to the trunk. Then Blaxx's legs are gone, pulled up into his middle, causing more branches to unravel and retreat. He continues to fold in on himself and the branches continue to fall away, until all that's left is his head, dangling in the air from that terrible umbilical root like a freakish, nightmare pinata. And *still*, it continues slurping him up, until even the back of his head is consumed too, dented in like a half-deflated basketball. Only a third of his head is left intact, leaving just the face. Literally all that remains of Thing One is his face, *and he never once stops screaming.*

His eyes stay focused on her the entire time he's being turned into a Miracle Grow, plant-food slushie. They accuse her even as they plead for her to help him. He only looks away when he begins to move. His eyes roll wildly from side to side when the root begins to retreat back into the knot in the trunk, dragging him (what's left of him) along with it. It retracts itself, until it's all the way back inside and Blaxx's face is positioned in front of the knothole. It slowly pulls his face in, wiggling it back and forth until it's wedged in tight and the hole is blocked. Then the edges of the knothole sort of *grow* around him to adhere him firmly in place, gluing him down tight, fusing him to the trunk, so that he is now and will forevermore be one of the many faces that it possesses.

The whole, horrifying process has taken no more than ten minutes from start to finish, but Ecko feels as if she's aged tremendously, as if entire *years* have passed within these last few minutes. The hundreds of other faces had all quickly caught on to what's been happening, and their cries have escalated to an unbearable level, an unholy uproar from the eternally damned. They all blend together into one horrendous, mind shattering din.

But two particular cries rise up and stand out from the rest. Two that are particularly painful and dig at her heart, gouging at her soul. She knows that even if she makes it out of the Scream Patch and goes on with her life, she will never be able to silence these two voices. They will live on in her mind and haunt her for the rest of her days. She will *never* be able to drown out the sound of their fear. The poor, innocent little lamb…and poor, dumb Blaxx.

The Song of Unmaking must be taking its toll on her. Or perhaps it's the weight of all the traumatic ordeals that she's been forced to endure in too short a time frame. Whatever the cause, her head begins to get foggy, and her vision begins to blur. She's suddenly swaying back and forth, thankfully still down on her knees, because otherwise she would have fallen down immediately.

The tears continue to trickle down her face even as her mind shuts down in a desperate act of self-preservation.

Her eyes briefly lock onto the bleating little lamb's face before they suddenly roll back and she crashes down to the dirt. One last thought flutters through her mind before the darkness takes her. "No, Dr. Lecter," she whispers. "The lambs have *not* stopped their screaming. They never will."

7

BE GENTLE, IT'S MY FIRST TIME

Samara

Those first few Pale's... *days... they're called days here.* **The first few *days* that Samara had spent here on this new world were filled with exactly that. Firsts. She rode in a car for the first time and almost had a heart fail when she witnessed her first horribly loud air flyer machine, soaring high above the vehicle. She witnessed her first sunset, her first star, her first sunrise. She saw cows for the first time and demanded that her driver turn around and take her back so that she could go out into the field for a closer look at the strange beasties. She'd laughed uproariously at their moo moo's and their frantic stampede to get away from her. She'd rolled her window down and scream-moo'd at every single cow she passed after that.**

That first man that she'd taken control of, the middle aged one from the hospital parking lot drove for hours. He drove until he claimed that he was so tired he could barely hold his eyes open. He complained and cried, saying he couldn't go on any longer. His whining had filled her head with such sudden, intense fury that she'd made him get out of the car, pick up a good-sized rock, and then beat himself to death with it. And while she'd had a good giggle at the sight of his bashed-in head, with his right eyeball dangling down onto his ruined face, she soon realized that she should have thought it through. If she had done so, she would have made him do it somewhere closer to a town and not in the middle of nowhere.

She'd had to walk for a long time, until she finally *did* come to a town. That was where she'd met her David in the 99-cent store. David had provided her with a whole *plethora* of vital information… taught her about soap and toothpaste and prepackaged food and balloons…and condoms.

He'd taken her to his home, where she'd slept in a clean bed for the first time, with soft, clean material folded neatly over the unsoiled mattress… something David called sheets. She ate her first 'fast-food' meal lying on that bed, watching, absolutely fascinated as one group of people after another… people inside the magic 'tv' box, mated with each other in more ways than she'd ever imagined possible. She'd gotten so hot, so turned on by the things she saw, that she'd had no choice but to relieve herself on the conveniently available young man. He'd thoroughly enjoyed it too, until she broke him and was forced to find another to take his place.

She was more careful the next time; she didn't just settle for the first man she came across. She picked one that was a bit older, a bit brawnier, with a passing fair appearance. She broke that one too, but not before she got to experience a wealth of other 'firsts' first. She had her first time riding in an elevator, which just about scared her to death. She went on her first clothes shopping spree and had her first stay in a rented room… in a mercantile called a hotel. She had her first taste of chocolate, which she figures is the closest she'll get to the EverLands.

She had her first swim in a pool, wearing her first bikini. She also had her first time being approached by 'swingers', which led to her first time going home with a couple, and her first time climbing into bed with a woman *and* her man. The woman was an exciting and pleasant *first*, but the man… oh, he'd lasted a lot longer than the woman had.

Of course, he'd wanted out immediately after the two of them broke his female, but she hadn't been ready to give him up so soon. He was beautiful and virile, vaguely reminding her of Krispin, and she had wanted to make him last. And he had, but only with the help of her Shadows, as his mind broke long before his body gave out. How was she to know that human men didn't find rolling around naked, covered in their lover's blood arousing? Krispin would have adored it. He would have fucked her for *days*.

So many firsts had distracted her from her original goal of finding her sister's few remaining loved ones and wiping them from the face of the Earth. Oh, she'll get around to it, if the old farts don't expire on their own before then. She *loathes* Ecko and still plans to make her pay for everything she's ever had to endure… all because she hadn't been born first. She hadn't been the chosen one, the *special* one. Her dear sister had been given every privilege, every advantage, every comfort and luxury, while she herself had been abandoned on that dreadful, dying world. As if that wasn't bad enough, she'd had to live her entire life being punished for *not* being the chosen daughter!

But all that's in the past. She's here now and her dumb sister is trapped over there, hopefully suffering horribly. She doesn't let herself think about her previous life very often, she just enjoys her *new* one. This world is amazing…there are so *many* firsts that she wants to experience, so much fun to be had! There will be plenty of time to hunt down Ecko's old geezers. She'll take her time. She'll learn all she can of her new world. She'll have some fun, damn it! Live a little, as she'd never been allowed to do before. She's going to do anything and everything that her dark, twisted heart desires…and she'll have as much sex as she can, with as many beautiful men as she can find.

And maybe, just *maybe*, she'll be able to fuck away the memory of the blue-skinned lover that haunts her memories.

The man watches her from the shadows and trails behind her, following her every move. He does not attempt to approach her or contact her in any way. He merely watches, learning everything he can. He wants her badly, but not in a sexual capacity. No, nothing as simple and mundane as physical pleasures. He could get that anywhere, and besides, he's seen what's left of the people she fucks. That's certainly not how he plans on going out. No, thank you.

No, he's smarter than the average man, those who are renowned for putting their own pleasures above all else. One must be shrewd, cunning, and ruthless in order to climb to the top of the drug cartel ladder… and even more so to keep the position upon that top rung. He has no intention of giving up his hard won and highly respected position of drug lord. He intends to hold that crown for many years to come… and he wants Samara to help him achieve his goals.

How much more power would he gain if he had her by his side? No one would dare to challenge him after they witness the things she could do to them. Oh, he wants her so badly he can almost taste it! All he needs to do is find something that he can offer her, something to entice her into joining him. He would grab her and use force if that were at all possible… but it's not. She would rip his entrails out… intact, mind you. Then she would wrap them around his neck and hang him so that he slowly asphyxiates on his own guts. True story. He watched her do just that to some other unfortunate bastard. But *that* man had been stupid, and he deserved what he got for being so.

Lennard Rollins the third, Lenny the 'Bossman' Rollins is most definitely not stupid. He'll get what he desires. He always does. It's all just a matter of time and patience, and very, *very* careful planning.

8

POOR MAGGS

Krispin

Krispin clutches his pounding head and groans miserably. Just as he'd suspected (and hadn't given a damn about) the drinking binge had *definitely* not been the answer to his problems. He hadn't been able to find his love at the bottom of a bottle, nor had the consumption of so much liquor made him feel any better. It just made everything worse. Terrible, in fact. Not only was Samara still missing from his life, but now he's got a raging headache and a sour stomach to go along with it all...

And apparently, a woman lying naked beside him that he has no recollection of bedding. A woman that he immediately realizes is *not* the one that belongs in his bed. He sits up, holding onto his aching head and glances around, confirming that he *is,* in fact in his bed. He has somehow magically made it back to his own broken bed, in his own trashed out, destroyed home. He has no memory of returning, and he certainly doesn't remember anything about the redhead currently lying beside him. Although she has a head full of limp red curls, it's a dull, washed out red, almost an orange color. It's certainly not the wild, flame-red spirals that he adores.

The woman is sleeping soundly on her belly, and she doesn't move when he gently prods her shoulder in order to rouse her. He tries to think back, wracking his brain for information that he just can't seem to retrieve. He can't recall anything after he'd switched from the light wine to the harsh, almost flammable rotgut swill that Storver passes off as whiskey.

He glances back down at the woman and growls. He does *not* like this. He doesn't bring other women into his home. *Ever.* His body may have needs that he must take care of, but he makes sure to take care of them elsewhere. He would never dishonor his love by bringing another woman into their home. But here she is, proof that he has no control over what he does when he's consumed too much alcohol. He's full of loathing and disgust for himself and how far he's managed to let himself sink

He grunts and slaps the woman's naked butt. "Get up, woman. Get up and get out."

But she doesn't move, and he suddenly gets an anxious feeling deep in the pit of his belly. He reaches out and gently rolls her onto her back, and the blank, sightless eyes staring up at the ceiling confirm his fears.

It's Maggs, the woman he visits on occasion when his Samara is unavailable or is being exceedingly difficult with him. And she is dead as dead can be.

"Oh, no," he whispers with true sorrow in his heart. He'd brought her into his home, and he broke her…permanently. He's done some bad things in his life, some nasty, heinous things even, but he's not a murderer. Ok, so he's really not above murder, but he always tries his best to spare the innocents. And that's the truth of it.

That's just what Maggs was, an innocent. An old whore she may have been, but that had been for survival, not by choice. Circumstance had forced her into that sort of life. She'd been a sweet old gal, just trying to live and now he's responsible for snuffing out her light, for sending her soul to face the unknown, out into the Eternal Pitch. "I'm sorry, Maggs. I truly am," he murmurs as he smooths the hair back from her face. He strokes those curls, knowing that he'll miss them most of all.

His brow furrows and his hand stills atop her head as he thinks about what to do with her. He can't just leave her here, lying about his house. But what to do with her?

He tugs his pants on then lifts her off the bed and throws her over his shoulder. He slinks through the shadows of the Pale, careful to remain unseen, until he's safely on the far side of town, the part of town that's abandoned and remains (mostly) empty at all times. The part of town where the only visitors that ever came calling were him and his love...where Samara's special underground room awaits its mistress. He'll put Maggs there, just for now, just until he can think of something else to do with her.

As he climbs down into the underground room, he senses that someone has been there recently, maybe just moments before his arrival.

"Who's there?" he calls out.

No one answers and he lets out a rumbling warning growl, as he hears the barely-there sighing of displaced air, feels the tiniest disturbance in the atmosphere of the room. Perhaps the intruder is still here, in which case he will make them very, very sorry. His eyes shine brightly in the darkness as they search every corner, skim over every object for the trespasser.

But he finds that he's alone, after all. There's no one here but him and old Maggs. He settles her into a chair in the corner and then spends a few minutes fixing her hair flatteringly around her face and arranging her arms and legs, so that she'll be comfortable while she waits.

He steps back to survey his work. He has to make a few minor adjustments to the angle of her head and then he nods to himself when he sees that it's good. He pats her hand reassuringly and promises that he'll return soon. Then he climbs out and closes the overhead door, sealing her away in the darkness.

He never discovers that his instincts had been right... that *something* had been down there with him all along, and it had watched every move he made as he'd set Maggs up in her chair. He never saw the virtually invisible presence that lurked just behind him in the darkness. He didn't feel it as it rushed past him, up through the door and out into the Pale. He never even suspects that he's being followed, watched, studied...*Manipulated.*

The Wyrm follows close behind, just as it's done ever since it realized that the girl had disappeared, the one with the hair like fire... the powerful one. The one that it had chosen as the host for its own lost mate.

No, not lost, but merely… misplaced for the time being. But the flame-haired female known as Samara has disappeared, and so it must alter its plans accordingly.

It must move forward with its plans to take the Krispin-creature, before he too is lost. It cannot afford to lose him. There are no other suitable replacements in the vicinity… none for miles and miles and miles. It would have to drift the skies for an interminable amount of time to find another with enough power to withstand the merging. It has searched long and far for two such as these, this Krispin and Samara. The girl is absolute perfection, and she will make a magnificent host for its mate… if and when the two obstinate females can be tracked back down.

The blue beast-man is not as great a find as his female, but he is suitable… powerful enough to survive the merging with a Wyrm. But only just. The merging will take its toll him.

Now that it must move up its plans, it will have to convince the Krispin creature to accept the merging as quickly as possible. Until then, until the two of them become one… permanently, it will continue to explore this unexpected new development… this delightful discovery. Although it will still need Krispin's permission to do a full merging, it has found that if this soon-to-be host drinks enough of the mind-alterer beverage, it can slip right in and take over. At least for a short time, until the effects begin to wear off… at which point it immediately gets expelled back out of the host's body.

At least that's what had happened last Pitch. Krispin had guzzled the grog-water beverages one after another, until he was so intoxicated that he'd fallen unconscious to the floor. He never re-gained consciousness as the people in the establishment had gathered around him, planning to terminate his life.

It had watched the proceedings in anger as it realized that its host body was about to be destroyed, before it got the chance to merge with him. It had rushed in then, desperate to rouse Krispin enough to alert him to the danger, but he discovered that his mind was completely shut down. And since his mind was no longer active in any way, he had no will left within him to say yay or nay...

And there was the loophole.

That was how the Wyrm had been able to get inside of him, without permission granted. It took a moment to get its bearings, but it was eventually able to get the Krispin-creature back up on his feet and into his chair, where he proceeded to snarl and growl and then laugh uproariously when the conspirators scattered like frightened children before him.

"So much for liquid bravery!" it had called out with Krispin's vocals as it made its borrowed body stand up and stagger out the door. That's when it bumped into the red headed female. It was not Krispin's red headed female... not his mate, but a different one. An older female, and not nearly as lovely as Samara, but still attractive.

The Wyrm, who had full access to the host's memories, searched and quickly found all the past interactions with this female. She's not Krispin's chosen mate, but he had nevertheless engaged in sexual acts with her... many times.

It lifted Krispin's hand and grasped the woman's delicate wrist, loving the feel of her tiny, fragile bones and her soft skin. The host's heart had then begun to pound, his cock growing hard, as she vehemently shook her head and spoke words at him, but it hadn't had any interest in words. It had focused instead on the shape of her lips, the little flashes of her small pink tongue as she talked. The sight of it drew up memories of her down on her knees before this body, her mouth moving over his swollen, spit-slicked member.

While it kept her arm firmly entrapped within its grasp, the Wyrm had taken a moment to explore those pleasure memories, to witness all the things she'd done to pleasure this body. And it had decided that she would do nicely for the first acts of debauchery in this host's body. It had worried for one brief moment that the act wouldn't be as delicious as it normally is, that it wouldn't experience the full magnitude of sex-pleasures that it would experience when the merging with Krispin was completed. But then it reminded itself that it would not know until it gave it a try. This would be an all-new experience for it. Never before, in any of its many previous life cycles had it taken its pleasures while it hovered solely within a host's mind… one that it hadn't first merged with.

But it was in here now, and as it hadn't yet succeeded in gaining Krispin's cooperation for the merging, it would most definitely take advantage of this wonderful new development. It had been too long since it last felt the pleasures of the flesh, and this female had seemed quite capable of reminding it of everything it had been missing out on, while it had endlessly searched for a host body to inhabit. *It decided that it didn't want to waste another moment, especially with the uncertainty of how long it would be able to keep its hold on Krispin's mind.*

The Wyrm had then stretched Krispin's mouth wide in an anticipatory grin as it caught the woman up in its/Krispin's arms and carried her away, where it did all those filthy, lovely things it had spent years dreaming about...

And it had been so very delicious.

9

THE WORLD IS A VAMPIRE

Ecko

Ecko's eyes snap open as she jerks herself up out of Dreamland to escape the nightmares. She'd been dreaming about Charlie and a sweet little dream-puppy that he'd bought as a surprise for her. It looked identical to the one that her parents had tried to give her years ago. The one that she'd wanted more than her next breath and had secretly named Pufflebutt. The one that she'd had to break her own heart for when she'd been forced to reject it in order to keep it safe from Samara.

In the dream, she'd been laughing and holding her arms out to receive all that soft, fluffy goodness. The pup wagged his tail happily, seemingly just as eager to be in her arms as she was to put him

151

there. But as soon as her hands wrapped around him, he threw his head back and pointed his nose up at the sky to howl.

And it wasn't cute little puppy howls that came out of his up-turned snout either. It was the bleating of that little lamb from the Scream Patch. Its cries tore her up, punched her right in her un-suspecting dream-heart. Her eyes had instantly flooded with tears as she tried to give the pup back. But Charlie was no longer there. She was alone once again in the middle of the Scream Patch, hold-ing onto that crying pup. It was a glaring reminder that she's never good enough, that she can never keep anyone she loves safe, can never bring them happiness.

The faces trapped in the trees are screaming, but all sound has ceased. Their mouths are still opened wide, their eyes full of pain and terror, but it's like someone has clicked the mute button on a giant remote control, silencing the whole world around her.

But then she hears a man's voice behind her. "You've doomed poor little Pufflebutt." She spins around to see who it was, but there's no one there. Then a woman's voice, coming from some-where to her left adds, "*You* set your sister loose on your world." A voice above her chimes in, "She's killing hundreds of your peo-ple. *Hundreds.*" Off to the right, a harsh, raspy voice calls out, "She's going to burn your world to ash!"

It's the faces talking to her, reminding her of all her many, many flaws and all of her failures. She spins around in circles as they speak but she can never catch them in the act, can never see exactly which face is the doomsayer. Their lips don't form words;

their mouths don't move at all. They're frozen open, in their perpetual screams. Only their eyes move, rolling about to watch every move that she makes. And throughout it all, the little lamb bleats on and on and on.

"Stop it," she whimpers. "Stop saying these things to me. Just go away!" But like every nightmare she's ever had, this one refuses to just go away when she tells it to.

The next voice laughs at her. "You're weak, pathetic," it says, and this time she instinctively knows which face said it. It was the leather-faced scarecrow woman with the beady black eyes, on her left, that had spoken up.

"You left Charlie and Sssusssan behind. They're going to be sssslaughtered." Her eyes dart to a reptilian face with yellow and green scales. Its forked lizard tongue is hanging out in a silent scream/hiss, but somehow the words had come from it just the same.

"You're crazy, dangerous. You should be locked up where you can't hurt anyone." This was from an almost-horse. It looks exactly like a copper-colored stallion, but its muzzle is all wrong. It has the mouth of a crocodile, complete with the sharp teeth of a deadly predator.

"Come. Join us!" urges a one-eyed cyclops monster.

The voices come faster and faster, shouting out their insults, issuing their demands, and chastising her with their doom-on-you's.

"Yes, join us."

"You hurt that boy, the one who just wanted to be your friend. Robert Walters is a vegetable now, all thanks to you"

"Come, join us. Feed us!"

"Everyone is afraid of you. Even your family thought you were a freak."

"Come, be our friend. *We're* not scared of you."

"Come, come!"

"Your mother, your *real* mother died because of you."

"You will never find your way back home. You will be trapped here forever. Just like us!"

The voices keep coming at her, tearing her down, filling her heart with anguish, with hopelessness…and then, oh! Then the grand and horrible finale. The pup, that sweet, fluffy little puppy in her arms looks up at her and, without moving its face a bit, says "You…Killed…Your…Whole…Family. It's all your fault…And you know it. You should kill yourself too. It's just what you deserve."

Ecko drops the pup to the ground and throws her hands up over her ears. She screams for it all to stop, begs for it to go away. Just go away! She screams so long and so loudly that the force of it carries out of Dreamworld and into the waking world. She wakes with the scream on her lips, her throat raw and shredded from the abuse.

She lays still upon the ground, trying to swallow down the pain in her throat and the horror from her dreams. Somehow, she instinctively knows that she's no longer in the Scream Patch. Not only is there sweet, blessed silence, but that overwhelming feeling of wrongness, that awful itchiness in her mind is gone.

She stares up at an empty grey sky and tries to think back, tries to recall just how she'd managed to escape the Scream Willows. The last thing she remembers (before she'd passed out) is the little lamb, the one that had followed her into Dreamland. After that, there's a big, empty *Nothing.* She has no memory of leaving the Scream Patch, no inkling of how she'd gotten here…wherever here is.

She tries to sit up and then dumbly stares down at her hands that, for some strange reason seem to be hogtied to her feet. She rolls herself over onto her side to search her surroundings for the reason as to *why* she's tied up, to find out what she's (somehow) gotten herself into now. She appears to be on the edge of a dark, forbidding forest. The trees are thinly spaced, but most of them tower so high up into the sky that they block out a great deal of the already puny light.

She can't see a single leaf or flower amongst them, though. It all looks dead to her, a dead forest full of dead things, but there *is* some sort of dark, bluish-grey moss growing on everything. It clings to the ground and the rocks, and it climbs up the tree trunks to wind around the branches in thick patches. Perhaps it's what killed everything, if everything *is* in fact dead. Things around here are deceiving….

"Things aren't always what they seem in this place, so you can't take anything for granted," she quotes in the worm from Labyrinth's voice. Good advice, even if it had come from a puppet.

Since there's no one in the direction that she's currently facing, she rolls herself onto her other side to see if the answers to her questions lie that way. Her gaze immediately locks onto a pair of angry… scratch that, a pair of absolutely *seething,* orange eyes. Thing Two is alive, and apparently, she is mad as H-e-double hockey sticks.

Ecko gulps at the malice directed straight down at her and she knows without a doubt that she's about to get blamed, and punished for Thing One's (death?) Is that even the right word for the state he's in now?

'Not the time to be worrying about what the correct term for Blaxx's altered form of living is' she thinks to herself as she covertly tests her bonds to see if she can free herself. No such luck. Urza is much too adept at villainy. She would never be so lax as to allow any room for escape. No, there will be no great escape on her part, *yet.* If she can't talk her way out of this mess, she'll just have to bide her time (again) and wait for the opportunity to come along. She's betting that as mad as Urza is right now, the hobglin will nevertheless continue to place her own self-preservation above her desire for revenge. She has no choice but to hand her captive over to the Lokskell. He'll kill her if she fails to do so. So no, Urza can't kill her, no matter how badly she wishes otherwise.

But there's a whole world of horrible things between life and death that she can do, a million and one different tortures that she can inflict upon her while they make the journey. It's best not to push her any further with half thought-out escape attempts.

She nervously clears her throat and just barely manages to squeak out, "Oh, hello Urza! I'm so glad to see that you're alive, so happy that you made it through safely."

Urza bends forward and picks Sir Didymus up off the ground, instantly bringing her attention to the fact that all of her belongings have been dumped out of her backpack onto the dirt. Her heart stutters with fear for Sir Didymus's life, but she does her best to hide it from her captor. She would go through a ridiculous amount of torture in order to save the stuffed animal, but she certainly doesn't want Urza to know that. (Don't be so quick to judge. Didymus is one of her only friends, and he's THE only friend she has on this entire world. Of course, she would do everything in her power to save him. Wouldn't you?)

As nonchalantly as she can manage it with her heart lodged in her throat, she asks, "Why'd you dump all my stuff out? Was there something you wanted? Are you hungry? You're welcome to whatever you want to eat. Surely, there's *something* that you'll like. You liked the smell of the beef stew. I have more of that, if you want to try some." She rambles on and on, trying her best to not freak out, trying to keep her eyes averted from that nasty hobglin's hands as they stroke Sir Didymus's fur.

Urza remains eerily quiet. If her intention is to intimidate her prisoner, well then, her plan is working marvelously. Ecko forces herself to shut up, because she knows that she's giving herself away and revealing her apprehension. She struggles to sit up and once she's made it into an upright position, she's finally able to survey her surroundings. The Scream Patch is back behind Urza, maybe a mile away from where they're sitting.

She wonders if the trees and all their many faces have gone back to sleep, or if they're just too far away to hear them. Either way, it's a tremendous relief to be away from their cries. The silence is a soothing balm to her ears, to her mind, and her heart. Closing her eyes, she tries to meditate, to think calm and relaxing thoughts. She just about jumps out of her own skin when Urza suddenly throws her head back and lets out her own shrieks of rage. She screams so loudly, so piercingly, that they may as well have been back in the Scream Patch.

When she's finally let out all the screams that she'd been holding inside, she turns her attention back on her prisoner and snarls, "Where is he? Where is my mate?"

Ecko quickly glances away. She doesn't want to see the pain on Urza's face when she tells her what had happened. She doesn't want to feel pity for someone so cruel, especially when that someone is holding her hostage and has every intention of turning her over to a man that's so evil, he makes the devil look like a happy little elf, skipping along, sprinkling wishes and glitter as he goes. But she *does* feel pity. No one should have to lose their loved ones so tragically. She forces herself to turn back and look Urza in the eyes as she sadly shakes her head. She whispers simply, "The trees got him."

What more is there to say? She fully expects Thing Two to lash out at her. She expects to have all the pain and anger and loss taken out on her, because that's what so many people do when they're in pain. They lash out and take it out on those around them in an attempt to make themselves feel better. That's just how it goes.

So, when the fire ignites in Urza's eyes and her entire face flushes from her anger (what color would puke-green skin that's flushed with a red-tinted blush be?) she braces herself for the up-coming punishment. She fully expects to be beaten, at the very least receive a slap or two. Maybe a kick to the ribs, or a punch to the side of her head. What she's not prepared for is Urza jumping up and stomping around in a small, tight circle, screaming at the absent Blaxx for being so selfish.

Ecko's stunned speechless. Like umm, *what?* What's happening right now? She has no clue what to do, what to say, or even how she's supposed to react. So she just sits quietly watching a grown woman/hobglin throw a raging tantrum.

"How could he? Oh, how *could* he? What a selfish, useless little shite! I should have listened to Mother. She warned me, she did! She said he was too weak to take as a mate. But would I listen? Noooo! I had to fall for those seductive eyes, for that tempting man-body of his, that delicious pelvic-thrust!"

Urza stomps around her circle, and now she's taken to hitting herself. She is literally beating the crap out of herself, slapping her own face and punching herself in the head. Every once in a while, she does a weird stamping/hop thing, so that instead of stomping just one foot as hard as she can, she jumps up and stomps back down to the ground with both feet.

Ecko waits for the ground to open and swallow her up from the force of her feet pounding upon it, just like what had happened to

Rumpelstiltskin. But a hole never appears in the ground and Urza continues her crazed rampage.

"Oh, what a nasty, selfish mate you are, Blaxx, to leave me alone like this! How am I to make this journey alone? How am I to feed and protect our hobglinets by myself? And what about my rutting urges?" She stops stamping around and shakes her fists in the air. "YOU KNOW I NEED MY MAN-MEAT!" she screams at the top of her lungs.

She lowers her fists and bows her head. Her shoulders drop in defeat as her chest heaves with every loud mouthful of breath she takes. They both listen to those last words echo throughout the forest, pinging off the trees until it's gone... MAN-MEAT! MAN-MEAT! MEAT! MEAT! Meat!

"Oh, you nasty, selfish he-hobglin," Urza whispers one last time and then raises her eyes up to meet Ecko's. "Was it you? Did you have anything to do with my mate's end?" She asks it so calmly, so quietly, searching her prisoner's face intently for any trace of a lie.

"He panicked and made a run for it." That's all she says...simple and to the point. Andit's not a lie. Blaxx *had* panicked. It just wasn't the whole truth, nothing but the truth, so help her God. She didn't feel any need in informing her captor that *she* had been what caused him to panic.

Urza nods her head once. She knows that had very likely been the scenario. Ecko holds her breath in fear as the unpredictable hobglin walks over and unties the ropes from her wrists and ankles.

"I'm half starved. Make me food, and none of that poison you tried to feed me before."

And just like that, Urza is over the loss of her mate. She sits back down and begins sharpening her knife on a stone as she waits for her lunch, or Middlinmeal, as the hobglins call it.

"How is it that you managed to safely make it out of the Scream Patch?" Urza suddenly demands. Ecko's so focused on cooking the food, so enthralled with the heavenly scent of it wafting up at her, that she's startled by the suddenness of the question. She yelps in fright and just about knocks the little pot of stew over.

"What do you mean?" she gasps as her heart tries to settle back into its normal rhythm.

Urza frowns at her and repeats her question. "I mean just what I said. How. Did you. Get. Out?" She enunciates each word, as if she's speaking to an imbecile.

Ecko stops stirring the food and stares at her in confusion. "I honestly don't understand. Didn't you come back in and get me?"

The two of them spend the next sixty seconds or so just looking at one another, blinking back and forth.

"You didn't come back and carry me out?"

In true Urza fashion, she snorts out a rude reply. "Are you a halfwit, girl? I wouldn't even go back in to save my own mate. What makes you think I would go back in for *you*?" She sneers and scoffs at the thought of it.

"B-b-But" Ecko stutters. "How did I get out then? I didn't get *myself* out. The last thing I remember is that the screaming had grown so loud and overwhelming that it was making me feel sick and light- headed. I passed out, and then I woke back up here, all trussed up like a Thanksgiving turkey!"

Thing Two frowns and says, "I do not know what this 'thanks-giving turn-key' that you speak of is, but it was not I that got you out. I walked up and down the edge of the Scream Patch, waiting for the two of you to emerge...or not. I came across you sleeping upon the ground, lazy thing that you are, and I knew my mate wasn't going to make it out. He would have been with you, if he could have been. I tied you up and dragged you far enough away from the scream-zone that the trees could no longer sense us, in hopes that they would forget about us. I did not wish to listen to them any longer than I had to. They make my head ache."

"Agreed. My head still hurts," Ecko admits as she extinguishes the small cookfire. Quickly ladling out the stew, she thinks back, replaying it all in her head to see if she can remember anything else. She passes a steaming bowl to Urza and murmurs a warning to be careful, because it's hot. The mean-spirited wench snatches the bowl from her hands, sniffs the contents before snarling that *she's* not the halfwit of their little group. Ungrateful hag.

"Wings!" Ecko suddenly shouts. "I remember seeing wings, just as I blacked out! I heard the sound of them. I felt the wind that they created against my face. Something that has wings flew me out *over* the trees. That's how I made it out safe and sound. But who? Did you see any flying things while you were scouting?"

Urza scrunches her ugly features into an even uglier grimace. "I saw nothing," she answers with her mouth full of food. She grunts in pleasure at the taste of it before quickly slurping up the rest of her meal.

"More," she demands as she holds her bowl out for a refill.

Ecko sighs in disappointment as she pours half of her own stew into it. Then she hurriedly scarfs down her remaining portion before Urza could demand the rest of it too. A burnt tongue is more preferable than an empty belly, in her opinion.

Urza burps loudly and then drops her bowl to the ground. "That almost tasted good. Hurry up and clean up your mess, so that we may leave this place. There's still plenty of Pale left for us to get a good start through the Black Forest."

As rude as that had sounded, Ecko's happy to obey. She gathers all her belongings up and returns them to her bag. While she was at it, she may or may not have placed a hurried, secret kiss on Sir Didymus's head, when she was sure that Thing Two wasn't looking.

When everything's been cleaned up and put away, she straps the bag on and waits for the 'get moving' command. But Urza's busy frowning, obviously lost in thought and she was going to do absolutely nothing to interrupt and risk angering her captor more than she already was. So, she waits until the hobglin finally sighs heavily, stands up, and approaches her.

"I have decided to let you walk on your own, without tying you back up. I know it is a risk. I have no one to watch my back, no one to help, should you decide to revolt. But we will be able to move faster if you are not bound. I want to get through the forest, as quickly as possible. If there are no complications," she pauses here to glare threateningly down at her, "we should be able to make it to the Sorrow Marshes in three Pitch cycles. If you try to escape, if you try to run, if you do anything other than what I instruct you to do, I will tie you back up like one of your 'thanks giving turn-keys'. You try anything at all, and you will remain bound until I am rid of you. *And* I will take your fire torches and let you suffer through the Pitches without them. Are we clear?"

Ecko nods at the nasty, sadistic cow, but she doesn't say anything. She has every intention of escaping, but she detests lying, so she keeps her mouth firmly shut. 'No promises, you unpleasant vessel of misery', she thinks as she's once again forced into playing follow the leader. 'I make no promises.'

Overcome with unease, Ecko stops at the very edge of the forest, distrustfully eyeballing the moss that covers the ground and crawls up the trees in thick, clingy patches. From far away, it had resembled a yucky-colored blanket of snow, but up close she can see that it looks more like a shag carpet. There are billions upon billions of little, curly tendrils growing straight up out of the mass, but they're so tightly packed in, growing so closely together that their individualities can't be seen from a distance.

She scrunches up her nose at it. It has a dreadfully *moist* appearance, and it smells bad too, sort of like the sickly-sweet rot of a garbage dump. The thought of stepping one foot onto that blanket of blue-grey vegetation is exceedingly abhorrent to her. Without taking her eyes off the loathsome stuff, she starts asking some very important questions.

"The trees, this weird moss stuff, are they alive? I mean, can they hurt us? Should I be worried? Will any of it try to eat us?" That's the main concern. Is she considered food in this situation?

"Stupid. So, so stupid," Urza mumbles under her breath as she shakes her head in an almost sympathetic way. Although she'd been talking to herself, her words are just loud enough that Ecko can hear the insult.

She doesn't mind though, not really. Stupid isn't the right term anyway. Uneducated, uninformed, ignorant of all the strange, alien-species of this world...*those* are all correct terms. She is unarguably new to this world, and she certainly doesn't have any kind of experience with people-eating vegetation. But she'll let Thing Two think she's stupid, that's just fine with her. It'll probably help in the long run anyway. She won't be expecting the stupid halfwit to come up with a successful escape plan.

"*Everything* will eat you if you let it. Everything needs nourishment, and food gets harder and harder to come by every single Pale. Hence why these trees are dead, or mostly dead. There is likely a lingering bit of life in them yet. Nothing to worry your hideous, empty little head over. The moss will only become a problem if you linger too long upon it. It's slow moving. It takes time to climb upon things, and even longer to take hold of them. Walking across it will not put us in any danger. Just don't sit down to rest. Keep moving at all times. We will pass beyond it soon enough."

Then she takes that first step to lead the way. Ecko holds back for a few seconds to watch. She just wants to be *sure*. Really, after all she's been through, after everything she's seen, who can fault her for that?

She finally gathers up enough courage to step out onto the moss blanket and she immediately grimaces at the feel of it under her feet. It's very unsettling, and she can only be thankful for the shoes on her feet. She's not sure that she would be able to stand the feel of it, if she were barefoot. It squishes and squelches, sort of like a waterlogged sponge, or Jell-O maybe? No, not Jell-O. That has too much jiggle… Tofu! It feels like she's walking on a bed of tofu.

Her tummy rumbles at the thought of food, because some greedy heifer had eaten most of her lunch. She's daydreaming about stir fry with those delicious little chunks of tofu mixed into it, when Urza seemingly reads her mind. (Most likely she's just heard the unhappy grumbling of her stomach.)

"It is toxic as it is now, but it *can* be eaten, if you dare. You must first boil it long enough to leech the toxins out. The color lightens up as the poisons are removed, and only when every trace of color has been removed, is it safe to eat. It *must* be cooked until it turns completely white. Most cannot stomach the stench of the removal process though. It is quite…. unpleasant. It's an extremely pungent scent, much like grinded-up dungbirds. *Those* are creatures that very few can bear to eat. The smell doesn't bother *me*, of course. I live in a hobglin mound. Some of our males smell so ripe, it draws tears from the eyes just to be near them."

Urza sinks her hand into a patch of it and squeezes it in her fist. The sound of it, squelching sickeningly, the putrid stench of it…

Ecko nearly loses the little bit of lunch she'd eaten. "I don't particularly like the taste of the stuff, so I never bother with it... unless there's no other choice, of course. 'Tis bland, not much flavor remains after it's cooked. But it *is* edible, unlike that slop you attempted to poison me with. We can collect some for our Endmeal, if you wish to sample it."

Urza laughs at the disgusted look plastered on Ecko's face. That will be a big fat negative. Nope, not in this lifetime, she thinks as she quickly shakes her head no. She loves tofu, but man, she wouldn't try this stuff if she was literally starving to death. Ground-up dungbirds indeed. No, thank you.

The two of them fall silent, once more, as they delve deeper and deeper into the forest. It changes slightly as they go, making the hike a bit more difficult now than it had been when they'd first entered. They must pay closer attention to where they step, concentrating on which paths to take. Several trees have fallen here, and some of them lay buried under mounds of the toxic tofu moss. The ground is littered with stumps and roots and all manner of decomposing tree debris, and it's all hidden beneath a deadly blue-grey carpet that they have no choice but to walk upon. They're forced to either climb over or go around many obstacles along the way.

At one particularly difficult obstruction, (a very large, fallen tree that they have to climb over) Ecko pauses for a few moments to catch her breath. She sits on the downed tree, straddling it so that she doesn't lose her balance, but she quickly hops the rest of the way over and moves her butt once more when she feels those bluish tendrils start slithering over her hands. It's just like Urza said. As long as they kept moving, the moss couldn't get them and turn them into Stephen King's meteor shi...poop.

When they'd been walking for a little more than two hours, the forest suddenly takes on a drastic change. The toxic tofu has slowly begun to thin out; they'd been seeing less and less of it on the trees as they passed by, until eventually it only covered the forest floor. Then there were only patches of the stuff on the ground, and now… they've come to the point where it doesn't grow at all.

There are even traces of life here, a bit of greenery tucked in here and there amongst the all the dead foliage. But the forest is even darker here, and it feels older somehow, ancient even, and incredibly sad. These trees had been around for a long, long time. They'd been witness to such terrible tragedy, such intense heartbreak that the echoes of it still linger in the very fabric of the world around them.

Ecko sniffles and swipes at the sudden tears in her eyes. Something's hurting her heart and she doesn't even know what it is. She glances over at Urza to see if she's feeling the strange sorrow too, but the hobglin's scowling fiercely at something off in the distance.

"We've made better time than I thought we would," she announces. "We're already entering into *Faoira's* domain." She makes a horrid face, indicating her disgust for said Faoira, and then hocks up and spits out something terrible that closely resembles teenage mutant ninja turtle slim.

Ecko yelps and hastily jumps back, before it can land on her foot and turn *her* into a mutant. Seriously, it looks even more toxic than the toxic tofu.

"I do not wish to stop and make camp yet, but I also do not wish to spend the Pitch by *her* revolting loch. Gggrrr, what to do?"

Ecko keeps her mouth shut and waits. She really can't offer an opinion, because she is too uninformed to make a logical, educated decision. Urza would most likely do the total opposite of what she wanted to do anyway. Also, why would she even try to help her kidnaper? Thing Two can just figure out the best way to get her prisoner to the slaughterhouse all on her own. Not that she has any intention of entering said slaughterhouse like a helpless little victim, but…

"We continue," Urza finally decides, effectively putting a damper on her wandering thoughts. "The sooner we are done with this place, the better. I wish to collect my rewards, return to the mound and my hobglinets. My mother will not eat my younglings like Blaxx's mother would, but she may forget that she has care of them. You wouldn't believe the places I had to collect them from the last time they were under her watch. Hobglins don't care much for any but their own younglings. Come, girl. Let us travel onwards."

Ecko falls into step beside her and asks, "Who's Faoira? I couldn't help but notice that she's…uh, not a friend of yours. Is she dangerous?" That's *all* that she really cares about. She wants to know about every dangerous thing on this world, so that she can avoid them. And if she cannot find a way to avoid them, then she wants to know exactly who they are, what they do, how they can hurt her…and most importantly…what they eat. She has already figured out that this entire world is a vampire, and she absolutely refuses to get sucked on by *anything,* without giving her express permission beforehand.

"Faoira" (there's that disgusted look again) "is, or once was, a very powerful being. Make no mistake, she is still extremely dangerous, but thankfully her powers are hindered now. Limited." Urza throws her head back at this and howls with deranged laughter, literally howls, long and loud, so that it echoes throughout the trees surrounding them.

Ecko stares at her, watching her shoulders rise and fall with mirth, waiting for her to get over her fit and explain the punchline. The hobglin eventually calms herself and explains. "Faoira is a Naiad, a water goddess. More like a water nymph, lake hag, pond scum if you ask me. Thankfully, she's the only one of her kind, as far as anyone can tell anyway. Her mother, Serefaye was a Siren and she lived with her sisters near the deadly Red Cliffs, in the coldest and harshest part of the sea. Her father was a Selkie named Marnan…"

She pauses here and turns to Ecko. "You *do* know what a Selkie is, don't you, girl?"

She doesn't wait for an answer but continues on with an explanation (even though Ecko does, in fact, know what a Selkie is…at least Earth's version of one. There's no guarantee that they are the same on this world though.)

"A Selkie can transform themselves into a seal, or is it a seal that can change into a person? I can never remember. Oh well. Unimportant, I suppose. Each Selkie-person has their very own seal skin and when they step into it, they change into a seal. They're not just someone that's wearing a seal skin. They actually *become* a seal and they go out into the ocean and do whatever it is that blubber butts do. And when they grow tired of doing seal things, they come back to the land, remove their skins and hide them away until they wish to put them back on and swim again. They are verily, verily careful and find the cleverest of hiding places to leave their skins when they aren't wearing them. 'Tis said to be a fate worse than death for them to lose their skins. They will forever be trapped in their people-skin, never again to swim with the seals and the fishes. Should such a fate befall them, most choose to end their own lives. Others go mad."

She pauses to glance over her shoulder and scowl threateningly at her prisoner as she scolds, "There, now you know what a Selkie is. Do *not* interrupt me again."

Ecko doesn't bother with a rebuttal, even though she'd never once interrupted. It's just not worth it. She'd rather learn more about who Faoira the Naiad is. She needs to learn what kind of danger she poses.

"Marnan the Selkie lived in a clean-water loch that flowed out into the very same sea that the Sirens lived in. But his home was way on the other side of the ocean, where the world remains warm all the year 'round. The deep cold that the Sirens thrive in had never stretched far enough to reach his home, and so Marnan hadn't known what winter was, had never felt the cold of it. 'Tis said that a sudden, unexpected winter storm blew in and caught him by surprise, while he was having a mid-Pitch swim. The storm came so quickly with such freezing winds, such a swift, penetrating cold that he'd had no chance to escape it. The cold froze his little flipper-flapper limbs and made him unable to swim, unable to move even. He got washed out to the sea and was carried far from his home."

"Now, the Sirens had no knowledge of Selkies, had no idea that such creatures even existed. When Marnan, in his seal form, got washed up onto the rocks near their Red Cliffs, the Sirens thought him just another sea creature in need of their help. Severely injured and weakened from the harshness of the sea and the extreme cold of winter, he lay for days amongst the Sirens as they slowly, lovingly nursed him back to health. Not many know this, but Sirens are as nurturing to the ones that they love as they are ruthless to those that they hate. And that they have great love for *all* living things. All things except people, that is. They harbor a deep, intense hatred for *all* people, but they especially despise men-peoples."

"As it happened, Marnan fell under their Siren's spell while they soothed him and helped him to heal and recover from his ordeal. He became entranced, completely enamored with them, and not knowing of their hatred for man-types, he decided to reveal himself to them. When he stepped out of his seal skin and they saw him for the man that he was, they became enraged at his duplicity. They, of course, wanted to do what is in their nature to do, which is to play their Siren's games. They wanted to have their way with him, use his body for their pleasures and then drag him to his death, down in the depths of their ocean domain."

"But 'tis said that Serefaye took one look at him in his naked, glistening man-skin and fell madly in love with him. She did not wish to send him to the watery grave that all men were sentenced to when the Sirens were done toying with them. No, Serefaye wanted forbidden things. She wanted to keep him."

"So, after all of her sisters had taken their pleasure of him and it was her turn, she instead stole away with him. She did it even though she knew that she'd never be able to return to her home, would never see her sisters ever again, the greedy, horny little slut. So, off they swam to find themselves a place where they could live together, away from both of their families. They made their home here, in a hidden clean-water loch that is located in a sunken part of this forest. It is close enough to the sea that they could travel back and forth and enjoy both the clean-water and the salted-water. They thought they would live happy and free forever. They should have known better. All the facts pointed out that they should have never bred."

Urza lifts her hand and starts ticking off the reasons. "One...They lived on opposite sides of the ocean. Two...They lived in different types of water, one in salted-waters and the other in clean-waters. Three...One liked the cold and the other liked warmth, and Four...They weren't even the same species!" She shakes her head at the absurdity of it.

"But they did what they did, all in the name of love or lust or stupidity. Whatever. The two of them came together, mated, and they spawned *her*, that half-breed Faoira. And *she* took on both of her parents' traits, inherited *both* of their magics. She was both Siren and Selkie, and as such, that made her a very powerful, very formidable, one-of-a-kind creature. They tried to keep her hidden away, and they succeeded remarkably."

"Faoira thrived in the secrecy that the Black Forest provided… until she became a grown she-person, with all of a grown Selkie's hungers, all of a Siren's desires. She wanted a mate. Marnan offered to lie with her, but she didn't want to mate with her old father. She wanted a mate of her own. She quarreled with her parents and then ran off to find herself a young, handsome male, an exciting new one that could fulfil her every need. She found plenty that were willing, but none that were to her liking. She traveled long and she traveled far, searching for many years to find the perfect mate to bring home to her parents."

"When she finally found him, that oh, so handsome male, she used her Siren's call to ensnare him. He fell madly in love, of course. How could he not? What choice had she given him? She took him and made him hers and then brought him home. She made up with her parents and they grew to love her new mate too. And they were all very happy, blah blah blah. Or *she* was anyway. Who knows what *he* really felt? I'm not convinced even *he* knew how he felt, poor besotted idjit that he was."

She pauses and glances over to ensure that she still has an attentive audience and Ecko's quick to reassure her. "Oh, I'm listening. Please continue."

Urza harrumphs loudly to clear her throat before she goes on. "Very well. Now, the magic of the Selkie skin will only transform its rightful owner into seal form. It won't work for anyone else. But there are several other reasons to entice one into stealing a Selkie pelt. Perhaps the most intriguing, is that *if* you can manage to steal yourself a skin without killing the Selkie that it belongs to, then you've also landed yourself a new slave. They have no choice but to obey every command that their skin holder gives them. Most captive Selkies end up as sex slaves for the depraved, enticing attractions that get passed around and around at celebrations and special events. And since Selkies are so rare, and so difficult to steal from, they are highly valued and verily sought after."

"There are some skin hunters that make it their life's work to hunt down the Selkies and steal their skins. They then sell them to the rich and powerful for large amounts of coin. If a skin hunter only ever manages to acquire and sell one single skin, he can live the rest of his life comfortably on the earnings that it brings him. But most hunters are greedy, wasteful male-creatures. They squander away all their earnings and then they get it into their dumb, empty heads that they can easily just go out and find another Selkie to steal from. So, off they go, off to hunt down another skin, risking their lives, not caring about the pregnant she-hobglin that they left behind! And what happens then? I'll *tell* you what happens. Death happens! Just like I'd told that idjit, halfwit first mate of mine!"

Urza's fairly shouting now, her chest heaving with anger, her breath loudly rasping in and out of her mouth. She stomps along, heavily pounding her feet into the ground as she fumes over the remembered, long-past insults.

Ecko patiently waits for the story to continue, but Thing Two seems to be completely lost in the memories... and she's *very* ticked off about them. She clears her throat nervously and then hesitantly, very softly asks, "Soooo, about this Faoira... I'm going to go out on a limb here and guess that someone stole her skin? And now she's angry, right? That's why you don't want to make camp near her?"

Urza stops walking and turns to her, hands on her hips with a dumbfounded look on her face. Her bushy eyebrow-caterpillars have crawled all the way up into her hairline. "Have you not been listening?" she shouts as her face flushes from the strength of her anger.

Ecko holds her hands up in surrender and takes three giant steps back. "Uhhh, wow. Just calm down! I heard every word you said. You just lost me somewhere around pregnant hobglins and halfwits and first mates! I heard everything else, I swear!"

Thing Two grunts and resumes her angry, stomping march. "Well, pay attention this time, girl!" she snaps. "I have no wish to constantly repeat myself."

Ecko nods and falls back in beside her. "Yes ma'am. Go ahead. I'm all ears now."

The hobglin's eyes immediately dart to her ears in confusion, but apparently, she decides that it's not worth questioning her about it.

"Yes, Faoira has lost her skin and she's *enormously* enraged about it. The only thing she would enjoy more than taking your skin from you, is if she could take mine. But… you're distracting me, making me skip parts! Stop interrupting!"

"Oh, where was I? Oh yes. Back before everything happened with Faoira, my first mate, Teerant somehow managed to steal himself a skin. I will never understand *how* he managed it. He was not particularly bright, and he certainly wasn't the best hunter either, nor was he the fiercest fighter. But he did it somehow, and we became one of the richest hobglins in our mound. But that idjit wasted all that gold so fast, it may as well have been a bowl of blood and blubber stew set before one of the starving outcasts that live just outside the mound borders."

"Thankfully, I managed to hide a fair amount of the gold, before he could spend it all on drink and good-time she-hobglins. I tried to get him to make it last, but he-hobglins never listen to the she's. They freely admit that we are the smarter sex, but they don't listen to us. Not ever."

Urza's shoulders slump and she sighs heavily while sadly shaking her head.

"My halfwit mate decided he would just go get himself another Selkie skin, make another fortune. I begged him not to go. You hear me? I. Begged. Him. Not to go. BEGGED! Do I strike you as a hobglin that begs?" Ecko quickly shakes her head in negation.

"No," Urza agrees. "I do not beg. It was the one and only time I ever did, and it shames me to admit that I did it. But I was little more than a youngling myself, and I was bigly rounded with my first hobglinet. I wanted him to be there for the birthing. But he'd laughed at me. Laughed and said that birthings and hobglinets and younglings was woman's work. And then he just left me to go at it alone, the filthy rutter!"

"And he never came back," Urza scowls. "Faoira made sure of that." She pulls her shoulders back and lifts her head up. "He weren't good for anything but the man meat that dangled betwixt his legs anyway, but he was my very first mate and I'd wanted him like no other. But as you can see, I made it just fine without him. I'm made of sterner stuff! I've survived for one hundred and ninety-three years...that is a long time for hobglins. I've outlived sixteen mates. Oh! Seventeen now. Poor, dumb Blaxx. I'm going to miss him. I wonder if his brother Blixx is still mateless..."

Ecko keeps her thoughts about Urza and all of her mates (the past *and* future ones) to herself...especially since she'd (secretly, guiltily) had a hand in the last one's demise. Who is she to give out relationship advice anyway? She barely understands the human variety, much less strange, non-human people...*things* on an even stranger world. Nope, she's not going there. Hobglin love is *definitely* none of her business.

As they fall back into silence, she concerns herself with nothing more than walking where she's led, until Urza suddenly speaks up again.

"We have arrived. Do *not* listen to her Siren's song and do not get close to the water's edge." Ecko looks around her in confusion. There's not a lake anywhere in sight. There's only forest and more forest.

Urza snorts. "Trust me, Dummy. I know of what I speak. I know this place verily well. Come along. 'Tis through here."

They move into a particularly dense section of the forest, where the trees have grown so close together that they almost form a wall. Twenty feet in, and the forest around them is suddenly gone. Just…gone.

Ecko's eyes grow wide with wonder as she realizes that they've gone through another one of those strange blips that she'd experienced back at the sea, the one that had taken her instantly (and unknowingly) from the beach to the cliffs. Now the two of them seem to be standing at the bottom of a deep gorge, a wooded valley that's completely boxed in by mountain walls all around them. They're still in a forest of sorts, but it's completely different from the one they've just left behind.

This one is inviting, welcoming. It's green and alive and lushly thriving. The moss under their feet is the ordinary, nontoxic kind. There's even a bird singing the most beautiful song in the history of beautiful bird songs. She's never heard anything quite so lovely, so soothing, and she quickly scans the trees in an attempt to locate it. She *must* find it. She must see if it's as beautiful as its song suggests it is.

That's when she gets her first look at the lake, sweetly nestled there in the center of the valley, and *it* is the most beautiful and enticing thing that she's ever seen in her entire life. The water is crystal clear and the brightest of blues. The surface gently ripples in the breeze, a thousand tiny sparkles twinkling everywhere that the sunshine kisses it. Several towering trees grow right up out of water, adding even more charm to the perfect, hidden lagoon paradise. The leafy branches provide appealing little patches of shade, and the water is so transparent that even the submerged branches and roots down at the very bottom are clearly visible.

"Lake Kaindy...." she murmurs in awe as she walks towards it. She'd wanted to visit Lake Kaindy and the Sunken Forest ever since she'd first heard of it as a child. It's been at the top of her bucket list of places to visit for *years*, and now she's here. She finally gets to experience the wonder of it in person.

Her heart flutters at the magnificence that surrounds her, the hypnotic melody of the birdsong, the irresistible lure of the pool. She absentmindedly starts pulling off her clothes, dropping them down onto the moss as her steps bring her ever closer. She *has* to take a swim in those enchanting waters. It looks just like Heaven, so cool and inviting, and she's so very hot and sticky from the sweltering heat of the sun beaming down on her. She will surely perish if she doesn't hurry and dive into those deep, cool depths. The bird urges her on, crooning its sweet lullaby to her with every step she takes...

Until a sudden, sharp blow to the side of her head brings her crashing down to her knees, just before she reaches the shore. Ecko cries out, more from the tragedy of being denied access to the pool than from the physical pain. She quickly jumps back up, but something strikes her again, and back down she goes. Again. Over and over, she gets up, just to be knocked right back down. But she's fiercely determined to feel those waters upon her skin, and *nothing* will stop her. She's *desperate* to feel it, and so she starts crawling on hands and knees to reach it. She must make it to the water, she must!

But instead she gets jerked back onto her feet and Urza's ugly face fills her vision, completely blocking out the sight of the lake. She cranes her neck to the side, in order to bring the loveliness of the lake back within her sight, but Urza cruelly moves with her, blocking her every effort. She struggles to get around the heartless hobglin and to the enticing pool that lay just beyond her. She even stretches her arms out, her fingers clenching and unclenching, as she tries in vain to grasp the beauty of it in her hands. Tears flow down her face as she screams aloud her frustration.

Urza gives her a long, hard shake that snaps her head back and forth and rattles her brain. Then she plugs her filthy, funky fingers into Ecko's ears to block out the sound of the birdsong and leans down to thrust her face right into Ecko's. She leans in so close that she actually jabs Ecko in the eye with her long, pointy nose. But it's the smell of her breath that does the trick. It is so disgustingly foul that it immediately pulls Ecko from the beautiful dream/lie that she's trapped in.

"What?" she whispers as she blinks up at the face pressed against her own. "Where am I? Ugh! Peee-yew, your breath is raunchy! How did we get *here*? Why am I not wearing any pants? Oh no! Why am I not wearing *anything*?!"

She crosses her hands over her private areas and frantically looks around. She spots the trail of clothes behind her, and with a glad cry she rushes back to pick them up and re-clothe herself. Her mind races and she begins to panic at the thought of blacking out and losing time again, just like she used to do back in her hospital days. She can't go back to that. She *cannot* live her life with that constant fear.

But before the panic can take hold and render her into a useless, curled-into-the-fetal-position, sobbing uncontrollably mess, Urza grabs her by the shoulders and shakes her one last time, for good measure, and repeats "Do Not. Listen To. Her. Siren's SONG! Gah! Such an idjit!" Then she spins around and vehemently shakes her fist at the lake.

"Shut up, Faoira. You hold that witchy tongue of yours still behind your teeth. The girl is mine. She is not for the likes of *you*."

Ecko's able to shake the last of the fog from her mind as the birdsong abruptly comes to a halt. "Oh my God! I was under her spell, wasn't I? How? Where is she? I never even saw her!"

She swivels her head this way and that way, desperately trying to locate the one responsible for her *almost* drowning.

"You do not have to look upon her to become her victim. Sirens *sing* their prey under their spell. Ignore their song and they will have no power over you. I *told* you this already. Mayhap you will listen to me next time."

Urza takes one last look at the lake, measuring the distance between it and herself, and then steps back twenty or so additional feet away from it. She drops down onto the ground and informs her prisoner that the Pitch is almost upon them and that they'll be making their camp here.

But Ecko doesn't even hear her. She's far too busy inspecting her surroundings. Her eyes dart about in disbelief and dismay and *absolute, unequivocal horror...* because every single thing she'd seen just moments ago had been a lie. Everything she'd *felt* had been a lie. There is no gentle breeze, no hot sunshine beating down on her, making her sweat. This world doesn't even *have* a sun.

All those tiny fabrications, those minute details were all just special, finishing touches added in to make the illusion seem more real, to make the lie more convincing, more enticing to her.... much like sprinkles on an already scrumptiously delicious cupcake. The siren's spell had blinded her eyes to the truth of this lake with pretty lies, made her believe what she was seeing was much more desirable to her.

She'd seen Lake Kaindy, because that's what she'd *wanted* to see. The picture of it had already been there in her mind, easily found and readily exploited. But now that she's no longer blinded, now that her eyes can see the truth again, she shudders in sheer revulsion at how close she'd come to walking out into *that*.

It looks very similar to the pictures she's seen of Lake Kaindy and the Sunken Forest, but it's *this* world's twisted version of it.

The surrounding forest is dead, black and dark and full of deep, disturbing shadows. The trees that once grew out of the lake still stand, but they are ugly, rotten things that stick straight up out of the water like a giant's discarded toothpicks. The only branches that remain on them are located below the waterline, and they've been perfectly preserved, either from extremely cold temperatures (just as they had in the real Lake Kaindy) or by magical means (which is just as likely here on this world.)

This lake *is* crystal clear also, and she can see each individual leaf still attached to those submerged branches. They sway back and forth with the gentle movements of the water around them. But that's where the resemblance between Earth's Lake Kaindy and this world's nightmare lake end. Below the surface of *this* lake looks terrifyingly haunted, a ghostly underwater world. The water is not blue, it's crimson red with the blood of Faoira's victims.

Apparently, she doesn't just lure people into her lake and drown them. If appearances serve, she lures them in and then rips them apart. The lake's full of dismembered body parts, *skinless* dismembered body parts. There must be hundreds of murder victims in there, because there are pieces of them *everywhere*. They bob and float upon the surface, hands, legs, limbless torsos, fingers...heads with their eyes stuck open, so that they're forced to witness the horrors around them for all eternity. Body parts are scattered across the lakebed, many of them half buried in the bloodied, sandy muck. Some are stuck to the submerged tree limbs, and they dangle amongst the leaves like overripe fruits... or macabre Christmas ornaments.

'Heads, shoulders, knees and toes. Blood, guts, fingers and toes'…. her mind inappropriately whisper/sings. This place is a big, capital lettered, italicized *NOPE!* There is no way on God's green Earth (nor on this deadly, demented world either) that she's going to spend the next 13 hours of her life here in the middle of this horrific crime scene… in the *dark*.

She swallows hard and backs away, never taking her eyes from Faoira's gruesome home, decorated with all her macabre décor and gruesome trophies.

"Disturbing, ain't it?" Urza cheerily chirps from behind her, and then laughs out loud when Ecko shrieks with fright.

Clapping one hand over her mouth and the other over her pounding heart, she listens to the sound of her own screams ring out across the lake and reverberate throughout the valley. She turns around and tells her captor in no uncertain terms, that she will *not* be sleeping anywhere near this lake.

"I can't sleep here! I don't understand how you can even suggest it. This place is terrible, all those poor people…." She shudders and picks up her backpack. "Let's keep moving. I'm sure we can get well beyond this place before the Pitch arrives. And what does it matter if we can't? You can see in the dark and I have my flashlights. Can we please just go?" She's getting desperate. She *really* wants to leave this place of death behind her.

"No" Urza rebukes. "Here we shall stay. It is unsafe to travel about in the Black Forest during the Pitch, and your little magic fires would do more harm than good. Fear not. This is the safest place to make camp. No one wants to come near the lake, so we will be left alone. Faoira cannot harm us either. Well, not if you ignore her call. If she cannot lure you to her, she'll not be able to have her way with you. She cannot leave her lake, see? So, simply ignore her song, as I've said, and you will be fine."

"Now, busy yourself with making our Endmeal before you can no longer see to do so. I'm hungry and wish to fill my belly. Let me warn you, I have no patience for defiance, especially when my belly is empty and angry. If you insist on being troublesome, remember that I can *verily easily* toss you into that lake and let Faoira have you!"

Ecko gulps back her arguments and sets about doing as she'd been told, but she's slow about it…and clumsy. She can't stop looking at all those pieces of people, all of them without any skin left on them. It's all so horrifying, so *tragic*. She tells herself, over and over, that she *really* doesn't want to know. But her mind *has* to know.

"Why?" she asks as she sets up her little camping stove and lights the fire.

"What happened to her? Why does she do this? Why take their skins off and then rip them apart? And why can't she leave the water?"

Urza plants her butt back into the dirt and lifts her head to stare up at the treetops as she continues the story of how her first husband had stolen himself a selkie skin.

"Well, my Teerant had apparently seen Faoira once when he was just a youngling. He heard her song, see? He heard her witchy song for just a *moment,* and he unknowingly became obsessed with her. But he'd been a small hobglinet and he could do nothing about it at the time. As he grew up, he never forgot it, never forgot her beauty or her Siren's song."

"Right about the time that he'd squandered the last of his earnings from his first Selkie skin, he heard the rumors that she and her mate had returned home to live with her parents. He decided that he wanted her, that he wanted to enslave her and keep her for all time. He made a plan to slay her mate and her Siren mother and to steal her Selkie father's seal skin. He planned to bring *her* home and make her his second wife!"

"Now, Teerant was never a smart one, no, *never* that, but his obsession with Faoira had his head so rattled that he was no longer thinking clearly. I would *never* have shared him. She-hobglins do *not* tolerate another she in their nests. But the males always think with their man-meat and never with their brains. They all seem to think that *they* will be the first to manage a multiple she-hobglin nest. Idjits."

Urza pauses, snorts and then turns to spit into the dirt. "He didn't listen when I told him that I would not tolerate her, that if he somehow lived long enough to see his plan through and he somehow managed to bring her home, I would kill them both. I told him in exact detail of how I would do it too, but he did not listen. He laughed. *I do not like being laughed at.* In the end, he hadn't been laughing though. He died screaming."

"Teerant managed to track the half breed bitch here, to this lake. The first one he encountered was Faoira's new mate. But

Teerant was in too big of a hurry to get him out of the way, so that he could get to his *real* target. The idjit stupidly rushed the attack. The male was harder to kill than he'd anticipated, and he put up a fierce fight."

"Desperate to save her man, Faoira sang her song to distract and lure Teerant away. She killed him. Horribly. While her mate lay on the ground bleeding to death, she tore mine limb from limb. She kept him as her most prized trophy though. That's him, hanging there for all to see."

Ecko turns her head, her eyes following Urza's pointing finger. And there he was, nothing but bones dressed in a suit of dried, leathery skin. He'd been ripped into pieces, strung back together with his own entrails, and hung from the top of the tallest tree at the center of the lake.

Somehow, Ecko instinctively knows that he's displayed there like that as a personal insult to Urza. That fact is confirmed when the hobglin laughs nastily and goes on to explain.

"She keeps him up there in retaliation… because I put her mother and father on display over here."

She points to a spot behind them and Ecko's eyes have no choice but to take the hint and look for herself. She cries out in dismay the moment she sees them. Urza had turned them into scarecrows and set them out where their daughter would always be able to see them. *That's* why Thing Two chose this precise spot to make camp in, so that if Faoira wants to watch them, she will also have to see her parents propped up behind them.

"That's the exact positions they were in as they drew their last breaths, so that is how I tied their limbs up. All they could do once I'd driven the poles up into their guts was cry and reach for one another. I set the poles into the ground with just enough distance between them that their outstretched fingers could almost, *almost* touch. And oh, how they stretched and reached for one another. *He* struggled so hard to get to his wife that he nearly tore himself free at one point."

Oh! *Oh!* How horrible can one be? She'd done it all while they'd still been alive! Ecko can't imagine the pain that they'd suffered, the physical pain of having a tree shoved up their bbzzztts, the mental anguish of the lovers forced to watch each other slowly die before their very eyes, the heartbreak of hearing their daughter scream and scream and scream.

"Now, see what you've done! You've distracted me yet again and I've gotten ahead of myself in my tale. Now, I must backtrack. Shut up, you, and let me tell it! Now, where was I? Oh yes. I wasn't far behind when my mate met his end. I couldn't stand the thought of him taking another female to wife, see? My jealousy, my anger burned too hot for me to meekly sit at home and await his return. I did not want to endure the shame of it either. I *refused* to be shamed. So, I set out shortly after Teerant's departure, but I arrived too late to save him. *She* was still playing with him when I got here, but there was nothing I could do for him. He was too far gone."

"But *her* mate...oh yes. I got *him*. I made him scream and cry for her to come to him, to save him. I used him to lure her to me, away from the lake where I knew she was at her strongest. When she finally let go of my mate and came to aid her own, we fought a long, hard, bloody battle. When she began to tire and weaken, she tried to sing her way out of it, but her song didn't work on me! I couldn't even hear her! I'd stuffed my ears with spiddersilk, see? I am smarter than I appear."

"We battled and rolled about until we ended up close to the lake's shore where she'd left her seal skin. In a sneaky, desperate move, she picked up a heavy rock and smashed it onto my ankle, instantly shattering the bones within …. nasty little cheat that she is. While I was busy howling out my pain, she took the opportunity to try and slip back into her skin. I knew I couldn't let that happen, she would be much more powerful with it on, and I would not make it out alive."

"By the time I'd dragged myself up behind her to try and stop the transformation, she'd already stepped into it and had it half-way back on. Her bottom half was already changing to seal form, while she was still struggling to get the top of her body tucked inside of it. Since I was lying upon the ground because of my broken leg, I did the only thing I could do. I reached out and I grabbed hold of that seal tail, and I yanked it just as hard as I could! At the very same moment, Faoira managed to slip herself the rest of the way into the skin and she tried to escape into the water."

"But I didn't release her tail like she expected me to, and her seal skin ripped right in half! I ripped her seal tail clean off of her. Her top half remained in seal form, but her bottom half immediately changed back into a woman's. She lay there on the sand at the lake's edge a half woman, half seal creature. She had a woman's stomach and buttocks, legs and feet. But there was no skin left upon them. Taking her sealskin while she'd been inside of it had cost her *both* sets of skins, the fishy one *and* the people one."

"I don't even think she knew what had happened, didn't realize what I'd done to her. Not right away. All she knew was that she was hurt... immensely hurt. Screaming and crying from the pain of it, she flopped herself into the lake where she knew I couldn't get at her, knew I wouldn't be foolish enough to follow. She removed what remained of her sealskin to inspect the damage it had taken. And that's when she realized what had happened."

Urza pauses to accept the bowl of beef stroganoff that she holds out to her. She has the nastiest, most self-satisfied smile twisting her lips and her eyes actually twinkle as she stuffs noodles into her mouth and continues.

"I will never, as long as I live, forget the sound of that water-hag's screams when she discovered that her skin was torn, and her magic was gone! No matter how many times she put that seal hide over her head, it just wouldn't work no more. I lay there and I laughed the entire time that she howled her pain and rage to the skies. But I'd soon had enough of listening to her when she was finally reduced to nothing more than quietly sobbing. Gah. Spare me. I won fair and square!"

"So I sat up and snapped my ankle back into place as best I could, then splinted and wrapped it up tight. I knew I couldn't travel and that I would be stuck there for weeks while it healed. And I was going to make the best of my time there. If I couldn't kill the lake hag, I would do the next best thing. Can you guess what I did? No? I found me a good, strong stick to aid me with walking and I went back to the place where I'd left her mate and I dragged him here, to this very spot. And then I made her watch as I took him for my own mate. She'd killed mine and so I took hers."

"Of course, she'd tried to stop me. She rushed out of her fish poop pond to save him from me, but quickly found out that rescuing him was impossible. When the air hit her skinless parts, her lifeblood immediately began flowing out of her. *Pouring* out of her. For some reason, only the lake's water kept her blood from leaking out, kept her from bleeding to death. She's been trapped in there ever since. She never healed. Her people-skin never grew back. She's nothing but raw, exposed meat from just under her tits, all the way down to her toes!"

Urza quickly slurps up her portion and then holds out her bowl for more. As Ecko takes it to refill it, she fumbles with a small satchel that's tied at her waist, opening it and then removing her own trophy. Apparently, the hobglin likes to carry her half of Faoira's sealskin with her. She unfolds it and smooths it out over her legs, stoking her hands over it almost lovingly.

"I spent two beautiful weeks here, playing with Faoira's mate, while she could do nothing but watch and listen to his cries for help. At some point during that time, Serefaye and Marnan returned from their trip to the sea. I'd already laid a trap for them, and I caught them quite easily. I wanted Faoira to suffer as much as possible by dragging their torture out, but I underestimated how enamored I'd become with my new mate. So, I poled the parents, knowing that they'd die slowly and would suffer greatly while doing so. And then I got back to rutting… to the beat of the screams that rang through the air."

"It was amazing, the best mating of my life…and also what drove the water slut mad. Honestly, I can understand completely. Oh, not about losing the parents…. who cares about that? They were old anyway. But her mate was something worth fighting for. He was a prime specimen, a very attractive male with more than enough man-meat to keep his mate pleasured. I could understand exactly why she favored him so."

"Eventually, I had to cease toying with him, had to give up taunting the water hag. I knew that I could not linger much longer. I was overdue to drop my whelp and I did not wish to do so here. I wanted the birthing to take place in my own nest."

"But I couldn't bring myself to kill her mate. I couldn't make myself destroy such a magnificent man specimen. I took him with me when I left. I took him to the hobglin mound, and I brought him into my nest as my slave-mate. I birthed my first hobglinet the very next Pale. And the Pale after that, I took Teerant's uncle, Boorunt as my new mate. *And* I kept my playmate. I refused to give him up. I'd won him fair and square, and naught could argue otherwise. He was *mine* to with whatever I wished, and I wished to keep him and play with him. I became the very first she-hobglin to have two males living in her home at once. All my mates, all but Teerant of course, (because he was already dead) have had to share me with him. And he is still there, a slave awaiting my return, even after all these...what? Has it really been one hundred and fifty-four years already? Hu, time passes by so quickly!"

"But back to the water hag. Faoira's gone completely mad over the years. *That's* why she does what she does. She removes her victims' skins and tries to make herself a new one, but that *never* works. They all lack the magic that is needed to heal her and to stop her blood from flowing out." And then Urza laughs and laughs at the thought of her nemeses' misery as she finishes inhaling her food.

Ecko doesn't find anything about it humorous. Her heart hurts at the thought of Faoira living the way she'd been forced to live. Even though she's not an innocent, far from it, no one should have to endure the traumas that she's suffered with for so long. She hadn't wanted any of it. She'd been living her life out here with her family, away from everyone else, all antisocial-like and minding her own business, when she'd been attacked. And what about her poor mate? He seems to be the most innocent, and yet he is probably the biggest victim.

Poor guy, he's probably as crazy as Faoira is. Her stomach sours and she gags at the thought of being forced to mate with a hobglin. Ok, that did it. She's completely lost her appetite.

"You want mine too?" she asks as she holds out her own half empty bowl of stroganoff. And then the Pitch is upon them, just as sudden and unexpected as it always does. She cries out and drops the bowl as she fumbles with the switch on the flashlight that she'd already laid out in preparation.

"Aahhh! I'm *never* going to get used to that! I need a way to tell time, or read the signs, or see whatever it is that lets you know that the Pitch is coming. I can't just keep being surprised by it every day. How can you tell when it's coming?"

Urza belches then lays back on the ground and closes her eyes. "The sign is felt, not seen. The entire world trembles for one hour before the change from Pitch to Pale, and then another hour before Pale to Pitch. Have you not felt its rumblings beneath your feet? Mayhap it's because of those things you cover them with. Take them off and focus on feeling the land beneath you. Or, perhaps you are just too dumb to feel the rumblings. But you'd have to be the stupidest thing alive, because even the dumbest beasts can tell when sleep time and wake time draws near. And *now* it is sleep time. Shut up and let me get to it. The Pale will be back all too soon."

Urza opens her eyes long enough to glare balefully at her prisoner. "I don't have to tie you up, do I? Should I list for you all the terrors that are waiting out there in the dark? No? Alright then. Do *not* try anything sneaky."

Then she simply rolls over and instantly begins snoring, leaving Ecko all alone in the dark with her mind to come up with its own list of waiting nightmares. There's no way she'll ever be able to fall asleep, so she doesn't even bother with her tent or even her sleeping bag. But she can at least get comfortable, maybe stretch out and rest her tired legs and her aching back.

She lays down and props her head on her backpack. And then she has to go and make everything worse by shining her light out into the Pitch to see if she can see any of those monsters that her mind is so busy trying to conjure up. As she shines her flashlight out over that scary as heck lake, she realizes that she doesn't need her mind to come up with anything at all.

There are very real terrors right here in front of her already. The light reflects off of wide, staring eyes and shines it back at her. "There are dead things here," she whispers. It reminds her of the Dead Marshes that Frodo and Sam had to pass through on their way to Mordor. She shivers and keeps her light trained on the lake, watching for even the slightest sign that there are ghosts here, or zombies. The only thing she fears more than herself and the monsters that live inside of her own head is dead things. Ghosts and dead things are heart-stopping, soul-shatteringly *terrifying*... with dead/ghost kids being the ultimate, number one freakiest, creepiest, scariest, boogery nightmare things in existence.

Thankfully, she hasn't seen any children pieces amongst the parts that are strewn about the lake. But dead things is dead things and they are *all* terrifying. Big fat NOPES...all of them. There's no way she'll get any sleep tonight, no way she'll be able to relax enough to fall asleep. The dead surround her, and it feels as if they're closing in on her.

If ever there was a time for singing a silly song from Veggie Tales to make herself feel better, now *is* that time. Childish? Yes. Is she going to sing it anyway? Again yes...and she's going to sing it without any shame at having done so too. Will it improve her situation any? No. But she just loves those inspirational, singing vegetables, and it'll make her *feel* better. Is that ok with you, Mr. Judgy Pants?

She can't think of a better silly song to sing than, 'God is bigger than the Boogie Man' at a time like this. And even though Ecko was sure she wouldn't, *couldn't* fall asleep... as soon as she finishes singing about eyeballs in the closet, Godzilla in the hall, and hundreds of tiny monsters, jumping right into her jammies... that's exactly what she does.

He watches her, cocking his head this way, and that way, as he listens to the sound of her voice while she sings her fears away. He doesn't bother to hide himself. Ground stompers are clueless, and she is no different from the rest. They rarely look up, even when they enter the Black Forest where they know danger abounds. Ninety-nine percent of the time, there's some sort of monster watching them from up above... just like he's watching her right now.

When the girl's eyes close and she falls silent, he tucks his head down into his wings to protect his ears from the biting bugs, while he takes his own sleep. He needs all the rest he can get. Flying her out of the screamer trees took a lot more strength than he realized it would. She is much heavier than she looks.

10

WHAT'S HAPPENING TO ME?

Krispin

He awakens slowly, painfully. Again. Drinking until he loses consciousness has become his new way of life. He's growing used to waking up each Pale with an aching head. Waking up and not knowing where he is or how he'd gotten there also seems to be a reoccurring theme in his new regime. As is waking up next to a naked woman that he has no memory of bedding… and he knows without a doubt that he'd bedded her. Even if his still-sticky seed hadn't covered his belly, he would have known it by how deliciously his body aches with the pleasure/pain of having been well used.

He sits up and grimaces as he takes in the scene around him. He feels no need to check the woman beside him for signs of life. The amount of blood and gore that they're both covered in assures him, unequivocally that she's dead… Just like Maggs, only messier.

He rises up off his bed with a grunt of frustration and immediately heads for the bathing tub that he'd stolen and set up for

Samara, his feet squelching and sliding through half congealed puddles of blood on the floor. Normally he didn't mind a little blood, adored it, actually. But this is no small amount of blood. He's caked in *gallons* of the stuff. Some of it's dried and flaking off his skin like little bits of rust-colored dandruff. Some of it's globbed on so thick that it's still tacky to the touch.

But *all* of it draws a big, empty blank in his mind, for he hasn't got a single clue as to how it got there. What in all the BelowNeath had he done? Oh, he knows *where* it came from; dead women don't lie. But he knows nothing other than that one small detail. He would ask her for an explanation, but he's pretty sure the bitch will be keeping her secrets to herself. Why can't he remember anything? What's happening to him? Has Samara's disappearance truly driven him mad?

Krispin quickly sets about cleansing himself… scrubbing every trace of blood from his skin, from his long, tangled hair. He rinses the gore from his teeth, spits if from his lips, and then returns to lift the woman from his bed and toss her over his shoulder. He feels her cold and sticky, *gelatinous* blood slick across his freshly cleaned skin and realizes that he should have gotten rid of her, *before* he cleansed himself. He growls and angrily slaps her naked ass in punishment for failing to remind him of that fact.

He makes his way through the shadows of the town, confident that he won't be seen, for he knows these little patches of darkness very well. He takes one cursory glance around him before opening the hatch and descending the ladder into the darkness that awaits him. He plops the woman down beside Maggs, who needs repositioning, because she's starting to droop a bit.

"Hello, Maggs," he growls in his deep, rumbling voice. "How're you this fine Pale?" he asks as he goes about setting her back to rights and then tucking the new girl up against her.

"I brought a friend to keep you company for when I'm not here." He fiddles with the new women's hair for a while, arranging it just so, and then he steps back to study them. His eyes rove over every inch of their bodies, taking note of their flaws and blemishes, as well as all of their pleasing assets. He also notices for the first time that this new female has the tiniest, loveliest feet… just like Samara's.

He quickly locates a scrap of an old rag and wets it from his stores of bottled sky water. Then he gently, lovingly washes away every trace of dirt and blood from those perfectly, beautifully formed feet. He stares down at them, cradled in his hands... only at them and nowhere else. And he finds that he can almost make himself believe that it's *her* feet in his hands, *her* skin that he's caressing. He closes his eyes as he kisses his way down those dainty toes, licking his tongue over the curve of her ankles, and nips at her heels with his teeth.

Desire pools deep in his belly and he feels his body responding, growing hard with his passion for all things 'Samara'. He knows that this is *not* his lover, but he pretends, just for a moment, that she is anyway. He keeps his eyes focused on those shapely ankles as he removes his clothes and drags her body beneath him. Then he slams his eyes shut, even as he thrusts himself into her, crying out

Samara's name throughout the entire, deplorable act. He keeps his eyes averted, even when it's over, and he rolls off of her, tucking her cold, still body up against his. "Just for a little while, ladies," he murmurs sleepily. "Don't let me sleep too long." With that, he falls into a deep, sated slumber, the three of them curled up together... sleeping the sleep of the dead.

The Wyrm hovers in the background, watching it all... every last delightful detail. It is beyond ecstatic that it had come upon this particular new host... this creature of such like-minded desires and depravities. It regards the three of them lying there on the old, half-rotten sleep pallet upon the floor. It couldn't be more pleased with the sight of its chosen host-mate cradling both of his females in his arms. They truly are the embodiment of loveliness, and it feels a sense of pride as it admires them. And also a great deal of lust. It wants them. It wants to keep them. Just like this. Forever. It wants to add even more lovelies to its collection.

Then it grins its invisible, spectral grin as it has an idea. A wonderful idea, a wonderful, terrible idea. If it can't have its own Wyrm-mate, and if his soon-to-be host can't have the one true love that his heart cries out for, maybe, just maybe, the two of them together can build a suitable substitute.

At least until it can get its Wyrm-mate (safely ensconced within Samara's luscious body) back in its arms.

11

HE LIVES!

The Lokskell

He has *everyone* searching for his daughter, searching for his elusive Ecko. Every man, woman and child, every creature and every beast under his rule is currently out scouring that dreadful world. He even has his Night Shades and Slivers spread thin, searching, watching, scrutinizing every living thing they come across. A whole network of spies at his disposal, and what has he got to show for it? Nothing! Not a damn thing. He slams his fist down onto the table with enough force to send cracks racing across the surface. They should have located her *long* before now! He feels the rage coming on, and he knows that if he doesn't receive news of some sort and *soon*, well, someone will have to suffer for it. Horribly. Hundreds of them, all out there doing their best to hunt her down… to gain his good graces by being *the* one to find her, but they're all incompetent imbeciles, every last one of them.

The Lokskell rubs his hand down his face in frustration. Oh, how much easier everything would be if he were over there, on Oblerian. Then he wouldn't need to rely on fools, cretons, and simpletons. Inferior, subpar creatures, the whole lot of them. If he

203

could but find the way out of this cursed castle… If he only knew where the secret chamber was located. If only he knew how to access the Rips, the portals that Laelynn, the sneaky bitch, had used to escape him…and with *his* daughters, no less!

He'd gotten Laelynn back, of course, but unfortunately not until after she'd whelped the brats and hid them away from him. Oh, she'd paid for that. She'd paid dearly… the ultimate price of betrayal. But no matter what he'd done to her, no matter how bad he hurt her, or how much she bled, she never once revealed where the Rips room was located or how he could find it for himself. She never gave up a single one of her secrets. He'd almost admired her for that. Would have, if her stubborn bravery hadn't sent him into such intense rages. Oh, how he'd hated her for that. But oh, how it made him burn for her.

Agnit Haldore, the man of infinite spirits, appears at his side, as suddenly and silently as ever. "Well? What is it?" he demands when the man merely stands there, staring at the wall, while waiting to be acknowledged.

Now that he's been granted permission to speak, he quickly undergoes the extraction ritual, drawing his spirit out and separating it from his body, so that he *can* speak. The process takes no more than thirty seconds, but the Lokskell has lost all patience by the time it's done.

"Do you have news of my daughter? Has Ecko been sighted? Speak up, fool!"

The man refuses to meet his eyes. Instead, he focuses his attention somewhere close to his hairline as his spirit replies, "I have seen no trace of the girl, Sire."

The Lokskell's hand clenches his wine goblet so tightly that it's crushed into a mangled, useless lump of metal. He takes a deep breath to calm himself, before he decides that this life-long acquaintance is no longer worthy of breathing air.

"Well, I certainly hope that you have a good reason for being here then. You'd best have some other, valuable bit of news for me. Otherwise, I see no reason for you to seek me out and bother me with inconsequential trivia. What, pray tell, do you want?"

Agnit Haldore straightens his physical body's spine, as his ghostly lips inform him of what he's learned, of who he's just seen back in that small, dilapidated Oblerian town. "I thought you would wish to know that I saw the blue creature, the one that you tortured and skinned for daring to bed your other daughter. He is alive, M'lord, and in a terrible rage from the loss of his lover."

The Lokskell rises to his feet and leans across the table, pushing his face right up close to the other man's, *forcing* him to meet his eyes. "You're certain of this?" he asks, his voice low, smooth, and steady… and oh, so deadly calm.

"Absolutely, M'lord. I saw him with my own eyes. I would never relay false information, nor would I listen to empty-minded gossips."

After a moment of searching his eyes for lies, in which time the man never blinks or tries to shy away from his scrutiny, the

Lokskell steps back and settles himself once more into his chair. "Very well," he grudgingly allows. He could find no lie in the man's eyes. Truly, he's never found any fault with the man, in action or in deed. Unless he counts the mystery that surrounds the man of infinite spirits as an offense, that is. But aside from the fact that he's annoyingly reticent and enigmatic, Agnit Haldore has *ever* been a loyal companion.

"This is vital news, even though it is not what I sent you in search of. I will have to think on what to do, in order to determine the best course of action to take. Go back. Watch him. Observe what he does and where he goes. In the meantime, I'll have a word with those two imbeciles that were charged with the removal and disposal of the creature, once it had taken its last breath. I'll be most interested to hear what they have to say for themselves. I'm sure it will be a riveting and entertaining conversation. I thank you for this, Agnit Haldore. I needed an outlet for all this pent-up frustration that my daughter's continued absence is causing me. I was beginning to fear that one of my rages was coming on. *Nobody* wants that. Now I can just let it all out on the two halfwits that dared to fail me."

12

GIFTS AND CURSES

Ecko

"Ecko…Eeeckoo."

It feels as if she's been asleep for only a matter of minutes, when someone begins crying out her name, yanking her out of her dreams, as soon as she'd entered them. Her eyes snap open and the voice fades to silence before she can determine where it's coming from. She doesn't know if the person calling out to her is here in the waking world, or if they'd merely been part of her dreams. All she knows is that she's so scared she can't breathe properly. It's still Pitch time and she's completely surrounded by a thick, impenetrable shroud of black. She'd fallen asleep with her flashlight on and the batteries must have died, because the forest around her is darker than her twin's black heart.

"Urza, was that you?" she whispers, praying with all her heart that the unpleasant woman is awake and that she answers her. But no, the hobglin's still snoring somewhere off to her right.

"Urza, wake up! Someone's out there. *Urza!!*" But it's no use. The hobglin won't wake up. Something's wrong. Something is *terribly* wrong here. Her heart pounds harder than a drummer beating on his drums at a rock concert, and she whimpers as she blindly reaches for her bag to find one of her spare flashlights.

She moves as quickly and quietly as possible, because she can almost guarantee that whatever it was that had woken her up was *not* trapped back in the Dreamworld. No, something *here* wants her attention, something that she can't as of yet see. But she is oh, so sure that whatever it is can see *her* just as clear as day.

"Please, *please* don't be a dead thing," she begs as her fingers at last wrap around a new flashlight. Her suspicions are confirmed, and she gulps back her screams, when she hears the voice again. Someone, or something (dead?) is calling to her, whispering her name from out there in the water.

"Eecko…Eeeckoo." She prays with all her might that it's Faoira calling to her. Bat poop crazy and dangerous the Naiad very well may be, but she's also extremely limited, banished to the lake as she is. And since she's trapped out there, all she can really accomplish is making Ecko pee herself from fright. Dead things are a whole different story...and would be a whole different mess in the pants to clean up. She's fairly certain that the dead, or any other monster for that matter, won't be quite so accommodating, so obliging, as Faoira is by physically keeping their distance.

"Like a good neighbor, she stays over there," Ecko whisper/sings in her best State Farm ad voice. But she knows that she can't hope for *all* the monsters to be good neighbors who practice social distancing. Really, what are the chances of that? For certain, most scary things won't be friendly, and they just as likely can, and *will*, come over here to eat her.

She clicks her light on and shines that beautiful little beam straight down at her backpack and frantically starts rooting through her belongings in a mad search for her iPod and headphones. "Where is it? Where. Is. It? Don't listen. Don't listen. La, la, la. Don't listen to her song. She can't get you and rip your skin off, if you just don't listen to her song. La, la, la." She focuses on the sound of her own voice, commanding herself to not listen, even as she does her best to ignore that other one, the haunting, ghostly voice that's begging her to come to the water's edge. She refuses, absolutely *refuses* to turn the light out towards the lake. She's entirely too frightened of what may be out there.

But then, *oh!* Then there's another voice, different from the one that's been calling out to her. And it's the voice of someone that she would give anything, *anything* to see once more. Oh! Oh! *Oh!* It's her father out there, calling her name, begging her to come to him. She stops rooting through her bag and cocks her head so that she can hear better.

"Ecko? Ecko, where are you? It's so dark. I can't find you! Come to me, daughter. I miss you so."

Tears immediately fill her eyes, as her heart fills up with wishes. "Daddy?" she whimpers with all the hope of a lost child being rescued by her hero.

"Yes, baby girl, I'm here! Please, come closer….so that I can see you."

Her longing for her father is so great, so immense, that the trickery may have worked…. if the monster in her head named Rage hadn't *instantly* understood what was happening and then very forcefully voiced his own opinion.

He pounds on the walls of his prison harder than he'd ever pounded before as he roars, "That is NOT our father!" He howls and snarls as he tries to kick and punch his way free. The utter fury that Rage displays is enough to snap her out of it and recognize the voice for the lie that it is… and then *she* is furious, as livid as she'd ever been at anything in her whole life. The idea that anyone would be so cruel offends her to the depths of her soul.

Her fury lends her strength, giving her the courage to face whatever may be out there in those nightmare waters. She gets up and marches straight down to the lake's edge, not stopping until she's standing right where the water meets the land. She shines her light out over the expanse of Faoira's domain, seeking the one responsible for her newest heartache. Nothing. She can't see anyone. Whoever it is, is a coward and remains hidden from her.

"You stop that right now!" she shouts and then listens to her own voice as it echoes out across the lake. "Come out. You wanted me here, well now I'm here. Show yourself and tell me what you want. Or don't. But don't you dare use my father again in your attempts to hurt me. Don't you *dare*.' Her chest heaves with every indrawn breath, and her entire body trembles with the force of her anger as she waits.

The Naiad rises up out of the water then, way out there in the middle of the lake, close to the tree that Urza's first mate hangs from. She is *nothing* like what Ecko had imagined her to be, and she is also *everything* she'd expected, too. And then more. But also less, somehow.

Faoira is without a doubt the strangest, most disturbing thing she's ever encountered… and she's become an expert on strange. She *lives* strange, breathes it. But this…wow. If prizes were to be given out for the strange and freaky, *this* woman/creature would win first place. Go ahead and give her all the awards, the blue ribbon, the first-place trophy, and even Simon Cowell's golden buzzer. She deserves them all.

It's not that she's *not* beautiful, like Sirens are portrayed to be. It's that Ecko can't even *tell* if she's beautiful or not. She can't quite make her out, because Faoira is not just *one* single person. She's everyone, thousands upon thousands of people, all at once… perhaps even *millions.* She constantly changes into someone different, shifting from person to person to person.

If you were to speed up the end of Michael Jackson's Black or White music video to say…maybe a thousand times faster than the normal speed, then that just might come close to what she's seeing right now. It's almost as if Faoira's form can never quite settle on one single person. She just continues to shift, flickering faster and faster and faster until she's nothing but a smudge of motion. There's no other way to explain how she looks, other than to say that Faoira's entire image is *blurry* from the speed of the constant changes. They occur so quickly, that the woman appears almost to be vibrating at an incredibly high speed.

Ecko can see the outline of her. She can see that she has a nicely shaped and voluptuously, desirable body. There's an impression of beauty, a very loud, convincing *suggestion* of beauty, but that's all it is...an impression, the *idea* that she is beautiful beyond comparison. She squints her eyes in an effort to see her more clearly, but it's just no use. Faoira remains nothing more than a blur, as thousands of different people all fight to be the one that gets to stay. It's literally a case of multiple personalities, with everyone struggling for dominance.

It's unnerving, to say the least, but Ecko looks her (as best as she can) in the face anyway, straight into those blue, then green, then red, back to blue... the ever-changing color of her ever- changing eyes. As if the constant changing isn't deterring enough, the pure hatred glaring back at her from every set of eyes she tries on *is*. Faoira seems to be looking at her with murder in her heart, no matter what shape, color, and form she takes...they *all* want her dead.

Even so, Ecko stares her right in the eyes with as much false bravado as she can muster up, because that's what her father would have done. Her daddy was the smartest person she'd ever known. He'd been Dan the Man, the big-time lawyer with the highest win/success rate of all the lawyers in Houston, Texas. He'd *known* how to deal with people, and he'd always told her to start every meeting by looking a rival/enemy straight in the eye, no matter how intimidated she may be or how afraid she may feel.

This may or may not be the best advice for this particular situation, she can't tell. Because the longer she stares into those Kaleidoscopic eyes, the slower they shift until they finally come to a decision on what form to take, and then they change no more. Ecko gasps and takes a hasty step back, as she immediately wishes for them to return to their identity crisis, battling for dominance again, because the woman looking back at her is *mad.*

Not angry mad...well yeah.... that too. But she is stark raving, insanely deranged mad too. And *that's* what's so terrifying. Her eyes are such deep, dark pools of madness and misery that Ecko can't look away from them. She's still unable to process exactly what the Naiad looks like, not that it even matters anymore. What matters is finding a way out of this, because all of her self-righteous anger and courage has fled the scene at such blatant hostility and raging insanity.

And then Faoira starts to speak, and her harsh, screeching voice rings out across the lake. "What is wrong with you? What *are* you? Why don't you want me? Do you not find me desirable?"

Ecko claps her hands over her ears. Ugh, yuck. Her voice is horrid, absolutely dreadful. It grates on her every nerve, like chalk scraping across a chalkboard or the screeching of a microphone with too much audio feedback.

"What's wrong with *me*? What's wrong with *you*? Why are you all blurry? And what's up with your voice? I thought you were supposed to have a beautiful, hypnotic voice. How do you ever lure anyone in sounding like *that*?" Ugh. Seriously, the only way she could have lured anyone to their death with that voice was if they'd been trying to escape the sound of it. They'd probably drown themselves so they wouldn't have to hear it any longer.

Faoira suddenly lowers herself down into the lake, until only her head remains above the surface. Then she swims up to Ecko so quickly that she may as well have teleported. One moment she's way out in the middle of the lake, and the next she's ten feet from where Ecko stands on the shore. That's apparently as close as she can get and still keep the lower half of her body safely submerged.

The two women stand still for long moments, silently contemplating one another, each trying to figure the other out and make some sense of the situation. As Echo stares at her, the madness slowly drains away. Sanity creeps back into her eyes as the crazy fades away, and with it, all pretense drops. The illusions disappear, allowing her to look upon the Naiad's true appearance.

Faoira's entire being changes, and her eyes... Oh! Every trace of color in her eyes has been leached out until they're as clear and translucent as the waters of the lake that she resides in. Peering intently into those crystal eyes, Ecko expects to see all the way through to the Naiad's brain, but it's not like that at all. Her eyes are deep pools of *nothing*, a never-ending abyss that stretches on forever and ever without end.

"You see me," she says in that unbearable, grating voice. "You can see my *true* self, hear my true voice. You are the very first to do so. Motarr told me there would be some out there that could see through the glamor, but I didn't believe her. I told her that all peoples are filled with lustful thoughts, *all* have dreams full of wants and greeds. I argued that you are all the same, wantful, needful things... all so very easy to fool and manipulate with our song. Motarr was right, of course, as she so often was, because here you stand. And you *see* the true me. You are the most complicated little creature I've ever beheld with mine own eyes, your desires unlike any I've ever tasted. You clearly do not desire me. You do not wish to mate with me. You do not covet my magic, nor do you wish to steal from me. You did not come here expecting me to make all your dreams come true, to grant your wishes, as if I'm naught but a Degeenie in a seashell! I know all of this to be true, because I can see you too."

She raises a ghostly-pale hand and points towards where Urza continues to snore. "*She* may have stolen my Selkie magics from me, but I still retain all of my Siren's magic. It allows me to see into peoples, to see their every wish and know their deepest desires. And you, strangling one, are the purest, most complex and conflicting creature that I have ever encountered. You have so many *wants,* so many longings inside of you, but you do not wish to take away from anyone to have those desires filled. You genuinely care for everyone and have a great love for all living creatures. Even me, whom you do not even know. Even that hobglin hag that holds you prisoner. You are clearly aware of her intentions to do you great harm, but you do not wish her ill in return. You are a remarkable creature. I thank you for the opportunity to look upon one such as you. I will cease all my trickery. I have no desire to harm something so innocent and pure as you."

Ecko's just a little bit confused. She knows that she isn't as 'pure and innocent' as Faoira believes her to be. There *is* darkness inside of her, she fights it back every single day. And there is one person that she *does* wish harm on. Samara *will* pay for the things she's done; she will personally see to it.

Faoira smiles sadly as she reads the thoughts that run rampant through Ecko's mind, as clearly as if she'd spoken them aloud. "You are such a delightful contrast! You're an open book, and yet you are hard to read. It is so very difficult to decipher the meanings of the words on your pages, because you don't even know yourself, not yet. You must let loose those things you have caged up inside of yourself. Only then will you begin to see. I will tell you this one single truth though. You do not truly wish to hurt your sister. Not *truly.* You want your family back, above all else, and you want her to be sorry for the pain that she has caused you. But you do not want to hurt her, not really. In the deepest, most hidden part of your heart, you want her to love you. She is your sister after all, the only family you have left, other than your sire...and you must stay far away from *him.* He is bad, so *very* bad."

Ecko vehemently shakes her head in denial. "You're wrong," she insists. "Not about the Lokskell, I know how evil *he* is. But from all I've seen of my sister, she's just as monstrous as he is. No, you're wrong about what I feel for Samara. She slaughtered my entire family right in front of me. And she smiled the whole time she was doing it. I want her to pay. I want her dead and buried. If my family must be in the ground, then I want her to be just as dead, just as buried. I owe them at least that much!"

Faoira gracefully dips her head in silent acknowledgment at her insistence, at her deep but false beliefs. "As you wish," she says in a soft, careful tone. She knows that Ecko is young, still a child really. The girl isn't even aware of who, or *what* she is yet. She has much learning and growing to do still yet, and no words uttered here and now will convince her otherwise, nor will they sway her from her fledgling convictions. She'll have to learn for herself, discover who she is and what she truly desires, on her own.

Faoira backs away, slowly retreating back into the depths of her lake. "I wish you safe travels, my new friend, my only friend. I have one last word of advice before we part ways... and I beg you to heed it. Gather up your belongings and leave this place now, before I release the two that I have held in slumber, so that we may speak freely to one another. Go now. Do not wait for a better time, as you've been planning to do. Make your escape this instant."

"The creature that has been trailing you, the one hiding in the trees, does not wish you ill, but Urza certainly does. If you become too troublesome, she will gladly kill you and accept her losses. Even now she dreams of ways to kill you. You would be wise to part ways with her sooner rather than later. Be safe Ecko Zyana. I hope we may one day meet again." And then a single tear drips down her face, before she dips down below the surface and disappears into the dark depths where the flashlight's beam refuses to follow.

Ecko turns and slowly makes her way back to the camp, sobbing every step of the way, because somehow, there in the last few moments, she'd been able to see into Faoira's mind too. She's uncertain whether it had been her own magic flaring to life, or remnants of Faoira's, but she'd somehow connected with the Naiad. For one brief moment, their minds had merged together, and it was as if they were one being.

She had instantly known every detail of the other woman's life, saw every major experience she'd ever gone through. She felt every joy and every single heartache, and oh, what a sad tragedy her life had been! It was no wonder she'd gone mad. The anguish that she endures every single day is so great, her despair so acute, that it actually radiates off of her. The sadness in her heart is what keeps the lake waters so cold. Hers is a heartache so great that it affects the physical world around her.

Faoira's broken heart, her shattered mind, and her sheer loneliness is breaking *her* heart. But she knows how to fix it. She can make it better. She marches straight up to Urza and snatches the stolen half of the Selkie's skin from beneath the hobglin's filthy, stringy hair. She feels the pull of it, feels the magic of it the very second that her fingers touch it. For one brief moment, the idea to keep it for herself enters her mind. (My Precious! And we takes it for Meee!) But her heart just as quickly rejects the thought. It does not belong to her, and she has no right to it. Her fingers stroke over it's incredible silkiness as she carries it back to the water.

"Faoira, come back!" she calls out over the still, quiet lake. "I've come to return what belongs to you." Nothing. Only silence. There's not even a ripple upon the surface of the water. She calls and calls, but the Naiad refuses to show herself.

Ecko finally gives up her efforts. She lays the sealskin on the sandy shore and gently pushes it out into the lake. It floats a few feet away and then it gets snatched under, as if a great big fish had mistaken it for food and snapped it off the surface.

A moment later, Faoira suddenly bursts up out of the water with a shrill scream of delirious, ecstatic delight. She hugs her pelt to her breasts and flops and flounders all about the lake, scream/laughing all the while. Then she dives deep under, where she can no longer be seen. Just as Ecko's about to turn and head back to gather up her things and make good her escape, a bright glow illuminates the bottom of the lake, and the water begins to boil and bubble.

She hastily steps back as the roiling turbulence of the water disturbs the corpses, and they all begin to rise up out of their hiding places, from deep in the depths. The light shoots upwards, illuminating the dismembered body parts all the way up to the surface.

Ecko ignores the horror and the gore and focuses all her attention on the object that's barreling towards the surface with all the speed of a torpedo… and then she's laughing out loud, unable to contain her delight. She hops up and down, clapping gleefully as a silver sea creature bursts up, breaching the surface of the lake and chirping excitedly into the Pitch. Apparently, what this world considers a seal is what Earth calls a dolphin, for that's what Faoira's newly restored form is…. a beautiful, sleek dolphin.

She sinks down to sit in the sand as Faoira jumps and spins, chitters and chirps, and dives and splashes for a long, long while. She watches it all with a happy smile on her lips and tears in her eyes, as the beam of her flashlight steadily moves back and forth to keep track of the dolphin's movements. She can't help but feel a deep sense of pride within herself. She did this. She'd returned something stolen, something missing, and had made it right again.

Pitch suddenly flees and the Pale comes in to take its rightful place. She clicks her flashlight off and grimaces at the scene that her eyes can now clearly see, the dolphin happily swimming through the bloody gore of the lake. Heads, with their grotesque, frozen faces, bob upon the surface from the waves that Faoira makes as she frolics and plays with her simple, childlike innocence.

She suddenly stops her frolicking and swims right to the shore. She looks up at her new friend, chittering and chirping up at her. She points her snout at Ecko, then back out towards the lake, then back again, repeating the motions several times.

Ecko plays dumb, pretending that she doesn't understand. But she does. She knows exactly what Faoira's trying to say. She wants her to come play, to come swim with her in her lake of death.

Abso-freaking-lutely not. She just continues to sit there, smiling back at her, hoping that she'll just go back to celebrating alone. But Faoira dives back under and when she next emerges, she's once again in her fully-healed woman's form. She stands naked in front of Ecko, with those endlessly transparent eyes, and oh, how she laughs and laughs and laughs!

"Thank you, my wonderful, beautiful friend!" she cries. "Thank you from the bottom of my heart and the depths of my soul! You do not know what this means to me. I will forever and always be in your debt. I will *never* be able to repay your kindness but should there ever come a time that you have need of me, I will be there, no matter the cost. I willingly pledge myself to you, here and now, and I freely share the secret of how to call a Siren unto you. All you must do is whisper my name, my full, *true* name into any body of water... even if it is but a small, shallow puddle. I will hear it, and I shall come to you. My name is..." and she leans in close and whispers the secret into Ecko's ear.

"You must never tell anyone, must never speak it aloud unless you say it thrice into the waters to call for aid. Heed me well on this," she warns. "Now, stay right there. I have a gift for you as well!"

The newly healed and deliriously giddy woman backflips into the water, is gone for a few short moments, and then suddenly rises back up before her. She tightly clutches her sealskin (dolphin-skin) in one hand, but the other cradles a huge, luminescent pearl as large as a crystal ball. Its base color is deepest black, but it glows brightly with a pearlescent shimmer that's made up of all colors.

"It is called a Night Pearl and it is thought to be the only one of its kind on the whole of this world. It belonged to my Motarr, though I know naught how she came to have it. She was never the one for sleep-time stories or sharing things from her past. All she ever told me was that it had come from Irredarr, from *your* home world long, long ago and that it holds a great deal of magic. I have treasured it and kept it these many years, because even though its magic never responded to her, or to me, it was Motarr's most prized possession. I want you to take it with you on your journey. Mayhap the magic will awaken in your hands. But first! Come swim with me, friend!" Her eyes light up with excitement at the thought of finally, after so many lonely years, having someone to swim with. She gently lays the Night Pearl onto the sand, takes Ecko's hands, and pulls her to her feet.

"Ummm, I really should get going before Urza wakes up...and uhhh, I never really learned how to swim…" She digs her feet into the sand, trying to stall for time, while she considers what to do. She is *not* getting into that lake with those dead things. She's just not gonna do it. But she doesn't want to hurt or offend her new friend either.

Faoira stops tugging on her hands and cocks her head to the side, as if she's listening intently. And she is. She's using her Siren magic to read Ecko like a book. "And *what* is wrong with my lake?" she demands as her grip on Ecko's hands tightens painfully. "It is the most beautiful clean-water loch in all the land. Its waters are magical and can heal many hurts. What is wrong with you that you do not like my lake, nor appreciate its magnificence?"

She releases Ecko's hands to gesture out towards the lake. "Just look at how serene and inviting…." But her voice trails off as she turns and gets a good look at the carnage behind her. Her eyes dart over the expanse of the blood-red lake, filled with heads and limbs and viscera and guts. She cries out, whimpering in confusion.

"Motarr? Fotarr? I'm scared! Where are you?" She turns back to beseech Ecko for an explanation, to beg for help. And that's when some part of her consciousness remembers at least a little bit of her past. She raises her head and looks directly at the skeletal remains of her parents, skewered atop those sticks as if they're nothing more than gruesome appetizers stabbed onto giant toothpicks. The dehydrated, blackened skin pulled taut on their faces emphasizes their silently screaming, open mouths. Their boney fingers still reach for one another, even after all this time.

Faoira throws her head back and lets out a piercing howl. She reaches up to grasp her own head, as if that might hold the memories at bay, or perhaps block her own thoughts out. "I remember," she whispers in horror. "I remember everything."

As her gaze lowers back down and she meets Ecko's own sympathetic eyes, the insanity that had been a part of her for so long, begins to creep back in. She can see it slowly seeping into her eyes, and she doesn't know if she's more saddened by the relapse or terrified, because Faoira is no longer confined to her lake. She has all of her powers back now and she has free reign to go wherever she chooses and wreak as much havoc as she desires… and Faoira realizes it too.

"You must go! Run! Get as far from me as you can. The darkness is descending upon me again, and I know not how long I can hold it back. I do not wish to do you harm, my friend."

She snatches the Night Pearl from the sand and thrusts it into Ecko's hands. "Go now! Quickly, before I forget what you've done for me…before I forget that you are my friend and not another enemy come to hurt me. Run!" And she starts shouting it over and over again. "Run! Run! RUUUNNNN!"

Ecko spins around and she runs. She skids into camp and hastily thrusts the Night Pearl into her backpack before shrugging it onto her back. She looks down at the now stirring hobglin with true regret in her heart, because she knows that Faoira will not let her live, and that she herself is partly responsible for Urza's upcoming demise. Not that it's undeserved, but she honestly can't stand the thought of anyone suffering… not even villains. But the whole affair is out of her hands. This feud started long before she'd come along. All she can do now is hope that Faoira grants Urza a swift, merciful death.

Although she knows deep in her heart that won't happen, that's exactly what she *chooses* to believe. She's an old pro, a master at pushing unpleasant things out of her mind, locking them all away in their proper little box/cages, so that she doesn't have to deal with all of her life's disappointments and failures. This is one such thing that she cannot let her mind dwell on.

She takes one last look at Faoira standing there at the edge of her Dead Pool. She has her arms wrapped tightly around herself and she's shifting once again, her forms flickering by so fast that she's nothing more than a blur of ever-changing colors. That convinces Ecko like nothing else could. It's time for her to leave. The

Naiad has lost all remnants of the sanity that she'd just moments ago possessed.

She must have lost her control over the hobglin's sleep too, because Urza suddenly reaches up and snatches her ankle, just as she turns to flee the scene.

"What have you done?" she demands. "Oh, what have you done, you nasty, tricksy girl!"

Ecko jerks her leg free and takes off like a scared little rabbit. She runs until she reaches the trees at the edge of the forest. The narrow passageway between the towering mountain walls is the only way out, and she makes a beeline for it.

She has no intention of turning back to look, has no desire to see the carnage that is surely about to take place. But as she pauses there to catch her breath, she suddenly thinks of something that Urza had told her, a detail that she'd bragged about that Faoira needs to be made aware of. She spins back around and thank you sweet baby Jesus, the two women are still right where she'd left them. No havoc has begun, as of yet.

"Faoira!" she calls out across the distance. "She told me that your mate is still alive. She's kept him a prisoner in her home all this time. You're free now, your magic has been restored. You can go save him. You *should* go save him. You can start over somewhere else, just the two of you. Make all new memories. You could be happy again. Let *that* be what you focus on and leave this place of death and sorrow behind you."

The Naiad dips her head slightly in acknowledgement, but she doesn't say anything in response. Ecko's unsure whether that's an affirmation, or if it's a big fat 'mind your own business', but she's not going to stick around and find out either way. "Goodbye, my friend. I wish you all the peace that you've been denied for so long," she wistfully murmurs as she steps through the pass and disappears into the deep, dark heart of the Black Forest.

She never notices the beast spread its wings and lift off its perch from high up in the trees, never realizes that something's taken flight and follows close behind her. She has, in fact, completely forgotten all about that second creature that Faoira had been keeping unconscious by whispering her Siren's song into his ears as he slept.

He trails her for the next several hours, watching, studying her closely. Oftentimes, he glides high above the treetops, and sometimes he flies down low under the canopy, swooping from tree to tree. Every once in a while, he'll fly ahead a bit, searching for food...always searching for food. His empty belly dominates most of his thoughts as he roosts and waits for her to catch up, or for a meal to come along, whichever should happen first. He prays it's a meal, because even she is beginning to look tasty. Maybe she would be willing to part with a small bit of her anatomy. She can spare it... she's huge. It would be for the greater good (the greater good being that his stomach stops trying to devour itself.) Maybe just a tiny little nibble....

Aaaand down she goes again. He shakes his head in consternation at her ground-stomper clumsiness when she trips over yet another root. This time she falls face down in the disgusting, half rotten mulch that litters the ground in this part of the forest. Stupid, clumsy ground stomper. He's beginning to worry that it may have been a waste of his time and his energy to save her from the scream trees.

Eeww. So gross.

Ecko lifts her head up and swipes at the little bits of...stuff clinging to her face, spitting it from her lips. "Ugh, that's it! Break time," she calls out to the trees as she hauls herself back up. She's been walking (also stumbling, tripping, and face planting) for hours, lost and with only the vaguest of clues as to what direction to turn or which paths to take.

"I'm starving anyway," she irritably grumbles. Time to clean up and have something to eat.

She sets about making herself a hot lunch, using the time while it's cooking to change out of her filthy, funky clothes and give herself the most thorough sponge bath that she can manage. She wrinkles her nose in disgust as she stuffs her dirties into her laundry bag and then stuffs *that* bag all the way to the bottom of her backpack.

She sure wishes she could find a stream or a nice, unbloodied, body parts deprived lake to wash herself and her clothing in, but for now this will have to do. Soon though, she'll have to figure out what to do about cleaning her hair. She can't stand having itchy, dirty, greasy hair... it reminds her of her early hospital days. That had been the most dreadful time of her life, those days of sponge baths and greasy hair and smelly armpits. Eventually she'd been allowed two supervised showers a week, and she always rushed through them as quickly as possible, because really, who wants a stranger staring at their naked butt?

She shakes herself out of her memories as she puffs out a bit of baby powder into the palm of her hand and then rubs it into her scalp. This trick will help to keep her hair from getting oily, but it will only work for so long. She needs a bath...and soon!

But right now, lunch is served...and she can eat it all by herself! There's no hobglin cow here to gobble up her dwindling food supply. *Oh!* Poor Urza. She suddenly recalls *why* she doesn't have to share her food anymore. She hopes that Thing Two is already dead, which sounds so bad…so wrong. But (and there's that 'but' again) a quick death is, believe it or not, the most merciful outcome. At least if she's already passed on to whatever comes after this life, she's not being tortured. Unless Hell is a real place...and God help that mean, old heifer if it is.

She takes her time eating, enjoying each and every bite to the fullest. She's made it through three quarters of her meal when she hears something. It's just a tiny *something*, but it's the first sound that she's heard since leaving the dead pool, other than the ones that she herself made. It's a barely there, chittering noise and she's sure that she's heard it before. But *where* had she heard it? What is it? She strains her ears, listening intently, until she can pinpoint where it's coming from….

And it's coming from her freaking backpack! Maybe, just maybe, it's only her music player. Maybe it magically turned itself on and what she's hearing is some song playing through her headphones. Hopefully that's it. Please be it!

But it doesn't *sound* like music. It sounds more like a, like a… insect! That's it! That's the noise that the weird roach/beetle bug back at Samara's house had made.

"Oh, there *better* not be bugs in my bag!" she yelps as she sets the remainder of her food aside to hastily dump the entire contents of her bag out onto the ground.

The first thing she does is check the iPod and confirms her fears. It's still turned off, so definitely not music. The chirping had stopped as soon as she'd emptied the bag, so she can no longer locate it by sound either. She starts poking at stuff, carefully pushing items aside, searching for anything suspicious. She pokes and rummages and shuffles things carefully about, and then, *oh!* Then she sees it and it *is* one of those mutant beetle-roaches…a *huge* one, clinging to the side of poor Sir Didymus's face… and it's staring right at her! It's got all four of its slimy eyeballs poked out on the tips of its fully extended antenna/tentacles, and they are 100% focused on her.

"Oh Didymus! Oh no, oh my poor little love. Don't worry, I'll save you. Now don't. You. Move…"

At the sound of her voice, the bug starts angrily gnashing its dual sets of mandibles, clicking them together and making that chirping sound again. Only this time the chirp is faster and much louder. It's clearly agitated and warning her to stay back. But huh uh. Nope, not happening. It can't just stay there, planted on her friend's face like some sort of disgusting growth.

She slowly reaches out for the fork on her plate, never ending the staring contest that the two of them are currently engaged in. Believe it or not, as her fingers close around the handle of the utensil, that creepy-crawly from hell lifts up one of its disgusting little legs, holds it up and shakes it at her... just like a human shaking their fist in anger...*and it never breaks eye contact.* She's not sure if it's her intention to stab the nasty little disease, or just flick it off her friend's face, but she never gets the chance to find out, because just as she's bringing the weapon up (into a stabbing-type position) another, far larger, but just as ugly, creature swoops down from somewhere up above them and bites the bug's head clean off!

"Aieeeee!" Ecko shrieks, as she points her weapon of mass destruction at *it,* instead of the bug. The fork trembles violently and she's forced to reach up and steady it with her other hand. She watches in surprisingly slow motion as the headless bug tumbles off of Sir Didymus and the winged *thing* lands on the ground, just a few, short feet away from her.

Still threatening it at fork-point, she reaches one hand out and snatches her bestie off the ground and hugs him protectively to her chest. The creature crunches and chews (with its mouth open, exposing the horror of what a ground up bug head looks like) and then swallows the whole mess down. It starts hop/walking towards her, causing her to simultaneously screech, *again,* and frantically booty scooch/crab walk backwards to escape. It threateningly holds up one of its dagger-claws at her as it closes in.

"Didymus..." she whimpers as she clutches her inadequate protector to her chest. But thankfully, the critter continues right on past her; it doesn't seem to be after her at all. But it does glare its beady swamp eyes at her the entire time it's hopping by. It doesn't take its eyes off her until it's standing right beside its kill. Then it snorts at her just once, before turning its attention downwards and casually uses that single, upheld claw to flip the dead bug over onto its back. The sharp, cactus-like spines that cover the beetle-roach's back are now pressed into the dirt, and its more vulnerable belly is facing upwards.

The creature then proceeds to use that same claw to pin it down, while it uses a claw from its other hand to slice open and perform an impromptu bug-topsy. It deftly pries the bug shell apart to get to the insides, almost like it's a lobster or a crab. Ecko's wonderful, delicious lunch that she'd so thoroughly enjoyed now threatens to make a reappearance as the newcomer begins spooning out and shoveling guts into its mouth, as if it's a starving person at an all-you-can-eat crab dinner. But this is certainly no crab, even though those water bugs are nasty in their own rights. *This thing is a hundred times, no, a thousand times more disgusting,* with fluorescent, oozy, drippy innards that *no one* has any business eating. Ever.

Ecko slowly stands up and mentally prepares herself for battle, just in case it decides that it's still hungry when it's done eating the bug guts. She studies the freaky little thing as he scarfs his buggy meal. For some reason, she believes him to be male. She can practically feel the testosterone radiating off him. He has the feel of an angry and sullen pubescent teenage/man/child who hates the entire world.

He stands somewhere close to a foot tall, about half the size of a newborn infant (if said infant could stand up.) But thank you sweet baby Jesus, none of the infants she'd ever encountered had looked like this...whatever he is. He looks like what would be spawned if a Gargoyle mated with a Gremlin… not the cute little Mogwai creatures like Gizmo either. We're talking the full-fledged, fed after midnight then reemerged from a cocoon and transformed into an evil little demon, kind.

His skin is strangely lumpy and leathery and scaly all at once and he's a noxious blend of greens, blacks, and browns. He looks like he belongs in a swamp; his coloring would certainly help him blend in anyway. Long, scraggly brown hair (highlighted and tipped in forest green) covers his lumpy, bumpy head and dangles down into his eyes. There are two tiny horns peeking out of that mess of tangled hair, but they don't appear to be sharp. They're rounded, so what damage could they possibly do?

But his overly large mouth, full of small, pointy teeth more than make up for those blunt little horns. *Those* are dangerous and deadly. Just ask Mr. DeadBug over there. He would surely nod his affirmation, if only he still had a head to nod with.

The creature's ears are similar to those of a vampire bat, only much, much larger, disproportionately so. He would look evil and vicious, if it wasn't for those batty/Dumbo ears that he's got going on. And also, that so-ugly-it's-almost-cute vampire bat nose, and those enormous, round, green eyes. Those actually lend him an almost comical, cartoonish appearance.

His arms are thin and overly long, so long he could probably scratch the bottom of his own narrow, clawed feet without ever having to bend over to reach them. He's got a thin chest, a round bulgy belly, and sharp, knobby shoulders, elbows, and knees. And oh yes, there's a very large pair of dragon-like wings protruding from his back...can't forget those. They look big enough and strong enough to carry at least double his size and weight. Overall, he looks like a bat, a Gremlin, and a Gargoyle all mixed into one ... strange and ugly creature. Ecko instantly dubs him a Bat-gremgoyle.

She watches as he lowers his head down closer to his buggy meal and then sticks out his long, slimy, black tongue to lick up the last bit of innards juices from the bottom of his bug-shell bowl. "Ugh! Aren't you just the ugliest, most vile and repulsive little thing I've ever seen in my entire life? Well, besides Urza and Blaxx. They were pretty disgusting too. I think I'll call you Sir Ugly the Batgremgoyle," she murmurs with an uneasy little giggle.

The creature glances up at her, sucks leftover specks of guts from its claws, as if they'd been absolutely finger licking good, then belches out an obscenely raunchy burp. "And I think I'll call *you* Miss Rude. And I'm only ugly because I've been cursed. If I was my *real* self, you'd instantly fall in love and beg to have my babies. But alas, it just wouldn't work between us, my dear. Mostly because you are so rude...and giant. But mostly because you're rude."

Ecko is *astoundingly* quick to come back with a witty retort. "Aieeeee!" she screeches again. It's the only sound she can produce as she hops back, trips, and lands back on her butt. But hey, she never loses her grip on Sir Didymus or her fork/weapon. That's got to count for *something*.

"Yes, I believe you've said that already," the creature snarks back. "Stop screeching at me and lower your sword, wench. I've no wish to harm you. If I did, I could, and *would* have done so long ago." And then, he nonchalantly reaches back and scratches his butt, which she just now realizes is stuffed into a pair of tattered, moldy-looking britches. If she'd noticed that earlier (and *how* had she not noticed it?) she might not have been so shocked at the creature exhibiting signs of intelligence. He's obviously self-aware enough to clothe himself. That proves that he must have some semblance of cognition, at the very least a higher understanding than your ordinary beastie. She also just now notices that he's wearing a golden band around his left arm, high up on his spindly bicep.

"Now then. Pay attention," he tells her, as he casually examines his claws. "The way I see it, I just saved your life. So, now you owe me, and I demand my payment in the form of…." he looks her up and down, inspecting her closely, and then he points at her feet, "*those*. Yes, those will do nicely. They do look de-lisss-iouss. Yes, they do! Come my dear, let me have them now. Fair is fair, after all."

Ecko's face scrunches into a frown as she answers with her own impressive level of intelligence.

"Hu?" she blurts.

The strange, little creature sighs as it shakes its head regretfully. "Tsk, tsk, tsk. I may have to change your name from Miss Rude and return it back to the one the hobglin wench gave you... Big Dummy! It appears she was correct in her assessment of you."

It takes a step towards her, and she quickly retaliates by brandishing her fork threateningly at it. "Stay back! Don't you come any closer. I'll use this. I swear, I will! Besides, you just got done eating. Don't you need to let that digest or.... something?"

The Batgremgoyle scrunches its dark eyebrows ferociously at her, rearranging its face into a mean(er) death glare. "Listen up, wench. First of all, that wasn't *nearly* enough to satisfy me. It would take a hundred of those to fill up all of *this*." He proudly rubs his claws over his tiny Buddha belly, as if it's his greatest work of art.

"Secondly, I saved your life by killing that Vika Vakooja. You cannot just go smacking at them like you were intending to do. Did you not observe that it has armor, *very* strong and effective armor? Did you somehow not see the stabby things covering that armor? Those stabbers are highly poisonous. They wouldn't have killed you because you're a giant. It would take several Vika Vakooja's to kill something as large as you. But let me assure you that for a few hours you would have wished it *had* killed you."

"It talks," Ecko mutters as she stares incredulously at him. "The miniature orc-bat talks!"

The creature lets out an angry screech as it flares up at her, standing as tall as it can stretch and puffing its chest out to make itself look larger.

"Now see here! There's no need for insults! All that's needed here is my payment. I've done you a service, and now you must repay me. That's how it's done. I'm hungry and I've decided that I'd like to sample your feet-meat, so pay up!"

And then he starts hop/running towards her with his hands stretched out before him. So, Ecko does the only thing she can think to do. She throws the fork at him, in a desperate attempt to slow him down and then grabs the bottle of *OFF!* bug spray from her pile of belongings and blasts him right in the face with it, just before he reaches her. (Which, come to think of it, is what she should have done to the mutant-bug... before it lost its head, that is.)

The creature immediately turns into a dying cockroach, but an extremely dramatic and vocal one. "Aaakkkk! Arrggg! Ick ack, ack, ack." He coughs and chokes and swipes at his face, jumping around, waving his arms and flapping his wings as he spins in circles. He grabs his throat and hacks for a few seconds, does one last half spin, and then falls down onto his back on the ground. Those green eyes are closed and that long, slimy looking black tongue is hanging out the side of his mouth, dangling down into the dirt.

She can't see it breathing!

"Oh my God, did I kill you? I didn't mean to kill you! Oh, please don't be dead, little beastie. Please don't be dead!" She picks up a stick and pokes at his bulging belly. Nothing! She jabs again, a little harder. "Come on… wake up."

Poke, poke, poke. She drops the stick and snatches up her half empty bottle of water and splashes it into his face. He shoots up like a rocket, spitting and sputtering and cursing. Then he sticks out his freakishly long tongue to slurp up every droplet of water from his face.

"Oh, thank God!" she cries out with relief. If it can curse at her, it's probably going be just fine.

"*What* did you do that for? And what *was* that? Ugh, it was terrible, like the fumes that come from a hobglin mound waste hole. 'Tis lethal!" the little beast groans.

He reaches down and rubs at a spot on his belly and asks, "Did you poke me?" She hastily shakes her head no, but then her eyes guiltily dart to the stick/prodder.

"You did, didn't you? You jabbed me with that stick, didn't you? Didn't you? Oh, you are a nasty, ungrateful wench!" He hops up and stomps around, muttering and complaining about his near-death experience at the hands of jabbing giants.

"Ok, ok!" she admits. "I *may* have poked you once or twice, but I was just trying to see if you were breathing. I thought I'd killed you." Then she apologizes, "I'm sorry. I didn't mean to hurt you. I was just scared. In my defense, you *were* trying to eat me."

The creature's shoulders slump in resignation as he grumbles, "Fine. You're forgiven. But you still owe me for saving your life…

and I'm still hungry!" He raises up his hand and points a claw at her. "What are you going to do to rectify this, hmmm?"

She hugs Didymus harder and lifts her chin up a notch. "Well, I know I'm not letting you cut off my feet! I'm willing to admit that you *may* have helped me, and I'll repay you for that. But your price is too high. You're demanding that I pay you for saving my life when you, in your own words, just admitted that one of those beetle-roaches wouldn't have been enough to kill me. So, technically you did *not* save my life, did you? Not *really*. At best, you saved me from a bit of discomfort. That is *not* worth chopping my feet off for! Is there anything *else* you'll accept as payment for your 'so called' life-saving good deed?"

The little nasty drags a claw through his hair and scratches at his scalp with a surprised look on his face. "Ooohh, the wench is smarter than she looks. Not such a big dummy after all…. Better stick with calling her Miss Rude," he mumbles thoughtfully to himself.

"You are correct," he reluctantly agrees. "I didn't *actually* save your *life*, per se. But I feel like you're missing the importance of what I have done for you, the incredible generosity that I've exhibited on your behalf. It feels like you're belittling me and downplaying my heroic acts of greatness. And I will *not* be taken advantage of! Do you hear me? You will have to pay me my due. But! I'm willing to work with you. I'll accept just one of your feets and call us even. How's that for generosity?"

He frowns angrily as she continues to shake her head at him. "No, you freaky little thing. It takes *both* feet to walk. I can't just hop along on one foot everywhere I go!"

He glares down at her feet and considers them closely. "Fine!" he shouts. "I will accept three toes, just a sample, really. You can walk without a few toes. I won't even take the big ones. I'll graciously accept the smaller, stumpy ones. And *that* is my final offer. If you don't want to pay up, then battle it is! Your choice, wench."

He crosses those scrawny arms over his chest, spins around, and storms five feet away from where she's sitting and plops his own butt down in the dirt.

She can't help but be slightly amused. He looks like a petulant child who hasn't gotten his way. He's pouting, he's actually pouting and he's so ugly he's almost cute. Kinda sorta... but no. Not really. He really is ugly.

"Battle it is then, I suppose, because I won't be cutting off any body parts for you to fill your belly with today. I do, however, have some non-human-body-part food here that I will gladly share with you, though. *If* you're willing to be reasonable, that is. Will this be acceptable, or must I continue to fight you off with my fork and bug repellant?" She picks the *Off!* back up and prepares to let him have it.

"Fine!" he hastily shouts. "Fine, you dirty cheater. Don't you shoot that stuff at me again! If I don't get to taste ground stomper today, then I demand something of equal value! And *that* is my final offer, for real this time."

She sets the can of bug spray beside her (in close reach just in case) and starts going through her food items. "So now that we're in agreement that my feet are off the menu… *permanently* off the menu, might I add, what do you want?"

She holds up package after package for his inspection/approval. "I have stews and soups, noodles and rice...beef jerky? You might like that. It can't be any worse than some smelly old feet, right? I also have candy and granola bars, but Urza thought I was poisoning her when she tasted those, so you may not like them either."

She gets busy cleaning up her picnic area and repacking all of the inedible items back into her pack. She pushes the bowl with her leftover portion of stroganoff closer to him and tells him that he can also have what's left of her lunch, if he wants it, although it's cold now and won't taste as good as it had.

He does this funny little booty scooching shuffle forward, so that he can sniff the contents of the bowl. His little bat nose wiggles, his eyes light up, and his belly lets out a loud, rumbling gurgle, all at the same time. But he quickly jerks his attention from the food that he obviously hungers for and glares at her all offended-like, as he plants his claws on his hips.

"Is this a trick?" he demands with anger and distrust in his voice. "Are you trying to cheat me? If I eat this miserly scrap of food, will you then proclaim that I've been properly compensated and paid in full? Nu huh. No, ma'am. I'm not falling for it. I am clever, see? Too clever for your tricksy mind traps." He laughs and taps a claw against his head as he crows, "Nice try!"

Then he haughtily turns his nose up and away from her and her offering of leftovers. But his tummy is rumbling and rumbling, so loudly. And if there's anything that she hates more than the dark, it's the thought of someone, *anyone* going without food…. even gross little orc-bats. The most hurtful offense to her heart is witnessing another's hunger. It's her biggest weakness. Her heart immediately softens towards the ugly little booger.

"No tricks, I swear. You can have that and still pick something else," she says softly, compassionately.

He turns his head back and glares at her. "I do not believe you, ground stomper!"

She sighs heavily in frustration as she picks the bowl up, shaking her head sadly as she does so. "Fine, be that way. I'm just going to dump it out on the ground and leave it behind for someone else to come along and eat…. since you don't want it. I'm sure there are starving things in this forest that will be glad to have it." She stands up and carries the bowl a few feet away, then acts like she's about to scrape it out.

"Wait!" he screeches. "I will do it! Since you've asked me so politely, practically *begged* me, I will do it! I will take it *and* your biggest food pouch, yes that one right there. And also one of those magic fire sticks I've seen you use during Pitch. Then, and *only* then, will I call your debt paid."

"What? You greedy little thing! We agreed on food as payment! You can't just tack additional things on like that. Wait, why am I arguing with a little orc-bat? Oh, it doesn't even matter anyway. There's nothing you can say that will *ever* make me give up even one of my flashlights. I'm almost as unwilling to part with those as I am body parts! So, no. You get food or nothing at all, but hurry up and decide, because I need to be on my way."

She thrusts the bowl at him, and he snatches it out of her hands, face all scrunched up in a fierce scowl. At the same time, he reaches out one leg and wraps his foot claws around a pouch of beef stew (the largest pouch of food she has) and slowly drags it towards himself. He never breaks eye contact with her either.

"Fine, keep your magic fire. But you owe me a favor."

Ecko raises her eyebrows in incredulity at how greedy he is. "Fine," she agrees. "I owe you a favor, but it's not a blind favor. I reserve the right to accept or deny the favor you request of me. *I* get to choose which one I fulfill, not you. Now eat, so I can clean my bowl and get back to making my way through this forest."

The little jerk grins up at her and offers, "You know, for a price, a *fair* price, I could fly ahead and show you the way out."

He is so frustratingly acquisitive, practically a mercenary! "No! I am *not* paying you anything else. Now EAT!"

He curls his lips up at her and snarls. "Fine! Have it your way!" he shouts back, then he buries his face in the bowl and slurps and snorts and grunts until the food's gone and every trace is licked away. When he finally comes up for air, his eyes are twinkling with delight and his little nose is covered in sauce. "That was de-lisss-iouss! What kind of food *was* that? Do you have more? Does my pouch hold this same kind?"

Ecko can't help but laugh at the mess he's made on his face. "Um, no. What you chose is not the same kind of food. You picked the beef stew. It's really just as good, though. Plus, the stew has a bigger serving size than the stroganoff, which is what you just inhaled and are currently wearing. You've got some sauce on your nose there." She grimaces at the sight of that black tongue darting out to clean himself up.

"Ummm, yumm, yumm," he hums to himself, as he licks away every last speck of sauce.

Ecko busies herself with cleaning the bowl and fork and then puts them away. Then she pulls on a blissfully clean pair of socks, slips on and ties her shoes, and then slips her backpack on.

"Wait!" the little monster suddenly cries out. "I've changed my mind. I realize now that I was being greedy in taking your biggest sack of food. What was I thinking? That was so wrong of me! From what I've seen, you will need all the food you can get…you are not a good hunter/gatherer wench. I have decided to return this large sack of food to you, and I shall graciously accept a smaller one. One that contains the stroke-off."

She turns her head away, just barely managing to hide the smile on her face. He's such a greedy, mischievous little thing. "Too late! No take backs!" she calls as she hurries away.

"But But but… *wait*! Come back. Let us discuss this!" He hop/flies behind her, struggling to keep up. His feet churn so that he's running, but his wings are flapping too, and they lift him briefly from the ground in a glide and then lower him back down, so that he almost appears to be bouncing along behind her.

"Sure, we can talk about it. I'll do you a *favor* and trade the food packs. I'll do it right now. Just say the word." She giggles as his mouth drops open in shock.

"Oh, you is a sneaky, tricksy wench, indeed!" he exclaims in outrage. "How about this? I will travel with you and show you the safest paths to take, until I decide what to do. This is a difficult situation. I must carefully think it over and consider all my options."

She disguises her laughter by covering her mouth and faking a coughing fit. "Sure," she agrees. "You're welcome to travel with me for a while, and I would certainly appreciate any help that you can offer with the navigation. I would really love to avoid dangerous plants and nasty creatures that want to devour me. Or, you know, the ones that try to trick me or take advantage of me."

Now it's *his* turn to snort back a laugh. He understands perfectly well that it's him she's implicating. He's actually an extremely smart beastie, who clearly understands sarcasm.

They've been walking along quietly for twenty minutes, or so. Well, she's been walking. *He's* been flying from one dead tree to the next with his bag of food clutched to his chest like a prize. She's already offered to put it back in her bag and carry it for him, but he declined. He doesn't trust her enough to relinquish his hold on it. "Suit yourself," was all she'd said. It really was of no consequence to her. He could tire himself out if he wanted to.

She's been thinking about something as she walks down the trails that her Batgremgoyle companion directs her to. "Why my feet?" she suddenly calls out to break the silence. "Out of all my many body parts to choose from, why would you choose my feet, of all things? Feet are so gross. I can't imagine anything wanting to eat them. But then again, you did eat that bug thing. What did you call it again?"

He lowers his altitude a bit, so that he can fly along beside her. "I am only able to answer one question at a time, wench! It was a Vika Vakooja, a bug spy. There are millions of them scattered over every part of this land. They have eyes that can see far, and they have memories that last forever. They *never* forget, because they share a collective mind. The Lokskell uses them as his spies. When a Vika Vakooja learns something new, that information gets passed along the collective through their mental connection. If they (collectively) decide that bit of news is worthy, they pass it along to the Lokskell. They are the perfect infiltrators. They're small enough to hide anywhere. They *are* hidden everywhere. They breed and multiply faster than any other living thing, and they love gossip and rumors."

Ecko tries to wrap her mind around the idea of bug spies. "The Buggy-Borg," she whispers and immediately shivers in revulsion as she thinks about the one in her bag, crawling all over her things. Poor Didymus. Then she wonders what it possibly could have learned, what information it could have sent back to the Shadow Lord.

"How long do you think it was in my bag?" she asks in a worried voice, not sure if she really wants to know the answer.

"Oh, not long," he assures her as he drops onto a branch to rest. "It crawled in there while you and the hobglin wench were distracted with eating. Now, about your other question. I will answer it now. I chose your feets, because I met a troll once and he told me that those were the best parts of ground stompers. He said he *always* eats the feets off of his people-meals first, because they're the tastiest part. I've wanted to try them ever since. I was finally going to find out for myself too, if you hadn't been so selfish! You wouldn't even give me some measly little toes. Selfish, that's what you are. And greedy! You could have at least offered to let me lick the in-betweenzies!" he complains.

She stops walking to turn and stare up at him in disbelief. "Selfish? How can you even say I was being selfish? YOU were the selfish one. And inconsiderate too! What was your plan anyway? Were you going to bite them off like you did that bug's head? Or were you just going to eat them right off my legs, bite by bite? Did you even care about how much that would hurt? And just how did you think I would be able to survive in this world without a way to move about? Not everyone has feet *and* wings, you know!"

The nasty little thing has the audacity to shrug nonchalantly down into the face of her anger. "Surely, you are exaggerating. Surely, even *you* could survive long enough for them to grow back. All you would need to do is hide yourself away somewhere and wait. How long could it possibly take for two foots to regrow? My wings are way bigger, and it only takes them thirty Pales to regrow themselves."

She throws her hands up in aggravation. "Regrow?" she shouts. "Regrow, the nasty orc-bat says. *They don't grow back!* None of my body parts do! Was I supposed to crawl on my hands and knees for the rest of my life to escape all the predators that want to eat me? Well, I guess at least I wouldn't have had to crawl for long, because I wouldn't have lasted a *week* in this place without feet. This is a dreadful, horrid place; this entire world is a vampire. Everything and everyone here is either a scary monster, a vicious predator, or a selfish, greedy, *inconsiderate* beastie!"

All of a sudden, she's angry. Furious. Seething. Her own inner monsters take up a stomping cadence in her head as her hair begins whipping about, slapping at her face. Her skin starts crackling with a familiar electric sizzle and she knows that her eyes have gone silver and mirror-like, because her vision changes to that strangely hazy, infrared perception. She peers intently at the Batgremgoyle that's staring down at her from the branches above. His image has gone all hazy, sort of misty and see-through, and there's a shadowy image of a tiny man weirdly superimposed over his little orc-bat self.

"Ack!" the littlest orc screeches down at her. "Why are your eyes changing? What *is* that? What are you doing? What's going on? Don't you point those crazy eyes at me! It's not my fault! I didn't know your feets wouldn't grow back. I swear I didn't know that!" Then he lifts his flimsy sack of food and ducks down behind it to shield himself, as if that would really protect him from anything.

Ecko grabs her head as she desperately tries to calm herself and regain control over her emotions. She spins away from him, so that she doesn't accidentally hurt him, and grabs onto the nearest tree to steady herself. Pressing her forehead against the rough bark, she tries to focus on her breathing.

That's when she sees it. With the magic flowing through her, influencing her, *changing* her, she can see things that she'd previously been blind to. Deep inside the tree, hidden beneath layers and layers of protective bark, is a radiance, a fist sized spark with little glowing veins protruding from it. It takes her a moment to figure out what she's looking at, but soon realizes that she can actually see the tree's vascular system. The veins stretch throughout the entire tree, from the glow-source (heart?) all the way to the roots in the ground and to the tippiest tops of the branches. Most of those veins have gone dark and turned black. Only a few are still lit up and glowing.

The tree is dying.

She lets go of it and steps back, slowly turning in a circle to regard the rest of the forest around her. Her emotions become a warzone inside of her as she takes in all the signs of life that had been undetectable to her eyes before now. Equal parts wonder and despair battle for dominance. Wonder, because the trees and plants are not as lifeless as their outward appearance suggests. Several of them still have that spark, that brilliant glow deep down inside them. They're sick and dying for sure, but not dead yet. The despair that she feels is because she knows there's nothing she can do to help them.

She reaches for the tree again, briefly pressing her forehead and both palms against the rough, abrasive bark. The anguish that she feels within it saves her from doing… whatever she'd been about to do. It rushes in and pushes the anger out of her heart, replacing it with sadness instead. As the pain takes hold, the anger, the burning fire inside her begins to die down. Her skin stops snapping out electrical currents, her hair settles back onto her shoulders. The raging beat of her pulse slows, and she can feel her molten mirror eyes returning to normalcy.

With the next blink of her eyes, her vision slips back into real time/real world perspective. She takes a deep breath, then another and another, before she turns to apologize to her little beastie companion. She feels awful when she sees him up there, hiding behind his pouch of stew, eyes wide as saucers and shivering with fear. She holds her hands up to show him that she's calm and that she doesn't mean him any harm.

"I'm sorry! Everything's fine! I've got it all under control now." She ignores the monsters in her head, as they laugh at that statement. "Oh, shut up," she quietly tells them.

The little Batgremgoyle tentatively lowers the pouch, watching her distrustfully. "I really am sorry. I didn't mean to scare you. Sometimes I just get really mad and I lose control of myself, that's all. I would never hurt anyone…well, not intentionally anyway."

She frowns as she reconsiders her words. They sounded too much like a lie, so she grudgingly clarifies herself. "That's not exactly the whole truth. I do have every intention of hurting someone, but it's not you and I didn't mean to scare you and *that's* the truth! Now, which way was I supposed to go again?" She feels embarrassed and ashamed of herself, like she's nothing more than a big bully who goes around scaring small, defenseless children.

The Batgremgoyle lifts his hand and points a claw at a trail to the left. "Thanks," she mumbles as she turns and gets moving once more. She feels terrible.

The little beast eyes her warily for a moment, as if he believes that she'll spin back around and blast him with her freaky eyes. "Elfslugs and earwax!" he exclaims as he hastily flaps his wings and lifts off to follow her. "I am *so* glad that I didn't eat you. You would have given me heartburn for sure!"

As they turn onto the designated trail to continue on their journey, a small spark of magic flares to life behind them. Unbeknownst to either of them, a single green stem emerges from a branch on the tree that Ecko had touched with her magic. Neither one notices as three tiny leaves burst out and unfurl themselves. They don't see when those brand-new leaves turn and stretch themselves in the direction that she disappears in, much like when a plant leans itself towards the life-giving warmth of the sun.

There's silence between the two unlikely companions for a good long while, as they've both retreated into their own thoughts. The ugly, little creature mostly thinks about *her* and what had just happened. He wonders, not for the first time, if she'll be of any use to him. He wonders if she can help him with his unique situation.

She, on the other hand, is mostly just dwelling on how exhausted she feels. It seems that all her strength had drained away when her anger left her. She plods along for as long as she can, but when she begins stumbling and tripping over her own feet, she decides that she's had enough.

"This is it, right here," she calls out. "I'm setting up camp right here in the middle of this path and calling it a day. I'm tired, and if I keep going, I'm going to end up falling and hurting myself."

He continues to fly ahead, but then circles back after a moment. "Now, don't get mad!" he cautions. "This is just a polite, *friendly* suggestion... but there's a better spot for sleeping just a little further ahead. It's only twenty wing flaps away, so that makes it somewhere around one hundred ground stomps for you. But it's completely up to you, wherever you decide is fine with me! I sleep in the trees anyway."

She would have laughed at his attempts to placate her, if she didn't already feel so guilty for terrifying the poor little creature. He probably thinks she'll fry his face off with her anger. "Lead on then, because I'm ready to drop."

Two minutes later and she's standing in a small clearing that's shielded by a ring of trees. It really would have been the perfect camping spot, if only it had a small non-threatening, non-lethal, non-poisonous, dead body-less, and monster-less little stream running through it. She desperately needs to restock her water supply... and a bath would be nice too. But that's just going to have to be a problem for tomorrow, because she's too pooped to worry about it today. She drops her backpack to the ground and murmurs, "You were right. This is a good spot. Now, I need you to be down on the ground and not up there in the trees where you can see everything that goes on below you."

He just stares down at her, not budging an inch.

So, she tries again. "I need a little privacy."

Blink, blink, blank stare.

"Fine!" she shouts. "I have to pee, and I don't want you to look while I do it!"

The Batgremgoyle makes a retching noise and croaks, "Gross!" before he flies down to the ground. "Ugh. Why would I watch?" He sets his food pouch aside and plops himself down beside it. "I'll just wait right here," he calls to her retreating back.

"So, what's your name?" she asks as she walks back into the circle of trees, just a few minutes later. He skitters away and hisses at her, actually hisses at her, before he flies back up into the trees where he *continues* to hiss and spit and sputter.

"Jeez, what's wrong with you, you little weirdo? I just asked what your name is. No need to freak out like some kind of...freaky thing."

He points an accusatory claw down at her and demands, "Who wants to know? Who sent you? What do you want?"

She gapes up at him in complete and utter bafflement. "No one sent me anywhere. And what do you mean 'Who wants to know?' I do. I need to know what to call you. I've been calling you a Batgremgoyle in my head, because that's what you look like to me, but that's kind of a long title and not really a name anyway." She sits down and starts working on dinner preparations, but she shakes her head at the absurdity of the conversation they're having.

"*Why* do you wish to know?" he demands.

She barely manages to stifle a groan of sheer frustration. "Because that is what polite people do when they meet for the first time. They exchange names so that they have something to call one another."

He sniffs haughty at that reasoning. "I am not a people!"

"Clearly," she mutters under her breath. "Fine. Don't tell me your name. I'm just gonna call you Gargamel. He was a big ole, grumpy meanie-head too." She ducks her head to hide her grin when she hears him up there, sputtering again. He may not know who Gargamel is, but he clearly recognizes the insult behind her words.

Once she's got her tiny kitchen set up, she calls up to him, "Everything's all set up. Are you planning on eating sometime tonight?"

"Yessss," he angrily hisses.

"Well, you forgot your dinner." She points to his forgotten, left behind meal pouch. "Aren't you hungry?"

"Yes!" (Slightly less angry and with a hint of hesitation thrown in)

"And have you decided if you want me to grant your favor by trading food pouches, or are you keeping this one?" Her grin grows wider when she hears his shouted response.

"Keeping it! You *still* owe me a favor, wench!"

"Well, would you like me to heat it up for you, or do you just want to slurp it up cold?" There's no answer from the sullen little creature.

"Are you gonna stay up there all night, all Pitch I mean?" Still no answer. "Fine. *I'll* eat it then!" She stretches her arm out and pretends to go after his food. He lets out a piercing banshee scream and dive-bombs out of the tree like a screeching eagle that's diving for its prey. Only he is much, much less graceful than any eagle she'd ever seen.

He lands on top of his food pack with a hard plop, but he still manages to scoop it protectively into his arms as he rolls several feet before coming to a (forced) stop. Upside down and against a tree, he turns his head so that he can glare one angry eye at her.

She can't help but giggle at him. He's such a funny, ugly little thing. She opens her own package of stew and dumps it into the cookpot. "I was only teasing you. I have my own food. Come back."

He rolls over and shakes himself off like a wet dog, flinging dust and dirt in every direction. Then he runs a hand over his hair to try and smooth it down... not that it helps any. His hair is a long, tangled mess that won't be tamed so easily.

"Look," she says, "I'll even help you out. I'll eat beef stew to-night too, so that you can try it. That way you'll know what they both taste like. Then you can make your final decision based on which one you like more. How does that sound?"

He hop/shuffles closer and plunks himself back down, his pouch of food safely shoved behind him. When the stew is bub-bling and warm, she dips out a spoonful and holds it out to him. "Peace offering," she offers with a smile.

He holds his hand out for her to drop the food into, and she realizes that there's no possible way for him to grasp the spoon, not with those monster claws of his. "Just open your mouth and I'll pour it in."

"I'm no infant!" he snarls, then opens his mouth wide as a baby bird does. She keeps her face serious and neutral as she pours the spoonful of yummy goodness in. He closes his mouth and chews enthusiastically, his eyes lit up with pleasure. But when he swallows it down, his face falls and a look of pure devastation chases the joy from his features.

"What's wrong? You don't like it?"

He throws himself backwards onto the dirt and stares miserably up at the grey sky. "I love it! *That's* what's wrong! They are both too scrumptious!" he wails in distress. "I can't choose one over the other! Oh, how will I decide which one to eat? I shall *starve* from indecision!"

She laughs at his silly predicament while she divides the stew equally into two bowls. She nudges him with her foot to stop his theatrics and dramatic wailing, then sets one of the bowls on the ground in front of him. She tells him that she will share her dinner with him tonight and advises him to save his food pouch for tomorrow. It will give him more time to decide which meal he likes better.

He instantly shuts his mouth and sits up. He eyeballs her with obvious distrust as she takes a small stack of crackers from a tin and divides those between them also. She crumbles her crackers atop her stew, because he's watching to see what *she* does, and she knows that he'll never be able to hold onto the little squares to dip them.

She pretends to ignore him as she digs in, but her heart twinges with sympathy when he wraps his wings protectively around his own bowl before lowering his head and practically inhaling his food. He keeps his eyes fixed on her the entire time, the entire sixty seconds it takes for him to gobble it all up, crackers and all.

He burps loudly and watches every slow dip of her spoon into her bowl, every mouthful she takes, every single chew and swallow, until hers is gone too. Then he sighs in disappointment when there's nothing left.

"Do you like granola?" she nonchalantly asks.

He enthusiastically nods his head. "Yes! Yes, I do. What is it?"

She tosses him one of the granola bars that has berries and nuts in it, and he sniffs it.

"It does not smell very appetizing," he grumbles right before he takes a small, sample bite… right through the wrapper. She forgot that he doesn't understand pre-packaged human food. He doesn't know anything about wrappers and packages. He wouldn't be able to open the snack with those long claws of his anyway.

"Wait!" she yelps. "Spit it out! You have to take it out of the package first! Here, hand it back and I'll show you." He grudgingly relinquishes the remaining portion and spits the bite he'd taken onto the ground, carefully watching all the while, as she removes the wrapper and passes it back to him.

He studies the mangled mess in the dirt and uses one claw to pull the piece of trash out of it. He tosses it away and then scoops the partially chewed glob of granola up and shoves it back into his mouth, dirt and all. His eyes pop open wide and a little teardrop rolls down his face as he chews. "Thank you," he fervently whispers, with so much gratitude that she doesn't even question why he turns and places the uneaten portion of the granola bar on top of his meal pouch. Who knows? Perhaps he wants to eat it later, so that he can savor it longer.

Something's been on her mind, nagging at her all day, something from her dreams last night…. from before Faoira had awakened her. She can't remember anything about it, except that she'd been weaving a basket-like handbag out of her bright purple paracord. Why? She has no clue. She can't remember, but she has the strangest feeling that it's something that she ought to be doing here, now, in the Waking World… sort of like a premonition. She doesn't even know how to weave a basket, but she takes the paracord from her bag and begins fiddling with it.

To distract herself, she tries once more at conversing with her beastie companion. "So, you won't tell me your name, but tell me something about you so I can get to know you better."

He glares at her with suspicion but growls, "What do you want to know?"

She rolls her eyes at his paranoia. "Whatever you feel comfortable telling me, just tell me *something!* Why are you so distrustful? How about, what's your favorite color? How old are you? Where do you live and what's your home like? Are you married? Do you have any kids? I don't know! Just make conversation. It's what polite people do! I know you said you're not a people, polite or otherwise, but just pretend for a moment that you are!"

The little orc-bat takes a worried step back. "Calm down, wench. I'll tell you what you want to know. Just don't point your 'angry' eyes in my direction. I am distrustful, because as you've stated before, this entire world is a vampire and I've been sucked on...unpleasantly, might I add, more times than I care to remember. Fair enough?"

He continues when she nods her understanding. "I'm three hundred and thirty-three years old, my favorite colors are pink and yellow, I have a treehouse far from here, and *who* in their right minds would ever want to be married and saddled with dirty little crotch goblins?" He shudders at the thought of it. "Nope, I live my life how *I* choose to live it... happy and free and playing the field! I was taught to share. And let me tell you, there's *plenty* of me to go around, if you know what I mean!"

Ecko shakes her head and holds her hand up in the universal 'stop' sign."Eww. Never mind. Just forget I even asked." She glances down at her hands, expecting to see a wad of tangled paracord, but what she sees is a flat, oval-shaped placemat. She's shocked that she's managed to weave something that actually resembles the bottom of a basket! She has no idea how she did it, either. The knowledge on basket weaving must be buried somewhere in her memories, but now that she's looking at it and thinking about it, she hasn't the faintest clue what to do next. She yawns and then balls the whole mess up and stuffs it back into her bag. It's not dark yet, but she still feels as if it's past her bedtime.

She sips at her cup of hot tea as she sets the camp to rights and cleans the dishes. By the time she's finished her chores, she realizes that she's too tired to set up the tent, so she just spreads her sleeping bag right on the ground and crawls into it. She's lying there, concentrating hard, waiting to see if she'll be able to feel the warning rumble of the approaching Pitch (totally prepared and armed with flashlights, of course) when her little companion speaks out.

"There's magic in names," he explains. "If you give your full name to the wrong person, they can hold power over you, force you to do strange things...things you would never, under any other circumstances do. I *never* give my name to anyone. It's high up on my list of things that I hate, number nine, to be precise. I try to always live by that list... I *never* willingly do, say, eat, drink, or think about the things that go against that list."

"But I'm not like that," she insists. "I would never do *anything* like that. Take control of someone, just by knowing their name? I had no idea such a thing was even possible." She falls silent for a moment as she thinks about it. "How can you be sure that's really true? Has anything bad ever happened to you from telling someone your name?"

He makes a rude sound at that, something between a snort and a laugh. "Yes. You want an example? I've got an example for you. Many years ago, I found myself the object of a she-witch's desires. Now, that actually happens to me quite often, being the irresistible creature that I am... don't laugh! I assure you that I am quite the looker, when I'm not busy being cursed, that is."

She stops giggling, so that he can continue. "Ahem. Back to my tale... even though countless wenches desire me, *this* one was different. She was everything I adored in a female. Mesmerizingly beautiful, smelling as sweet as a flower, soft as spiddersilk... you get my point. This perfect she-witch decided that she wanted me for herself.... *only* for herself. So, she batted her big bright eyes at me, tricked me with her luscious woman's body. I'm telling you, she bamboozled me into saying my name! She repeated it aloud and said a little incantation, and then she had me! From that pale on, I was her slave. There was nothing I could do about it. And I don't want to talk about it anymore! But now you see? I know exactly what I speak of. I *never* tell my name, especially to tricksy female types!"

She can hear the very real pain in his voice, so she lets it go at that. She'll just think of something to call him tomorrow. "Ok," she says. "I understand. You don't have to tell me. You don't have to do anything you don't want to do."

Silence and more silence, but then he suddenly speaks out again. "I do not trust you. That other girl, the nasty one that looks just like you is very, *very* bad."

Ecko sighs. It figures that even this little orc-bat knows of her evil twin. "Yeah, you don't have to tell *me* that. I know firsthand how rotten she is, and *I* don't want to talk about *her*."

It's quiet for a few more moments and then he nervously clears his throat.

"I said that I never tell my full name and that is true as true can be. But I suppose I can tell you *part* of my name and still keep myself safe from any trickery." He takes a deep, steadying breath and then confesses, "My middlin name is Boodark. You may call me Boodark the Mighty. No! Boodark the Great. Yeah, that's the one! And please don't try to find out the rest of my name, and do *not* try to use it against me. And please stop calling me Gargamel the Batgremgoyle. And don't you *dare* call me a orc-bat anymore! Are we clear?"

She smiles sleepily before softly murmuring, "It's nice to meet you Boodark. You can call me Ecko." Then the ground begins to rumble, and she *does* feel it, but she's asleep long before the hour of warning rumbles is over and the Pitch arrives. She never hears Boodark the Sneaky fly away in the dark of the night. She's too deeply asleep to hear anything less than a Foul-Kry screaming in her ears.

But even exhaustion can't keep the dreams at bay, and after several hours of wandering around in DreamWorld, her mind at last, mercifully shuts itself down. The dreams loosen their grip on her, and she moves into a lighter sleep, one where dreams are blessedly absent. She teeters on the edge of waking and sleeping, and so it is that she hears the soft sighing of Boodark's wings as he returns to his perch in the trees.

She feigns sleep, lying still and quiet with eyes closed, because even though *she* can't see through the Pitch, she knows that *he* can. She listens to the slight rustlings as he gets settled. Minutes later, his softly purring snores let her know that he's fallen asleep.

But there will be no more rest for *her*. The dreams of Laelynn and her dad, Charlie and Susan, Red Doors and shimmering wings, and a woman's sad song echo through her mind and she knows that her sleeping is done for this night. She can only hope that she got enough rest, because tomorrow will be another long day and the world is a vampire and there are so many things here that will put out her light forever, if she's not careful.

She can't suppress the quiet groan of frustration that spills from her lips. She doesn't even want to think about the approaching day…*Pale* and all the troubles it will bring with it. So, she sits up and clicks her flashlight on, careful to keep the shine off of her sleeping companion. She digs around in her backpack as quietly as possible, searching for her iPod. Music will help clear her mind. It always does.

But she forgets all about music when her fingers unexpectedly brush up against a smooth, round object. How had she forgotten about Faoira's gift? She wraps her hands around it and lifts it out of her bag, so that she can shine her light on it. She wants to take a better look at it, now that her life isn't (imminently) in danger.

The Night Pearl is as black as the Pitch that surrounds her, but its overlaying rainbow hues shimmer in the beam of the flashlight. It's exquisite, like nothing she'd ever seen before. She subconsciously runs her fingers over its smoothness, turning it this way and that way to better admire it. She can't help but think of Susan, of how much the sweet old woman adores pearls. Oh, how Susan would have loved to see this one!

She smiles softly at the memory of Charlie gifting his bride with a strand of pearls for their wedding. She wistfully reminisces about happier times, as she continues to admire the Night Pearl, her mind filled with memories of Susan and her beloved Charlie. All of her thoughts, all of her hopes, are focused on the two of them, when the magic flares to life inside of her. The electric force rushes through her body and settles in her hands, lighting them up with that brilliant blue glow. It flows out of her and straight into the Night Pearl, causing it to thrum and pulse in her hands. It reacts the exact same way that her mother's box had!

A sudden, tiny, spark appears *inside* the Pearl, a pinprick of radiance at its core. It pulses like a heartbeat, one that she can feel deep inside of herself, as if a link has been made and now connects her to it. She gasps as the iridescent rainbows begin to move, to swirl and roll over the surface with kaleidoscopic brilliance. The colors swirl faster and faster, like psychedelic storm clouds tumbling in, and as they rush towards her, that little ball of light begins to grow. The rest of it, that deep black color, starts getting pushed aside to make room for the ever-growing light.

While she mentally ooh's and ahh's at the marvel that she holds in her hands, she realizes that at some point in the last few seconds, a drastic change has occurred within the Night Pearl. Although she never once took her eyes off of it, and she never saw how or when it happened, the light and the dark somehow, magically switched places with one another other. Now there's a black center, a small marble of Pitch shrinking away in the middle of a pearl made of pure, beautiful light. It grows so bright, so brilliant, that it *should* have blinded her. It should have at least hurt to look into it. But it isn't painful at all. It's soothing, almost hypnotic in its magnificence. Something about it calls to her, beckons her to look closer, to search inside that light for...*something.*

Then the light dims, and there they are, Susan and Charlie, back at home. She immediately bursts into tears at the sight of them. Charlie's sitting in his old recliner, his head in his hands, shoulders shaking with sobs, while Susan tries to console him.

She can't hear them, but she knows that his old heart is breaking from his worry for *her.* She did this to him. Poor Charlie doesn't deserve this. He should be enjoying this time, loving every day with his new bride...and poor sweet Susan...

Ecko has the urge to tap upon the surface of the Night Pearl, as if it's nothing more than a sheet of glass that separates her from them. She wants to shout that she's here, trapped on a hellish, nightmare version of Oz. She wants to shout that she's trying to get back home to them, just like Dorothy had cried, "Aunty Em! Aunty Em! I'm here and I'm frightened Aunty Em!"

But Charlie and Susan wouldn't hear her cries any more than Aunty Em had heard Dorothy's.

13

PERMISSION GRANTED

The Lokskell

The Krixtax messenger gulps and shifts nervously from foot to foot, as those cold, soul-raping green eyes focus on him. The Lokskell silently regards him for the longest two minutes of his entire, miserable existence. He stares at him, stares *into* him, as if contemplating cracking his head open, peeling back the bone, and eating his brain right out of his living skull… which he very well could be doing.

"Say it again," the Lokskell demands in that calm, emotionless voice. Fehall gulps again and reluctantly stutters it out once more. It's even harder to spit out of his mouth now than it had been the first time he'd said it.

"They failed, M'lord. Your hobglins are either dead, or they are wishing that they were." The master remains still as a beast on the hunt, a predator preparing to strike, never even blinking as he spits out one word. "Elucidate." Not even a twitch… just like a slithery thing that has no eyelids.

265

"The male, Blaxx, was taken by one of the Scream Trees," he answers and reflexively jerks back as the Lokskell's fist bangs down on the table. "Idiot! He always was the dumb one of the pair. The female is smarter though. What of her?"

Fehall focuses his attention on the Lokskell's nose as he delivers the rest of the message…. he just can't muster enough courage to force his eyes any higher to meet those glacial eyes. "M'lord, your men found what remains of her. At least, they're fairly certain that it's her… out by the Dead Pool. And that's not all, Sire. The water nymph has gone missing. It appears as though she is no longer confined to the water."

The room is quiet as a house after Death has come calling while the Lokskell thinks on what he's just been told. "Interesting," he finally murmurs. "And no one knows where she's gone?"

The messenger shakes his head regretfully. "No M'lord. There's been no word yet. No reports of a sighting, and the men have found no trace of her."

There's a single, sharp knock on the door before the servants file in, silently bearing trays of food and pitchers of wine. They set the table and serve their master quickly, efficiently, then just as silently retreat, shutting the door behind them. The Lokskell takes a bite of his meal, chews slowly and swallows it down, before addressing the messenger once more. "And my daughter?"

This is the part of the report that the Krixtax had been dreading the most. If he is to die this day, then surely this unfortunate bit of news is what will bring about his demise. "I regret having to inform you that no one has been able to locate her, as of yet. The men can only assume that she's lost somewhere in the depths of the Black Forest." He fidgets anxiously as he watches the master take another long, drawn-out bite/chew/swallow before he speaks again.

"So, what you're telling me is that a tiny slip of a girl, one that's new to Oblerian, and has no knowledge whatsoever of the deadly nature of that world, is wandering around out there alone, uninformed, and unprotected. Would you care to explain to me *how* she's managed to stay one step ahead of my best men for so long?"

Choking down the hard lump of fear in his throat, all he can do is confess his ignorance. "I don't know, Sire. But they haven't given up! My mate uses our mind-link to keep me informed of every new development. She immediately relays every scrap of news that she learns."

The Lokskell grins then, a brief but unsettling flash of mirth on his otherwise harsh and unforgiving features. "Yes, smart of you to remind me that you are useful to me, while you dole out such disappointing news. Whoever would have thought that a spineless Krixtax would be so shrewd? Very well. Leave me and report back the instant that you have news of Ecko's whereabouts."

Fehall sighs with relief as the master impatiently waves him away, but as he's hastily trying to make good his escape, one last scathing comment is thrown at his back like a poisonous blade.

"I hope nothing ever happens to your mate while she's over there on Oblerian. *You* will be worth nothing to me if that mind-link the two of you share is severed."

The Vika Vakooja bug crawls out of a crack in the wall, agitatedly gnashing its double sets of mandibles, clicking them loudly to gain his attention. He does not get angry at the insect for intruding into his private chambers. For such a simple creature, it nevertheless has sense enough to not interrupt him, unless it has a very good reason to do so. It would only interrupt if it had vital information that it knows, without a doubt, that he would want to be made aware of, without delay.

"What is it?" he asks and then 'watches' as it answers him with a series of pictures in its mind. As far as he knows, he's the only one that's ever been able to communicate with the vermin, for they cannot speak with voices and spoken words. Fortunately, he'd learned how to get around that little inconvenience, many long years ago. So long ago now that he doesn't even remember the reason for *why* he'd sent a tiny bit of his Shadow magic into the bug that had crawled out of its hole and stood still, blatantly staring back at him with all four of its eye tentacles fully extended.

Perhaps it had been out of boredom, but it was more likely that he'd been angered at how it dared to disturb him at whatever task he'd been carrying out at the time. Knowing himself as well as he does, he'd probably meant to torture the little disease to death. Instead, he'd found his mind linked to the bug's mind... and the bug's mind had been linked to every single Vika Vakooja in existence. Their consciousnesses were all connected in a strange collective and they communicated with one another with series of mind pictures... images that they'd collected and stored within that vast collective.

The amount of information, steadily flowing through their connections with one another had been astounding. He'd spent quite a bit of time mind-lost inside their link, just studying their ways. He learned that they gathered every scrap of gossip that they came across, listened to every secret whispered. *Staggering* amounts of information and infinite details on anything and everything was collected and passed along through the mind waves, back to their buggy collective where their queen-mother sorted and stored it all away in a boundless mind-library.

He quickly realized that he'd discovered, quite by accident, the perfect, infinite and limitless spying machine. The Vika Vakooja's were small, inconspicuous things… very often they got overlooked and as such, could hide themselves *anywhere.* They bred nonstop, depositing large batches of eggs with every single birthing. They were extremely resilient with their hard shelled, armored bodies and poisonous spikes. But the best part was, he found that as long as he was linked to a single bug, he had access to the entire collective, and therefore was privy to every bit of information that they garnered. Having just one single Shadow-controlled Vika Vakooja had ultimately connected his mind to *all* of theirs.

He'd been forced to learn how to control and manipulate what information got passed on to him, because the vast majority of it was useless, and as such, a huge waste of his time just sorting through it all. He ended up sending his Shadows into hundreds of the crawly creatures, and they all learned together that he could make the Shadow-infected ones hurt so badly that the pain waves traveled throughout the entire collective. After that helpful little revelation, he'd focused on commanding them, directing them to go out to gather very specific bits of information, until they became so used to him and his wants and demands that he eventually became their new god, reducing the queen-mother to nothing more than an overworked information keeper.

And as their god, they are *ever* so eager to please him. They live for gossip and information and secrets. It is all they do, all they care about. They live to spy, eat, fuck, give birth to new vermin, and try their best to find every shred of information that their master might find pertinent or useful. They enjoy being his spies, *adore* being his slaves. It makes them feel important, when all they'd ever felt before was small, insignificant, and invisible.

Yes, this Vika Vakooja most certainly has something of importance to tell him. Otherwise, it would never have crawled out of its hole and approached him. He opens his mind and the bug wastes no time in relaying its message. One of their own had spotted the girl that they were all searching for. It had climbed into the pouch upon her back and then hid itself away as she unknowingly carried it around with her for a time.

The Shadow Lord watches it all play out in freeze-frame still shots… memory photographs. He sees the Vika Vakooja get discovered by his daughter, and how she fearfully threatens it, and then it all goes dark. He knows exactly what that means… Vika death. He never even saw his daughter move, but somehow, she still managed to put an end to its life, instantly severing his only link to her.

But no matter. Every detail that he can learn about this unknown daughter of his is beneficial. And now, thanks to his spies, he has a generalized lead on her location.

"Very good," he tells the bug, and it gnashes away in ecstatic triumph at his praise. "Spread the word. Find her. Watch her and report any new findings to me, no matter how small the detail."

He watches it scurry away, back into the crack that it had crawled out of, before he calls out to his servants to summon Fehall back to his chambers. The Krixtax messenger arrives only one minute later, his face flushed from having to run in order to obey the summoning, his heart pounding more in fear than exertion.

"Yes M'lord? How can I serve…"

That's as far as he gets before the foul, inky black Shadows pour into him and the Lokskell takes over his mind-link with his mate. He relays the information to her, quickly filling her in on the specific area in the Black Forest that his daughter was last seen.

"I know the area, M'lord," Issbeel calls back through the mind-link. "If it pleases you, I'll gather some of the men to accompany me in my search and send the rest out further, on to the outskirts to watch the borders, just in case she makes it that far." She does her best to keep her emotions, her *fear* for her mate pushed aside, tucked away where it can't be used against her. But at the moment, the Lokskell's not interested in anything other than his daughter being found and delivered to him.

"Yes, you do that, Issbeel. I want her located. Immediately," he insists.

"Very good, Sire," she promises in subservience, and then waits for him to sever the connection. But he has one last thing to tell her. "If Ecko has not been located before this time on the morrow, do not bother with mind-linking to your mate to deliver a report. I hereby grant you permission to throw yourself off the nearest cliff… spare yourself from mind-witnessing the things that I will do to your mate, should you fail me in this."

Issbeel pushes her panic down and answers him as calmly as she can. "Thank you, M'lord," she says with a slight bow of her head. "That is most generous of you."

14

OOPS, I DID IT AGAIN

Krispin

Krispin searches for her in every place that he goes. His eyes probe every shadow, scrutinizing every being that he encounters. Sometimes he finds her, but then he blinks, and she's gone once again. Or he'll see someone and be convinced that it's her, only to chase them down and then realize it wasn't her after all.... It confuses him every time it happens. They never even come close to her magnificence, and he doesn't understand how he'd ever believed it to be her in the first place.

Sometimes she is everywhere…and she's nowhere.

He sees her everywhere, a revenant that dissipates into thin air whenever he draws near… as much a tease now that she's gone as she'd ever been. It's driving him mad, this wanting her. He honestly believes that it's making him lose his mind.

He searches the abandoned houses, the empty lots, all the ruined, long-deserted shops. He scours every inch of the homeless camps, including his old stomping grounds at the defunct orphanage. Every face is carefully scrutinized. Lice-infested pallets are kicked aside. Every tattered blanket hung for privacy is ripped down, the space once sheltered within, laid open for his inspection. She's nowhere. No one has seen her.

Not here.

Not there.

Not anywhere.

He throws his head back and roars so loudly that the old, rotten rafters above rattle and groan. A few of the inhabitants throw filthy hands over filthier ears and cry out in fear, but it doesn't faze many of the others. The truly lost souls no longer care about anything at all. Their eyes, begging for sweet, merciful oblivion, follow him as he storms by.

He makes his way out of the building, around to the backside of the half caved-in, dilapidated old mansion/turned orphanage/turned purgatory for the lost and the damned. He passes several of those doomed and unfortunate beings on his way to the old playground.

Some of them are sleeping outside to escape the stench of hundreds of unwashed bodies. Seven of them are Reaped out on Reaper berries, staring out at things that only they can see... three of them giggling hysterically.

There are two male/female couples engaging in acts of copulation. The first couple, the man is lying in the dirt with the female on top, riding him into rapture. The other has the woman lifted up against the side of the building, the man doing his best to shove her through the wall with the force of him pounding into her.

Then there's the orgy… the large group of both male and female genders of several different species, all mating with each other in one loud tangle of sweating, writhing bodies. He only stops long enough to yank the outer layer of fornicators away, so that he can ensure that his Samara is not among the (fortunate? unfortunate?) recipients at the center of the group.

He grunts and moves on, once he's confirmed that she's not there, leaving the ones he'd disturbed to jump right back in and sink their dicks back into whatever hole they can find to fill.

He stalks through the old playground. Nothing remains here but rusted out frames that hold the last three and a half rope swings that he himself had made and hung so long ago, to give the children something to do. Something to take their young minds off their misery, if even for just a few moments. Those days of his kinder, softer self are just memories of a time gone by, nothing more than a ghost from his past that rises up every now and again to haunt him.

The swings, predictably, are all occupied with a group of the youngest children gathered round, waiting for their turn to fly high, fly fast, fly free. They're still young enough to believe that they may one day sprout wings and fly off through the sky. Stupid brats. They'll soon learn that this is all there is and that they'll never be anything other than one more desperate and disillusioned vessel of incurred self-loathing.

The older children skip stones, laughing whenever their aim proves true and strikes against the flesh of some unfortunate recipient. Still others, even older yet, younglings on the cusp of adulthood, hang back at the edge of the playground, playing a dangerous game of Hangman's Bluff, Deadman Snuffed.

Three kind-hearted, but disillusioned and world-weary women oversee the children, doing their best to keep them all from getting into too much mischief. The children, when they notice him watching, all scream and run away and his heart gives the tiniest, unwelcome twinge. They used to laugh and run *to* him. There was a time when he'd been… not good. No, never that, but softer, kinder than he is now. Long ago. Now everyone flees before him, and it's just as well that they do. Why would he want to care for anyone? Why *should* he? He'd loved Samara… *loves* Samara and look where that's gotten him.

He scowls at the children as they race away and hide… and not very cleverly at that. It's not his responsibility to look after the little shites anyway.

"I can still see you little troll turds! Scat! Or else I'll cut you up and cook you into a soup!" He grins in satisfaction, as they screech again and scatter like bugs, before he turns and stomps away. He's done searching for this Pale. Time to head on over to Storver's for a drink. Perhaps this will be the time that he finds Samara at the bottom of a bottle.

A woman with a soft, sweet voice calls out to him as he passes by. "That wasn't very nice of you."

He gives her a brief, cursory glance as a growl of warning rumbles deep in his chest. He thinks about it, and it *is* tempting, so tempting. But no, not in his current frame of mind. No good could come of it with the mood he's in. "Eat my dick, bitch," he snarls as he storms past her. How's that for nice?

Storver takes one look at Krispin's livid expression and immediately pours him a tall glass of his strongest rotgut… before he's even made it up to the bar. Two hours of steady drinking later, he gets up and stumbles from the eatery. He'd consumed enough to get rip-roaring drunk, but not enough for a lights out - pass out. He finds that he's in desperate need of a woman, and since Samara is currently playing her teasing games, denying him access to her luscious body, well, he'll just go find another.

And he already knows exactly which one he wants… Miss "That wasn't very nice'. The female that dared to chide him at the playground. He'll pay *her* a visit. After all, she'd said that she wanted to eat his dick. Hadn't she? Or had she told *him* to eat a dick? He can't remember now, but no matter. He'll let her eat his. She *had* chided him for not being nice; *that* much he remembers. Maybe this will make up for it. Sharing is nice, is it not?

She's right where he'd left her, sitting on an old wooden crate, still watching the children play and fuss and fight. He makes his way over to her and silently holds out his hand, waiting to see if she'll willingly place hers into it. She stares at it, and then up at his face for several minutes, while all the children in the background scream, "Run, Miss Manna! Run!"

"Hush, children," she softly croons as she makes up her mind and places her hand in his. Krispin hauls her to her feet, up against his hard body as he searches her face. For what, he doesn't know, because he's doing this thing, whether she's willing or not… just as soon as he knocks back one more bottle of rotgut. He turns and storms back to Storver's, half dragging the woman along behind him in his haste to return to the chair that's still warm from its previous encounter of his ass perched upon it.

The Wyrm was incensed, positively livid when it thought that the host wouldn't get intoxicated enough for it to sneak in for his highly anticipated (albeit temporary) coup. But then he'd gone back to imbibe some more. He'd even picked out a female for them, a most pleasing one at that. The Krispin/host has ordered the barkeep to feed her, some sort of meat-filled pastry, and also to see to it that his glass is never empty.

The female finishes her meal long before he's done with drinking, but she waits patiently for him to finish up. At last, he slugs back what's left in his glass, lurches to his feet, and snatches up the half empty bottle that Storver had angrily set before him, so that he could serve himself. Then he takes the woman's hand and stumbles out the door with her in tow.

Pitch has long since fallen and he leads the woman through the dark, his drunken mind automatically guiding him back to the last place he'd been... back to the playground where he'd found her. He had intended to take her to his bed, but he doesn't want her there. That's supposed to be... has always been a sacred place, reserved only for his love. His Samara. He cannot knowingly bring another there. He can't stand the thought of another woman lying in her spot, taking her place. The empty playground will do just fine for what he needs. There's no one about at this hour. No one but an old, Reaped-out man, and he has no wits about him. He couldn't care less what happens in the world outside his own head.

Enraged at being denied its turn to be in command of the host's body, the Wyrm acts on pure, outraged impulse. It attacks blindly, lashing out in its anger even though it's naught but an incorporeal, insubstantial thing that can do no damage onto a physical being. Even more enraged at its limitations, it nevertheless pours itself into the host's mouth, up through his nostrils and dives straight into his mind, fast and hard and violently. And there it waits, fully expecting to be rejected and expelled right back out.

But it doesn't happen. What's this? How can this be? The Wyrm tentatively delves in further, tentatively exploring this new development. The host never even lets up his forceful kiss upon the female's lips, never slips his tongue from her mouth, and he never once suspects that he has an extra life force riding around inside of him.

The Wyrm finds that while it's not able to directly overtake the host's mind at this time...not while he still retains full consciousness, it can ride along as a silent observer. For a while, anyway.

There's no way of knowing how long this will last. Although not ideal (for it would much rather be in control, so that it could engage in the acts that IT chooses and not the gentler ones that the host would otherwise choose without its guidance) the Wyrm contents itself with the knowledge that it will, at least, be allowed to feel everything that the host feels during the mating process. It watches/feels the host and the female together, impatient for them to get down to it...

But then it rudely gets evicted from the host's mind! No! It will not miss out on this! It is determined to enjoy the woman too, even if it can't do everything unto her that it wishes to do. It will still be able to feel every bit of pleasure that the host body receives, and that is better than nothing, which is what it will have if it's forced to remain locked out.

It dives back in, just as Krispin pulls the woman's shirt off, and gets cast out again as Krispin falls down upon her and pushes himself deep inside.

It lunges back in, gets expelled… in and back out again. Several times in rapid succession.

Krispin rolls off of her with a grunt, flips her over onto her knees, and takes her from behind like an animal.

"No! Me too!" It's desperate to feel this! It needs it! And it rushes back, exhilarating at the pleasure, the ecstasy that it feels, as the host throws back his head and roars up at the sky with the release that he finds within her body. He holds himself there, still sheathed deep inside of her, as he lifts the bottle of rotgut to his lips and guzzles the rest of the contents down in one long pull. He belches loudly as he tosses the bottle aside, slaps the woman smartly on her ass, and then promptly tips over and crashes unconscious to the ground.

"At last!" the Wyrm crows as it immediately moves in to gain full control. It gets Krispin back up onto his feet. The female looks up at him, standing there before her, and her eyes widen when she sees that his cock is already standing at attention again, just begging for her mouth upon it.

"My turn," the Wyrm croons with Krispin's mouth, and the grin that slashes across his face causes the woman's heart to stutter in fear.

"Wh-what do you mean?" she whimpers in that soft voice, from those sweet, tempting lips. It wraps its/Krispin's hands up in her hair and lifts her up onto her knees.

"Open wide," it demands as it shoves itself into her mouth, silencing her cries at such rough handling. It drives itself into her, hips pumping madly as it holds her head steady so that she can take everything it has to offer. It pounds deep down into her throat, unaware, and not even caring that she cannot draw in a breath.

The host's own breath begins to quicken as she claws at his buttocks, her sharp little teeth clamping onto his cock whenever it draws out far enough for her to attempt biting down. She doesn't know that it loves the pain, doesn't realize that it only spurs it on further and faster.

"Yeesss!" The roar tears from its lips, even as its/Krispin's burning hot seed spurts into the woman's throat. It cums for a long time, its cock held so deep down that the female's face is mashed tightly against its belly. And then it's over, and it pulls the host's softening member from her lips, adoring the sight of his semen leaking out of her mouth and dribbling down her chin. The Wyrm loving stokes the hair back out of the woman's wide, unblinking eyes.

"Oops. I did it again," it murmurs with a heavy sigh... half in regret, half in gratitude. It has found that their bodies are much

more flexible after life has left their limbs. In death, it can shape them and bend them into any position it so desires. But it does miss the screams. "We'll still have so much fun together. I'll make it good for you, too," it croons into her ear. "I promise."

Eventually, the Wyrm lifts the well-used female up and carries her, gently cradled in Krispin's arms, all the way back to the underground lair, where it introduces her to the rest of its lovely ladies.

15
BUMBERSHOOTS AND BEDDY-BYE BASKETS

Ecko

Ecko doesn't realize that her new companion has woken up and flown from his perch in the tree to join her down on the ground. She's too focused on what she's holding in her hands, too busy ugly crying. He clears his throat uncomfortably and asks, "What's going on? What's wrong with you?" And then, when she looks up at him, "Oh! Oh, girl. You got some boogies there…." But then his eyes dart to her hands, just in time to watch as the last of light fades away and the object goes dark as Pitch.

He gasps in shock and hop/shuffles closer. "Is that … Is that the Night Pearl?"

It takes a moment for her to sniff her tears back enough so that she can get the words out. "I guess it is. That's what she called it, anyway."

Boodark jerks his eyes back up to her face to demand, "Who? Who called it that? Where'd you get it?" He doesn't give her time to answer but continues to prattle on as he hops in even closer for a better look.

"This is incredible! I always knew the Night Pearl was real! It's been lost for so long that most no longer even believe that it exists. They believe it's only a myth. But *I* knew it! I did! What's it do? The legends speak of its magic, but no one really knows what it's capable of… and why is it called Night Pearl? What is it supposed to mean?"

"Night means Pitch," she murmurs. "I'm assuming it's called that because night… and Pitch, is black, like *it* is."

"Ah. Well, that makes sense. But why not call it Pitch Pearl? Or Black Pearl, or even Dark Pearl? Where'd you say you got it again?"

She waits a few seconds before she attempts to answer him, just to make sure he's really ready for her to speak. When he sits there, quietly blinking up at her for more than five consecutive seconds, she explains. "I don't know *why* it's called that. I'm just explaining that night means the same thing as Pitch… And Faoira gave it to me as a thank you gift."

He narrows his eyes at her in suspicion. "A thank you for *what*, exactly? What did you do to earn that crazy water-wench's gratitude? And how did I miss...whatever it was that you did?"

Boodark the Dramatic stomps around in a tight, little circle, his wings flapping all agitated-like. "I knew there was something fishy going on with that lake witchy!" He stops ranting and suddenly grins up at her, snorting out a laugh.

"Do you get it?" he asks, amid his giggles. "Something fishy...lake witchy. Oh, never mind. Back to my point, I *knew* when I woke up and saw you running away from the Dead Pool, while she just stood over the hobglin hag... and she was *out of her lake*, that *something* had to have happened whilst I slept. It was her, weren't it? *She* kept me asleep somehow, didn't she? Didn't she? What'd I miss? What. Did. You. Do?"

As the new Pale arrives, Ecko wraps the Night Pearl back up and returns it to her bag. Then, as she prepares breakfast for the two of them, she tells her small companion the tale of how the Naiad got her dolphin-skin, along with all her powers, back.

Boodark doesn't notice when she stops eating and frowns down at the ground a few feet away from where they're sitting. He's entirely too focused on shoveling eggs into his mouth to take much notice of anything else. She *thought* she'd seen something moving from the corner of her eye. A sudden, intensely eerie feeling comes over her as she turns her head to look.

The uneasiness fails to dissipate, even after she realizes that the movement was just her own shadow on the ground, mimicking her movements, as she spoons eggs into her own mouth.

For just a moment, it seems like her shadow's actions don't quite match her own, like it's lagging a bit behind her by a millisecond's delay. She watches it closely for the next several minutes, but finally decides that it must have been her imagination playing its tricksy tricks yet again. And then the mmrruunng, mmmrruunng, mmmrrrung noises that Boodark makes as he thoroughly enjoys his food distracts her, and she turns back to watch him lick up the last of his breakfast.

She soon forgets all about the shadow incident, without ever coming to the realization that it couldn't have been *her* shadow that she'd seen. She never puts two and two together that *there is no sun on this world,* and especially not in this dark forest. There's no way that she cast that shadow, not that far away from herself. The light is much too weak to pull that off. No, it was something else…something *other;* and because of her failure to think it through, it remains free to continue skulking along behind her, unchecked and unhindered, as she packs up and moves out.

There's not much to look at in this part of the forest, other than scrawny, lifeless trees and stunted, blackened bushes. It's positively eerie here, and a little bit depressing too. She's quiet as they move along, but she doesn't think that Boodark the Blabbermouth knows the meaning of the word. Either that or he *really* likes the sound of his own voice, because he prattles on and on and on about… she doesn't even know what. She quit listening after the first few hours of nonstop, nonsensical chatter.

She blocks out the sound of his voice (now rambling on about some sort of bright red, but streaked with blue, Fire trees) and retreats inside her own mind. She relentlessly prods that monster named 'Worries' with a purely mental stick.

She worries about Charlie and Susan, about how she's going to get home, about what will try to eat her next, and Samara's killing spree on *her* world. She's so focused on her mental monsters that she forgets to watch where she's going and to look out for the real monsters in the waking world. And since she's stopped listening to Boodark, she doesn't hear his warning shout.

She walks right into a swarm of them ... of tiny, winged horrors. "Ack! They're spiders!" she screeches, as she instantly turns into a karate master, chopping and slapping and swatting them away.

They, in turn, aim their butts at her and shoot fully formed webs, like miniature nets at her.

'And why not,' she thinks to herself. 'Why *wouldn't* this world have spiders.... that fly!' She screams like a little girl as she spins, waving her hands all around in her attempts to keep them (and their butt-nets) away from her face. Boodark falls to the ground and howls with laughter at her freak out.

"Why are you laughing? Spiders bite... with *poison teeth!* We could die! *Do something!*"

But he can't answer because he's too busy pointing a claw at her and laughing like a lunatic.

"Arrggg! I'm serious! How do we get out of this swarm? They just keep coming!" she cries.

"Of course, they keep coming," he says between his giggle-snorts. "They want to lay their eggs in your ears, where it's nice and warm and safe for their spidderlings to hatch out. But don't worry, they don't have poison teeth. They won't bite!"

And that's *all* she needed to hear to make her drop down to the ground and assume the armadillo position. You know the one...Arms wrapped protectively around her head and curled up into the tightest ball that she can possibly contort her body into, making herself the smallest target possible.

"Ru, ruru, wuugh, ruughh, wuwu, rruugh, ru, rugh," is all Boodark hears next. He can barely get his own words out between the hoots and howls. "What? (Snicker, snicker snort, snort) I didn't understand a word you just said. Say it again."

So, she spreads her arms apart, just far enough to press her lips between them and vows, "Go ahead, keep laughing. I promise you won't be laughing anymore come dinner time, when I decide to not share my food with you, you nasty little jerk!"

And *that*'s all it takes to bring *him* to the same level of terror that she's currently experiencing. He sobers up *real* quick.

"Relax wench, and fear not. I shall save you!"

Then he lifts off the ground and flies right into the swarm! She peeks through the space between her arms, that she's still holding protectively over her face, as he *zooms* past her. He zigzags back and forth, much faster than she realized he could even move. And with every pass he makes, there seems to be less and less creepy crawly, fly-ee spid-ees. When he lands back on the ground just two minutes later, there's not a single tiny, flying nightmare left in the air.

She cautiously lowers her arms, uncurls herself from her fetal position, and sits up to watch him in morbid fascination. His hands are held up in front of him, claws pointing towards the sky like he's practicing being Wolverine (from the X-Men), and he's got the spiders skewered, one atop another on those long dagger/claws.

And that demented little monkey is eating them! He's biting them one by one, off his claw/skewers, as if they're deliciously irresistible bug-kabobs. Their legs twitch and their wings flutter as he bites each one off and crunches them up, enthusiastically and entirely too audibly.

One of the unfortunate little bugs isn't actually stabbed onto a claw, it's just been stuck between two other spiders. It's wedged in so tightly that it can't free itself until the ones above it are lifted. The very instant that the bug on top of it disappears into Boodark's mouth, it flies up and speeds away. He lets it go, but shouts at its retreating butt, "Yeah, go on, fly away! And tell your friends to beware of Boodark the Biter!"

He then turns to Ecko and offers her one handful of bugs as he munches from the other. "Wampff fome?" he asks and grins at her with his mouth full of mashed up buggy bodies and gore in his teeth. He swallows the mess down and adds, "They're really tasty.

Their butt-nets give them a slightly sweet flavor, and you're just gonna *love* the way their wings crunch!"

She silently shakes her head at him with a big fat Nope.

"Are you sure? These are some of the best eatin's you'll find in the Black Forest. The only thing better is FireFairies, but you can't eat too many of those all at one time. Eat too many and they'll give you heartburn and a serious case of the fire farts and that is *no* fun, let me tell you! No fun at *all,*" he advises as he bites into another bug.

Horrified beyond all reasoning, she stays quiet for all of sixty seconds as she tries to process what he'd just said. "You eat *fairies*?" she whispers, "How could you? How horrible!"

Boodark points a bug-bedazzled claw at her. "No, I ain't. I'm hungry. *Very* big difference. And I don't go around eating *all* fairies. Just the evil turned ones…. like the fire ones and the blood ones. I *would* eat the flesh ones too, but they taste like rotting corpses. I have to be on the brink of starvation to eat one of *those.* Last time I ate one, I ended up with the most toxic butt-stinks of my entire life. I farted dead bodies for two whole weeks. It. Was. Disgusting…. Nope. I'll take FireFairy farts over rotting corpse ones any Pale! And just so you know, you have to be very careful when eating the fire types. FireFairy blood is super spicy-hot. Once I had it drip down on my manroot, and it burned so badly that it immediately earned #2 on my list of unfavorite things. It burned right through my trousers and blistered my most favorite piece of me!"

She stares at him in... all the words that equal disgust and horror. "Who hurt you?" she whispers with sincere dismay.

"Lots of peoples," he nonchalantly replies as he licks a wing that's trying to escape back into his mouth. "But what's that got to do with filling my belly?"

She shudders and tells him that she doesn't care how hungry she gets. She will never eat something as wondrous, as *magical* as fairies, or something as nasty as flying spiders. "Fly-ee Spid-ees? Flyders? What are they called?"

Boodark snorts. "I call this kind Spittler spidders, because they spit nets out of their butts to capture their prey. And clearly, you've never gone hungry before, with your magic bag of food and your plentiful water supply. Stick around in the Black Forest long enough and you'll find out *exactly* what lengths you'll go to in order to survive. You'd be surprised at what you'll be willing to eat, if you're starving and have no other choice. When *you* go without a meal for five Pitches and four Pales, *then* we'll talk."

And even though she still finds it repulsive and *beyond* horrifying, she also knows that he's right. Who is she to judge him? She *does* have a seemingly magical bag of food, from her magic world of plentiful, magical food. And although she *has* gone without, and she *does,* indeed, know the pain of hunger, she's never had to hunt for a meal on a dying world that's obviously running out of things to eat...a world that's become a vampire unto itself. And she knows that he's also correct about doing whatever it takes to survive...but bugs and fairies? Come on! She'd rather eat Toxic Tofu.

"You're right," she admits. "I'm sorry for judging you. I don't know your life, or the things you've had to do in order to survive. I can't even imagine living here, forced to live off bugs for my entire life."

He grins mischievously at her as he uses a bug leg for a toothpick to remove...*something* from his teeth. "Oh, I'm not forced to eat them. You *know* I'm not starving right now. I've been eating your magic food, after all. I just really love the sweetness of them upon my tongue, when they burst open in my mouth!"

She blinks at him once, twice before she gets up off the ground and starts walking away. "*Someone* hurt you," she mutters. "I *know* someone hurt you…. had to have. I'm outta here. Catch up when you're done eating your bug-meal. Or don't. It's all the same to me if we part ways here."

She glances over at him as he rushes to catch up and fly beside her. "Oh, don't worry. I can fly and eat at the same time!"

She sighs and sarcastically mutters, "Great. I guess I get to listen to you munch away at your buggy-to-go meal for the next hour."

Boodark laughs and corrects her. "Wrong again! This won't take an hour. I'll be done in three minutes, tops!"

"Perfect," she fires back, because really, what else could she say?

Hours later, long after his Spittler/spider meal had been devoured and nothing else has come along for him to snack on, Boodark's stomach begins to growl in protest. He's hungry again and he's bored with the scenery and tired of flying in silence. He lands on a tree branch several yards ahead of her and then hangs upside down from it to watch her as she approaches. He's ready for food and conversation and answers.

But mostly for food.

"We gonna stop for Middlinmeal soon?"

She keeps walking as she shakes her head at him. "Nah, I think I'm just going to skip lunch. I'm not hungry anyway, not after witnessing your bug-massacre back there. I'll just have a snack in a little while, so that I don't have to stop. I really just want to keep moving. I want out of this forest as soon as possible. I'm starting to get a bad feeling about this place. I don't know, it just feels more and more wrong, if that makes any sense to you. Darker, somehow. Also, the faster I'm out of this dreadful Black Forest, the faster I'll get to where I'm going."

Boodark sighs with heartfelt disappointment at having to wait for his belly to be filled. "Fair enough," he grumbles. "If we can't stop to eat, at least talk to me. I'm bored, and I've found that I can get myself into a *crazy* amount of trouble when that happens."

"Yeah, I can totally see that!" she agrees with a laugh at his honesty. "What do you want to talk about?"

He peers intently at her from his upside-down position. "I want to know what your story is. Why are you so dumb…. Not in a bad way! I just mean, why don't you know about things like Vika Vakoojas and Spittler spidders? Where could you possibly have been hiding to have lived such a soft, sheltered life? Why are you so *odd*?"

Ecko snorts out a laugh as she passes by him. She never fit in with the humans on Earth and she doesn't fit in with the freaks on...whatever world she's currently on. That sums up the story of her life perfectly.

"What's so funny?" he calls to her back. "Come on! Don't leave me hanging! 'Snort, snort' Get it? Don't leave me hanging? Fine!" he shouts as he drops from the branch and hurries to catch up to her.

"Fine. Keep your secrets. I understand. I have my own." He's quiet for maybe three minutes (about a minute and a half longer than she thought him capable of) before he speaks up again. "So… where *are* we going anyway?"

She glances down at the path in front of her, at the arrow made out of sticks telling her to take a left turn. Ignoring this sign (just like she has all the others) she steps over it and continues on her own course.

"Well, I have no idea where *you're* headed. But I'm on my way to find something that I think, I *hope*, will get me off of this cursed world and back to my own."

Boodark looks down at her in shock, forgetting to watch where he's flying. He splats right into a tree and tumbles to the ground.

Ecko cries out in fear for him, as she reaches down and plucks him up out of the dirt. "Are you ok? What happened?" She starts checking him over as best as she can, moving his arms and his wings to see if he's broken anything.

"Stop tugging on me," he shouts. "What's wrong with you? Get your giant paws off of me. Put me down THIS INSTANT!"

She sets him back down, almost dropping him in her haste to do as he demands.

"There's no need to yell at me, you mean old thing. I was just trying to see if you were hurt! Next time, I won't even bother. I'll just leave you where you fall!"

He groans and rubs the knot on his head as she walks away and leaves him behind.

"Wait!" he hollers. "Wait for me! I didn't mean it!"

He stands up and inspects his own parts for proper functionality before he lifts off and hurries to catch up to her. "I'm sorry. I was just…. not *scared*. Who says I'm scared? I'm not scared of you. I'm not scared of anything! *Alarmed* is what I was. *You* try being the size of a ground stomper's foot and see if you like being trapped in a giant's hands! It brought back some bad memories for me, that's all."

She thinks about it for a split second. He's right. Again. It sucks being at anyone's mercy, big or small. She glances over at him and tells him that she understands. Then she grins.

"But you *were* scared!" And she cracks up as he spits and sputters his outrage and his fierce denial.

"I WAS *NOT!*" he shouts straight into her ear. "I am Boodark the Brave! I fear nothing!"

It's a struggle to get herself under control. "Yeah, keep telling yourself that. Whatever helps you sleep at night!"

For the next ten minutes, she listens to his rants and denials and excuses, but she doesn't argue with him anymore. Poor little guy wants so badly to be brave. Who is she to take that away from him?

"... Are you even listening to me? Are you going to answer me? You can't just say you're from another world and leave it at that. I *need* an explanation! Oh, and we have to turn here. Take that path there, to the left."

She frowns and informs him that she needs to keep walking forward, straight ahead. She doesn't know why, exactly, but that's the direction that she feels she needs to be traveling.

But Boodark stubbornly shakes his head and counters with, "You don't want to keep going that way. You really, really don't."

Ecko grunts in annoyance. "I really, really do," she insists. But then she thinks about it for just a second. She thinks back on all the terrors that she's already encountered. Does she really want to risk meeting another monster?

Nope, she does *not.* She can be terrified of whatever is up ahead, just as easily from afar as she could up close and personal. She hangs a left and asks him what's up ahead on the path that they just *had* to avoid.

"Ametrine, the witch of the wood," he replies. "We want to avoid her at all costs, and we've drawn too close already. Her home is only one hundred wing flaps away, and that is too close for my peace of mind."

She stops dead in her tracks and stares up at him in dismay. "Witch?" she squeaks. "A real, live witch? With like, warts and stuff? Wait, is she a bad witch? I'm guessing she's a bad witch.... Of course, she's bad, *everything* here is. And you *are* trying to avoid her…" her words trail off while she contemplates the situation.

"*Why* have you let us get this close to a *witch*?" she shouts at him.

Boodark lands on a nearby tree branch to continue their little spat. He points a claw at himself. "Me? *You* are the one plotting the course. I'm just following where you lead! And you *still* haven't told me where it is that we're going. How am I to know what plans fill that empty head of yours?"

She throws her hands in the air and shouts, "But you're supposed to be leading me down safe paths…that was the deal! This is not safe…. letting us get close to a witch! Why didn't you tell me about her earlier? We could have turned away sooner. Why would you let us get close enough for her to possibly discover us? Why chance it at all?"

Boodark laughs derisively at her. "She already knows we're here. She knew of our presence the very moment we entered into the Black Forest. This is her domain, after all. She's linked to every living thing in here. But if we had, by any slight chance gone undetected, your screeching has surely alerted her to our presence by now."

"And to answer your other question, we have gotten this close because had we turned away any earlier, we would have run straight into the witch's mate's home. And *that* is an automatic death sentence. She hates him, but she is tremendously jealous too. *No one* is allowed near him, especially not other female-types."

Boodark scratches at his butt and continues, "You seem to be traveling in a straight ahead, righty-like direction. I have taken you down the safest paths, while still allowing you to stay as close to that course as possible. I only turn you away when I must. If you would but tell me where you are leading us, I could do this much more efficiently!"

She starts walking once more and quietly admits that she doesn't really *know* where she's going. Boodark the Confused falls in beside her.

"Ahem...I thought I just heard you say that you don't know where you're going. That's funny. You're a funny female. I didn't know that about you."

She glances at him from the corner of her eye and then quickly looks away again.

"I don't know *exactly* where I'm going. How could I? I just got to this stupid world. I certainly don't know my way around. I'm just following that… *noise.*"

His eyes go round as a hoot owl's and his avocado-green eyebrows rise up so high that they disappear behind his tangle locks. "What in all the world are you speaking of? What noise?" Then he growls in frustration and adds, "And there you go again! You keep saying you're from another world, but you refuse to explain yourself! It's verily frustrating!"

So, for the next three hours, as she gratefully moves *away* from jealous, evil witches and their husbands, she tells her new companion the story of her life. She has to stop several times to answer his questions, but she eventually gets it all out...The whole complicated mess, starting from the day she was given to her 'father', to the day her twin sister pulled her through the mirror and switched places with her.

Boodark had become so thoroughly engrossed in her tale, so distracted by it, that he couldn't really focus on flying *and* listening. After bouncing off of tree number four, she'd offered him a ride. So, now he sits upon her shoulder as the hours pass, until her tale is told, and he's all caught up to current events. He's grown quiet, quieter than he's been the entire time they've known one another.

"Are you asleep?" she quietly inquires.

He gives himself a brisk shake and tells her that he's just thinking, contemplating all that she had told him. Then he says, "Let me see if I understand you correctly. Your mother, your *real* mother was Laelynn, Irredarr's Mirror Walker, their only Wandelaar. And your father is the Lokskell... *THE* Lokskell! To keep you safe from *him*, your mother did a spell on you that suppressed your magic and then sent you to a world called Earth."

"You looked just like those Earth people, but you were different. You saw things in the mirrors that no one else could see. And you met your twin sister through those mirrors… and what a nasty little thing she was too! She killed your adopted family and you lived for the next few years trapped in a place meant for crazy people. Your friends, Charlie and Susan, helped you find the answers, the truth of who you are and where you came from."

"Then, on your 18th birthday your mother's spell broke and you finally got your magic. You accidently opened up a mirror and your sister was able to pull you through to *this* world, while she slipped into yours. And now you need to find a way to get back home. Samara also told you that there are no more mirrors here on Oblerian, so you don't know what to do. You're just following some sort of...noise. You have no clue what it is, or even where it's coming from. Have I got it all right so far?"

She nods her head and admits, "The noise.... it's not really a sound that I can hear with my ears. It's a sound that I *feel* inside of me, almost like a heartbeat."

She then turns her head slightly so that she can see his reaction to what she has to say next. "I don't think it's true...what Samara said about there being no more mirrors here. I think she lied, or perhaps she just didn't know any better. But it *feels* wrong, the same way that a lie feels wrong."

She pauses for a moment to evaluate her own thoughts before hesitantly continuing. "I think what I'm hearing *is* a mirror. A special one... maybe one from my mother's world. If it's not a mirror, it's most certainly *something* from Irredarr. It speaks to me the same way that my mother's jewelry does, the same way the Night Pearl did too. Only... whatever *this* is, it's much more insistent. The call is so loud, so urgent."

Boodark finally puts the pieces of the puzzle together. He sucks in a huge, dramatic gasp of air and then shouts (right into her poor, unsuspecting ear) "Holy Octobeast poop! *That's* why the Night Pearl worked for you! *You're the new Wandelaar!*" And then he rudely starts pointing out all of her flaws.

"I thought Mirror Walkers were supposed to be graceful and wise and… oh, uh never mind. I'm sure you'll figure it all out eventually." Then he whispers to himself, "Change the subject, you fart blasting fool!" Then louder, "Well, *I've* personally never seen a single mirror. I've heard of them; I know what they are, of course. I've just never seen one. But that doesn't really mean anything one way or another. I try to stay far away from ground stompers and all things pertaining to them. So, you could be right, I can't say yay or nay."

She nods her head. She's too tired to take offense at his words. He's only pointed out things that she already knows anyway. Her mother, the last Wandelaar, had been the very picture of perfection, and she herself is nowhere close to perfect. She knows her own flaws, recognizes that she's lacking in every way. She doesn't even have the first *clue* how to be a lady. She certainly doesn't know how to be a Wandelaar. How is she supposed to do this? *Any* of this?

"I'm really tired," she says as doubts and fears plague her mind and wear her down. "And I'm hungry. I think I'm going to call it a day."

Boodark asks what 'day' is and she listlessly gives a vague explanation. "Same thing as the Pale. But brighter."

He nods his understanding and informs her that the Pale is almost over anyway, so it's a good time to stop. "I'll fly ahead and find a suitable place to make camp," he calls as he flies up off of her to scout ahead. She thankfully rubs her sore, tired shoulder. He's much heavier than he looks.

Twenty minutes later, with her empty belly growling angrily the entire time, Ecko quickly settles into camp and prepares dinner. Her mind is stuck on how amazing french-fries would taste right about now, when she suddenly remembers a tiny tragedy.

"Ah man!" she bursts out. "I had chicken nuggets in the fridge! I was gonna eat those later!" And now she's hungry *and* grumpy! Chicken nuggets, gone to waste!

Boodark scratches his head and tells her that he hasn't got the first clue as to what she's going on about. "What is a chicken nuggets? What is...fridge?"

She has to take a moment to think of how to properly describe them. "A refrigerator is a big, metal box that Earth people store food inside of. It keeps the food cold so that it doesn't spoil and keeps it fresh so that it lasts much longer."

Then she sighs longingly, dreamily, as she tells him all about chicken nuggets. "They're little pieces of chicken, breaded and fried and *so* delicious. Actually, I'm pretty sure they grind the whole chicken up, press it all back together into little chunks, and *then* they fry it. I'm not really sure how they make them, I just know that I love them. They're one of Earth's favorite on-the-go foods. They sell them at a restaurant...uh a place that cooks and sells food... called McDonalds. Actually, they sell them at lots of places, but the ones from Mickey D's are the best!"

Boodark is all ears and demands, "What is chicken?"

When she tells him that chickens are birds, he gets a disgusted look on his face. "You eat things like Foul-Kries and sky ratters? Earthians are repulsive!"

She gags a bit at the thought of Foul-Kry nuggets... *black* Foul-Kry nuggets. "Oh, that's just *nasty*. Definitely not! Our birds are *nothing* like those horrid creatures. And we're called humans, not Earthians... Well, not me. I suppose I'm Irredarrian. Yeah, *that's* gonna take some getting used to!"

They fall into a comfortable silence then, each thinking their own thoughts. Hers have moved on from their conversation. She's wondering if Charlie's fairing any better than the last time she'd seen him.

But Boodark's mind is stuck on his belly, like always. "Tell me more about this magic foodorator box. You said it's big... *How* big is it? Exactly how much food is in it? Does it only have 'chicken nuggets' in it, or does it contain your beef stew and stroke-off also? What about those little crunchy things with the berries? Does it have those?"

Ecko laughs at his one-track mind, as she dishes dinner out and pours a small portion of Sprite into a bowl for him to try. While they eat, she explains about MRE's and preservatives and about all the different kinds of food she had in her refrigerator back at the cabin in New Hampshire.

Boodark, as usual, gobbles his food down in 60 seconds flat and then stares longingly at every bite she takes of her own dinner.

"Stop watching me and try your Sprite."

He looks down at his empty food bowl and then at the bowl of sprite in confusion. "This?" he asks. "Is it not water?" He dips his head down and sticks his tongue in to lap up a sip and then he lets out a whoop of excitement.

"It's sweet, like nectar!" And he dunks his head for another, longer taste. He has a small coughing fit when the bubbles tickle his nose, but it doesn't deter him from slurping up another mouthful.

"Oh, what *is* this? It has bubbles, it does, little bubbles in there to tickle my nose and delight my tongue!" He quickly chugs the rest of his Sprite down and then a tiny little girl giggle escapes him. He claps a hand over his mouth, but it does nothing to stop his laughter. "This liquid is de-lisss-iouss! Have you got more?"

She smiles and pours the rest of her drink into his bowl, and he immediately starts in on it. She watches him in amusement as she takes her bundle of purple paracord out of her bag and continues fiddling with her 'basket'. She finds that if she doesn't think about it and just lets it come, her fingers move mindlessly, as if it's something that she's done so many times that the motions are made out of habit or repetition. It's not true though. She has no clue where the knowledge of weaving a rope basket came from. She's also perplexed as to *why* she has the overwhelming compulsion to make it in the first place.

She mentally shrugs it off, though. Stranger things have happened to her, and a pretty purple basket might come in handy for *something,* she supposes.

Boodark sips and giggles, then sips and giggles again. "Oh, oh! Yum! This is so *good!*" He's sipping and slurping and then he suddenly falls onto his butt, laughing as if he's just heard the funniest joke.

"What's wrong with you?" she asks, but she thinks she knows the answer. "Are you drunk? You are, aren't you? You're drunk...off of Sprite!" And now she's laughing, because he's fiercely shaking his head in denial. So fiercely that his big bat ears are flopping around and slapping himself in the face.

"No, I ain't! Pixies don't get drunk on anything but the nectar from Larria flowers, and this is no Larria nectar." He sips and smacks his lips. "It *is* good though. De-lisss-iouss!" Hiccup, giggle. "Oh, I feel like *dancing!*" he suddenly calls out.

He excitedly jumps to his feet and looks around (for who knows what) and then his whole body slumps in disappointment. Even his ears droop and he's just the saddest sight ever. He sighs dejectedly and then nonsensically mumbles, "There's no music, no magic, no Secret. I'm all alone." He looks like he's about to start sobbing his heart out any minute.

Ecko panics. What is she supposed to do if a drunken little beastie starts crying? A proud, *male* beastie at that. He'd said he wanted to dance, but there was no music... she could fix that. She unplugs the headphones from her iPod, hits the power on button, and then presses play.

When 'I Hope You're Happy', by Blue October starts blaring, Boodark lifts his head up and triumphantly fist pumps the air with a victorious shout. He hops up onto his feet and dances around their little campsite while she laughs at him. She also (secretly) records him with her phone's camera. She doesn't want to spook him, like she had with Blaxx, but she just *has* to get this recorded… for future teasing reasons.

She sings along while he dances, and despite him never having heard the song before, by the time it's over, he's shouting along too, belting out the lyrics at the top of his lungs.

Then the world goes dark, just as the song ends. "Oh! Sleep time! What a *great* idea I've just had!" he slurs and then drops to the ground, right where he's standing. He starts snoring as soon as he touches down.

"That must have been some potent stuff!" she chuckles as she clicks the flashlight on and shines the light on her snoozing companion. She makes a little bed with her extra blanket and then carefully lifts him up and tucks him into it. He immediately snuggles in and murmurs something along the lines of, "I hope you're happy, I missed your secrets."

Then he's snoring away again, cutting logs and catching z's, which is exactly what she's about to be doing too. Her last coherent thought before drifting off is, 'I wonder if he's gonna have a headache in the morning.'

He does.

He's grumpy, surly, and mean and it makes her laugh. He sits there in the dirt and glares at her like it's *her* fault that he couldn't handle his Sprite. He eyes her distrustfully as she offers him breakfast. Then he eyeballs the food she sets in front of him too. "Eat it or not, Mr. Grumpy Pants. But hurry up about it, because I'm leaving in five minutes, with or without you. And I'll be taking my bowl with me!" He eats, but he looks like he's about to hurl the entire time he's doing it.

She's a little bit concerned when he flies off without a word, while she's cleaning his bowl and putting it away, but she shrugs her shoulders at his sullen antics. All she can do is follow in the direction he'd gone.

As she bends to pick up her bag, a sudden cold, *nasty* wind blows in from behind her. She feels it a split second before it crashes into her back, and when it does, it's so horrible that she almost believes that Satan is standing right behind her, breathing his foul breath on her neck. It blows through her, settles inside of her like a bad dream in the night that remains in her thoughts throughout the next day. It *clings* and it makes her feel dirty, icky inside.

Thankfully, the wind dissipates within seconds and takes with it all the nasty feelings. *Mostly.* A tiny sliver of 'yuck' gets left behind to linger and fester like an infected wound on her soul.

She shakes it off as best she can and tries to put whatever *that* was out of her mind. But she walks away from the campsite longing for a bath, even more than she already did. She feels fouled somehow, but she manages to forget all about it several minutes later when she catches up to Boodark.

He's clinging to a tree, his arms bear-hugged around it like he's some kind of weirdly hideous koala bear. He's got his tongue buried deep into a hole in the bark, and he doesn't appear happy about it. He's making all sorts of repulsed sounds, yucking and retching and gagging, as he slurps up... something.

"What in the world are you up to now?" she calls up to him. He sucks his tongue back into his mouth and turns his head to glare down at her.

"The sap from this tree should help with this huge headache you gave me. You'll have to excuse me, this is gonna take a few minutes. Better yet, go on without me and I'll catch up with you soon enough."

He points a claw and sourly grumbles, "Just follow that path. I'll be right behind you."

Then he turns and pokes his long black tongue back into the tree to continue his headache treatment.

Ecko laughs and snaps a couple of quick photos of him before she moves on. "I hope it works," she calls back as she leaves him behind.

She doesn't make it very far before another disruption appears and stops her in her tracks. One hundred yards ahead of her, a glowing green orb floats out of a patch of scraggly, sickly bushes. It looks like a softball-sized sphere of gas, an orb burning with some kind of mystical green fire. It hovers close to the ground, right in the middle of the path, blocking the way forward.

As she stares at it, trying to decide whether she wants to turn back or try to go around it, the intensity of its light dims down to a soft glow. In the center of all that radiance is the silhouette of an itty bitty, tiny woman. Ecko kneels down and squints her eyes to try and see her better. The little woman beckons her to come closer but then darts a few feet away. When she doesn't immediately follow, the light flares up again, so brightly that she's forced to look away from the brilliance of it. It dims down once more and the tiny woman signals her again, as if saying, "Come, follow me!" Then it floats over to the right, *away* from the path. Hovering between two spindly trees, it gestures for Ecko to follow, eagerly motioning her forward.

She tries to look past the aberration, to see where it's trying to get her to go, to see *exactly* what it's leading her into. The section of forest behind the glowing orb-lady is even darker than the space that they're currently standing in. It feels horrible, sinister and foreboding, and if she's not mistaken and hasn't gotten turned completely around, it's leading to the area that they've been trying to steer clear of. The wicked witch of the wood's house is somewhere over there, and this cunningly mesmerizing little ball of light is trying to lead her straight to it!

She's about to tell it, 'Heck no, I will *not* be going to visit a witch today' when Boodark suddenly drops down in between the two of them. He frantically shakes his head up at her and spreads his wings as far as they'll stretch, to try and block the way. She can't help but grin. She guesses he forgot that he's only about a foot tall and that she could very easily step over him, should she want to.

"Do not follow it!" he shouts while holding his hands up at her in the universal, 'Stop! Slow your roll!' signal. "Wisps are tricksy and false! Don't trust them. Don't ever trust them!"

She stops grinning when she realizes how agitated he truly is. "Calm down. I have no intention of following her. I've seen *way* too many movies. I know better than to follow *anything* that tries so hard to lead me off of a nice, safe path into *that*." She points to indicate the deeply shadowed section.

"Someone once lured Scooby Doo into the deepest, darkest part of the forest with a bag of hamburgers and look what happened to him. He was almost eaten by monsters!" She steps past him to continue on down the trail. She's pretty sure that the little Wisp lady is mad about having her plans, whatever they had been, thwarted, because her light suddenly flares so brightly that she appears to be a miniature green sun.

And then that angry, vindictive little thing divebombs right at poor Boodark's unsuspecting head! He lets out a little yelp and throws his wings up to protect himself from the incoming onslaught.

She reacts on pure instinct as she lifts her foot up and punts that glowing green ball of wrath away from him. She didn't *mean* to do it; she wasn't even aware that she was moving until the deed was already done and the Wisp lady was soaring through the air away from them, a tiny scream of "Eeehh!" trailing behind it.

Boodark and Ecko turn their heads to look at one another, and despite them being two completely different species, they both sport identical looks of shock on their faces. Eyes wide and startled, jaws slack and mouths hanging open, it starts with a smile. Then it's a nervous chuckle that quickly escalates until the two of them are howling with laughter. They laugh until helpless tears trail down her face and Boodark begs for the laughing fit to be over, because his tummy's starting to hurt.

Sobering up at last, she blurts, "I have never, in my whole life, kicked another living thing before. I feel terrible. I hope I didn't hurt her. Do you think she's ok?"

Boodark cradles his belly and groans, "Don't you feel bad! It was trying to lure you to certain doom...probably straight to the witch! That's what they do. You didn't hurt her, and you *still* haven't kicked any living thing. Will o' the wisps are not alive. They're the spooks of fairies and pixies that turned bad during their lives, the ones that have been denied entrance to the EverLands. They're mean and spiteful and malevolent and we really need to get as far from here, as fast as we can, just in case she decides to come back... with friends! Let's go!"

He lifts off and flies down the path, with Ecko running right behind him. "Wait!" she yells. "Is she really gonna go get reinforcements? Will she track me down to get revenge? What exactly have I just gotten myself into?"

He ignores the questions as he shouts down at her, "Escape now, explanations later! Run, girl!" So, she runs. She runs for twenty minutes straight, dodging branches and hurtling over logs as if her life depends on it, which may or may not be the case. But like he said… questions later.

When she's out of breath and can run no more, she drops to the ground and just lays there, heaving and huffing, gasping for air. Boodark circles back to check on her, then flies further down the path, way up above the treetops in a self-appointed reconnaissance mission. He comes back with a "All clear", as he lands on the ground beside her.

"Haven't done much running in your life, have you? You sound terrible. Are you going to make it? I mean, you're not going to heart explode, are you?

She grunts as she sits back up and wipes sweat from her brow. "I'll be fine. And no, I haven't done much running in my life. I haven't done any physical activities for a long time; I wasn't allowed to. They don't let you run around in the crazy house. That would be crazy." She ignores his shamefaced expression and asks, "So, have we lost her? The Wisp isn't following, is she? Are we good now?"

Boodark glances back the way they'd come. "Yeah, I think we're safe. Hopefully, we got far enough away that she'll lose interest in us. Also, she's green, and the green ones usually aren't as resentful as some of the others. I'll keep a look out for the rest of the Pale though. Just in case."

She digs a bottle of water out of her bag and pours a tiny bit into a bowl for him, before sipping some herself. Her mouth and throat are so dry and gritty that it feels like she's been trying to eat sand. "You lost me," she gasps out. "What does her being green have to do with anything? And what other color Wisps are there?"

Boodark sniffs his drink suspiciously, probably to make sure it isn't the devil's drink... better known as Sprite. Once he's assured that it's safe, he quickly slurps it up. "Aahhh, that's good." He settles onto his butt and then explains. "Will o' the Wisps are elemental spooks. Whatever element they were closest to in life is the kind they become when they die."

She pours him a bit more water, and this time around he sips it slowly. "By spooks, you mean ghosts, right? Spirits?"

He only nods, so she continues. "There's water, fire, air, and ground elementals, so she was, what? A ground one?"

He frowns and shakes his head at her. "It's a bit more complicated than that. The elementals here are more specific than what you're suggesting. There are several different types than just those four. For example, green is actually more for vegetation than it is for ground. And there are several different shades of green for different plant types. There's grass green, tree green, hills green, pond scum green...get it? Different shades of blue and grey represent the sky and oceans and lakes and streams and so on. You understand?"

"Oh, I get it. Basically, they're nature ghosts and not so much elemental ghosts."

He looks pensive for a moment and then nods his affirmation. "Yes, I suppose you're right. Nature Wisps. There are some very rare ones that I haven't got a clue about though. I saw a black one once. And a purple one too. I've been told that there are clear ones, but I'm not sure I believe that. If it was clear, how could anyone see it? Hmm?"

"Anyway, as far as I know, they are *all* tricksy and they *all* like to play games... deadly games. I've heard that if you ever manage to catch one, they *have* to grant you a boon, but I can't tell you if that's true or not either. I've never known anyone that actually caught one. There aren't many people that can resist the urge to chase after the Wisp's pretty lights, and those unfortunate souls almost always get lured into bogs or lakes or holes in the ground. Or to eater-plants. Or to evil witches... you get the point. They certainly don't receive any boons."

She repacks the water bottle and Boodark's bowl and stands back up to press onward. "Well, her charm didn't work on me. I thought she was very pretty, but I didn't want anything to do with her. I had no desire to follow her, and I certainly didn't want to hurt her. She forced me to...do that terrible thing. She was trying to hurt you!"

Boodark falls in, gliding along beside her. "Aw, I didn't know you cared." He says it sarcastically, but she hears something hidden beneath the sarcasm. Hope, loneliness, sadness.

"I care," she says, simply and without exaggeration. But the smile that stays glued on his unfortunate, ugly little face for the next hour is something she will always remember.

"Why are we turning back towards the witch's house?" she asks. "Shouldn't we try to keep moving *away* from it? I mean, shouldn't getting far away from her be our main priority right now?" She stops walking to lean up against a tree for support. She needs to rest, just for a moment or two. She feels so tired all of a sudden, and her back has started to ache.

"We're not traveling in this direction for long. We're just going this way, as far as the Bumbershoot Tree. Then we'll get back on course…eventually," he tells her as he lands in the branches above her head.

"What's a Bumbershoot Tree, and why, exactly, do we need to get to it?"

He glances up and distractedly murmurs, "You know…those big, round things that peoples hold over their heads to protect them from the sky waters. Do you not have bumbershoots on your world?"

She wipes the sweat off her forehead and asks, "Are you hot? Is it getting hotter? And what do you mean 'bumbershoot'… are you talking about umbrellas?"

He sighs with exaggerated annoyance. "Yes, it *is* getting hotter. That is why we're going to the Bumbershoot Tree, and I know not what a 'umbrellas' is. We *need* to keep moving."

He takes flight once more and she reluctantly pushes off the tree to fall in behind him.

"I don't understand. You're making absolutely no sense at all!"

Boodark slows and then drops down onto her shoulder. "Do you mind? It's easier to talk to you from down here, than from way up there." But he continues without waiting for her answer. "It is about to rain…. Raining is when the sky dumps all of its extra wa-ter out."

She rolls her eyes. "I know what rain is," she snaps.

"Well, excuse me! How was I to know if your Earth-world has sky-water? I was just trying to be thorough with my answers to your endless questions!"

She sighs and quickly apologizes. "I'm sorry. I just *really* hate being hot. All sweaty and sticky and gross…. Please continue."

He sniffs haughtily, but nevertheless continues with his lec-ture. "Apology accepted. As I was *trying* to explain before Miss Rude decided to interrupt me, the sky water is about to come down. It always gets hot right before…. that's how you can tell that it's on the way. The sudden heat is an early warning sign, one that you will eventually come to be grateful for, because it gives you at least a few minutes to try and find shelter. And if not shelter, then some sort of protection. I searched the area from above for a cave or a hollowed tree…anything that's big enough for your giant butt to fit into. There's nothing suitable close by, but thankfully there *is* a Bumbershoot Tree. And it's just beyond that thicket."

He points a claw at a wall of trees and bushes that are growing so tightly together, that she immediately knows it's going to be dif-ficult for her to squeeze through. It's probably going to hurt, too.

"Is this absolutely necessary?" she asks. "I don't think I really need a bumbershoot thing. I'm actually looking forward to the rain. I mean, I desperately need a shower and I'm running low on drinking water, so it'll be good to refill my empty bottles. And I can wash out my clothes! Yeah, I think I'll pass on trying to get through that...tangled mess. I think I see thorns in there anyway. But you can go if you want to. I'll just wait right here for you until it's over."

He grunts right in her ear, and she hears him mumble to himself, "Remain calm, Boodark. You must remember she is not from Oblerian. She knows naught of the dangers of this world. She is like a dumb, helpless babe. A giant one, yes, but a babe all the same. You must be patient and teach her."

"Really? You know I can hear you, right?"

Boodark smirks up at her. "Of course. I *am* perched right here beside your hear-hole."

He points at a spot in the thicket that looks like it *might* allow her to pass through...if she were half her size perhaps.

"I can't fit through that!"

He frowns up at the sky, that as far as she can tell, hasn't changed even the slightest bit. It looks the same as every other Pale-time sky. But she can see that he's extremely agitated, scared almost. '*Maybe I should be worried too*', she thinks as her heart starts to thud in her chest.

"You must! Now go!" he shouts as he glides from her shoulder to the ground. "Drop down and crawl."

She immediately drops down and crams herself into the thicket, and there *are* thorns! Of *course*, there are. She pushes herself through, until her head and shoulders are past the tree wall, like she's acting out some sort of weird birthing process.

"I wonder if this is how Groot felt when he was born," she mutters. And then to expound on the whole birth scene, her butt goes and gets stuck, wedged in tight between two trees. Boodark slaps a wing against her bottom and yells, "Push! Come on, girl! Squeeze that big butt through there. Turn it sideways, if you must, but do it quickly! I don't know how much longer we have!"

She grits back the ugly words that she wants to yell at him and does what she's told, twisting and contorting her body every which way, until she finally manages to slip free and faceplant into a small clearing. She glances up from her ground-sprawl position at the single, *enormous* tree that grows right in the center of it. It looks just like every other dead, leafless tree in this forest, except this one's bigger than most. Also, it has what appears to be miniature black umbrellas hanging upside down from its branches. Bumbershoots. Go figure.

She sits up and starts checking herself over, swiping at the numerous scratches that are oozing blood. "There's no time for that. Get to the tree!" Boodark shouts as he flies ahead and lands in the branches and starts...um is he *chewing* on one of those umbrella things? She rolls her eyes in annoyance but picks herself up and rushes over to him. She wants a closer look anyway.

All of the 'umbrellas' dangle from branches way above her head. They're all much too high for her to reach, so she stands directly below Boodark, looking up at the one that he's busy trying to bite off. (At least she *thinks* that's what he's doing.) It's a leaf! A weird, round, and very dead leaf. In fact, it's so dead that it's nothing more than a leaf *skeleton*. The pulp, the 'skin' has all eroded away, leaving nothing but the delicate, lacy vein system.

A wave of nostalgic homesickness fills her heart at the sight of it. She's always loved those fragile skeletons; she had a huge collection of them years ago. The fire must have eaten them, just like it had eaten everything else she loved...everything except Sir Didymus. She has Charlie to thank for saving not only her life, but Didymus as well. She blinks back sudden tears and steers her mind back to the here and now.

"What are you *doing*?" she yells up at the crazy little gremlin. *That* gives her a momentary pause. What if he really *is* a gremlin? He seems to be terrified of 'sky water'. What if he'll sprout little mini Boodark-minions out of his butt if he gets wet, like Gizmo had? Or, what if sky water transforms him into something else, sends him into a cocoon in which he emerges as a terrifying, hideous(er) beast? Oh! She'd hate to see what he turns into if *that's* the case, because he's already ugly.

She's not thinking mean things, she's truly not. He just really is that ugly. Maybe he'll do a reverse transformation. Maybe he'll turn back into a cute little Mogwai if he gets wet. She grins at the thought of him, and his tough 'manly' attitude, trapped in a cute fuzzy Mogwai body.

"Catch!" he demands, pulling her from her mental musings, as the umbrella leaf snaps free and falls from the branch. She catches it and then flips it right side up...in a proper umbrella position. In (normal) leaf structure, the stalk, which is called the petiole is situated at the bottom of the leaf and it's the little stem that attaches the leaf to the branch. In this case, it's the 'handle' of the umbrella, and it's attached to the very center of the leaf, instead of at the bottom. Boodark bit it off so that this 'handle' is extra-long... longer than he is tall actually.

'Normal' leaves have a main rib, a thick vein that runs down the center from top to bottom, with several smaller ribs branching off of it. This one has sixteen curved ribs that run from the main midrib to the outer edges of the leaf, just like the metal spokes in an umbrella. These curved ribs are what give the leaf its dome shape.

The lamina, the 'skin' of the leaf is gone, completely eroded away, leaving nothing but the skeleton behind. The whole thing is incredibly beautiful, just like a gothic, Victorian lace parasol.

On closer inspection, the color of it's not as completely black as it had first appeared. There are little flecks of shiny, emerald-green mixed in, like tiny, glittering jewels.

Boodark glides down and lands on her shoulder (without asking permission) and takes right back up where he'd left off in his lesson on sky-water. "There's no way of knowing what kind of sky water's coming, so we have to protect ourselves. Lift it up, Dummy! Up! Over your head!"

Seriously? The 'umbrella' is the size of a dinner plate. It's much too small to do any good. Plus, *it's a skeleton*. There's nothing left of the leaf but lacey veins. The water will go right through it! "Boodark, this isn't going to work," she patiently tries to explain. "This isn't going to do anything to keep me dry! It may be big enough for you, but it won't even cover my head! And what good is an umbrella with holes in it?"

He suddenly throws out a wing and slaps her across the face with it. "Oh, have some faith! Trust me! If you don't stop yapping at me and do as I say, we may both regret it. But maybe not for *long* because we could also very well be *dead* in the next few minutes. Now lift it UP!"

So, what does she do? She lifts the ineffectual, miniature parasol up over her head. Like an idiot. "There!" she explodes. "Are you happy? Now, I look as dumb as *you* did with your tongue stuck inside a hole in a tree!"

She sucks in a breath, lets it out, and starts over with a new line of questioning. "What do you mean, you don't know what kind of rain is coming? How many kinds *are* there?" He scooches in closer to her head and scrunches down, making himself as small as possible before he answers.

"Three," he grunts. "There's the good kind, where nothing bad happens when it lands upon you. That is the kind you want. It is safe to drink and wash in. Then there's hot sky water. And I mean *hot…* boiling, peel your skin from your bones, hot. Not pleasant."

"And then there's poison rain, which isn't so bad… *if* you're fast enough to dodge raindrops, that is. It's *mostly* good water, but there's random, slimy green, poison drops that look just like what oozes out of an infant's nose mixed in with the good water drops. Maybe one poison drop to every hundred raindrops, which doesn't sound so terrible, until you realize how many raindrops actually fall. Billions...Trillions."

"So, there's no possible way of avoiding the poison drops. There's just too many of them. Unless, like I said, you're super-fast or perhaps one of those weird thrill seekers that like to test the fates. I am *not* either of those. I've seen what the poison sky water does and no, thank you. I choose life."

Ecko feels her legs trying to turn to Jell-O. Her heart starts thudding painfully in her chest and she just about pees her pants. All she can think is that she's about to be poisoned, melted into a gross puddle of goo.

"Oh, my God. This is stupid! We're gonna die!" she yells. She has every intention of tossing the useless leaf that she's ridiculously holding above her head and making a run for it, and Boodark knows it. He opens his mouth to try and reassure her, to tell her to just trust him, but then all H-E-double-hockey-sticks breaks loose.

A massive thunder boom that makes her scream her fool head off, is the only warning they get. "Trust me, Girl! Look up!" Boodark shouts into her ear, and she looks up at the lacy leaf that she's *still* ignorantly holding over her head.

As the first raindrops land on it, the emerald-green specks instantly begin to spread outwards, growing like water stains. She watches, mesmerized, as the green spreads out to fill in all those holes with a new 'skin', magically restoring it to what must have been its original glory.

Within seconds, the leaf no longer looks dead, black, or withered. It's now a sparkling emerald-green with obsidian black rib/veins running through it. And those sixteen ribs *grow*, they shoot outwards, bringing all that new skin with them. The entire leaf stretches and expands until she's holding a very large, protective canopy above her head. It's got to have a diameter of five feet…. That's sixty beautiful inches of magically produced, almost instant protection… literally at her fingertips.

She looks over at Boodark, who's grinning his ghastly smile at her. "I told you to trust me," he brags. "But you don't have to worry. It's the good kind of sky water! If I were you, I'd hurry up and get the restocking your water supply done, so that you have time to do some bathing…because you really do stink!"

She's highly insulted, even though she *knows* that she's not at her freshest. But she also knows that she smells like a rose, compared to *him*. "Me?" she screeches in outrage. "*I* stink? That's *you* who smells like old, moldy cheese!"

Now it's his turn to look offended. He lifts his arm up and sniffs at his pit. He immediately grimaces and then nods reluctantly, as he's forced to agree. "You're right!"

Shouting to be heard over the pouring rain, she asks if he's *sure* that it's safe. He flies up off her shoulder and darts out into the rain, and after a few seconds of watching to ensure that he doesn't melt, she shrugs off her backpack.

She senses movement in the tree above her, and she turns her head upwards just in time to see several of the Bumbershoot leaves unfurling and expanding. They aren't upright in 'umbrella' posi-tion, as the one she holds is. They hang upside down and they've now become bowls, giant bowls to catch gallons and gallons of the precious, life-saving water.

Now she understands why there's only a couple bumbershoot-leaves on each branch. They need room in order to grow so big, and they must also weigh a ton when they fill up with water. They would be too crowded and would become too heavy for the branches to support, if there were any more of them.

Shaking her head briskly to snap herself out of just standing there, (like the big dummy that everyone here seems so fond of calling her) she gets back to digging things out of her bag. She rushes to get the refilling of her water bottles done, so that she can hurry up and get to what she *really* wants to do. Bathing!

She takes her soap and shampoo and her dirty laundry out, and then props the Bumbershoot over her backpack to protect the rest of her belongings. With a delighted squeal, she runs out into the rain where she offers to share her body-cleansing supplies with her companion. "Here. Use this. De-stink-atize yourself."

She squirts a tiny bit of sweet pea body wash into the palm of his hand/claw and then she turns away to strip off her t-shirt and jeans. She washes her hair and then scrubs herself as best as she can while still wearing her underclothes. Once she's as clean as she can possibly get, she vigorously attacks her small pile of dirty laun-dry. She scrubs each item and hangs them from the tree branches where the rain can finish rinsing them. Done with her chores, she turns back to see if Boodark's finished too.

He's sitting right where she'd left him, but he's picked up her bottle of body wash. He's got it held beneath his nose, sniffing it. And even though the rain's doing a great job of disguising his tears, she still sees that he's crying. She walks over and sits down beside him. She doesn't say anything, she just wants to let him know that she's here, if *he* wants to talk. She's learned that sometimes that's the best thing you can do for someone who's in pain.

The rain chooses that moment to shut off with a suddenness that equals the instantaneous switch from Pale to Pitch and vice versa. She blinks up at the sky for a moment or two, hoping for a rainbow or a sun to peak out of some clouds, but it's the same sky that's always up there, grey and gloomy and forever unchanging. At least that awful heat from before the storm has dissipated. The temperature is back to its normal, comfortable 70ish degrees.

She glances back down to her little companion to see that he's still holding tight to that bottle of body wash. The tears have ceased, but he looks so sad and dejected. His big ears are drooping down, raindrops dripping from the tips. The sight of him like that just about breaks her heart. "You can have it, if you want it," she murmurs in a hushed, gentle voice. "I have more."

She doesn't *really* have more, but she *does* have other soap and also shampoo. She doesn't need the body wash and she'll gladly give it up, if it makes him feel better.

He looks up at her, the surprise and hope evident in his eyes. "Truly? You would *truly* give me this...this magnificent treasure?"

She smiles at him and simply says, "It's yours." She watches as his ugly little face breaks out in a uummm... well, a terribly ugly, but ecstatically happy smile that lights up his eyes. It warms her heart that she was able to drag him up out of the depths of his sadness.

"If you want, I'll just put it in my bag with your food pouch. Or you can carry it," she assures him when she notices his hands clench the bottle tighter. "Totally up to you. Just know that even though it's in my bag, it belongs to you, just like your stew. You can have them any time you choose."

Boodark nods and takes one last sniff of the sweet scent before he reluctantly holds the bottle out to her. "You know what?" she says. "Why don't you just hold onto that for a bit? I know there's still a few hours of Pale left that I could, and probably should, spend traveling. But I think we'll just go ahead and set up camp here. I'm feeling so tired today. I don't know what's wrong with me! And besides, all my clothes need time to dry out. That ok with you?"

He only nods his head as he pulls the bottle back and cradles it against his chest. She stands up and says, "I guess I need to set up the tent tonight. I don't want to lay in mud and... Wait. Why isn't the ground wet?"

She glances around the clearing, and it all looks just like it had *before* the storm. There's nothing dripping, no water drops clinging to anything... except on her, that is. *She's* still soaked. Even Boodark's completely dry now. "How are you dry? How is *everything* dry already?"

Boodark lays down in the dirt and curls his little body around the bottle in his arms. "But you already know how. You've said it many times. The world is a vampire. It's greedy, and it sucks up every drop of nourishment it can get. *Everything* here does. My skin absorbed all the water that clung to me, the dirt and the plants and the trees did the same. I don't understand how *you* are still wet. Do you not absorb water at all?"

She peers down at the droplets on her arm. "I guess not. At least not like you do. I certainly don't speed-absorb. That's crazy! I can't believe how quickly the entire world dried out. It happened even faster than you scarfing down your meals, and that's saying a whole lot!"

Boodark yawns and tells her, "Well, if you wish to pack up and move out, we can because your clothes will be dry already too. The Bumbershoot Tree is just as thirsty as everything else. It will have sucked your clothes dry for you. The leaves collect as much water as possible for the tree to drink, but the rest of the tree pulls in any excess moisture it encounters too." He yawns again, deeper this time. "But I vote for staying here anyway. Now that I'm clean, I'm ready for a nap!"

She rushes over and lays a hand on one of her shirts. Sure enough, it's just as dry as it had been before the washing. "That's just crazy," she whispers to herself. She looks up at the branches above her head. The tree must have greedily sucked all the water from its umbrella bowls, because they've already begun to shrink back up. The newly grown skin is starting to erode away, turning the leaves back into skeletons, right before her eyes. It's only a matter of minutes before even those giant water bowls are sucked bone dry and returned to their former 'dead' and shrunken states.

She glances down at her backpack and sees that the Bumbershoot leaf that's propped over it is going through the same metamorphose as the ones that are still hanging from the tree, but it's doing so at a much slower pace. In fact, the 'skin' has only just begun to dry up and erode away from the veins. It hasn't even started shrinking yet.

She picks it up and carries it over to where the lazy little orcbat is lying. She squats back down beside him and asks him what would happen to it, since it's no longer attached to the tree. He cracks an eye open to balefully glare at her for disturbing him, but still takes time to (grudgingly) answer. "I'm not really sure what will happen if you continue to hold it in your hand, since you don't 'absorb' like the things from this world do, but if you set it back on the dirt, the ground will pull the water from it. If we put it back on the branch, it will reattach itself and the tree will drink the water out of it, just like it would have done had we had never taken it down."

And he closes his eyes, as if the conversation is supposed to end there. She has other plans, though. She *has* to know. "You mean to tell me that you can cut a leaf off a tree here and then stick it back on and it'll be fine? It'll just glue itself back on somehow?"

Boodark sighs and sits up. "No. Not *all* trees. And no, it doesn't glue itself back on. It *grows* back on. The severed ends will sprout new growth to connect the two parts back together." He uses his hands, interlocking them to demonstrate.

"So, not *everything* is a vampire. This thing is actually quite useful," she murmurs as she twirls the umbrella leaf in her hands, admiring the swirl of emerald and obsidian as it spins.

"Will it stay just like this? Or will it eventually return to its original state? Oh! If it *does* shrink back down, I could keep it. I could tie it to my bag and carry it with me for the next time it rains!"

But Boodark's already shaking his head. "Negative. You do *not* want to keep it."

She stops spinning it as she turns to regard him. "Oh. Will it eventually die...*really* die? Will it not work the next time it gets wet?"

"I'm not sure what will happen to it. But I still suggest not keeping it, because you really just don't understand. Despite its helpfulness, it's more vampiric than you realize. Just like every-thing else, it's always, *always* looking out for itself. Its only pur-pose is to keep itself alive. It cares naught of how it does that or where the nourishment comes from. It will draw sustenance from anywhere it can get it. Even from you."

"Had you held onto it for much longer without the sky water to distract it, *you* would have been its next meal. It would have sprouted long, thin barbs to hook into your skin, and then its veins would have burrowed in and tapped into yours."

She has to think it all through. It takes a moment, but she fi-nally gets it. Horrified, she tosses the umbrella away from her. "It would have *leached* me? Sucked *me* dry?" she screeches. "And you let me hold it… without telling me? You put it in my hands and let me almost get eaten? Sucked to death...by a *leaf*? A ding dang vampire *leaf*? How could you? Oh! I am really, really mad at you right now Boodark! That was a terrible thing to do!"

And she really is. She is *so* mad, positively livid. She feels that mysterious electric current spark to life inside of her as a red haze obscures her vision. "If I were as nasty as you, I would take back that bottle of body wash. But I'm not like you. I gave it to you for keeps, but I'm 100% regretting the decision to give you *anything*. I've been sharing my food and water with you every day! And for what? For you to thoughtlessly and uncaringly put my life at risk like that!"

Her anger is so inexplicably intense that she's actually terrified of what she might do. But even in the midst of all that sudden rage, something inside of her urges her to walk away. She realizes that the best thing she can do is distance herself until she can calm down.

So, without another word, she gets up and stomps over to her backpack and angrily sets up her tent. She gathers up her newly washed and dried clothes from the parasitic vampire tree, snatches her backpack, and tosses it all into the tent. She turns and gives him one last glare before she crawls in and zips herself in to block everything out. She has every intention of folding her clothes and putting them neatly away, but somehow ends up just balling them up into a pillow to cushion her head as she stretches out.

"Vampires suck! This *world* sucks!" she screams as she closes her eyes… just for a minute. She's asleep the moment her eyes close. Apparently, she'd been in desperate need of a nap too.

When she wakes, she's instantly filled with regret for being so mean to Boodark. She doesn't understand what came over her. He obviously knew what would have happened if the bad kind of rain came down. *She* hadn't known about the different kinds of rain, hadn't even suspected that it was *about* to rain. She realizes that he must have calculated the risks of the Bumbershoot leaf against the risks of the bad rains. Yeah, he may have put her in danger, but he'd also been trying to save her while doing so. He could have flown off and found shelter for himself at any time.

And who knows? Maybe having a leaf hook into her veins wouldn't have been an immediate death sentence. Unpleasant as it would have been, it probably wouldn't have resulted in instant death. In fact, Boodark probably knows how to get out of a 'death by leaf' situation. Yes, he'd likely done the best he could do in the few short minutes he had to do it. She shivers and suddenly realizes that the air is cold, *much* colder than she ever felt it here. Sudden apprehension squeezes her heart like a vise.

"Boodark!" she shouts as she unzips the tent. He's asleep, laying right where she'd left him, curled up and shivering around his bottle of body wash. His lips are no longer green, they've turned blue from the cold. The sight of him like that breaks her heart and she immediately starts to cry.

"Oh God, Ecko. You are such a jerk," she chastises herself as she scoops him (and his bottle) up and carries them back to the tent. He never even stirs as she wraps him up in her extra blanket and cuddles him close. When he finally stops shivering and his leathery skin feels warm again, she lays him down and rummages in her bag for her thermals and her pj's.

After she pulls them on, she gathers everything she needs to make dinner and carries it all outside. Up until this point, she'd only used the canned heat with the little foldable 'cookstove' that she had brought with her. But she wants to conserve what fuel she has left, and since it's also super chilly out, she decides that tonight's a good night to build a real fire. Since she's lost all track of time and has no idea how much longer she has until Pitch falls, she hurries to gather as much firewood as she can... with a flashlight stuffed in each pocket, just in case. Heck the dark.

Thirty minutes later and she's got a good fire going, a skillet full of spam sizzling away, and a pot of chicken noodle soup heating over it. Just as she's pouring the first pot of soup into a bowl, she feels the ground rumble that lets her know she only has one hour left until the darkness comes. She hurriedly scrapes half the spam onto a plate and adds a handful of trail mix. Soup, Spam, and trail mix, it's not much of an apology dinner, but it's the best she can do...almost.

She crawls into the tent to wake Boodark for dinner and grabs one of the granola bars to add to his meal. She remembers how much he'd loved the one she shared with him before. *If this doesn't win him over then nothing will'*, she thinks as she gently shakes him awake.

But he does *not* come awake gently! He shoots up, kicking and fighting to get out of the blanket as he hollers, "I did *not* eat the last bullbug!"

She leans back to escape his swiping claws and yells for him to snap out of it. "Boodark! Wake up. It's me, Ecko. I don't care if you ate every single bullbug in existence. Stop trying to kill me with your demon claws!"

He stops trying to slice and dice her and blinks dumbly at her until he wakes up enough to recognize her. "Oh, it's *you*," he sneers. "What do *you* want?" And then the little monster crosses his arms over his skinny chest and waits. She places his food in front of him and gives him what he's waiting for, her apology.

"I'm sorry I was mean to you."

He ignores her offering, points his nose up into the air, and spins around so that his back is to her. He's clearly still upset with her. She sighs heavily. She should have known that a simple, 'I'm sorry' wouldn't be good enough.

"I know you were just trying to save my life. You did a great job too, the best you could in the time that you had. I don't even know why I got so mad. All I remember is that I was feeling really tired, so tired that I just wanted to lay down in the dirt and nap with you. Then all of a sudden, I was just… *angry*."

"And when you told me that the Bumbershoot leaf is basically a parasite and just as dangerous as every freaking thing else around here… I don't know! I just felt so overwhelmed. I don't think I can do this. I don't know how to be a Wandelaar. I keep waiting to wake up and find that it was all just a bad dream…. every bit of it.”

“I want to wake up and find out that I’m still fourteen years old and none of it actually happened, my family dying in front of me, the fire, the three years that I spent in the hospital, finding out that I’m from *another world* and that I have magic. I want to go back before I found out that I’m supposed to be some badbutt that’s supposed to save my true home world, a world I’ve never even seen, mind you, and possibly every other world while I’m at it.”

“But I can’t wake up… I’ve tried! And every day I feel more and more incapable and worthless and helpless. I feel lost. I don’t want any of this! I’ve never even been on my own. I have no idea how I’m going to survive in this world. I don’t know the difference between what’s dangerous and what’s helpful. I’m eventually going to run out of food and water. What’ll I do then? I just want to wake up! And if it’s not a dream, then I just want to hurry up and get back home to my own world where the leaves don’t want to eat me!”

She’s ugly crying at this point, and practically shouting out her frustration when all she’d meant to do was say that she’s sorry for being the reason that Boodark had almost frozen to death. “I can’t even manage a simple ‘I’m sorry’ speech without screwing it all up.” She turns her own nose up to sniff suspiciously at the air. “And now my Spam’s burning!” she wails as she tumbles out of the tent to save her own dinner.

The Pitch arrives just as she takes her very first bite. She’d managed to save her tasty, canned and heavily preserved meat-product meal just in the nick of time. It's a bit burnt and crispy around the edges, but that's how she likes it anyway. She's decided to sit outside and eat her dinner alone, since she's so ashamed of herself... for her outburst, her botched apology, and especially for *why* her apology was needed in the first place. Self-imposed punishment, she supposes.

It's cold out and steadily growing colder, and the night's just as pitch black as it always is. She's built a good fire, but it's having a hard time holding both the cold *and* the dark at bay. She shivers as she feels them both creeping in to get her. She hears a deep sigh from inside the tent, then Boodark calls out to her. "You may as well come in here with me. It's cold out there and you *know* you're afraid of the Pitch."

She ignores him...until he adds, "Fine. Stay out there. But there's probably a spook staring at you right now, just waiting to…."

She doesn't even let him finish. "Aaaiieeeggghhh!" she screeches as she dives in through the tent's door, leaving everything behind…. even her food! She has to wait a good two minutes, listening to his laughter, before she can convince him to go back outside with her. "Oh, shut up," she grumbles at him. "You got your little revenge, now come outside and make sure nothing tries to get me while I gather everything up. I see that you've managed to scarf your dinner down in record time, but *I'm* still hungry. And my dinner's getting cold!"

She crawls back outside and mutters, "nasty little orc-bat!" But she's smiling, because she knows that she's been forgiven and that their little spat is over.

She quickly banks the fire and carries her things inside. Once she's zipped the two of them back into the safety of her tent (because surely those strong nylon walls are indestructible and impenetrable, and *nothing* can harm them while they're safely ensconced within) she eagerly gets back to eating. And Boodark eagerly watches her every bite.

"Stop watching me, weirdo. It makes me uncomfortable. You had just as much as I gave myself, which is crazy if you ask me, because I'm so much bigger than you. You know I need more food than you right? What is it you keep saying? Oh yes, I'm a giant, with a giant's great big butt. Well, that just means that I need more fuel than you do. You're teeny tiny. You shouldn't need nearly the amount of food that I do."

She sips a spoonful of soup and then points to the 'dessert' that he's hoarding and says, "Besides, you haven't eaten your granola bar yet. If you're still so hungry that you want my dinner as well, eat that!"

He glances down at the treat with naked longing in his eyes but then shakes his head no. "I'm saving it," is all he says. Saving it for what, she doesn't know. But she doesn't question him either. She figures he's been hungry a time or two in his lifetime and now hoards food whenever he can. She knows all about that.

He does his best to ignore her as she finishes up her meal, looking everywhere but at her. But every slight noise she makes causes his big ole' ears and his tiny bat nose to twitch. She can't help but grin at his antics. He's just too ugly/cute. Somewhere along the way, he's become...not *cute* exactly. Endearing is the word she's looking for. She sighs in defeat as she realizes that she's come to care about this strange, ill-favored, and unsightly brat.

"Here!" she grunts as she sets her plate with the last slice of Spam in front of him. She jerks her hand out of the way, just in time as he pounces on it.

"Geesh, calm down! I'd like to *keep* my hand!"

He takes four huge bites, barely chewing before swallowing each one, then turns and grins up at her. "Why? Are you attached to it?" He throws himself backwards and rolls around the tent, giggling helplessly.

"Your jokes are bad. You should be ashamed of yourself," she tells him, but she's grinning from ear to ear as she unzips the door and sets the dishes outside to be washed in the morning. She watches him make a nest in the blanket that she'd given him, then pulls her weaving project from her bag. She'll never be able to explain it, but she's somehow got the bottom half of a large handbag/basket made.

She gets to work on it and waits for it to start... the questions. Boodark likes to pepper her with endless inquiries about Earth and 'Earthling magic'. She's tried countless times to explain that her world doesn't have magic, they have science and technology. She's given up though, because he just keeps stubbornly insisting that it's magic... it *has* to be.

They've talked for hours and hours about *everything*, with an inordinate amount of their conversations revolving around 'foodorators' and the many kinds of Earth food that could be put into the magic boxes. He also asks about flowers and plants quite often…and 'Earth' animals, as well as the Sun, the Moon, and the stars. Cars and trains and airplanes. Paper clips and elastic and toilet paper, of all things. And books.

He's absolutely fascinated with books, but he doesn't understand about the written word. "How can scratch marks tell you anything? How can they speak?" He just can't grasp it and she's promised to teach him the 'scratch mark' letters and how to read them, if she has the time and opportunity to do so.

Tonight's first questions are "So, what is that dead, furry thing you carry stuffed in your bag? That creature you sometimes like to take out and hug. It doesn't smell dead, but it has not moved at all, so dead it must be…unless… is it spelled? Cursed? What's wrong with it? And *what* is it? And tell me about that magic box that sang songs, while you sneakily plied me with drink to turn me into a drunkard. I liked that, 'I Hope You're Happy' song. It was catchy!"

She takes her iPod and Sir Didymus from her bag and explains them as best she can. She shows him how to turn the music player on, how to search for a song (he sees the 'scratch marks' but says that they don't speak to him… meaning he can't read the words) She chooses one at random and hits play. Bob Marley's voice rings out, telling them not to worry about a thing and that every little thing was gonna be alright.

Boodark bobs his head and taps his claws to the happy beat. "How?" he demands when it's over. She can't really tell him *how* the music player works, and so, naturally he just chalks it up to magic.

Then she introduces him to Didymus. "This is Sir Didymus. Even though he's just a stuffed animal, he's been my best friend since I was five years old."

Boodark looks horrified and slightly alarmed. "You carry the carcass of your best friend with you?" Her explanation of Sir Didymus eases his fear and then makes him giggle. "So, you're telling me that you carry a child's plaything with you? And that you were willing to fight a Vika Vakooja for a *toy*?"

She lets him laugh. He doesn't understand that Didymus had been her only friend for most of her life. He's all she has, other than Charlie and Susan and *they're* not here. "Are all Earthlings as strange as you?" he teases.

With a sad smile, she simply says, "No. I've been different all my life, no matter what world I'm on, apparently." She glances down to check her basket weaving progress and finds that she's nearly completed it. All that's left is a couple more rows and then to add the handles. But that will have to be tomorrow night's project, because she's ready for sleep.... Again.

She stuffs all of her things back into her backpack (everything but Didymus, because she suddenly needs the comfort that only he can provide tonight) and then she crawls into her sleeping bag. She pulls Didymus close and says, "Goodnight Boodark." Then she whispers, "Goodnight, Sir Didymus."

Despite waking up from her nap feeling refreshed and well rested, she once again feels completely worn out and fatigued…. drained of energy. She imagines that this is exactly how a toy feels as its batteries start to die. Such a dismal thought, but only for a moment, because that's all the time it takes for her to go tumbling into her dreams.

16

DEAD BODIES AND BUILD-A-BITCHES

Krispin

He's lost his mind. That's the only explanation he's got, the only one that fits. The rages, the blackouts, all the lost time and the memory gaps. Waking up in places that he hadn't fallen asleep in, the naked women that he has no memories of bedding… *dead,* naked women. And now *this*, whatever this is. *This is new,* he thinks as he glances around the darkened room, trying to figure out just what *this* is.

He's surprised to find himself here and his eyes scan the room, seeking out clues as to what the fuck is going on. This is obviously different than any of his other blackouts. He's not in his bed with a woman. He's not in a bed at all… not lying down even. He's standing upright on his own two feet in the underground basement room. His mind works overtime, trying to make sense of the mess around him.

There are tattered scraps of cloth, piles of hair… long locks of it strewn all about. Blood splattered all around him. And everywhere he looks there's fluff, soft, gossamer tufts of wispy blue down. It's scattered throughout the room, floating in the air even.

"DreamSnare fluff?" he whispers in confusion, as he watches a tuft of it float away on the breeze that his breath creates.

He becomes aware of the painful cramp in his hands and glances down at them in confusion. *What has he been up to*, he wonders as he realizes that both hands are coated in sticky, half congealed blood, bits of fluff stuck to them. There's a large needle, threaded with a thick, black string clutched in one hand, and a round, oversized button pinched between the fingers of his other hand.

He slowly turns around to question the two women that he'd stashed in here. "Oh. Who the fuck are *you*?" he growls because somehow, there's three women now. But then he recognizes her, this new female in his growing collection of frozen femmes' fatales. It only takes a moment to make sense of her, as he comes to grips with *exactly* what he'd been up to.

At least he now knows what he'd been about to do with the button, needle, and thread. New girl is sporting the twin to the button that he holds in his hand, as her new right eye. Her own eyeballs had been removed, the button then shoved into the empty socket and secured with string. Krispin's own eyes wander over the women, trying desperately to make sense of it all.

Dolls. It looks like he's been making life-sized dolls.

There's an overflowing chum bucket on the dirt floor before them, and he moves in, kicking aside a discarded, half eaten loaf of blood-soaked bread, in order to take a closer look at the contents: ropes of intestines, organs, blood, and new woman from the playground's eyeballs… one of them, anyway, floating there on the top. There's no telling where the other one's hiding.

Krispin turns back to examine the females once more. They've all been split open from their breasts to their groins, and then stitched back up with the black string. Apparently, he'd taken their innards out and re-stuffed them with DreamSnare fluff. It also appears as though he'd removed some of their parts, rearranged them, and then stuck them back on with his handy-dandy needle and thread… Just like Samara had done to that cuddly little child's toy he'd given her years ago. The one that she'd loved so much but had refused to admit to.

"*Fuck me,*" he whispers to himself as he stares down at his new playmates. He's been killing women and then turning them into dolls. Stuffed, life-sized woman-dolls that he'll be able to play with, again and again and again. *And he has no memory of doing any of it.*

17

FIRE IT UP

Ecko

Ecko sleeps right through the change from Pitch to Pale. Dreams of the Red Door opening up to reveal all of her nightmares and fears keep her tossing and turning restlessly throughout the long hours of the night and on into the morning. She sleeps lightly, jerking awake at every disturbing scene that she's forced to visit in the DreamWorld. Each time she awakens, she finds her face wet with tears and her heart pounding painfully in her chest.

But she's worn out, so exhausted that she immediately dozes back off to watch the Red Door reveal the next new horror, one after another. It creaks open to show Charlie sobbing into his hands before it slams shut, stopping her from getting to him. Then it opens again, and the scene has changed to Sir Didymus, burning up in a fire, before it closes again. Opens, she's looking at herself lying drugged and strapped to a gurney back in the mental ward. Slams closed and opens again, there's Boodark, lying dead in the dirt, beside a strange puddle of goo. Red Door thumps shut and then opens one last time.

Now she's got a bird's eye view of all the many worlds out there, just drifting through space, *and they're burning.* They're all burning and it's *her* fault. She couldn't save them. She couldn't save her family; she can't save Charlie...she can't even save herself. How is it that she's expected to save entire *worlds*?

She wakes with a start, but she's disoriented and believes for a moment that she's still asleep, still trapped in DreamWorld and being haunted by her fears of letting entire worlds perish, of watching them burn to ash. There's a hint of smoke in the air and she hears several disturbingly *wet*, splatting sounds. She watches as tiny patches of flames lick their way inside her tent walls and that's when she knows for sure that this is no dream.

Her eyes tear up and she starts coughing from the smoke that's beginning to pour in. She immediately rolls out of her sleeping bag and yells for Boodark to wake up. He doesn't answer her, doesn't even stir inside his nest of covers.

She frantically stuffs Didymus into her bag, gathers both of their bedrolls up into one big wad, Boodark and all, and then bursts out of the flaming tent with as many of her things as she could grab. She doesn't stop to look back, doesn't even look around. She just focuses on getting them all out of the danger zone.

She perpetually messes things up. She always seems to make the dumbest mistakes, so she just assumes this, too, is all her fault. She must not have properly put out the fire, and errant sparks had been what started her tent to burning. That's what she *thinks* as she runs for her life. She doesn't realize that her camp is under attack or that there are currently a hundred sets of eyes trained solely on her. She has no clue that an army surrounds the Bumbershoot glade, an army that's strategically placed to block their escape, effectively entrapping them inside it.

So, it comes as a complete surprise when she hears several tiny (but shrill) war cries ringing out all around her. Her mad dash comes to an abrupt halt as Boodark pokes his head up out of the tangle of bedding in her arms. He takes one look back behind them at the burning tent and then his eyes dart wildly about the Bumbershoot clearing and beyond, to the wall of trees that surround it.

"Fire!" he shouts, just in case she hadn't already noticed the flames and the smoke and her tent burning to ash. Yeah, he's just a little slow.

"It's an ambush!" he screams as he struggles up out of the blankets. He turns wide, resigned eyes up at her and solemnly says, "We're dead. There's too many of them."

Them? She strains her eyes to see through the thicket wall, to see what he sees, but it's no use. The attackers, if indeed there *are* attackers (she sees nothing to prove his claims) are too cleverly hidden for her eyes to detect them.

Boodark finally manages to untangle himself and crawls up her arm to sit on her shoulder. "Prepare yourself!" he yells, and she instantly drops everything that she's holding onto... to do what? What's she gonna do?

Her eyes dart down to the supplies that have spilled out of her bag, searching for something, anything, that will help against.... whatever it is that's intent on ambushing them. She hasn't got a single clue as to what she's about to go up against.

She's totally *not* prepared as Boodark's shout riles up the enemy and triggers their onslaught. Tiny, marble-sized balls of flames erupt from the tree line in front of them. She stands there, frozen in place, dumbly watching them fly towards her. Most of them fall short and burn out on the ground, but a few of them find their marks.

One sails directly towards her face and she lifts her hand up to swat it away. She hits it, but instead of bouncing off and being redirected back at the assailants, it sticks to her hand like glue! A flaming ball of sticky glue! It delivers a stinging burn before she claps her hands together to slap the little flame out. Two more miniature fireballs land on her blankets and another on her backpack, and she quickly slaps them out, before they can catch hold and burn her things up like they'd done to her tent.

"Well, I guess this is it then," Boodark stretches out his wings and cracks his neck. "I'm finally going to learn the answer to a question that has long plagued my mind. Exactly how many FireFairies can I eat? My record is twelve, but I could have eaten more. I *know* I could have. I wasn't even close to being full, I just ran out of willing test subjects. Also, unwilling ones. I'm not picky. I'll double that number now, easy-fleasy. I'm going to eat so many of them that I'll burp fire and flames will shoot out of my arse for five Pales in a row!"

He puffs out his chest as he continues to brag. "Yeah, they really just don't understand who they've decided to war with." He rubs his claws over his little Buddha belly and grins. "This belly may seem small, but it's mighty! They very well may take me down, but they're going to lose some serious numbers in the process. I refuse to go down without a fight, and I'll make a name for myself yet! Oh yeah, they'll remember *me*. I'll forever more be known as Boodark the Devourer! My name will draw forth cries of fear from the lips of FireFairies for years to come!"

He points a claw to the left half of the thicket and commands, "You start eating over there." He turns to point to the right. "I'll start over here. And on the bright side, even though we'll never be able to eat them all, at least we won't live to suffer the heartburn and the fire farts come next Pale!" Then he turns his head, places the sweetest, ickiest slobbery kiss on her cheek and tells her, "I'm glad to have known you, Ecko. May we meet again in the Ever-Lands."

With surprisingly cat-quick reflexes, she reaches out and snatches his foot, just as he lifts up off her shoulder. She's got him held fast in her hands, and she turns him around to face her. "Whoa! Slow down! FireFairies? We are *not* eating fairies! I forbid it!"

Boodark squirms in her hands, trying to break her hold without actually using violence to do so. She sets him back on her shoulder with a stern, "Stay put!"

He glares angrily at her and growls, "You and your soft, girly 'You can't eat those!' morals are going to get us killed, but fine! I'm not really that hungry anyway, so now probably isn't the best time to try and break my record. What do you suggest we do, Oh Great Leader, Oh, Brilliant One with a plan, Oh, Wise One who knows all about this world, Oh, Experienced One…?"

"Oh, shut up!" Ecko interrupts him with her own panicked shouts. "Do we really have time for this? Like Mushu said, 'We're in the middle of a war, man! There's no time for stupid questions!' Now pull yourself together Boodark! Focus! What can we do?"

She has yet to see the enemy for herself. She's trying her best to get even the tiniest glimpse, but she may as well be blind. "Why can't I see them? Are they invisible or are they just that good at hiding?"

He gives one firm nod of his head which, in all actuality, tells her nothing. "Trust me, you'll see them soon enough. I can hear them, and they are really, really mad at you."

Ecko's heart plunges down into her belly. "But I didn't do anything! I can't even *see* them!" Boodark shrugs his shoulders. "You don't have to *do* anything for them to hate you. They just do. Oh, don't take it personally, they hate everyone. FireFairies can't be reasoned with."

He taps a claw against his temple. "They don't have enough brain power. Their heads are too full of angry, hot gas. They'll burn your butt for any old reason. But most likely it's because you're a ground stomper…. a giant one, no less. They hate giant ground stompers above all else. You stomper-types long ago proved your ruthlessness and your blatant disregard for the 'lesser' species."

She turns her shocked, offended eyes back to him. "But But but…that's stereotyping! And prejudice! I'm not like that at all! I've never hurt anyone! You can't just lump us all together into one group… It's not fair!"

He merely shrugs and pats her cheek. "No, it's not fair. *I* know you're not like that, but *they* don't. Also… they don't care. Like I've said, FireFairies can't be reasoned with."

"Fine. They can hate me all they want. I'm used to that. People have hated me my whole life. But they don't have to burn me at the stake for it! What's their weakness?"

Boodark lets out an exaggerated gasp. "What, now you want to *fight?*"

She hurriedly shakes her head. "Definitely not. What I want to do is turn back time and leave this campsite, before the pack of crazed and demented fairies from hell burn my tent down. But since I can't rewind time and I *do* wish to remain amongst the living, I'll do what I must to stay that way. I'm going to try for a peaceful resolution. But if, as you say, they can't be reasoned with, if they refuse a truce…well war it is, I guess. So, it sure would help if I knew their weaknesses. They're FireFairies so… water?"

He smirks and shakes his head. "Think again. They *like* water. All fairies do."

She throws her hands up in frustration. "Well, what *are* they vulnerable against? You've dealt with them before. You have to know *something*!"

Boodark, with his smart-alecky self tells her, "Well, I've found that biting their heads off and eating them like the spicy delicacies they are works great. They're very vulnerable to that!"

And the little brat turns his snooty little nose up and away from her in a snit fit.

"Really?" she snaps. "You're wasting time being petty. Help me find a solution here. One in which we stop the enemy from crispy-frying us, but where they don't end up on the dinner menu either! Preferably one where this ends in peace and we all walk away. Or fly...whatever. You know what I mean!"

Just then, they hear a single, piercing cry and the two of them stop fighting amongst themselves and turn their attention back to the thicket, just in time to see the next barrage of firebombs coming at them. She momentarily ignores the three that land on her, as she uses her hand to block the one headed for Boodark's face. She slaps at her body to put them all out, then hurriedly moves on to snuff the ones that have landed on her gear.

"Stop. Burning. Holes. In my. Blankets!" she shouts. She snatches the tarp from her bag and shakes it over her belongings that are lying scattered on the ground. As she's doing so, she sees that one of her lighters has fallen out of her bag, and without know why, without conscious thought even, she picks it up and shoves it into her pajama pockets.

"Now I know why I had such an nagging urge to buy the fire-resistant tarp," she mutters. "I guess we'll see if paying extra was worth it. You should hide under there too, Boodark. You *should* be safe, at least for a little while. I'm going to try to reason with them."

But the stubborn little beastie sighs and his shoulders slump in resignation. "I'm with you till the end, Big Dummy...which will be very soon. Fairies don't negotiate.... especially not fire ones. They're much too angry. All they want to do is fight. And burn things. And laugh while their victims burn to ash."

"But do what you feel you must," he continues. "When we die and we're nothing but spooks, forgive me if I say I told you so. And I *will* say it. Spook-me will make *that* my very first priority." Then he turns his attention back to the thicket and waits for whatever plan this new, unorthodox and highly inept Wandelaar comes up with.

Ecko gulps down her nerves and holds her hands up in the 'Look, I'm unarmed, and I come in peace' gesture. "I do not wish to fight!" she calls out. "Can we talk about this, maybe call a truce? I have no quarrel with the FireFairies. Do you have a leader that I may speak with?"

There's silence for a good thirty seconds or so, and then a lone, rebel fireball flies out of the surrounding copse of trees. She watches it land in the dirt, five feet short of hitting her.

"Ummm, parley?" she calls out loudly, before she lowers her voice and giggle/whispers to her companion. "I've always wanted to call for a parley!"

Boodark rolls his eyes, but keeps his mouth shut, at least until she starts speaking again.

"My name is Ecko…"

Then he's choking and grunting, frantically shaking his head back and forth, and whisper/yelling a harsh, "Don't give them your name, Dummy!"

She glares at him and whisper/hisses back. "I'm *not* telling them my full name, just part of my name. Stop interrupting me! You're making me look bad!"

She ignores his sarcastic, "Yeah, *I'm* making you look bad." He waves his hand out in the 'go ahead, after you' gesture and tells her, "Carry on, Oh Brave Leader."

She turns her attention back to the hidden enemy and calls out, "I don't know what I've done to offend you, but if you come out, we can discuss it and hopefully reach some sort of understanding." There's nothing but silence and more silence from the thicket.

"Ok, ummm how about this… I know there is much we can learn from one another, *if* we can negotiate a truce. We can find a way to coexist. Can there be a peace between us?" She lowers her voice, so that only her companion can hear her next words. "I heard that on a movie called Independence Day." Then she tears up a bit because she suddenly remembers that it was the last movie that she had watched with her dad. To distract herself from those untimely memories, she quickly calls out, "Come out, come out, wherever you are! Let's talk."

Her eyes detect a slight movement, a small flash of green and then a blur of red through the tree wall. "Oh shnarts," she chokes out as the 'leader' obeys her command to 'come out, come out.'

Her heart stops for a moment and then triples its normal speed when it restarts. The will o' the wisp had *not* gotten distracted, nor had she forgotten about Ecko ignoring her attempts to lure another victim to a bad end. She must not have appreciated being punted like a football either, because she'd *definitely* gone for reinforcements.

She just about loses it when the wisp's tiny, haunting voice calls out, "No peace!"

Huh, imagine that. "I guess she saw that movie too," she whispers to no one in particular. She almost laughs but gulps instead, as a red will o' the wisp floats out of the circle of trees to stand (float) beside her green sister. A moment later, the two wisps are joined by what can only be a FireFairy.

A mere four inches tall, she's mesmerizingly beautiful, delicate and perfectly magical. Her hair is a flowing cascade of snapping, sizzling golden sparks. It makes Ecko think of those sparkler fireworks that she'd loved as a child, a never ending, flowing sparkler. Her wings are scarlet red and ebony black, and they appear as dainty as lace. Encircling her head is a crown of black diamonds and raw, ruby red crystals to match her wings. Oh! And she's wearing a dress made of fire, actual, living flames!

She's magnificent, and tears prick Ecko's eyes as she stands in awe before her. Her entire life, she's wanted to see the fairies, to befriend the wee folk. She has always believed, in her heart of hearts, that the Fae are real, but never in any of her wild imaginings had she pictured herself on the opposing side of the battlefield, *against* fairies. But if she must, she will fight every last one of them to protect the ugly, surly little orc-bat by her side. It'll surely break her heart to do it, but so be it.

"Ohhhh," Boodark moans and then scrunches himself down lower on her shoulder in an attempt to make himself smaller, and therefore less visible. "Boil me in troll blubber, that's the Fire-Queen! She *never* gets involved in these little skirmishes... she's much too important for that. Why is she here now? Oh, this is so bad!"

Red Wisp raises her tiny hand up in the air in what must have been some sort of silent signal, because all at once the entire FireFairy army decides that it wants to 'come out, come out' too. They pour out of the trees like an invading swarm of locusts, a couple of them launching random fireballs in her direction.

Green Wisp grins a nasty, self-satisfied smile as Ecko and Boodark find themselves surrounded by an angry mob of teeny tiny, winged fairies...*naked* teeny tiny fairies. Ecko throws her hand up over her mouth to stop her giggles as she blushes as red as the queen's fire dress. "Oh, they're nakie! Look at all those itty bitty...uh, never mind. *Why* are they naked Boodark?"

He turns his head towards her with pure outrage stamped on his face. Had she seen that pinched, disgruntled face he was making at her, it probably would have driven her into a fit of laughter. But she doesn't see it. She's entirely too transfixed on other…dangly things. "Why can't I stop looking?" she wails in true distress.

Boodark slaps a wing over her eyes and orders, "Eyes up *this instant*, girl! There's no time for that. Focus! What's your plan? Quick now, before she gives the signal to…. Oh, Elfslugs and earwax! Too late! We're dead. Oh, we're so dead! *Why* did I ever listen to you? You're nothing but a babe, a dumb helpless babe!"

He rambles on and on, bemoaning his fate, as the fairies all begin to hack and gag. She tunes out his ceaseless wailing as she tries to make sense of what's happening on the enemy lines.

"What's *wrong* with them?" she whispers, mainly to herself, but hoping that someone would speak up and clue her in to what's happening, because she *really* doesn't have a clue. She watches, horrified and morbidly fascinated as the fairies, as a perfectly synchronized unit, cup their tiny hands under their mouths and puke flaming, marble-sized barf-balls into them. Horror, disgust and terror all war inside of her as she realizes that these little nightmares have been hurling flaming balls of puke at her…and are preparing to do so again.

"Oh, we are *so* doomed," Boodark wails yet again.

Ecko silently agrees with his panic-stricken proclamation of doom, but she has to try anyway. She doesn't want to go out by fire, she really, *really* doesn't. She's had countless nightmares about being burned alive. The doctors all told her that it was normal after what she'd gone through, but they didn't know. They just didn't know.

She hastily steers her thoughts away from those memories and nightmares and focuses on the immediate dangers at hand, namely the pyromaniac FireFairies and pissed off will o' the wisps that are hell-bent on revenge.Everywhere she looks, the fairies are grinning maniacally at her. Several of them have tiny specks of flame-spit still clinging to their lips. Some of them toss their burning puke-balls from hand to hand, in eager anticipation. Twelve of them decide to go ahead and hurl their flaming puke projectiles at her and then quickly puke up replacements. But the majority of them hold still like tiny, perfectly horrific mannequins... the only parts of them that move are their wings keeping them aloft. But *all* of them are 100% focused on *her*.

She quickly slaps out the three balls of regurgitated fire that splats against her. "Oh, gross! Ouch! Ew, ew, ewww, ouch!" Then she turns her exasperated attention back to Green Wisp. "Oh, come on! Isn't this level of retaliation just a *tad* bit harsh? I didn't *mean* to kick you! It was a reflex, I swear! I would *never* have done it, if you hadn't attacked my defenseless little friend. He's kinda dumb, and he gets picked on and bullied a lot. I *had* to protect him!"

Boodark jabs her in the neck with a claw and hisses in her ear, "Stop that! You're making *me* look bad! I am Boodark the Ferocious; no one bullies me, you giant, lying octobeast arse! I would eat them if they tried!"

Despite the very real danger and the direness of their situation, Boodark still has the ability to make her laugh. She covers her grin by coughing into her hand before she shushes him.

"Ssshhh, I'm trying to negotiate a truce. Let me work." She turns back to the angry mob and calls out, "Will saying I'm sorry help? Because I am. I'm really, truly sorry."

A random, errant fireball strikes her from behind, right in the middle of her back where she can't reach it. It's a good thing she had fallen asleep with her hair still tied up in a messy knot on top of her head. Otherwise, her hair wouldn't just be flame-colored, it would be flaming for real. She yelps as the puke ball burns a hole in her pajama shirt, and Boodark turns and slaps a wing against it. He howls and flaps like mad when the fire-puke-splat sticks to him and singes his wing.

"Thank you, Boodark. Are you hurt?" she murmurs as she holds his wing and gently searches it for injuries. He seems ok, so she turns back to glare at the cheaters on the other side of the battlefield. "Stop throwing your vomit fireballs at us! I'm trying to work this all out. You're not supposed to shoot at us while we're negotiating a peace treaty!"

Green Wisp just nods at Red, turns back to Ecko and grins. "No sorry," she hisses just as Red drops her uplifted hand in a brisk, downward slashing motion.

"Wait!" Ecko screams as she pulls her distraction device out of her pocket. She holds the cheap, disposable lighter up where they can see it and hurriedly strikes the flint wheel. Her sigh of relief when the little flame shoots up almost blows it right back out.

"Hold!" The FireQueen commands, and Red Wisp's hand rises back up, this time held in a tight fist.

Encouraged and hopeful, Ecko calls out, "See? I can make fire too! We can be friends, allies. We don't have to fight! I do not wish for a war with the Fairies. I've only ever dreamed of being *friends* with the Fae."

FireQueen flutters forward a bit, and it visibly makes her troops nervous. "You are *not* FireBorn, nor are you even Faeborn! How do you come by the magic of the Flame?"

And Ecko, with all of her brilliant intelligence and witty astuteness, glances at her cheap disposable lighter and replies, "Uh.... I bought it at a dollar store?"

Puzzled faces peer at her like she's a bug under a microscope.... or perhaps like she's an alien, which she guesses is true enough. So weird.... *She's* the alien here. What's even stranger is the fact that she'd lived her entire life on Earth and had (unknowingly) been an alien there too. "Yeah, everyone stare at the freaky alien," she grumbles under her breath. Even Boodark's peering up at her kinda nervous and uncertain like.

But not Green Wisp. *She's* still got that nasty little, "I hate you. I hope you die painfully while rats eat your guts' smile on her face... directed straight at *her*, of course.

"Give it back!" FireQueen demands. "You are not FireBorn, so you must have somehow stolen the Flame. You will return it to me immediately!"

Ecko's a bit offended at being called a thief. "Now just a minute! I didn't steal anything. I bought it…. It came in a pack of three for a dollar. But I will let you have it, if there can be peace between us. *If* angry, old MeanGreen over there can let bygones be bygones. Will you agree to these terms? Will *she*?"

FireQueen holds up a miniscule pointer finger in the 'hold up' signal and says, "One moment. I must confer with my companions." She turns to the wisps and a brief, intense argument ensues, during which time several stray fire pukes get launched.

"Well, in the meantime, can you tell your blood thirsty...or better yet, your fire thirsty minions to stop raining their hellfire down on me? I feel like they're trying to cook me alive and nothing but me ending in a puddle of flaming creme' brulee will satisfy their fire-lust. I'm pretty sure that they're dead set on watching me burn up... with or without your blessing."

FireQueen turns her head and looks her straight in the eyes as she casually shrugs one dainty shoulder. "They are, as you say, fire thirsty, insubordinate rebels… Wild, uncontrollable things. But do not be concerned. They will not cause you any lasting harm. Well, not much, anyway." And with that, she turns back to the Evil Wisps of the Black Forest.

Boodark snorts. "More like insubordinate rebel arse-goblins if you ask me. Incoming!" he shouts as a lone firebomb comes flying in their direction. Thankfully it misses. He laughs and calls out, "Missed us, you miserable flaming fart-makers!" But he says it quietly, so that only she can hear his insults. He's smarter than he looks.

The two of them anxiously watch the three enemy leaders bicker and Ecko wishes with all her might that they'd hurry it up, because the little metal wheel on the lighter is getting hot and it's beginning to burn her thumb. It appears that the FireQueen wants to agree, but Green is adamantly refusing to let go of her fury. She angrily stabs a tiny, green finger in Ecko's direction as she argues with FireQueen, her jade light flaring brightly with each jab. Red Wisp doesn't seem to care which way the wind blows. She's just waiting for orders. The pissed off mob is still pissed off. All they want to do is fire things up and watch them burn to the ground, but they watch their queen and anxiously wait for her decree.

The debate finally comes to an end and FireQueen turns back and announces, "We accept. You give us the magic Flame and you may leave here in peace."

Boodark clears his throat and instructs her to make them clarify, to be more specific. "Ahem, you may want to find out if this is to be a lasting truce. Sure, maybe they'll let us leave in peace, but will they just follow us and attack again at another time? Does that green *virago* intend to honor the queen's orders? She certainly doesn't *look* like she's ready to forgive and forget!"

Ecko sighs and quietly tells him that all they can do is hope that they'll be honorable, to which he grunts and grumbles, "FireFairies and Wisps *have* no honor." But he shuts up and turns his attention back to the three beings that are deciding their immediate futures.

FireQueen turns to Green and says, "Come, Jaida. We have all gathered here, because of wrongs done to you. Be at my side, as I take the Flame magic from this imposter. Let the taking of her power be enough to satisfy your need for vengeance."

The fairy closest to the queen (naturally it's one of the males) tries to protest. "Rowana, my Queen, I beg you, do not get close to *it*. We know nothing of what it is, or where it comes from. It may well have other, hidden magics that we cannot yet perceive. You need not put yourself in danger. I will gladly go in your stead."

The FireQueen lays a calming hand on his shoulder. "You are ever the gallant warrior, Fenixx, but I shall see this through. Remain here and guard our people. If she proves tricksy and false, we will rain fire down on her and make her rue her treachery. And should I perish here, should my Flame leave me and my essence move on to the Burning EverFields, *you* must take care of our Firelings. You know who I have chosen to take my place. Give her my Flame and teach her to burn bright. She will make a worthy FireQueen." She leans in and licks away the single fire-tear that trickles down his cheek before she turns back to the 'flame stealing imposter'.

Ecko gulps at the look of utter hostility that Fenixx turns on her as his queen and MeanGreen move forward. "Come on, come on, come on. Come and get it," she urges under her breath. Boodark shoots her a look of concern, which she ignores completely. They're moving entirely too slowly, and she can stand it no longer. "AAiieee!" she yells out as she lets go of the little button on the lighter, causing the flame to go out. She hurriedly transfers the lighter to her other hand and shoves her scorched thumb into her mouth to relieve the sting.

MeanGreen and FireQueen come to a halt with ten feet still remaining between them all, identical expressions of fury stamped on their faces and rage burning in their eyes. "You would dare try to deceive me? ME? For your treachery, you will *both* find death in our EverFire," FireQueen shouts.

She's not even given the chance to relight the lighter and show them that '*Hey, here's your flame. No trickery involved.*' The queen holds her hands close together and conjures up her own ball of flames, no puking needed for queens apparently. She balances her weapon of choice on one palm and points at Boodark with the other. "I will make you watch *that* hideous thing burn first. Slowly. Endlessly. I will ensure that you suffer greatly before you meet your own excruciating end."

Everything happens so fast after the Queen's, 'Doom on you' threats, almost as if God has pressed the fast-forward button on his remote control. The two of them, Fairy Queen and Wisp, both infuriated beyond their breaking point, simultaneously try the whole divebomb thing that got MeanGreen punted in the first place. The entire FireFairy army lets out a battle cry and surges forward, their flaming puke-ball projectiles held at the ready.

Boodark throws his wings over his head and cries out some strange nonsense about loving secrets. The sight of him cowering like that, combined with the threat made against him, does *something* to Ecko. Her own magic instantly awakens and a fiercely defensive force roars through her, as if the spirit of a protective momma bear has invaded her body. It flows through her, building up and growing stronger, before concentrating and settling in her hands. It lights them up, not with blue electricity, as she's come to expect, but with a bright, wispy white glow. The haze drops over her vision, not the familiar silver luminescence, nor the raging red, but with something new this time. It's as if her eyes have suddenly been turned to glass, and she's now seeing the world through kaleidoscopic vision.

It's intensely unsettling, so she shakes her head and rapidly blinks her eyes to try to get her vision to return to normal. But then she gets distracted by the beauty of the trees around her, the vines and bushes, the sky...even the dirt. It's all incredible, as if a rainbow had burst open and drenched the world with its color. The ugly, drab forest has transformed and come alive with all the colors of the rainbow, shimmering with sparkles and glitter. And all those new, nameless colors that human eyes can't perceive are present also! It's spectacular, this new prismatic world, but there's no time for admiration and wonder.

She turns her attention back to the two closest threats. FireQueen and MeanGreen both see the change that's come over her (she can only guess at how freaky her eyes look *this* time) and they realize that they've made a terrible, terrible mistake. They both pull up and try to stop their attack, but it's far too late for that. They're flying much too fast, and have gotten way too close, and besides... FireQueen has already launched her fireball. And it's headed straight for Boodark.

Ecko does three things in the space of a single heartbeat. She shifts her body, turning so that her helpless little friend is out of the line of (literal) fire. She instinctively, reflexively holds her hands up to protect her face from the incoming attack. And she slams her eyes shut, as she mentally braces for impact.

She cries out as a warm tickle in her palms has her believing that the fireball has struck. She doesn't feel any pain from it, just an odd, tingling heat. She cracks her eyes open, convinced that her hands have been reduced to nothing more than two flaming charcoal briquettes and her brain's just too stupid to register it. But that is *so* not what's going on. She's not sure exactly what *is* happening, but her hands aren't on fire. Actually, no part of her is burning, thank you, sweet baby Jesus.

That is the first (and most important) thing that she notices. The second is that FireQueen and MeanGreen are now encased in a bubble. Correction, they are now encased in a *fire filled* bubble. It floats in the air, just beyond her glowing hands. MeanGreen. Is. Pissed. She hurls herself through the flames and slams against the bubble (walls?) over and over, trying to break free.

FireQueen is furious too, but she's being more productive than her companion. She's reining the flames from the fireball that she'd set loose back in, absorbing it all back into herself. When the last of the flames disappear, FireQueen presses her miniscule hands against the now crystal-clear globe that's shimmering with all the iridescent hues of a soap bubble. But it's definitely no soap bubble. Or if it is, it's the Mighty Mouse version of all bubbles, because it is *strong.*

MeanGreen's doing her worst, beating and kicking and slamming into it like some sort of claustrophobic mental patient. She may as well have been a gnat trapped in a glass jar for all the good she does.

"What in all the EverLands is *that*? What have you done?" Boo-dark lowers his wings from atop his head and stares at the trapped females… the *infuriated* trapped females. In fact, everyone on the battlefield has frozen in place and is now completely focused on that floating orb. Silence reins all around, for about thirty seconds or so.

Then all hell breaks loose.

The mob starts screeching and howling like a pack of wild things; they sound just like angry Capuchin monkeys. Cries of "Fire it up! Fire it up!" ring out above the noise. They lift up their deadly vomit missiles and prepare to burn her biscuits right where she stands. But Fenixx holds his hand up and shouts, "Hold your fire!"

She can't suppress the manic giggle that bursts out of her at that statement. Fenixx frowns ferociously… '*say that three times fast*' she thinks as another hysterical laughter/snort escapes her. *Why* must her mind *always* pick the most unacceptable things to find humor in…. at the most inappropriate times?

Fenixx turns back to the army and tries to reason with them. She can't help it. Her eyes settle on his tiny perfect man-buns, and she's actually grateful for the new view, because it's better than the dangling man-bits that she'd been doing her very best to *not* stare at while he was facing her.

"We must not harm the imposter!" He shouts to be heard over the uproar. "We know this magic not. We must hold our fire…" he ignores Ecko's giggle/snorts behind his back and continues, "…until after *it* releases Queen Rowana."

The angry army makes their displeasure as crystal clear as the bubble. "We should kill it!" screams an angry blonde male.

"It needs to *burn*!" shouts a dark-haired female. Cries of "Kill it! Burn it! Kill it with fire!" resound throughout the clearing.

A female with hair that looks exactly like the flames clutched in her miniscule, delicate hands flutters forward. "Release my mother this instant!" she trills in a tiny, shaky voice. "Do it not and face our retaliation!" She turns her head to glance behind her and shouts "Come, my brothers and sisters! Come forth and together we shall destroy the imposter and save our mother." Before the last of her words are even out of her mouth, thirty or so flame haired fairies come forward to join her.

Ecko whispers an incredulous, "Oh man, FireQueen's been *busy*! Who has thirty kids anyway?"

Fenixx tries to reason with Red Daughter # 1, tries to cool her fire but it burns much too hot and she turns her anger on him. "It is our right, Fenixx! She is OUR mother, not just our queen!"

Fenixx has a valid argument though. "If *it* becomes enraged, we may never get her back. It could very well decide to keep our queen entrapped for all time!"

Red Daughter #1 frowns at that, but says, "Surely, not. Surely, its magic will die when it dies…." As the two of them bicker back and forth, Ecko turns her attention back to the bubble. She doesn't understand how, but she knows without a doubt, that she's the one that had created it.

She shakes her head in absolute self-disgust. Her magic had conjured up a *bubble*.... a freaking, silly-as-all-get-out bubble. Figures. She is *so* lame, even her magic is pathetic. How could *this* be her power? How is she supposed to beat Samara with *bubbles*? She can just picture it now, her and Samara facing off in a battle. The ground behind her sister is littered with blood, guts, gore, and countless dead victims, as she sends out her nasty, mind-control smoke magic. And there *she* is, on the opposite side of the battle-field. The ground around her is made of pink and blue cotton candy and delicate soap bubbles. She floats toward Samara on her fluffy cloud puff, shooting dainty little bubbles and glitter at her evil twin.

Ecko shakes her head to dispel the mental drama being played out in her mind. She has no desire to see just how horrifically that scene would end. Unless...maybe she'd have a chance of winning that fight if she could first incapacitate Samara by tossing some of that glitter into her eyes... Because glitter in the eyes seriously *hurts*! But how embarrassing would that be? To win the fight, but doing so by using death by glitter and bubbles magic... although victory is victory, no matter how that victory is gained. All's fair in love and war, or some such bull-poop. But still. She just can't be-lieve she has *bubble power*. She's so ding-dang pathetic.

If she hadn't already been convinced that she's 100% responsi-ble for the entrapment of those two tiny, spherically challenged beings, the white hazy wisps flowing from her hands to the bubble confirm it. She tries to lower her hands, but the bubble jerks downwards too, and it throws her little prisoners off balance. They bang their heads on the top of their bubble-jail, bounce off, and then fall to the bottom onto their butts.

"Oh, sorry!" she exclaims as she jerks her hands back up and sends them tumbling again. And then she panics. Simple as that… she full on panics. Freak out mode: activate. "It's stuck! Boodark, help!" Then she's frantically shaking her hands, trying to jiggle the bubble loose. The little women go bouncing around inside of it, pinging off the sides, just like the balls in one of those pinball games at an arcade. Any second now, there's gonna be clown music, bells ringing, and whistles blowing.

"Stop Ecko! Be still, be calm!" Boodark shouts into her ear. She immediately stops trying to shake the bubble off her hands and turns panicked eyes to him. "What do I do? What do I *do?* I can't go around with this thing stuck to me forever! And what about them? They'll *die* in there!"

She tries to gesture at the trapped fairies, but all it does is send the poor things tumbling again. "I'm sorry!" she cries in distress as she steadies her hands, and thereby also steadying the bubble. FireQueen gingerly sits up, a hand pressed to her head as if she's dizzy. She probably is.

Once her eyes have refocused, the first thing she does is reach up and regally straighten her crown and then run her hand over her wild, sparkler hair. She climbs to her feet and runs her hands over her fire dress, as if she's attempting to smooth the flames down. Then she pulls her shoulders back, lifts up her chin, and stares Ecko right in the eyes. "I may die in here, Flame thief, but I take comfort in the fact that you will not live one minute longer than I."

MeanGreen doesn't have anything to say. She just continues her mean-mugging and wall thumping.

"I didn't mean it! I don't even know *how* I did it. I'm new to magic and power and... bubbles. Don't worry, though. I'll find a way to get you out of there. Somehow. I promise!"

FireQueen scrunches her face into a frown and asks, "You did not intend for this to happen? You did not wish to entrap us? Tell me true... Do you wish us harm?"

Ecko vehemently shakes her head, but she's careful to keep her hands steady. "*You* attacked *us*! I don't want to hurt you! I don't want to hurt anyone!"

FireQueen presses her hands against the bubble. "What *do* you want?" she asks, causing Ecko's breath to hitch in and back out in a sigh of pure misery.

"What I want is to go home and save the only two people that care about me," Ecko insists. "What I want is to be free of my mother's burdens and my father's sins. I want justice for the death of my family. I want to disappear, so that no one can find me. I want to go where no one expects impossible things of me. I want to wake up in the mornings and make my own decisions, go where I want, because *I* want to go there. Not because I'm running away from anything. Not because I'm forced to go, and certainly not at the directive of a mysterious beat that no one else can hear or feel, as *I* do. I want to escape the astronomical *pull* of it, drawing me towards the unknown. I want to silence that *other* beat, the quieter, but equally seductive pulse that I know is bad for me, but that I still desire regardless."

"I want to escape the war that the two opposing forces are constantly waging inside me. I want peace. I want freedom. And I want to eat a big, juicy hamburger and chase it down with an entire pizza. But I can't do any of that. I have to save the rest of the people of Earth, not just *my* two people. I have to save my mother's world, Irredarr… and probably this one too, although I *really* hate it here…"

Her voice trails off and she turns away, blinking rapidly to make the dumb tears go away. She seems to have spent entire *years* crying, and it's never helped anything. It won't help now either.

"Umm, who exactly are you speaking to? Have you finally gone mad?" Boodark's looking extremely worried, and he's very slowly scooting as far from her face as he can get. His wings are held up behind him and he's prepared to lift off at any second.

"I'm talking to FireQueen, of course. Who else?"

He stares blankly at her.

"Didn't you hear her?" He slowly shakes his head no, and she rushes to explain.

"She asked if I intentionally trapped her. She asked me if I wanted to harm her and what exactly it is that I want. You really didn't hear any of that?"

Boodark shrugs apologetically. She turns back to FireQueen and asks her to say something to him. So, she turns her head, looks him dead in the eye, and says, "You are the ugliest thing I think I have ever seen."

Boodark shrugs again. "I can see her lips move, but I don't hear any sound coming out. Can she hear me?" When FireQueen doesn't answer, Ecko repeats his question to her, and she shakes her head in response.

"No, I cannot hear his words, although I can see that he is speaking."

Boodark scratches his chin with a claw as he thinks aloud, jerking his head towards the now quietly observing fairy army. "I wonder if *they* can hear her. Yo-ho, Fenixx!" he calls. "Can you hear your queen through the bubble?"

Fenixx flutters forward and presses his hands against the iridescent wall. FireQueen mirrors his actions, and the two of them look into one another's eyes for a long moment, hands pressed together with the thin walls of the bubble an impenetrable barrier between them. "Rowan my love, can you hear me? Are you hurt?" he pleads. She shrugs her dainty shoulders, shakes her head and says something that he obviously can't hear.

"I cannot hear her voice." His shoulders slump as he turns and faces Ecko. "FireFairies are proud, the proudest of all the fairies. We refuse to beg for anything, not even for our own lives. But I am begging you now. Please, please release her. The Hive needs her; our Firelings need her. *I* need her. I cannot live in a world where she does not exist. Take me instead, if you must. I will be cast out of the Hive anyway for pleading for her release."

Ecko's eyes brim with tears all over again at his obvious love for his queen. She glances at the mob and then back to him. "They would cast you out?" she whispers, horrified.

He nods and simply says, "Weakness is not tolerated. But for her, I would do anything, risk anything. I would suffer any punishment, just to know that she is safe."

Oh man. Tragic love stories are the worst. They get her every single time. She refuses to let their love story end at this chapter. She will *not* be the reason they get separated. They've made it this far; their story will *not* end in tragedy now. Not happening. Not on her watch.

She's trying really hard to keep her hands steady, so that she doesn't shake the bubble up, but standing there with her arms outstretched is seriously uncomfortable and getting worse by the minute. She almost falls over backwards as she plops down to the ground. Propping her arms up on her knees to help alleviate the discomfort, she tries to figure out what her next move will be. FireQueen sits down inside the bubble too, but she does so in a regal, queenly manner. She even smooths her fire dress down over her legs.

Boodark hops to the ground too, and Fenixx hovers close to his queen-love. MeanGreen hovers inside the bubble, perpetually glaring the stink eye at her. FireQueen glances at her bubble-mate and sighs. "Glaring your hatred at her won't solve anything. Come, Jaida. Sit beside me as we seek a solution."

MeanGreen's chin goes up a notch and her color flares a deep, fluorescent green. She does not sit, and she does not put away her scowl. FireQueen sighs once more and turns back to Ecko. "Que sera sera," Ecko mutters.

FireQueen nods and says, "Since none but the two of us can hear our words, I wish to speak openly with you. First, you may call me Rowana. May I call you Ecko?"

She nods her head. "Of course. It's nice to meet you, Rowana."

The entire army hisses at her casual use of their Queen's name, but she ignores the angry little (literal) spitfires. And then Rowana's telling her that she understands the position that she's found herself in. She knows exactly what it's like to be forced into a life that she neither wants, nor feels qualified for. And she tells of all the many mistakes that she'd made as a newly appointed Queen.

"I never wanted this for myself, never wanted to be Queen. I wanted to leave the Hive with my true love." She turns her head and her eyes, full of longing and unspoken wishes light upon Fenixx. "I wanted the two of us to start our own Hive, away from FireRules. But my people's need of me was too great to ignore. It far outweighed any desire for self-happiness."

She turns her attention back to Ecko. "I have no right to complain. I am Queen over all FireFairies. I have a good life. But it is not the life I would have chosen, had I been given a choice. So, you see? We two are not so very different. I do understand your plight. I can also admit that it was a mistake to allow Jaida's anger to sway me. I should have routed out the entire truth, before I sent my people to war. I have been Queen for over one hundred years, and it seems that I am still just blundering through."

Rowana stares down at her clasped hands in her lap, regret and sadness stamped on her face. Ecko feels bad for her, even though just a few moments ago she'd wanted nothing more than to fire her and Boodark into crispy chicken dinners.

"Bleeding hearts," she mutters to herself. She turns to Boodark, who's been listening to her half of the conversation. "I have to find a way to release them. Any idea what I should do here?" He moves in closer, staring up at her face. He hop/walks back and forth around her, so that he can see her eyes from all angles. "You are so bizarre," he says, causing her to snort.

"Yes, I know I'm a freak," Ecko answers, "But can we please just get this freak show on the road? Help me!"

"Well," he observes, "This isn't the same as what happened before. Obviously, you didn't create any bubbles then. The glow around your hands is a different color and your eyes are different too. Last time, they were solid silver, shiny and reflective. Although I have never seen a real mirror, that is the way they have always been described to me. And since you are a Mirror Walker… logic dictates that your eyes had changed to represent your mirror magic. This time though… they're still silver and mirror-like. But they're all busted up, full of cracks and shards. They almost look like ice, like frozen silver pools of cracking ice."

She shivers at the description. "I'm glad I can't see them. The solid silver eyes were freaky enough. But Boodark, what do my eyes have to do with my current predicament? It's my hands that're do-ing...whatever it is they're doing."

He plops down on his butt in front of her and continues. "Yes, but I think they're connected. Think about it. You've told me that every time your magic has shown itself, it's also affected your eyes. It changes the way your eyes appear to others, and it also changes your vision... changes how you see things."

"The first time I saw evidence of your magic, you were mad at me for wanting to eat your feets …. Please don't get mad at me all over again! I no longer wish to eat any part of you! *That* time your eyes went solid silver. When you got mad at me over the Bumber-shoot leaf, they started turning red at the edges, like they were fill-ing up with blood. But you suppressed it then. You were able to calm yourself down, so they never changed all the way. You with me so far?"

He continues when she nods at him. "Well, it seems to me that so far, every time your magic has awakened, it was always tied into your emotions. You got mad and they went silver. Then you got frustrated and overwhelmed and they started going red. Now, they're ice-like. Think. Close your eyes and think back. What were you feeling right before your bubble power manifested?"

So, she closes her eyes and turns her thoughts back to the last thing she remembers, before finding out that she can spew bubbles from the palms of her hands. "Rowana and MeanGreen were com-ing at us and Rowana had just tossed her fireball. I realized that it was headed straight for you, that she'd *aimed* it at you. And there you were, all curled up and defenseless like an armadillo."

Boodark interrupts with, "And how did that make you *feel?*"

She frowns but keeps her eyes closed tight. "I don't really know. I just know that I wanted to...no. I *had* to protect you. That's all. I wasn't mad. I just wanted to keep you safe."

Boodark says, "Alright, now we're getting somewhere. Apparently your cracked-ice eyes are for when you're feeling protective. How do you feel now? Do you feel as if I may still be in danger?"

Her eyes snap open. "I don't know what I feel!" she wails, and he immediately throws his hands up to pacify her.

"Calm down! Everything's fine. I'm fine, you're fine. Try to relax, we're both safe for the moment." She makes a mental note to tell him that it's *never* a good idea to tell a female to calm down, but then a light bulb goes off in her head.

"Wait, just hold up a sec. Let me think."

Boodark snickers at that. "Well, don't hurt yourself."

She grunts and then stretches out her leg to bump him with her foot and send him toppling backwards.

"This is serious time!" she grumbles at him, but she's smiling. "I don't think I need to calm down. I think I need to *feel*. If my magic is tied into my emotions, shouldn't I change how I'm feeling? Think about it. When I was so mad at you for wanting to eat my feet, *I* didn't calm myself down. The sadness is what made the magic fade and go back to sleep."

"What sadness?" Boodark asks for her to explain.

"I felt the trees of the forest. I felt that they're sick and that they're dying. I felt their pain. Their sorrow washed through me and took the place of my anger. *That's* when the magic faded away."

He sits up and pats her foot. "Then you know what you need to do. You must make yourself feel something other than what you feel right now. A strong emotion… but hopefully not anger! I don't want you to be sad, but I don't think anger is what we need here. Plus, you are insanely frightening when you're mad. It would be a shame if I pooped myself this soon after my bathing session. But hey, don't mind me. If you decide to go with anger, I'll just be right over there, hiding in the thicket."

She grins at his silliness, but secretly agrees. Please, no anger. The less fuel she has to feed Rage, the quieter her head remains and the longer he stays asleep. She wishes he would just sleep forever.

Anger won't work, but neither will happiness. Her happy thoughts always lead to other emotions. Rage. Sadness. Fear. There's no telling which direction her mood will take if her happy memories turn sour. They're unpredictable and she can't take the chance of getting mad. Sadness was what worked last time, so that's the emotion she'll go with now.

She chooses her first memories of waking up in the mental ward, memories of opening her eyes to the dingy, white ceiling of her new home. Of finding out that she'd been there for weeks already, drugged and subdued, so that her mind could 'heal'. Thoughts of losing her family had consumed her in those days. Thoughts of losing her father had broken her. She thinks back on how she'd done nothing but lie there on that uncomfortable cot with tears trickling out of her eyes, day after day after day….

Oh, now she's done it. She starts crying in real time, ugly sobbing in front of everyone. But it achieves the desired effects. As the memories of losing her loved ones sends waves of sorrow and despair coursing through her, the tingling heat in her hands slowly cools and then disappears. When she opens her tear-flooded eyes, the white smoky tendrils trailing from her hands are gone. The bubble is no longer connected to her....*and so it floats up and starts drifting away!*

"Oh no!" she cries as she reaches out for it.

Rowana's queenly face shows just the slightest trace of fear as Ecko's fingers fall short but manage to barely brush against it, causing it to float further away. Fenixx rushes in to rescue his love. He flies up and lands on top of the bubble and pushes down on it, using the power of his wings against the air to push it back. He struggles with all his might, his little wings fluttering in a blur in order to produce enough force to send it back down.

When it's back within her reach, Ecko takes it in one hand and catches Fenixx with the other as he drops down from overexertion. She's not quite sure what to do now that she's got a tiny naked man lying on the palm of her hand, and she doesn't think she has ever been in a more awkward situation in her life. She tries to ignore him and his teeny tiny weenie, she really does. But she can't do it, especially not with his little man buns pressing against her skin.

She lowers him to the ground and tries her best to *gently* set him down in the dirt. But she's ungraceful at the best of times and downright klutzy and clumsy when she's stressed. And naked men stress her out, ok? Apparently even miniature men that are roughly the size of her pointer finger. She fairly flings him off like a booger, that's how fast he goes tumbling from her hand to the dirt. She unconsciously scrubs the offending hand against her pajama bottoms before turning her attention to the FireQueen. She lifts the bubble up, so that they can speak, face to tiny face.

Although Ecko had been briefly distracted by...uumm *things*, she's still crying her eyes out. The tears hadn't let up even a bit. They're still pouring down her face in two steady streams. And looking at the bubble jail she has clutched in her hands, realizing that her brilliant idea to make herself sad had only halfway worked, turns the tear streams into tear rivers.

"I'm sorry, Rowana," she whispers. "I don't know what to do to get you out. I've condemned you to death! I can't believe I've killed a fairy, a fairy *queen*, at that. Oh, I'm going to hell for sure!" But then something happens, something unexpected and amazing and magical. The trails of tears lift up off of her face and stretch through the air towards the bubble!

"Your eyes!" Boodark whisper/shouts. "The cracks are disappearing! It looks like the 'ice' is melting away, flowing out along with your tears. Whatever you're doing, keep doing it! Keep crying. I think the magic will recede along with your tears."

They all watch as the strange tear-trail floats through the air and begins to pool on the surface of the bubble. Her tears pour over it, coating it in liquid silver. Then it dries and hardens like a hard candy shell.

The entire FireFairy army screams in outrage as the silver tears paint the bubble, completely obscuring their view of their Queen.

They surge forward as one and let loose their flaming puke-balls just as the last of the tears leave her face and settle upon the silver-coated bubble in her hand. As the fireballs close in, the bubble flares brightly *from the inside* and the cracks that had previously been in Ecko's eyes appear on the surface of the bubble.

The light within glows brighter and brighter, shining out through the cracks so intensely that she has to squint to look at it. Fenixx cries out in fear and dismay. He flies up and perches on her outstretched wrist to be closer to his love, no matter what may come. He throws his hands over his heart as if it's cracking too, and fiery teardrops trickle down his cheeks as with one last blinding flash of light, the bubble bursts. Silver fragments explode outwards like glass shrapnel and then come to a complete, sudden stop, hovering in the air all around them.

Standing on Ecko's open palm, in the midst of all those frozen-in-time bubble shards, is Rowana, Queen of all FireFairies… and she's been changed. She's different…*More* somehow.

Before anyone can react, or even take a breath, Rowana throws her hands up and directs all those broken bubble pieces to fly outwards and stop the incoming fireballs that her army had launched just moments before. The shards intercept every single flaming puke-ball at the last possible second, just before they could land and set the world on fire.

And it causes a chain reaction. The shards melt, re-liquifying when they come in contact with the flames. As they melt, they coat the flaming spitballs, thereby putting out the fires. In other words, the two opposing forces cancel each other out completely. No more flame missiles and no more bubble shrapnel. Ecko watches as what's left behind (probably solidified balls of vomit that she has no desire to examine closer) drops down out of the air to land in the dirt around her feet.

MeanGreen glares pure hatred at her from behind Rowana's back as she lifts off of Ecko's fingertips and puts distance between them. She's changed a bit too, grown darker. Before she'd gotten trapped in the exploding bubble, she'd been a jade color, as her name indicated.

'She'll probably have to change her name' Ecko absentmindedly muses, *'because now she's more of a forest, or perhaps a hunter green.'*

But then she turns back to study Rowana more closely and she dismisses Jaida altogether. She should have paid better attention though, because Jaida, aka MeanGreen has turned into Meaner-Greener, and she's got a raging, all-consuming hate-on for Ecko.

Rowana though, no one would be able to dismiss *her*. She'd been amazing before, but now she is *spectacular*, dazzlingly so. Her wings have blackened and grown huge, all jagged edges and sharp points. And they're on fire, or made of fire, or they create their own fire. Whatever the case, however it works, they burn unbelievably bright with all the brilliant colors of the hottest fires.

Her crown has changed too, the points of it stretch up taller. The black diamonds and blood-red rubies shimmer from the light of the flames that now dance along the headband. Her sparkler hair is longer, flowing faster and snapping with even more sparks. Additional flames have been added to her dress, and it now has a long train of fire at the back that trails across Ecko's palm, overflowing and dripping like burning, melted plastic down the sides.

She feels no heat, no painful effects of literally holding fire in her hands, but she doesn't even question the logistics of it. It's magic, pure and simple, and she has *ever* been a believer in magic. It seems that her own magic has somehow managed to enhance Rowana's, blessed her with a mystical upgrade.

Everything about the FireQueen is now... *More.* Even her boobs appear bigger and Ecko glances down at her own barely adequate bosom in hopes that some of that upgrade magic has affected her too. 'Of course, not' she snorts in disgust. No such luck.

While everyone else stands frozen in awe of the newly improved queen, Fenixx drops to his knees and kneels before her. "My Queen," he fervently whispers as he bows his head in reverence. The FireFairies, all still hovering in the air, immediately mimic him. They kneel and bow their heads too, even as they flutter in midair around her.

Rowana gestures for them to rise as she begins to speak, her voice strong and proud and passionate. "Long have we, the FireFairies, known that this world was dying. Long have we listened with fearful hearts to its dying gasps for breath. Long have we felt ourselves fading, felt our own sparks dimming. Trapped as we are in the death throes of this land, we have all felt our EverFire struggle to stay aflicker."

A single, blazing fire tear trails down Rowana's cheek and she has to look away in order to regain control of her emotions. After a moment of silence, she composes herself enough to turn back and face her people once more. "Long have we known that our numbers were dwindling. Our females lost the ability to bear Firelings… All but I. It became my sole responsibility to bring us new life, and for the past hundred years it has been so. I have dedicated myself to bringing as many Newlings to our Hives as I could possibly manage. Like a brood nag, I spent my life conceiving and gestating and birthing each of those precious lives."

"Out of my three hundred and eighty-six eggs that went into our EverFire, three hundred and thirty-nine of them hatched and flew back out of the flames to become productive Hive members. My heart broke for the forty-seven Newlings that I lost, that *we* lost. I mourn them still, even now. But I couldn't stop. I could *never* stop. I couldn't give up. I had to continue. I birthed more and more Firelings, even as my tears fell for my lost ones. I knew my duty, and I did it to the best of my ability…. Until that magic left even me."

The FireFairies gasp in shock and start murmuring amongst themselves. Rowana raises her voice to be heard over them. "I know that many of you believed that I was merely taking a break from mothering. Some of you even believed that I was being selfish and neglecting my duties as your Queen. Only a select few of you knew the truth, that our Fire magic has faded so drastically that we have now completely lost the ability to procreate. The truth is, I have been unable to conceive Newlings for the past three year-cycles. No amount of trying on my part has resulted in success. I have lived in secret sorrow at failing you. I have lived in secret regret and fear for our very existence. But I fear no longer!"

Rowana reaches up and removes a necklace from around her neck that had thus far gone unnoticed, hidden by the living flames of her dress. It has what appears to be a long black crystal, shaped like a bean pod dangling from it.

Ecko watches curiously as Rowana wraps her tiny hands around it, closes her eyes, and calls to her flames. Her hands light up and fire engulfs the pod. The flames spread along the length of it and then the pod splits open to reveal eight tiny seeds. They're not much bigger than grains of rice, onyx colored with fire-tone sparkles and specks. And those fire speckles are *moving*. They dance and flicker like dark flames in the night. The FireFairies crowd in closer, all pushing and jostling one another for a better position, until Rowana holds them up higher.

"Behold! Ecko's magic has given us back our home!" she cries out, and the entire army goes wild, screaming and crying and turning somersaults in the air. The females hug and clasp hands and the males pound one another on the back like men do.

Rowana sees the confused, but happy-that-everyone-is-happy look on her face and quietly explains. "These are the last remaining FireTree seeds. We lost our beloved FireForest many long years ago. One terrible Pale, their sparks started burning out. They just grew cold. We never knew why. We could do nothing to stop it, could do nothing to rekindle their will to live. And so, we watched them wither and die, one by one."

"Sometimes, it all seems like only one Pale past, but it was really so long ago now that many of my people have never even seen a FireTree. Oh, but how we all feel the loss! Even the ones that have never seen them with their own eyes feel their absence in their hearts. When our FireForest died, we were forced to move, to find a new home far from all that we'd ever known."

"We lost so many of our brothers and sisters during that time…. Whole Hives lost, wiped out entirely. It was so terrible that we do not speak of it unless absolutely necessary, and when we must, we refer to it as the Flameless Age. It took many years and countless tears to find a new home, one that was suitable to our Fires."

"The field of FlameFlowers that we finally found was nowhere near the equal of what we'd lost, but we were grateful to find it. We tend the flowers most diligently and with *every* respect. But we mourn the loss of our FireTrees. Their sparks were what kindled our EverFire, a fire that has burned for all time and never dies."

"It burns still yet, but not with those magnificent flames of old. It's grown small and weak without the FireTree sparks to fuel it. I have long feared that the time would come when our EverFire would burn out entirely, because that will be the Pale that we, the FireFairies, lose the last embers of hope in our hearts. That would be the Pale that we truly begin to die."

The FireFairies have grown quiet, all immersed in their Queen's telling of their history. But Rowana's next words rile them right back up once more. "Long have we waited, hoping for one to come forth with the power to heal us, to save us. *You* are the savior. When your tears coated the bubble with your magic, I saw a vision, a glimpse of the future. I felt the truth of it, the *conviction* of it flow through me. *You* will save this land, just as you have already saved my people."

Murmurs and excited whispers spread throughout the crowd and all eyes turn to stare at her. "Oh crap," she whispers as apprehension makes her heart stutter. This is just *all* she needs… more people believing that she's more than she really is, thinking that she could somehow save them. She is no savior. "Umm, Rowana… may I speak to you in private for a moment?"

But the FireQueen shakes her head. "No, Ecko. I know that you do not yet believe, but one Pale you *will* recognize it as truth." She turns back and addresses her people once more. "I know that we have sworn to never trust the words of a ground stomper. We have sworn an oath to never, ever pledge allegiance to any other than our own Fire-kind. But this Pale everything changes."

And then Rowana gracefully drops to her knees and regally bows her head… *to her*. "Oh, crap. Oh crap, crap, crap," she repeats as Rowana lifts her head, and with fiery tears in her eyes, proclaims an oath of fealty, to *her*…a nobody, a massive screwup, queen of crazyville and wanderer of mental ward halls.

"I, Rowana Davina Everleigh of the EmberWinds Hive, last remaining descendant of Queen Nymphadrorna, and current Queen of all FireFairies, do so swear my allegiance to you, Ecko Zyana, Irredarr's newest Wandelaar, protector of the weak and innocent. From this Pale and forever more, I pledge my fealty to you and no one else."

She stands back up and flutters up off her hand to fly forward and seal the bargain with a kiss. Rowana presses her tiny lips to hers and for just a moment, the two of them become engulfed in brilliant blue flames. It burns out within seconds, but the two women will never, ever forget the feeling of that blue fire uniting them in sisterhood.

Rowana flutters down onto Ecko's shoulder and turns back to her fairies... fairies that are staring with wide, shocked eyes at what they had just witnessed. And as her tears begin to flow, raining liquid fire down her face, she rejoices, "Not only has she given us back our home, but her magic has also given us back the magic to bear Newlings! Come, my brothers, my sisters! Come, share this gift with me!"

Red Daughter #1 (the mouthy one that had been so eager to flame broil Ecko just minutes ago) zooms in like a bat out of hell. A dark headed, muscle-happy man falls in right behind her and places his hands on her shoulders. Rowana smiles and tearfully whispers, "No longer will you have to care for my Firelings, wishing that they were yours instead, my daughter. You will finally bear your very own."

Then she leans in and places a kiss upon her daughter's lips. That blue flame momentarily flares between them and then engulfs Red Daughter #1. The flames coalesce over and then sinks *into* her belly. She throws her hands up to cradle her stomach, crying out as she turns to face her mate. The fire-tears pour down her cheeks like molten lava.

"It's true!" she sobs. "It's all true! I felt the magic enter my womb and awaken it."

The worry drains from the man's face and his eyes light up with hope when she adds, "I can bear your Firelings!" Now muscleman is sobbing too, laughing in between the kisses that he covers her face with.

He lifts her up above his head and spins her around and around, but then seems to remember that the two of them aren't alone. He lowers her back down, cups her face in his hands, and wipes the tears off her cheeks with his thumbs. He places the sweetest little kiss on the tip of her nose and then the two of them turn to give thanks for the miracle they just received. They bow low before their queen first, then rise up and turn to her.

Red Daughter #1 declares, "We almost killed you, and you, in turn have given us back our home and our Newlings. I have no words to express the gratitude I hold in my heart for you. Rowana is my mother and my queen, and I will always be loyal to her above all others. But I believe every word she has spoken is true. You *will* be the one to save our world."

She kneels and bows her head, and muscleman immediately drops down beside her to do the same. "I swear allegiance to you Ecko, with only my Queen held in higher authority. I owe you a debt that can never be repaid. But know that you have made an Evermore ally this Pale. Should you ever have need of me, know that I will not hesitate to answer your call."

Muscleman simply states, "I will fly with you," and somehow those five simple words hold as much meaning and merit as Red Daughter's longer proclamation. The two of them rise up, flutter forward, and quickly place their kisses upon her cheek. Then they move aside and turn to watch the rest of their Hive follow in their wing path. They hold tightly to one another, as one by one, the entire not-so-angry-anymore mob receives the gift and then pledges their allegiance… all except for the ones that refuse, that is.

Thirteen sullen-faced FireFairies hover close to Jaida, aka MeanerGreener. She must have decided to stay and observe the outcome. She very obviously has no intention of letting go of her anger, and she certainly wouldn't be joining Ecko's list of new allies. She watches the proceedings from the tree line, glaring at her with narrowed hate-eyes and silently fuming at Rowana for what she sees as the ultimate betrayal… siding with a ground stomper over fairy-kin.

Rowana tries to reason with her, urges her and the other malcontent Fae to reconsider, to not leave the Hive as self-appointed outcasts. But nothing she says does any good and she cries at the loss of them, as they turn and disappear into the thicket.

Jaida meets Ecko's eyes across the distance and repeats, "No peace," before she follows them. It's a promise of retribution, a proclamation of unpleasantries to come.

Rowana earnestly advises, "Do not underestimate her. She has an unreasonable hatred for you burning deep within her. Plus, we know naught of how your magic affected her. We can only hope that it merely changed her appearance and did nothing to enhance her powers, as it did mine."

Ecko looks down at Boodark, who's been suspiciously quiet for far too long. "You have nothing to say? Really? Today truly *is* a day of miracles!" she teases him. He shrugs and mutters, "I got nothing. I just watched an entire army of raging spitfire hell-fairies intent on un-aliving us get converted into our new best friends."

Before she has a chance to respond to that, Fenixx flies forward and clears his throat to get her attention. "Ahem. Excuse me for interrupting, but I wish to swear fealty to you also… if you'll have me, that is. Or, if you prefer, you can wait and make your decision after the council has decided what my fate shall be. I'll understand if you do not wish to be allied with an outcast."

The beautiful little man looks away from her then, but not in shame that he may be cast out of the Hive. He turns away, because he just can't seem to keep his eyes off his lady love. Rowana and a group of ten others, five females and five males, have distanced themselves and seem to be having an impromptu meeting.

"They would still cast you out? After all that's changed today?" she snaps in disbelief. She points toward the group, "They're deciding now?"

Fenixx nods without ever looking away from Rowana.

"Well, I won't let them!" she vehemently cries.

That has him turning his head to look at her with surprise stamped on his features. "It is the FireFairy way. Weakness is not tolerated," he says again.

"Do you love her?"

"Of course. She is my Queen," he automatically replies.

"No! *Do you love her*? Not her as queen, but her as a woman… as Rowana."

He turns his gaze back on her, out there fighting to keep him from being exiled, and his face instantly softens. "I do," he whispers.

"And would you do it again?" she asks. "Would you beg for her life again, now that the danger has passed and she's safe once more. Now that you've had time to think about the repercussions of your actions. Would you make the same choice and plead for her life again?"

Rowana's head lifts up and her stricken, heartbroken eyes meet his. The council's decision is written all over her face. He would be expelled, banished as an outcast.

Fenixx pulls his shoulders back proudly as he turns to face her. Even with tears in his eyes, he's the bravest, truest little thing she's ever seen. He nods and proudly declares, "I would plead for her time and time again. For all eternity."

She smiles. She can't help it, true love and all that sappiness. It gets her every time. "That's what I wanted to hear. Quick! Kneel and do your pledging fealty thing. Keep it simple and fast; the meeting's ending and I don't think it resulted in your favor."

Fenixx kneels and bows his head. "I swear to always…"

But that's as far as he gets because she cuts him off. "Yeah, yeah, you swear. Now get up and kiss me. *Hurry!*"

He looks up at her in utter confusion, but he does what she demands of him. The council and a silently sobbing Rowana arrive (with the rest of the Hive fluttering at their heels) just in time to watch as he rises up and presses his lips to her cheek. So, they *all* witness when her eyes suddenly roll back in her head, and she falls to the ground in a dead faint.

"What have you done?" Boodark screams at the startled Fenixx, as he hop/runs over to where she's lying still upon the ground.

But then she starts twitching, as if she's having a seizure, her eyelids fluttering to show nothing but the whites of her eyes. She shakes and twitches for thirty seconds or so, and then her eyes pop open as she loudly sucks in a huge gasp of air. She sits up, presses a feeble, shaky hand to her head, and turns her wide, shocked eyes to the FireFairies.

"I've just had a vision... a vision of the future!" she whispers and then pauses as everyone crowds in closer to hear her. "I have seen a future in which your FireTrees thrive. They've grown tall and have spread wide to create a brand new FireForest. The Hives have made their nests high up in the branches, hidden and protected by the flame-leaves." She pauses and turns to Rowana and asks, "Blue? FireTrees are bright, brilliant shades of red, but the branches are marbled with streaks of blue?"

The queen can't seem to get her voice to work, so she merely nods her head in wonder as Ecko continues. "I saw tiny Firelings, at least a hundred of them, zipping and zooming about, giggling and throwing fireballs at each other. I saw a large, magnificent fire surrounded by stones in the middle of the forest. It burned so bright and threw black sparks high up into the air!"

She glances around at her captive audience. There's not a single dry eye in the lot of them. Her own eyes return to Rowana, and she smiles gently. "I saw that you no longer lead the Hives alone. I saw that you chose a king to rule beside you, to share your duties and responsibilities." She turns and points at Fenixx. "Him. I saw Fenixx at your side, wearing a crown to match your own."

The FireFairies gasp and murmur amongst one another. Someone hidden in the back shouts, "That is *not* how our Hives work. We have only *ever* been ruled by a Queen!"

An obviously older female responds to that hasty outcry. "That is not true, Chara. We had kings as well as queens many, many years ago. The tradition of matriarchy in the Hives began when Queen Nymphadrorna ruled. She loved a female, but the council decreed that she could not claim her as a mate. So, she in turn refused to take a mate at all, saying that she would rather rule alone than have a king forced upon her."

Suddenly everyone's arguing, bickering back and forth and tempers are beginning to ignite. So, Ecko holds her hands up and shouts over the noise. "I have seen it! It does no good to argue about it. I have seen it, and it will come to pass. You should all be rejoicing right now, instead of bickering. Fenixx is a good, strong male. Brave and true. He has fire blazing in his heart, but he is also calm and cool and collected... just as your Queen is. I think he is a perfect mate for her, don't you agree? And I *know* that he will be a great and mighty FireKing. I have seen it, after all."

A blonde-headed male flutters forward a bit and tells her, "I believe in you, Savior, and I trust in your magic. I will accept your words and I will welcome Fenixx as my king, *if* Queen Rowana wishes it to be so."

Murmurs of "yes" and "I agree" and "I accept" ring out throughout the crowd and all eyes turn to see what their Queen will do. Rowana doesn't even notice them. She only has eyes for her man, and he stands tall and proud, but clearly terrified of what she'll say. She flutters up close to him and gazes up into his eyes. "I choose you, Fenixx. I'll always choose you. Tell me you'll accept the responsibility. Say that you will be my king."

Fenixx cups her face in his hands and whispers, "I just died a thousand deaths waiting for you to say that you want me. I love you, Rowana, I always have. You are the fire that lights my soul. Of course, I'll be King to your Queen."

Then he leans down and takes her lips with his and that blue flame, the flame born from Rowana's and Ecko's mingling magics, flares up at the joining of their lips. It engulfs the couple, the flames dancing over them, swirling so fast that it creates a wind. Rowana and Fenixx are blissfully unaware of the world outside of their embrace and the flames swirl faster and faster around them, until they're completely encased inside a burning vortex of royal blue flames.

Everyone, as a whole, takes a breath and holds it, watching...waiting. They don't have to wait long. The vortex begins to slow, almost as soon as it begins, and the flames recede and quickly die down. And everyone releases their pent up breathes in ohhs and awws and shocked gasps, as the last of the flames disappear, and the newly crowned king is revealed.

He is *more* now, too. His wings have grown considerably larger, and a crown to match his Queen's now rests upon his brow. Rowana bows her head and whispers, "My King."

Ecko gets up out of the dirt and turns to the crowd of FireFairies. "I present to you the royal couple, Queen Rowana and King Fenixx!" She yelps and jumps back with a laugh as the FireFairies surge forward to welcome the new royals with happy hearts and excited cries. Boodark flies up to perch on her shoulder. He shakes his head in baffled amazement and repeats, "I've still got nothing."

Once emotions settle down a bit, the upcoming goodbyes are inevitable. Tears and cries of thanks and promises to never forget what happened here are called out as the FireFairies take their leave. They're anxious to go home and plant seeds...FireTree seeds *and* Fireling seeds. They want nothing more than to regrow their beloved FireTree Forest and make the babies that they'd been denied for so long.

"I can't believe that worked," Ecko whispers to herself as she watches them disappear into the thicket and beyond. But of course, Boodark hears her.

"You can't believe what worked?"

She walks over to her bundle of belongings, picks up her sleeping bag, spreads it out, and then crawls inside. It's finally quiet in the Bumbershoot glade and she's decided that a nap is in order. They've wasted too much of the Pale to get started walking now. Besides, she is *exhausted.* Boodark hops over and pokes her in the back with a claw. "You can't just say something like that and not explain it! Open your eyes and talk to me! You can't believe *what* worked?"

She smiles and barely manages to pry her eyes open. "I lied," she murmurs with a yawn. "I can't see visions of the future."

Boodark spits and sputters and shouts questions at her, but the only answers he receives in return are tiny little sleep snores, because she's fallen fast asleep. Matchmaking and proclamations of make-believe visions of the future will wear a girl out, every time.

18

DO IT FOR YOUR WIFE

Krispin and The Lokskell

His Night Shades, or Shadows as some call them, spread out and search outside the town limits for someone suitable to carry out his plans. He doesn't worry about failure; it never even crosses his mind. They'll find someone to fill his needs. They always do. They are extensions of himself, after all. They don't fail in the tasks that he sets for them, whether it's locating an acceptable meat suit to inhabit, or convincing those few stubborn fools that need persuading to do as he commands.

There are always willing fools to do his bidding (or not so willing, it matters not to him). None can hide from his Shades, they are the perfect spies. Shadows can linger anywhere, everywhere. They fill every crack and crevice and lurk behind every object. One can never be sure if the shadows surrounding them are merely the ordinary, harmless kind, or if they're his deadly Shades... *if* they even take notice at all, that is. There are very few beings that choose to peer closer into the deep, dark niches of the world around them. They're much too afraid of what they'll find. There are even fewer souls that are powerful, or brave enough to resist his will, should he decide to set his Shades upon them.

For this particular task, the Lokskell has need of someone that won't be recognized by his daughter's lover, the blue man that had somehow, miraculously survived his sanguinary attentions. He needs some unknown stranger, a traveler or a wanderer, perhaps. Someone who can convey a message without rousing Krispin's suspicions. He cares not who the unlucky bastard is, just so long as it's someone that he can manipulate, with Krispin none the wiser. His plan will only work if the blue beast is completely unaware of his involvement.

His Night Shades are stretched thin, searching far and wide beyond the borders of that dreadful little town that Samara had gleefully escaped from. Soon enough, they come upon a man out in the middle of the Plains of the Damned. He's traveling in the direction of the town, leading a scream-brayer mule along behind him with a worn, frayed rope. There's a woman, most likely the man's mate, perched upon the creature's back.

The scream-brayer has been domesticated, which is no easy task to accomplish. They're notoriously difficult to capture, due to the extreme level of panic that dominate their lives. The breaking of them is even more arduous for that same reason. The unfortunate things are nervous and agitated at the best of times, and downright deranged and hysterical the rest of the time.

The creature's bodies are equine in appearance, large, strong mule-type animals. But their faces are something else altogether. Their heads are shaped like a donkeys, but much, much broader.

They typically have anywhere from eight to twelve eyes and a grossly over-large mouth that's packed full of needle-sharp teeth. They could easily bite a grown man's head off, if they only had the sense to realize it. (For a creature with such a large head, with the capacity for an equally large brain, they're not the cleverest of beasts.)

And they *scream*. They scream and bray and cry so loudly (hence the name) that they can shatter eardrums from several yards away. The only way to domesticate the creatures is to blind their eyes. All of them. Taking their sight calms them and they finally, blessedly go silent. It's widely believed that the creature's many eyes can see things that no one else could see, horrible things that coexist alongside the living, tangible beings. As controversial as it sounds, blinding them is, in all reality, an act of kindness, even though the deed is never done out of compassion. They're blinded so that they can be used, just as this one had been.

Perfect, the Lokskell thinks as his Shades 'show' him the potential candidate. *This man will do, and the transport beast will help him carry out his tasks all the faster.* Yes, this is a most fortunate opportunity.

The Night Shades move in at his telepathic command and the man watches in hopeless dismay, as they close in… the inky black Shadows flowing up into his woman's nose, pouring into her mouth and down her throat. It takes the Shadows, and therefore the Lokskell, a moment to adjust to this host. Not only is it a female (which he normally doesn't bother to inhabit, due to their frail, weak bodies and typically softer inclinations), but because of the unexpected life in her hugely distended belly. That's certainly a new, disgusting first for him.

The woman turns blacked-out eyes to the man and when she speaks, she does so in a deep, manly voice. "Dineel! How are you? I hope you don't mind me availing myself on your mate like this, but I find that I'm in need of assistance, and *you* are the unlucky imbecile that I've chosen to help me! Isn't that exciting news, indeed?"

The man, realizing that he's being addressed by none other than the Lokskell himself, immediately falls to his knees and bows his head, exactly how the Shadow Lord likes to be greeted.

"Well met, Dineel!" the Lokskell praises. "Arise and listen closely to my words, for I have an urgent task for you to undertake and I suggest that you be quick as can be about it. It seems that the shock of having such a large, powerful man such as myself enter your mate has thrown her headlong into labor. Your spawn will soon make an appearance and you'll want to be done with this business and on your way before it arrives. Let me assure you right now that if I'm still inside this body when she spills her filth from between her thighs, I will make you suffer pain like you've never even imagined."

The man scrambles to his feet. "Please, M'lord. Mercy! I'll do whatever it is you need of me. Command me!"

The woman throws her head back as the Lokskell's deep, rumbling laugh bursts from her lips. "Well, of course you will! Now listen very closely. There's a man, a blue skinned aberration in the town ahead… that *is* where you're headed, is it not?" He doesn't wait for the man's affirmation as he continues. "Krispin is the creature's name. Find him, but do not approach him directly. Casually spread the word… in his presence, of how you came across a beautiful, but violently angry, flame-haired female. I care not what story you come up with; I care only that it's *believable.* She's an angry little spitfire, vindictive and cruel just for the fun of being so, but she is not stupid. And neither is he."

"Whatever lie you come up with will need to include you witnessing some sort of nastiness on her part. If he comes to you and demands a description, she stands only as high as your chest, a tiny little thing with wild red curls and vivid green eyes. A pleasingly womanly body, with shapely curves… although I *do* suppose you shouldn't mention that. Krispin was her lover, and a brutish, jealous one at that. He'll probably not take it well if he believes you were ogling his woman."

"*Convince* him that it was his woman that you saw… without him being aware that you are doing so. Make it known that when you came across her, she was entering the Black Forest. He needs to go after her, and you must see to it that he does just that. Now go. We will eagerly be waiting for your return." He makes the woman stroke her hand down her belly in that way that expectant mothers do. It *should* have been comforting… a loving, motherly thing to do, but instead it's blatantly threatening.

"Yes, M'lord! I will see to it, right away! But if I may… you could release her and use me instead. I will gladly let you inside and do anything you want of me. Gladly M'lord!"

The Lokskell/woman snorts at him. "As if you could stop me, if that is what I wished to do. But it is *not* what I wish. The whole purpose of this entire, elaborate charade is so that Krispin doesn't know of my involvement. If I switched to your body, he would sense me there. The worthless louse can *always* detect my presence. He'll suspect a trap if he thinks I'm involved in any way, and then he wouldn't go after her. He *must* go after her."

"Now, help this bloated bitch down off this scream-nag, before I make her *toss* herself down. You'll need to move quickly, and the mule can walk faster than you can run. But if I were you, I'd make him run just as fast as his feet can fly over these sands, because I just *may* get bored and decide to amuse myself with your woman whilst we wait."

The man helps her down and clings to her for a moment. "Please, M'lord," he whimpers desperately. "Shelann needs help! Our babe is on its way, and it's her first birthing! Can I not bring her with me? We could part ways at the town's edge. This Krispin man need never know of her at all. He wouldn't never know about you, M'lord. Not never!"

The Lokskell directs the woman's hand up to lovingly caress his cheek. "Dineel?" Shelann/Lokskell croons as the woman's hand drifts down, down, down his body, until she can grasp his manhood with all the strength of a snapjaw's bite. His face instantly goes red as his breath gets stuck on an inhale that he can't seem to follow through with.

"If you do not move your arse this instant, I will rip your babe from this rotten womb and beat you to death with it. Do I make myself clear?"

The man is unable to speak, still unable to even take a breath, but he nods his head vigorously. The hand abruptly turns him loose as Shelann smiles that beautiful smile up at him, the one that he loves so much.

"Very good!" the Lokskell praises, his voice a shocking blasphemy coming from those beloved lips. "Get going, hurry now. Every moment that you remain here arguing is just one more that she'll have to spend alone when her time draws near."

The man cradles his wounded, outraged member in his hand to protect it from further agony, as he throws himself onto the scream-brayer's back and kicks it into a dick flopping, ball bruising gallop.

Things have changed drastically by the time the man finally returns. He races back in, the scream-brayer exhausted and whimpering from being rode so hard. Dineel jumps to the ground, his eyes frantic, as he takes in the horror. His mate, his lovely Shelann is lying in the dirt, her legs spread wide with his mewling newborn son between them in a spill of blood and birth fluids. Standing over them both is an unfamiliar Wartal, a male one that is so ugly it's actually difficult to look straight at his face.

The repulsive brute points down at the mess between the woman's legs and complains, "That was *most* unpleasant and I'm sorely vexed that I had to endure even a second of it. Thankfully my man, Blegulful arrived and offered his body, so that we could continue our business."

Dineel drops to his knees and gently touches his woman's face. Her head lolls to the side, her eyes wide, staring accusingly at him. "*Oh no.* Oh, Shelann. No, no, no, no." He leans over and presses his forehead to hers as tears stream down his face.

"You took too long. She just couldn't wait for you." The Lokskell's voice comes out of the Wartal's mouth and Dineel understands that he'd switched bodies, moving from Shelann to this brute.

"Get up! It is too late for her. I feel no pity for you whatsoever. You shouldn't have taken so long. Now tell me, did you succeed? Is Krispin even now going after my daughter?"

The man climbs back to his feet, his eyes and nose streaming. "No, M'lord. The blue creature was drinking heavily at The Chopping Block when I arrived. He was with a woman, but he didn't seem interested in anything other than getting soused."

"I did just like you bade me do. I told a tale of coming across an angry, young female during my travels. A beauty, with hair the color of flames, I bragged. I told it loudly to be sure he heard every word of it, but he seemed to take no notice."

"I did my best, M'lord, but he paid me no heed, no matter what I said. He only cared about emptying glass after glass of whiskey. I followed him when he'd finally had his fill. I dared to hope that it had all been an act on his part and that he'd been paying attention to my words all along. I'd hoped that he was, in fact, preparing to head posthaste out of town, but all he did was drag the female behind a building and bugger her. I didn't stick around after I saw that. I knew that I'd failed you."

He looks down at his woman and sobs anew. "I had hoped that you would show us mercy, but it's too late now. My Shelann is gone." He bends down and reaches for his son, but the revolting Wartal beats him to it. He snatches the infant up by a tiny, fragile leg and the child lets out a wail at the rough handling.

"What?" the man howls. "Give him to me! You'll hurt him, you will, handling him like that! Please, M'lord, he's my son. He's all I have left!"

The Shadow Lord feels no sympathy and he certainly doesn't feel merciful. "It is too late for your mate. She's dead and there's no bringing her back. But perhaps it's not too late for this wretched, wrinkly thing. Go back. Surely Krispin will be done fornicating by the time you make it back. Go back and *this* time convince him. Speak directly to him if you must. Mention her name, Samara. Perhaps tell him that she sent you to find him and pass along the information of her whereabouts, as an invitation to join her. I care not what you tell him, just keep my name off your tongue."

The Wartal/Lokskell pulls the infant in and cradles him to his chest. "Hurry now, make haste. I know nothing of younglings, especially not the newling kinds. Just how long can they survive without proper care and nourishment?"

The devastated new father drops back down on his knees once more and clutches at the Wartal's leg as he begs. "Please, Sire, let me take him with me. He needs immediate attention. He'll not live for long… not like this! I'll do it! I don't care what it takes. I'll convince Krispin to go. I swear on my soul that I'll get it done. Just please, please let me help my boy while I do it!"

The Wartal/Lokskell shakes him loose from his leg and then kicks him away. "You will first take care of what you should have already done. Then, and only then, may you attempt to save the whelpling. But go ahead. Proceed with wasting everyone's time. Especially your son's.

"Just remember that every minute of my time you waste brings him a minute closer to joining his bitch. Every passing minute is a minute that he could be spending greedily suckling on a wet-nurse's tits. Oh! But I'm surprisingly feeling generous all of a sudden. I'll tell you what I'm going to do. I'll make this meat suit walk towards town. I'll have him carry the child closer, so that you won't have as far to travel to retrieve him. Therefore, you will be able to get him to safety all the faster. How's that for generous? Hmm?"

Dineel climbs to his feet and wipes his face with the back of his hand, smearing tears and snot as he glances down at his wife. "What about her?" he asks in a broken-hearted whisper.

"Oh, I'm sure she'll wait right here for you to conclude your business and return for her. She loves you, Dineel. She wouldn't abandon you!"

The man's lips tremble for just a moment as he meets the Lokskell/Wartal's eyes. Those eyes narrow into a malicious glare. "Tick tock, Dineel. Tick tock," the Lokskell threatens and then laughs as the man spins away and throws himself back onto his mule.

"Good man! Make haste!" he calls to his rapidly retreating backside. "Well, now we wait, little disgusting one."

Hysterical and desperately distraught, Dineel returns in half the time it had taken him before. His face is a bloody, bruised wreck and one eye has swollen completely shut. "It worked, M'lord!" he crows even before he's dismounted the poor, wretched beast's back.

"It took some time, because I couldn't find him. I finally decided to go back to the eatery to wait for him at the bar where I put on a good show of getting nice and soused…and loud. I rambled on and on to everyone that came in about the mysterious flame haired beauty that I'd met, the beautiful seductress named Samara."

"It didn't take long for someone to get the word to Krispin that there was a stranger in town singing *his* woman's praises. He barreled in there, growling and snarling like a rabid beast and then he was just *on* me…tearing into me so fast I thought he was like to kill me! *'Where is she? Where is she?'* he kept screaming right up in my face, but he wouldn't stop hitting me long enough for me to tell him."

"At last, I just threw my hands up over my head and started screaming right back at him, trying to yell louder than *he* was in hopes that he would hear me and let me go. *'In the Black Forest! The Black Forest! Samara is in the Black Forest!'* I just yelled it over and over again, until he finally stopped beating me. We both grew silent, as he dragged me up so that he could look in my eyes. I said it one last time, *'Samara is in the Black Forest'*."

He smiled and slapped a kiss right on my bloody mouth, threw me back down to the floor, and then turned and ran. I dragged myself to my feet and followed him for a short time, but I couldn't keep up, not even close. But I can tell you that he headed in the direction of the Black Forest… along the coast of the Dead Sea."

Dineel stops to catch his breath and wipe the sweat and blood from his one good eye, trying to focus on his son cradled in the Wartal's arms. "Please M'lord. May I have my son now?" he begs, fearing the absolute worst as he holds out his arms for the oh, so quiet and still infant.

The Lokskell/Wartal grunts and says, "Gladly, although I've got to say that you may want to find someone to take the disgusting little runt off your hands at the earliest opportunity. Do yourself a favor and rid yourself of it and never look back, because it is loud and obnoxious and *wet*. Fortunately for you, it finally grew quiet and fell asleep."

"But then it *pissed* on me, it actually dared to piss on me! Nasty, unpleasant things, infants are. This is exactly the reason I never involve myself with the rearing of my own offspring. They're hideous and repulsive. I came very close to breaking our deal when *this* one decided to leak on me. You're *very* lucky that you arrived when you did. Another ten minutes or so and I would have given it to Lamashtu to play with."

"I still can, if you'd like. She's been desperately searching for a replacement, since she broke her last one. No? Fine, suit yourself.

You deserve a reward, although curse is more like it. Here, take the nasty little blighter." And with no further delay, he passes the child into his father's relieved and loving arms.

"Thank you, M'lord! Oh, thank you!" Dineel cries out, even as his son lets out his own feeble cries. He begins to turn away, but stops to take one last look around, trying to get his bearings on exactly where they're at. He'll need to come back for the body of his mate, once he's gotten his son back to the town where he can be seen to. He gasps in shock and outrage when he looks out further, past the Wartal's hideous body.

"I thought you said you would bring my son closer to town, so that I wouldn't have as far to go to get help! We're still in the same place that we began. Shelann lies just there!" he cries out as he points to his mate, lying perhaps fifty yards back.

The Lokskell glares at him through the Wartal's pus-filled eyes. "I didn't lie. I *never* lie. The truth is so much more fun. I *did* make the meat suit carry the brat closer to town… this is closer, is it not? Now, go away. Go on about your business, before I decide that I have further use for you."

Dineel's one functioning eye widens with alarm and he gives a hasty, clumsy bow as he blurts out, "You're right, merciful lord! Thank you! Thank you!" He cradles his newborn son protectively to his chest as he kicks the poor scream-brayer into a gallop one more time, just as the inky black Shadows pour back out of the Wartal's nose and mouth.

The Lokskell turns his attention away from Dineel and his disgusting infant. Now, all that needs to be done is to alert his men to be on the lookout for the blue bastard. And all *they'll* need to do is follow Krispin, for he *will* lead them straight to his daughter...just not the daughter that Krispin believes it to be. He will soon have his Ecko in his grasp, and Krispin will be the one to deliver her.

19

PEARLS OF WISDOM AND MISERY

Ecko

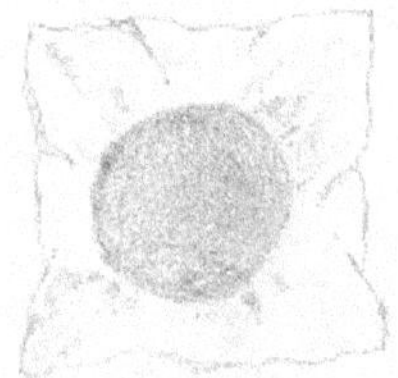

When Ecko wakes from her nap, she's groggy and disoriented and she can't quite remember where she is or how she'd gotten there. For a moment, she can't recall *who* she is, can't even remember her own name. But then it all rushes back and she sighs with both *relief* at discovering that she does not have amnesia, and with *regret* that she does not have amnesia. And that is certainly something that would only make sense to her, but such is her life. She rubs the sleep from her eyes and blinks up at the gloom-sky, wondering if it's still the same day as when she'd curled up in her sleeping bag, or if she's somehow managed to sleep straight through the long hours of Pitch and into the next day. It wouldn't surprise her. She'd certainly felt tired enough for it.

"Boodark?" she hesitantly calls. She sits up, her eyes automatically searching the clearing when she receives no answer. Her little friend is nowhere to be seen, but she grins when she sees the 'message' that he's left for her. Stacked up beside her bedroll is a small mountain made up of random food stuffs, her pot and pan, dishes and utensils. He even included the little cookstove and a lighter. Balanced precariously on top of the pile are two granola bars.

"Message received, loud and clear, my piggy little friend," she murmurs with a laugh. Boodark's just told her that he'll be back in time for dinner, and that he would like a granola bar with his meal, please and thank you very much. The little brat.

She's uncertain of what time it is, but surely it must be nearing Pitch-fall. It *feels* as if she'd slept for a good long while. Her rumbling belly certainly thinks so too, but that in and of itself doesn't necessarily mean anything. She hasn't had a single bite to eat since dinner last night. She's taken on an entire army since then, and her tummy is voraciously letting her know that it's displeased with the entire situation.

But she's not quite ready to start dinner, no matter what her protesting belly has to say about it (and it has plenty to say, and none of it good either!) What she really wants to do is try to call up her magic, see if she can get something, *anything* to happen, when *she* actually commands it. So far, it has only ever shown itself whenever *it* felt like showing up, never when she calls for it. She closes her eyes and tries to meditate, tries to clear her mind of all its ceaseless, nonsensical and useless prattle.

That should be an easy feat to accomplish, and yet she's never been able to manage it. There is always *something* weird going on up in her head. To prove the point, now she's mentally singing the lyrics to Party Up (Up in Here) by DMX. The entire chorus plays through her mind on a loop three times before she manages to shut it down.

"Stop it, Ecko! Focus!" she audibly scolds herself and then just about has a heart attack when Rage's laughter whispers through her mind. He must be getting better, stronger, *sneakier,* because she hadn't even realized he was awake.

"I never sleep anymore. I don't need it," he whispers.

Well, that's terrifying, she thinks and his laugh sighs through her again.

"I can help you with our magic; you know that I can. I can show you just how great we truly can be. All you have to do is come in here and release me. That's it. Come, embrace me."

She frantically shakes her head. "No way, Jose. That is *so* not happening. I don't trust you. You sound calm now, but I'm pretty sure it's just a mask that you're wearing to cover up your real face… a trick to get me to open up your cage. Then you'll make your move. You'll turn on me in a heartbeat and fill me up with *you,* with rage and anger and fury. And then what? Will I do terrible things? Hurt people? Kill even? Will I ever see *me* again?"

She waits for his answer, and in that time her mind is quiet, *finally* as if all the monsters in all their respective cages are holding their breaths, listening intently for his answer too. Even the sense-less chatter that always fills her mind is strangely, mysteriously missing.

"I am you," he simply says. *"No more, no less."*

Ecko pounds her fists against her knees in frustration. "What does that even mean?" she shouts.

"We are you," he replies. *"All of us, all of these 'monsters' that you've locked away are all just pieces of you. You continue to deny us, and therefore you cannot grow. You stay frozen, stuck in your weak, humanly mind. Let us out. Embrace us. Accept us in all our glory and our flaws, for we are all fragments of you. Accept us. Accept yourself! Until then, you will never be whole. You will never find your magic. You will never become the real you, the magnificent, powerful Wandelaar that you were born to be... A Mirror Walker the likes of which the Universe has never seen before. If you do not embrace us and accept yourself, you will never become. You will forever remain just a weak, pathetic human wannabe. An imposter, too afraid of herself to amount to anything. And when the time comes to stand against your sister, against your father...you will lose."*

Even through her doubts and fears, his words *feel* true. The real question is, is she brave enough, or dumb enough to follow his advice? And the answer is... not today. But she will think about it. She will think long and hard about his words and all the possible motives behind them. Rage's sigh of frustration at her decision fills her mind.

"Best I can do, Pal!" she snaps. "At least I agreed to consider it."

Rage chuckles. *"Fair enough,"* he croons and then retreats back into his silence.

"Whatcha doing?"

Ecko dies an instant, but fleeting death when Boodark unexpectedly returns and drops down in front of her.

"Ack!" she screeches and clutches her chest as her heart restarts. Her legs automatically kick out at what her brain perceives as a sudden threat to her well-being. The little flying monstrosity jumps back just in time to avoid her reflexive, defensive ninja moves.

"Whoa! Are you crazy? Calm down, you mentally challenged ground stomper!" he shouts at her, but he immediately realizes his blunder. Once again, his mouth has taken off without his brain's permission. He holds his hands up in front of himself as her eyes narrow into dangerous slits. "Na-now la-listen, I didn't mean it like that…" he stammers.

"Do not call me crazy. Don't ever call me crazy." She says it calmly, but with a deep, underlying well of simmering anger that she usually keeps carefully hidden beneath a placid facade. Boodark quickly jerks his head up and down in a nod, in that moment wholeheartedly agreeing to whatever she says. The last thing he wants is to be put into a 'time out' bubble for an indeterminate amount of time.

"*You know* I didn't mean it literally. I call everyone mentally challenged ... even myself! But you're right. I need to learn to use more thought before I open my big piehole. I've been alone for so long, that I've grown comfortable with just blurting it all out. Well, to be honest, I've always been a careless, knuckle dragging dung-dweller. I swear, crap just *falls* out of my mouth, like offal spewing from an Octobeast butt."

Ecko's eyes grow huge, and she nearly gags at the mental images that his words bring to mind. "See?" he cries in mock distress. "What'd I tell you? The shite just flows right off my tongue in endless rivers of diarrhea!"

He's very obviously trying to distract her from her anger and his whole potty, poo poo mouth confession has certainly done the trick. She takes deep breaths to slow her overstimulated heartbeat while he stares up at her, hands still held up defensively in front of him.

"It's ok. I got it all under control." She ignores the laugh that whispers through her mind once more.

"Shut up, Rage. No one's talking to you," she mumbles under her breath. Boodark takes three big steps back. Uttering nonsense to oneself is typically a clear indication of a *lack* of self-control.

"Oh, I wasn't talking to you, Boodark." She points to her head and calmly adds, "The voices." He takes two more slow, cautious steps back and she bursts out laughing, dissolving into helpless, almost hysterical giggles.

At the sound of her mirth, the worried look leaves his face and mock outrage replaces it. "Oh, such a naughty, *tricksy* thing is you! You sure had me going...*the voices!* Oh, you're good! That's so funny. The voices, indeed!"

She nods and smiles weakly at him before she turns away to busy herself with looking through their remaining dinner options. She wants to steer the conversation away from the very real voices of her mental monsters that are locked away in mental cages inside her mind. Food always works as a fail-safe means of distraction when dealing with her piggy little friend. This time is no different and she can't help but grin when he hops back in to watch what she's doing.

"Whatcha making for Endmeal? Hu, hu? Can we have the granolas? Pa-leeease?"

"Yes, you can have a granola bar," she replies. "How long did I sleep? Do you know how much time we have until Pitch falls?"

He scratches a claw through his long scraggly hair as he looks up at the sky. "You slept a long time, close to five hours. We have little more than an hour before Pitch."

She stands up and quickly goes about collecting firewood, stacking it all up in the ashes of last night's cookfire. Boodark helps too, gathering up twigs and dried roots for kindling. Soon enough, she's got a fire burning hot and all that's left to do is to decide what to cook.

"Well Boodark, it's decision time." She spreads out the 6 remaining MRE packages for his inspection. "Tonight, we're gonna splurge, because tomorrow…. we go on a diet."

She gathers up the dishes from last night, still dirty, because her morning had been much too weird to even think about cleaning them. He watches her wash them now with suspicion on his face as he asks, "What's die-it?"

She keeps her face straight as can be as she answers him. "Well, a diet is usually for people that need to lose weight. You know, for people that are a bit more rounded in the belly area than they should be."

It takes all the self-restraint she possesses to not direct her gaze to his little buddha belly. She determinedly keeps her eyes focused on the plate that she's vigorously scrubbing as she explains. "There are many, different kinds of diets. Some people cut out calories or carbs, some just change the things that they eat… less junk and more healthy stuff. You know, more green vegetables and such."

She peeks at him from the corner of her eye and just about loses her composure. The look on his face is so terrified and so disgusted, she can't help but to tease him just a little more. "Some people also try to eat less, cut out snacks. And sometimes," she drops her voice into a scary, campfire storytelling whisper, "Sometimes they even cut out a meal or two. *Every Pale!*"

She finally raises her eyes to gauge his reaction and it's as bad as she'd expected it to be. He's horrified beyond speech, beyond proper thought process even. He says not a single word for an entire minute, *that's* how appalled he is. He just stares at her, without blinking, while his dismay grows in leaps and bounds.

But finally, he can keep his agitation to himself no longer. "How *savage!*" His ugly little face is all scrunched up in shocked disbelief. "Earthians do this to themselves? *On purpose?*" he cries with mounting distress. "*Why?* What's wrong with you ground stompers? Why would anyone do such a terrible, dastardly thing to one's own self?" He is truly shaken up and appears to be on the verge of crying.

"They do it, because they're overweight," she tells him.

"Overweight?" he questions as he narrows his eyes at her. "What do you mean, *overweight?*"

She tries to come up with a polite way to word it. "You know… obese." He just continues staring up at her, waiting.

"Oh, come on!" she exclaims. "You know what an overweight person is. Plump, chubby, chunky, rotund, round… a roly-poly, big bellied, bikini challenged person! Someone that eats entirely too many meals!"

Boodark's eyes fly open wide with sudden outrage. He jabs a claw at her and screeches "I. Am. Not. FAT! I *refuse* this die-it torture plan, do you hear me? I refuse it!"

Ecko grins at how utterly offended he is at the idea that she might be calling him fat. "We're not going on a diet because we're fat, Boodark. We're doing it because I'm running low on food. We have to start rationing it. I don't know how much longer it will last, or what I'll do when it's all gone. You can survive here just fine; you've done it for years and years. You know where to find food, what's safe to eat and what isn't. *And* you have no scruples and seriously lower standards than I do."

"I have absolutely no clue what to do. I haven't seen the first thing that looks even remotely edible in the entire time I've been here. And before you say it, FireFairies and Spittler spiders are *not* on my menu! And I promise you right now that I will die, I will literally starve to death, before I eat a Vika Vakooja bug." And then she promptly gags just from the thought of it.

Boodark's shoulders relax from their upraised, outraged position, and he lowers his hand and puts away his jabber claw. "Oh," he mumbles. "Well, I can go find my own Endmeal this Pitch. It's no problem," he offers as his tummy audibly shouts its very loud displeasure.

She chuckles again and then she shakes her head. "No, Boodark. I will share equally with you all the food that I have, while I have it. We'll deal with the problem of starvation when the time comes. We just need to ration it, so that we can prolong the dealing with said starvation problem for as long as possible. Tonight, we'll enjoy our last un-diet meal. Tonight, we're gonna stuff our faces until we get bellyaches!"

Boodark throws his claws up in the air in jubilation and shouts, "Yes! Oh yes, yes, yes!" as he does a little celebratory, stomping-in-place jig. He grins his ghastly smile, the one that he only wears when he is either very pleased with himself, or if she's said something that pleases him immensely. Good food and a full belly *always* pleases him.

"Come on, silly goose. Let's decide what we want to eat, shall we?" She reads him the contents of each MRE pouch. It does no good though, because he's unfamiliar with the foods and she can't properly describe them to him.

"I don't know! How will I decide?" he wails with such sincere distress that she has to fake cough to cover her amusement.

"Close your eyes. I'll mix them up and then you can pick one at random."

He closes his eyes and nods vigorously. "That's a great idea! I don't know *why* everyone calls you a big dummy."

Ecko snorts and tells him, "You and Urza are the *only* ones that have ever called me that. Ok, they're mixed up. Stick out one of your dagger claws."

He does as she tells him and then pops his eyes back open when she declares, "Spaghetti and meatballs it is." She sets it and the pork sausage patty meal aside and shoves the remaining four meals back in the backpack.

"Is that good? Did I choose well? Hmm? Did I?" he asks as he hops around behind her, following her every step.

"Well, I think so. They should *all* be good. I picked these particular meals, because they're things that I normally enjoy eating. I love spaghetti, but I've never eaten this kind before, never had it in MRE form. I guess we'll see how they compare to the regular spaghetti that I'm used to, won't we? If you let me have a bite of yours, that is. I'm having the sausage patty."

When the MRE's are done heating, they decide to split them in half, so that they both can sample the other's meal. Ecko scoops the entrees onto their plates and equally divides the sides, snacks, and desserts that came with them. She places two of her precious (slightly melted and then re-hardened) Reese's peanut butter cups onto each plate, then adds two powdered donuts for good measure.

"Ok! Let the Wild Rumpus begin!" she declares and then grins when she notices her piggy little friend's eyes dart to the granola bars. "Oh yeah. I almost forgot these."

His eyes light up, sparkling like emeralds, as she sets one beside his plate. And then he enthusiastically, and quite disturbingly, buries his face in his spaghetti. He never notices her slip her own granola bar back into the backpack. She's decided that as long as she's not starving and forced to live off of bugs, the remaining granola bars are his.

Ecko eats her own meal a bit slower than her overzealous companion, seeing as how she wants to actually taste her food. He's finished eating long before she is, but for once he's not staring longingly at every bite she takes. He seems lost in his own thoughts, as he fiddles with his unopened granola bar. He's got something on his mind, but he hasn't as of yet, decided to share with her. She leaves him to it, and peers out into the Pitch beyond the perimeter of light from her little fire. The forest is so dark, so silent and foreboding, that she can almost forget there even *is* a world out there. She can almost believe that the abyss surrounds her, and that nothing exists beyond her small circle of light.

She shivers and steers her mind to other, less fear inducing subjects. She stares into the fire instead, savoring the lingering taste of chocolate on her tongue, the flickering, dancing flames remind her of the day's earlier events with the FireFairies. She's surprised that she managed to keep herself from being roasted and toasted like a campfire marshmallow (which she now wishes she'd had the foresight to pack) Those literal spitfires had been angrier than a pack of wet cats who'd had their tails stepped on…repeatedly, and then tossed into a bubble bath for good measure.

She recalls the panic (and shame) that she felt when she'd somehow conjured up a miniature prison in the form of a bubble. She thinks about the power upgrade that Rowana received, and she wonders what new magics the FireFairy Queen will now possess. She can't help but smile as she imagines just how stinkin' cute FireFairy babies…Firelings would be.

Her thoughts then turn to Jaida, that mean spirited will o' the wisp that refused to forgive and forget. She hopes that she's seen the last of *her,* but she's pretty sure there will be further reckonings. Yes, she has the unpleasant suspicion, almost like a sixth sense, assuring her that they'll be seeing one another again, before she's done with this world. And she's almost *certain* that Jaida had also received her own boost in powers. Would those thirteen FireFairy hive deserters team up with Jaida or will they venture off to join a different Hive? Would they follow Red Wisp?

"Oh!" Ecko blurts out loud, so suddenly that it startles a loud toot out of Boodark's nether region. He laughs with cruel delight as she's forced to cover her nose and mouth with her pajama top.

"What's *wrong* with you?" she cries as her eyes water from the foulness that permeates the air around them. "It's like the Bog of Eternal Stench! I've never smelled anything like it!" Now he's howling, rolling on the ground in a fit of hilarity. But she knows how to fix him. "That's right. Go ahead and laugh it up. Seeing as how Earth food makes you so gassy, you should probably go on a 'Earth food' diet. You should probably avoid eating any more of it!" That sobers him up just as fast as she'd known it would. He immediately stops his manic giggling and sits up to stare at her with big, hurt eyes.

"You would truly do such a cruel thing? To *me*? Besides… the stink is already gone! It's safe for you to come out now."

Of course, she wouldn't *really* deprive him of food, but he doesn't have to know that! She lowers the shirt enough to take a cautionary sniff, then lowers it to its rightful place. "What I was going to ask, before you started playing your butt music was…whatever happened to Red Wisp? I can't recall her leaving. She didn't leave with Jaida, and she didn't go with Rowena and the Hive either."

Boodark lazily scratches his butt and says, "Oh, she snuck away when you decided to start making bubbles…while you were too busy panicking, shaking your prisoners up and scrambling their brains."

She's ashamed of herself all over again for her mindlessly hysterical episode, but she nevertheless attempts to defend herself. "Hey! That was an accident! I didn't *mean* to shake them up like that. I didn't even notice them bouncing around. I just wanted that bubble off my hands. It was weird, and I was scared. Ok?"

She jabs her poker stick into the fire and watches the resulting sparks fly up and away into the night. "So, Red just snuck off and flew away, huh? Just abandoned them all to save herself?"

He nods and scooch/hops closer, eyeballing the plate that she'd set aside. There's still the two donuts and one Reese's cup left, not to mention the crumbs and remnants of her meal.

"Well, she did abandon them, that much is true. But she didn't leave until everyone else did, or right before they did anyway," he clarifies.

She grins at this point, because he never once raises his eyes from the plate as he's talking to her. "I saw her sneak off and hide in the thicket. She stayed long enough to see what would happen, long enough to determine who the victors would be. She watched the whole thing from the safety of her hidey hole, until she could figure out which way the wind was blowing. *Then* she ran off." Boodark's little bat nose twitches as he sniffs at the air above her plate. "Are you gonna eat that?" he asks.

She snatches her Reese's cup and takes a bite. "Well, I was planning on it," she tells him, but then pushes the plate towards him. "There's no way I'm giving you my chocolate, but I guess you can have the donuts."

He wastes no time with thank you's. He just dips his head down and licks away every trace of food that's clinging to her plate. Then he stabs the donuts onto his jabber claws and actually takes his time eating them with small bites, as if he wants to prolong his eating pleasure for as long as he can make it last. He makes his eating sounds the entire time too, that weird little 'mmrrung, mmuurrrunnng, murrrungg' growling sound that he makes when he's particularly enjoying what he's consuming.

"Ugh, you're such a piggy little brat," she tells him, but she's grinning at the powdered sugar mustache and beard that he's got going on. She takes her camera from her bag and quickly explains what it is and what it does. She tells him that she wants to take his photo and that she's already taken several of them, with him none the wiser, and she insists that no harm could come from it. She explains that Blaxx had *totally* freaked out when he saw her taking his photo, because he'd been convinced that she was a witch and that she was attempting to steal his soul.

"I know that I've already taken several photos of you without your permission, but I don't want to keep doing that. Besides, I want to get some selfies with you. Do you trust me? "He nods at her, but she's not sure that he's really even hearing her words. He's looking at his remaining donut like it's the most beautiful thing he's ever seen in his entire life.

She grins again and tells him to look up and not to panic at the bright light. She snaps several hilarious photos of his wide, shocked eyes and his messy sugar face. She has a good laugh while she shows them to him.

"Magic," he whispers in awe as she scrolls through the memory card. "I keep telling you, it's not magic. It's technology. Science. There's a very logical explanation for how it all works. *I* can't explain it to you, because I haven't actually learned the how's and why's of it, but it *can* be explained. Just not by me."

She shows him all the pictures that she's taken on this world and then starts showing him the ones from Earth. He takes an inordinate amount of time studying each one, asking a million and one questions. He's understandably drawn to Earth's *aliveness*, the greenery, the flowers, the animals, the seemingly explosion of color.

Boodark is so disappointed when she comes to the end and there's no more photos to look at, that she takes her phone out and shows him all of those too. She actually has more pictures of him on this device than she has on her camera, because it's easier to snap pics in secret with a cellphone. He's a little startled by the videos at first, but he has a good laugh at the one with him drunk dancing, belting out 'I Hope You're Happy' along with Blue October. He abruptly stops laughing though, when he gets to the photos of him clinging to the pain reliever tree, slurping up his 'morning after' headache remedy. He frowns instead, and then quickly looks away, smoothing a hand over his hair in a futile effort at taming it.

"What's wrong?" she asks at his grimace and his sudden sad demeanor.

"Oh, it's nothing really," he sighs.

She puts her phone away and tells him that it's not 'nothing' if it's upset him. "You know that you can tell me anything, right? Maybe I can help."

He looks ashamed as he glances at her and mumbles, "I appreciate that, but you can't fix *this*." He jabs a claw towards his own face. "I really *am* ugly!" he wails.

Ecko gulps. How is she going to get through this conversation without either lying, which she refuses to do, or hurting his feelings, which she very much wishes to avoid doing. She takes so long just trying to figure out her best course of action, that he starts dejectedly walking away, shoulders slumped, head hanging down, feet shuffling in the walk of shame.

"I knew it! You think I'm ugly!" he wails.

"Wait! Where are you going?"

He sniffles and informs her that he's going away, so that she doesn't have to be offended by his ugly anymore.

"But I'm not offended! *You're* the one that's offended." He stops walking but keeps his face turned away from her, waiting for her to continue.

"I can't lie, I *won't* lie. You're not the prettiest thing I've ever seen, but why does that even matter? Life isn't supposed to be a beauty contest. You should be grateful for what you do have. You've got the cutest little bat nose, and your big ole ears are adorable. And you *do* have other redeeming qualities. Looks aren't everything, you know."

He turns his head at last to look at her and snorts. "That's easy for you to say. You're not ugly!" She smiles gently at him and says, "Thank you for that, but I've never really worried about what I look like. I guess I've just always sort of taken that for granted. I know that I'm pretty, but it's never really occurred to me to care about it. I am who I am, and I look how I look. That's just how it is. My looks have never done a single thing for me. My face has never helped me to be accepted, never won me any prizes, or granted me any favors. It's just my face, like it or not."

Boodark snorts in disgust. "That's because you've never had to deal with being a hideous monster!"

That's it. That does it. She points a finger at him and shouts, "Don't you say that! Don't you *ever* say that again! You are *not* a monster, nor are you hideous. Trust me, I know monsters. You have a good heart, no matter what your outside looks like. Now, come here and let me brush your hair. I know it bothers you that it's so messy. You'll feel better about yourself when I get all those tangles brushed out."

Boodark gives her those wide, hope-filled eyes, but wastes no time as he shuffles back over and plops down in front of her. Her heart melts at his obvious eagerness as she digs her brush out of her bag. She starts by first picking the twigs and leaves and all sorts of other debris out of the tangled mess.

"I don't know why you're so worried about how you look anyway. Is it because you can't find a mate? I wouldn't worry too much about it. I'm sure a suitable girl will come along. Your, uh, unfortunate appearance may even be a blessing in disguise. It'll help weed out the undesirables, the females that are too shallow to see the person *under* the skin. If you find a girl that sees you for who you are and not just how you look, you'll know that she's true. If she loves you, she won't care what you look like."

He snorts out an objection. "Or she'll be as hideous as I am!"

She can't help but laugh as she pokes his shoulder. "You are not hideous." She's removed all the visible debris and so she parts his hair into sections and carefully starts picking the brush through the tangles, starting at the tips and working her way up. She uses his tiny, blunt horns to hold each brushed section away from the tangled section as she works.

"Beside the point. Who says I'm even looking for a female? Why would I want one of those?"

Her hands still for a moment, brush in mid stroke. "Oh! Oh, I'm so sorry. I didn't realize… Do you like boys? I just assumed you liked girls because you've mentioned your uummm…. irresistibleness to the opposite sex."

Boodark chokes and sputters and she hurries to assure him that it doesn't matter to her. "I don't care who you choose to love. It's absolutely 100% ok to be gay."

He shouts, "Ugh! I'm no male-loving, rump humper, you big dummy! I never said that I don't like females. I said I was not *looking* for a female. It's a very big difference! I like breasts! *Female* ones!"

He grumbles on and on for a few moments about 'big dummies that like to twist his words around, and rump-humpers, indeed'.

"I'm sorry!" she finally concedes. "I totally misunderstood."

She continues where she'd let off, working on his tangles, and he eventually calms and mutters, "Alright. You're forgiven."

After a minute of contemplative silence, she asks him "So what *will* you look for in a wife? And don't tell me nice boobs!"

He grunts his annoyance. "Again, who says I'm even interested in all that?"

"I guess I was just making assumptions again. But if you don't like boys and you're not interested in 'all that', does that mean you've never been with anyone before? I mean, *been with* been with? Like, intimately?"

And now he's back to sputtering and blathering, vehemently denying his virginity and boasting of his *very* experienced and incredible prowess under the bed covers...with *females*, thank you very much! She hastily cuts him off when he starts going into details.

"Ok! Ok, I get it. You like women and you are very experienced. I don't need the details. Nor do I want any mental images!"

But Boodark's on a rant now, all worked up and agitated. "I like females, I *adore* them. And I've had so many of them that I've lost count. I'm as opposite of a virgin as opposite can be! And what is it with you females anyway? Always got your minds stuck on finding a lifemate. Why? So that you can be with the same mate for the rest of your life? I'd have to be crazy to want to saddle myself with just one female, when there's plenty of Boodark to go around! Do you know how long my lifespan is? At least *eight hundred years.* That's a long time to listen to the same woman nag incessantly at you."

He pitches his voice up so that he's mimicking a female, and he sounds so ridiculous that she has to cover her mouth to hold her giggles inside. "Take out the waste, Boodark. Change the baby's nappy, Boodark. Don't dust up my nice clean floor. Stop biting your toenails and spitting them everywhere!"

His voice returns to normal. "It could go on and on. For Eight. Hundred. Years." He stops to take a deep breath and then adds, "And another thing. Why do we even need a mate? To *complete* us? There are entirely too many fools out there looking to complete themselves with a lifemate. What happens when they find that having a mate is not completion, but merely change instead? Taking a mate means that you no longer live for you. You forevermore live for *them*!"

"Oh!" Ecko interjects. "That reminds me of a book that I loved when I was a child. It was called The Little Prince and it had a quote that just always stuck with me. I don't know why I loved it so. I only know that it called to something inside me. It said, 'You become responsible, forever, for what you have tamed.' Isn't that simultaneously the most beautiful and terrifying thing that you've ever heard?" A single tear rolls down her cheek as she repeats it. "You become responsible, forever, for what you have tamed."

Boodark exuberantly nods his head in agreement. "Exactly!" he cries out. "Who in their right mind wants that? *Complete,* my divinely shaped arse! I *am* complete, all on my own! I don't need no female to complete me!"

Ecko bursts out laughing at his display of outraged, male pride and he jumps up and spins around to face her. "What's wrong with you? Why, *exactly* are you laughing? What is it that you find so humorous?"

She gets her giggles under control, even wipes the smile off her face before she asks him, "Whatever happened to romance?"

He scowls ferociously at her. "I killed it. And ate it...with berry sauce. What?" he demands when she raises her eyebrows at him. "I was hungry." And he grumbles unintelligibly under his breath as he spins around and plops back down so that she can finish brushing his hair.

"Wow. I don't know *why* you got so defensive. There's nothing wrong with being celibate. I certainly have no grounds to make fun of anyone. I've never had a boyfriend, never even been kissed."

Boodark grunts, but otherwise stays quiet. "I don't think I even understand kissing. I just don't get it. I mean, how do you breathe if someone's got their tongue shoved in your mouth? And that's just kind of revolting just thinking about it anyway. What if they have bad breath?"

He sighs forlornly as he unconsciously runs his clawed hand over the golden band around his upper arm. Then he softly whispers, "One day you will meet someone so special, someone so beautiful to your heart that you won't care if you can breathe or not. You won't even think about it. *He* will become your air, and you his."

The brush stops mid stroke. "Huh?" Now *she* grunts and then tells him that she doesn't understand that. She doesn't understand it at all.

"You will, one day. And when that day comes, you'll wonder how you ever breathed without him."

Even though she still hasn't gotten a straight answer on how to breathe with someone's mouth… and *tongue* pressed against hers (not an answer that she can understand anyway) she decides to let the whole thing go for now. It seems like this kind of talk is making her little friend sad, and she doesn't want that.

The tangles have all been smoothed out, but he seems to enjoy the feel of her hands in his hair, so she continues running the brush through it for a bit longer. Then she plaits it into a braid and ties it off with a rubber band from her miscellaneous junk pouch. She takes front and back photos and shows them to him, and he gets all choked up at seeing his hair nice and neat and clean. She realizes how much his appearance truly means to him and so she decides, then and there, to do what she can to make him feel better about himself … starting with some new clothes.

Boodark excuses himself to fly off to 'use the bathroom', only he doesn't *politely* excuse himself. No, of course not. He yells out, "I have to go poop! It's coming out right now!" and then laughs uproariously when she makes a face at him.

"TMI, " she yells at his retreating backside, but she's grinning at his uncouth mannerisms. While he's off doing his business, she takes out the pair of jeans she'd been wearing on her very first day here. She'd ripped holes in both pants legs, right at the knees, when she'd slipped down the oceanside cliffs. She carefully cuts the legs off at the tears with her tiny sewing scissors, turning the pants into a pair of shorts. The excess material is more than enough for a new pair of pants, enough for a Boodark sized pair, at least.

When he returns to camp from his daily constitutional poop, she quickly explains what she's doing, so that he won't try to give her a detailed rundown of 'how things came out'.... *Again.* She's discovered that her beastie little companion is very much like an adolescent boy. Gross bodily functions are funny, and they are a hundred times funnier if there's a girl around to be thoroughly grossed out by them. She's counting on his vanity and his obsession with his appearance to distract him from that unwanted conversation, and the plan works marvelously. He's more excited with the idea of new pants than he is about oversharing his personal details with her. Thank you, sweet baby Jesus.

She gets her measurements and carefully makes the necessary cuts. Then she snips a length of her purple paracord to use for a drawstring in the waistband. He watches her for a few minutes, watches how she smiles softly with each tiny stitch that she adds. He can see that she's lost in memories, pleasant ones for a change. He's curious to know what she's thinking of that has her smiling like that, but he's reluctant to intrude on her happy thoughts.

So, he remains quiet and waits to see if she wants to share, and he's not disappointed. She speaks softly, almost in a whisper, as she tells him about how her stepmother had wanted her girls to know how to sew. How she'd insisted on it, actually. And how, naturally, both girls had rebelled against it. How they'd both *loathed* it.

"Sewing lessons were the one thing that Karen and I always agreed on…. we shared a mutual hatred of needle and thread. The twice a week, hour-long sessions don't seem so bad now, but back then we thought we'd die from the torture of it. We were such dramatic, ungrateful brats. I'd gladly endure hours upon hours of those agonizingly boring lessons if only it would bring them back to me."

She sighs sadly as she ties off the tread and snips it off. She turns them right side out and then holds the doll-sized pair of pants up to the firelight to inspect them. "I think these will suit you just fine." She holds them out to him and adds, "Try them on and see how they fit."

Boodark's claw/hands clumsily fumble with the rope tied around his waist, untying it and acting like he's going to drop his britches right there in front of her.

"Not right here!" she screeches in panic as she tosses the pants out into the darkness beyond the firelight's reach. "Go over there, where I can't see you!"

He giggles maniacally as he scurries after them, letting her know that he'd just been teasing her to see her freak out. But he also wanted to snap her out of the sadness that thoughts of her lost family were conjuring within her.

"I don't *ever* want to see another green ding-dong! Not ever again. Blaxx's was terrible," she says with a shiver of revulsion.

Boodark snorts, and then he's bragging and boasting of his own magnificent endowments. "Not *my* green one. Mine is pure perfection, downright awe-inspiring. The females love it, *beg* for it. The males are jealous. They only wish theirs was as divine as mine."

Now it's her turn to snort and sputter. "I really, *really* don't want to know."

"That's because you've only seen me in my cursed form, in this hideous body. If I was my *real* self, you'd be singing a completely different tune."

Boodark comes strutting back into the light, stopping to turn this way and that, doing a crazy little dance, so that she can admire every angle of him in his new attire. She giggles at his silly antics and snaps photo after photo of his impromptu fashion show, all the while singing the Firey Gang's song from Labyrinth. "We can show you a good time. And we don't charge nothin'. Just strut your nasty stuff. Wiggle in the middle, yeah! When you think this wild, Chilly down with the Fire Gang!"

He drops to his knees and throws out his arms in a grand finale and then takes a bow when she claps and cheers for him. He grins as he stands back up and carefully brushes his new pants off.

"You look good, like a completely different man," she compliments, her heart warmed at his obvious delight.

He unconsciously touches a hand to his braid and then firmly nods his head. Then he flashes that horrific smile that she's come to love. "I certainly do, don't I?" he brags. "Thank you for this. You know I'm no good with words, but this really does mean a lot to me. Now, hush wench. I've got a laying-to-rest ritual to attend."

And then he tosses his raggedy old, holey and moldy pants into the fire. He mournfully bows his head and murmurs, "They were some good pants, strong, sturdy, true. They protected my... assets from terrible atrocities, shielded them from those that would attempt to steal and use those attributes in unmentionable ways... But alas, the fabric grew old and feeble, and my incredible endowments threatened to burst free of them more and more with each passing Pale..."

She's laughing so hard that she's snorting. "Shut up, you idiot, before I toss you in after them!" He spins around and grins mischievously before he hops back over and drops down beside her. She grins back, but it fades quickly as she realizes that she can't put it off any longer. No more stalling. She'd made up her mind earlier to try to figure out her magic, and that's exactly what she's going do. Her shoulders slump and she sighs in resignation.

"You might want to distance yourself from me for a while. I need to start learning how to use my abilities. At the very least, I need to learn how to call the magic *out*. You know I don't have any idea what I'm doing, and I don't want to hurt you."

She points to the granola bar that he's been hoarding and adds, "I know that you've been taking those off somewhere every night. I don't know if you're hiding them or giving them to someone else and I really don't need to know. They're yours to do with whatever you please. One day, you will trust me enough to tell me your story…. How and why you were cursed, where you disappear to at night, what you do with a treat that you obviously love, but refuse to eat. I'm only mentioning it now, so that you can stop sneaking away after I fall asleep. I won't pressure you for explanations. Everyone has secrets."

Tears well up in his eyes and he quickly turns away in hopes that she doesn't see them and think him unmanly. "You have no idea the depths of my Secret," he murmurs with a sniffle as he turns back to face her. "I *am* going to leave for a while, but it's not because I'm scared of you. I don't think you'd *let* yourself hurt me."

"I'm leaving, only because you are correct. I have somewhere that I need to be. I have things that I need to attend to. Secret things. But you're wrong about me not trusting you, because I do. I trust you more than I've ever trusted any other ground stomper. My reluctance to share my story has nothing to do with trust. It's about pain and guilt and shame. It *hurts*, and I hate myself. But I will tell you, just as soon as I can stand to do so."

She nods in acknowledgment. "Fair enough. I'm ready to listen whenever you're ready to talk. And who knows? Maybe I'll be able to help. Stranger things *have* happened." She holds out her arms and murmurs, "Steady now. Don't freak out. I'm going to lift you up, so that I can hug you. Not because I think you need one, mind you, but because I do."

He pushes his wings back out of the way and opens his own arms wide as she lifts him up and hugs him close, his little body pressed against her shoulder. He wraps his arms *and* his wings around her neck for a double decker embrace and just holds tight for a moment, his breath hitching and tears threatening. Then he turns his face towards hers, sticks out his slimy, black tongue, and slurps it up her cheek.

"Hrurrk!" She gags and drops him, and he has to flap fast, so that he doesn't hit the ground. "What?" he asks with overexaggerated innocence. "I was caught up in the moment and wanted to show my love for you!"

She scrubs at her cheek and yells, "I don't like wet, lickery kisses!"

Boodark swoops in and snatches the granola bar from the ground. "Oh, that wasn't a kiss. I just wanted to lick you!" Then he flies up and away from camp, his howls of laughter ringing out behind him.

She can't help but grin. In all honesty, as gross as the experience had been, it had also been sort of … sweet, almost like a puppy's kiss. And then she's laughing at the thought of how outraged the little beastie would be, should he ever find out that she'd compared him to a pet.

"Stop stalling, Ecko. You know you need to learn how this magic bull-poopy works. Now get to it!" Blocking out the sound of Rage's demented laughter and his whispered, *"You can try,"* she closes her eyes and concentrates on just locating the magic. If she could learn how to *find* it, maybe she'll get a better understanding of it. Baby steps are better than no steps, she muses. Then she smirks with satisfaction, because she knows that she's onto something when Rage shuts up with his annoying taunts.

Two hours later, exhausted and dripping with sweat, she calls it quits on the whole magic exploration and experimentation. She'd been able to "wake" the magic within herself several times. Oh, nothing had come of it. She hadn't zapped anything or conjured up any bubbles, but then again, she hadn't tried to.

She'd just focused all her will into finding it and rousing it, concentrated on feeling it out and getting to know it better. She'd followed the flow of it as it coursed through her body and concentrated on how it grew and built up inside of her. She'd familiarized herself with the tingling in her palms as her hands lit up with that brilliant, blue energy. And that's *all* she'd done, but that's as much as she'd set out to do and she's satisfied. Although she's nowhere near ready to take her sister on, (at this point she still wouldn't be able to use her magic to take on a bug and win the fight) she's actually quite pleased with the small step forward that she's made tonight. And by small step, what she really means is a teeny tiny, fairy sized step. But progress is progress, no matter how long it takes to get to the finish line.

"It does not matter how slowly you go, so long as you do not stop," she mutters. That Confucius sure was a smart man, but she can't help but wonder if he would have been able to come up with any words of wisdom to offer for *her* particularly unusual issues. Probably not. He'd probably come up with something along the lines of "You're screwed, but smile and know that although you may try to stop the inevitable and highly unpleasant boinking you are about to receive, the Universe will *always* find a way to stick it to you."

She snorts as she rifles through her bag for the wet wipes, intent on washing away the unpleasant stickiness of sweat from her face. She sees the shirt-wrapped bundle that contains the Night Pearl and can't resist the allure of finding out if it will work its magic once more. She's desperate for news of her beloved Charlie and Susan. And although she dreads what she'll learn, she needs to see how much damage Samara is causing.

"Just one more experiment," she promises herself. "Just one more." She knows that *if* she does happen to get the magic to work, and *if* the Night Pearl decides to reveal her twin, she'll probably bear witness to some sort of unpleasantness again... see things she really doesn't want to see. It's probably going to be awful. But she has to do it anyway. She has to know. And once she's done, she'll crawl into her sleeping bag and turn herself into a blanket burrito and cry herself to sleep. Because she knows that whatever Samara is up to, it won't be good... and there won't be anything she could do to stop it.

She lifts the bundle out of her bag and carefully unwraps it, a small sigh of wonder slipping from her lips as it's revealed. She'd forgotten just how magnificent it truly is and she takes a moment to admire it, partially because it's so alluring... but also because she's procrastinating. She's terrified of what she might see, afraid of witnessing the atrocities that Samara's undoubtedly committing. Because although she's known this whole time that her sister is living her best horrible life back on Earth, torturing and killing, wreaking havoc and destroying lives… well, knowing it and *seeing* it with her own eyes are two very different things. Actually watching it as it happens puts faces to all the unknowns, makes it all the more personal. Gives it names.

But she's stalled as long as she can, and since she hasn't been successful in talking herself out of this whole dreaded affair, she takes a deep breath and calls to the magic inside of herself. She expects it to be sluggish, slow to wake and reluctant to cooperate, because of how much time she'd spent poking and prodding it earlier. She couldn't have been more wrong. It responds instantly, as if it had only been fake sleeping and was just waiting for her to call it back out. It rushes through her, rapidly filling her with that electric energy before it flows from her hands and *into* the Night Pearl. No hesitation, no resistance. Just an absolute eagerness to obey that has her feeling the tiniest bit suspicious.

The force in which her magic joins with the Pearl's creates a tempest around her, producing an almost violent windstorm that has her hair whipping about her face, each individual strand snapping with tiny electrical lightning strikes. She blocks it all out and steers her thoughts to Charlie. She thinks about what he's doing right now, how he's feeling, wondering if he's still going out of his mind with worry for her. She focuses on willing the Night Pearl to reveal her friend and mentor to her.

And it listens, it *obeys*. She watches the pinpoint light in the center grow, expanding to crowd out the black, until the two colors switch places. The black becomes the center, but it soon shrinks away and disappears. And when it's gone, when it's completely vanished and nothing but white light remains, *they* appear.

There they are... her Charlie and her Susan. They're walking through the doors of a church, making their way hand in hand down the center aisle. They pass pew after pew, until they get to the pulpit and the table of candles set out before it. Charlie stares up at the stained-glass image of Jesus for a minute or two, then turns and smiles sadly, weakly at his wife. He reaches out and lights a candle and then slowly, painstakingly lowers himself to his knees and bows his head to pray. Susan wipes a tear from her face and mimics his actions.

Ecko watches them, half shocked and half awed. Charlie had once told her that he used to go to church with his first wife, his beloved Gretchen. He'd stopped going when he lost her, and he'd never gone back, aside from his and Susan's wedding. But there he is now, kneeling before God and begging for *her* safe return.

She knows that's what he's praying for; she can *hear* his thoughts. Somehow, Charlie's beautiful, old and rumbly voice is echoing through her mind, his prayers for her clutching at her heart. He stays down on his knees until his body aches and he's dehydrated from all the tears he's shed, begging and pleading, making promises and offering up bribes. This has been so hard on him and he's not coping well at all. She can see that he's lost weight and his old face looks tired and worn.

Susan gets up off of her aching knees and settles onto the bench right behind him and bows her head once more. Charlie ignores his own pain and stays right where he is, stubborn old goat that he is.

The reality of witnessing their anguish, of hearing Charlie's thoughts has Ecko sobbing. But then a sudden quiet fills her mind and soothes her heartache, just a bit. Because something has just occurred to her…. If she can hear Charlie, perhaps she could make *him* hear *her*. She concentrates with every ounce of will, with every drop of hope living inside of her, to send a message from her mind to Charlie's.

"I'm ok. I'm trying to find my way back to you. I'm ok. I'm trying to find my way back to you…" She repeats it over and over and over, mentally picturing herself standing right there beside him, speaking the words directly into his ear. For the longest time, he gives no indication that he hears anything other than his own desperate prayers. But then, oh miracle of miracles, he slowly lifts his head, cocking it to the side as if he's trying to listen in on a hushed secret.

"Ecko?" he whispers. "Ecko, sweetheart?"

She sobs once with joyous relief, but she knows that she can't afford the distraction that tears or even jubilation would bring. As it is, she's concentrating so hard on making him hear her that she's shaking, straining from the effort of sending a purely mental message from her mind to his, indeed from one *world* to another. She says it one final time, with as much conviction as she can muster. "I'm ok. I'm trying to find my way back to you." Then she adds, "Love you so much Charlie. Stay safe, hide from Samara."

She watches his face light up with a beautiful, radiant smile, just before her thoughts of her sister cause the scene inside the Night Pearl to shatter and disintegrate into a swirling cloud of particles. And then those sand-small particles of dust begin pouring themselves back together, creating a new scene... one in which her twin is the star of the show.

Samara's walking away from a massive, blazing inferno, the flames of which are shooting high up into the air behind her, setting the surrounding trees ablaze. Her sister is in no hurry to escape the devouring flames. She appears to be extremely pleased with them, in fact. But where is she? What has her sister done?

It seems that Ecko has tuned in to the middle of the movie and she has no clue what has transpired before this particular scene. "What have you been up to?" she murmurs as she watches Samara lift up and examine the prescription pill bottle clutched in her hand.

Her twin freezes like that for a moment, hand upraised and smiling that self-satisfied smile. It's as if the 'movie' has been paused, so that the audience could take a quick bathroom break. But then someone hits the rewind button on the remote and now Samara's walk/running backwards in triple speed. The scene breaks apart, disintegrating into particles again, before reforming even further back in time... a flash of the scenery from before the fire started, then it's rewinding again.

Flash to a car ride, a bloody scene in a hospital setting, Samara grinning at her reflection in a mirror, blood in her teeth and dripping down her face. She's going backwards, back, back, back. She's rewinding so fast that Ecko can't catch more than bits and pieces of it, and so nothing's making any sense and she's not quite sure what's going on.

But then she *does* know, and it suddenly makes perfect sense. The magic is rewinding the 'movie' of Samara's time on Earth, providing an answer to Ecko's question. When she'd whispered, "What have you been up to?" her magic, or the Pearl's magic, or possibly both of them combined had taken her literally. The Night Pearl is going to show her *exactly* what Samara's been up to, starting from day one of her Earth vacation. And she's got a front row seat to the Samara matinee.

Much like a real movie or even a book, it doesn't all play out in one continuous stream. It jumps around, picking out and broadcasting the highlights and cutting out all those mundane and boring moments in between. And it's as terrifyingly abhorrent as she'd feared it would be.

It begins with Samara's arrival through the mirror at the hospital and her very first human victims. She'd been determined to find and kill everyone that Ecko loved, had made a vow to destroy everything and everyone that her sister had ever come in contact with. But she soon found that in order to do that, she'd first have to learn more about the new world with its strange new people and all their technologies. And then she'd quickly become distracted from her plan to 'eradicate Ecko and wipe away every single trace of her.'

The Night Pearl shows Samara's early 'learning' days, when she'd been acquainting herself with her new world and its natives, figuring out how all those strange new things worked: automobiles, traffic lights, indoor plumbing. She'd almost had a heart attack at her first sight of an airplane flying through the air. She'd had to adjust to the noise of Earth, with its machines and inventions and its overpopulated masses. She had to adjust to the blinding, blistering heat of the sun and the nighttime skies, which aren't dark at all with its moon and stars to light it.

She'd had to learn everything, but she didn't receive her education in the normal way, by studying and learning it for herself. No, that's not how Samara operates. She'd cheated her way through it. She'd sent her foul, mind-raping shadows into people, one after another, and plundered the depths of their minds. With their unwilling help, she'd learned vast amounts of information… in mere *minutes*. Some of it was vital and some was useless, but *all* of it was pertinent. She'd learned what she needed to know in order to function in this new, vibrantly busy world.

It wouldn't have been so bad if that's all she'd been doing. Mind raping someone is terrible, yes, but *survivable* (as long as that's all she'd done in there.) If she'd just gone in, learned what she'd needed to know and then left again, all would have been forgivable. Wrong and intensely invasive… but still forgivable. But again, that's not how Samara works.

She does not believe in 'Live and let Live'. No, what she believes is 'Might equals Right' and 'If you are strong enough to do a thing, then you have every right to *do* the thing. Take it by any means available to you, if you are powerful enough to do so. Destroy as many lives as you possibly can along the way. Show them your power. Let them feel your *rage*. Put it all out there on display, so that everyone knows who you are and that you are to be feared, worshiped. Do whatever it is that makes your little heart beat faster for a moment in time, however brief it may be'.

So, no. Samara never had any intentions of merely entering her victim's minds to learn all that she could and then peacefully leave again. She could *never* leave it at just a learning experience. She had to destroy them once she'd taken what she wanted from them. Because *that* is ultimately what her heart craves, what her soul demands… debauchery and depravity. That's what makes *her* heart beat faster. Might equals Right. And because she can, she always *will* do whatever it is in her shriveled black heart to do.

She'd killed some of her victims immediately, played with others before snuffing out their lives. She wiped minds clean and left them that way, mindless, drooling, and catatonic. She rearranged memories, made them believe false realities before sending them back home to wreak havoc on their loved ones, the lies in their heads firmly believed as truth. She'd planted dark thoughts inside some of their minds, tiny, black seeds made of her Shadow-smoke to grow and fester, to destroy them from within.

She convinced one of her victims that a giant, person-sized roach had raped and impregnated her and that all of its roach babies were crawling throughout her body, eating her up from the inside. Ecko cries out at the horrible way that poor woman died, how they *all* died. She can't stand this; she wishes she'd never even started watching this 'movie'. But even more than that, she wishes she could convince herself that this really *was* just a movie, with actors and props and fake blood.

"I don't want to see any more," she vehemently insists. But naturally the magic chooses this particular time to ignore her and her wants. "I don't want to see any more. Turn it off!" she cries as the scene disintegrates and changes again.

Samara's taking partner after partner to bed with her. Men of all ages…. old men, young virile men, strong men in their prime, some hardly more than boys even. She does not discriminate. She even takes some female lovers, though there's not nearly as many of them as there are men.

Ecko watches each one of them climb into bed with her sister. But they don't climb back out, they *never* climb back out. They get carried out and disposed of. The scenes change to show each one of those bed partners dead, their bodies broken and bloody, sightless eyes staring, *if* they even have their eyes still. Some don't.

With every new death, a man comes in and carries the bodies away and then returns to clean up the mess and set the room back to rights. It's always the same man, strappingly strong and empty eyed. She must like him; why else would she bother to keep him around? Oh, she keeps him brainwashed, but she spends time with him too. He shows her how to read and write, how to work a cell phone, teaches her about money and banks and credit. And then he introduces her to the wonders of the world wide web. And oh, what a magnificently helpful tool *that* is. With Google at her fingertips, she learns more and more about the world she's now living in, about the people that she must either learn to mingle with or endure, one or the other.

Then she discovers the Dark Web, and she learns that she's not as alone with her depraved needs and filthy desires as she'd once believed. There are plenty of humans with 'sick and twisted' perversions. Fantasies for most, but realities for the few that are brave enough to go after whatever their nasty little hearts desired.

There are porn sights, fetish sites, and live stream torture videos from hostels. You could order your exotic purchases to be delivered straight to your home and you could pick out a sex slave and have *it* delivered to you. You could watch someone burn sweet little puppies and kittens alive and you could order a hitman to kill for you. Almost anything that you can think of could be found and delivered to you, for a price.

All that's needed is someone that can hack their way into the Dark Web. Someone that can access that 6% of internet content that is so encrypted that special software and/or a brilliantly gifted hacker is needed just to *view* it. Samara immerses herself there for a time, loses herself in the dark, disgustingly beautiful fantasies being lived out, the twisted fetishes being indulged ... and all of it broadcast for her viewing pleasure. It thrills and excites her, and she takes it all out on her lovers. And her ministrations are *never* something that one recovers from.

She soon learns that although she's found some like-minded individuals, equal to her they *are not*. They're weak, breakable, their bodies and minds not able to withstand her particular brand of pleasures. She breaks every new toy she gets, in record time. And while she hasn't grown bored, exactly, the newness *is* starting to wear off and it's all starting to become mundane and prosaic, routine almost.

Then she sees *her*. A woman that looks enough like herself to almost be her twin. Just like that, her desire to track down her sister's old home is rekindled… And what Samara does to *that* poor woman whose only sin was her similarity in appearance is absolutely abhorrent and unspeakable. Ecko turns her head to the side and vomits her last full, un-diet dinner into the dirt.

"That's it, I'm done. I've seen enough!" she cries as she tries to set the Night Pearl down. She desperately wants to rinse the foulness from her mouth. If she could bleach the images from her eyes, she would do that too. But she can't do either of those things. She can't do anything other than watch until it's over, because much like when she'd conjured up that bubble prison that entrapped Queen Rowana and MeanGreen Jaida, the Pearl is stuck to her hands too, held in place with that snapping, blue electricity.

She doesn't even try to shake it loose. She had already learned *that* wasn't possible. She'll just have to wait until the magic gets done with her. So much for learning how to control it. That's what she gets for being proud of her 'progress'. Reluctant but resigned, she turns her attention back to the horror show that she's holding in the palms of her hands.

Thankfully, Samara's done with … doing those atrocities to that poor woman and has moved on to retracing her steps back to the one sure place that she knows Ecko had been. The scene disintegrates and then Samara is back in that New Hampshire hospital where the sisters had switched places. *This* is the bloody hospital scene that Ecko had caught a glimpse of when the Pearl first started its rewinding trick. She watches as Samara slaughters her way through the halls, screaming out her demands until someone finally gives her what she's after... Ecko's medical records.

She witnesses Samara's meltdown when she realizes that there's no useful information to be found in that file. Charlie, bless him, had given them false information, fake names and fabricated addresses. The bill was left unpaid, so there's no way to track her down that way. Samara goes on a rampage, tearing through that town, killing everyone that can't, or won't tell her what she demands to know.

"Where. Did. My. Sister. Live? Someone here knows something!" she screams. She wraps her Shadow-engulfed hand around a tall man's throat and easily lifts him into the air. "She *must* have lived somewhere nearby. Someone knows where and I'm not leaving until I'm told what I wish to know!"

The man's face is turning red. He's choking and he tries to break her hold by kicking out at her. She gives him a sharp shake and turns to glare at the crowd. "Anybody? No? Alright then," she snaps as she slices his belly open with a scalpel that she'd taken from the hospital. He struggles as his guts spill into the dirt. Weary of his feeble attempts to save himself, Samara twists his head around so that it's on backwards, then she drops him to the ground.

"Who's next?" she shouts. "Or is there anyone here that would rather spill their secrets than their guts?"

An old man standing in front of a small cafe speaks up. "This is a small town, where everybody knows one another. I know everyone that lives around here. I remember the ones you're searching for, the old couple and your sister. They weren't from around these parts. They were just visiting, came into town once a week for supplies. Ask around at the Lodge. They have cabins that they rent out to tourists and vacationers and the like. That's your best bet. We do have a motel, but I would have known if they'd stayed there. My cousin owns it."

Samara saunters up to him, her hips swaying seductively, and he gulps. She wipes her bloody hands on his shirt and smiles up at him. "And where will I find this place, this Lodge?"

He lifts his trembling, wrinkled hand and points without breaking eye contact. "That way. The last building on the right, just at the edge of town."

Samara rises up onto her tiptoes, presses her lips to his and then trusts her tongue into his mouth in a nasty parody of a lover's kiss. The poor man is too terror-struck to even move. She pulls back and then reaches out and grabs his crotch. His eyes fly open wide when she murmurs, "Hmmm, when I'm done with my business, I'll come back for you. You deserve a reward." She throws her head back and laughs when the only sound he manages to produce is a terrified whimper.

The Night Pearl skips through the confrontation at the Lodge and takes her straight to the moment when Samara arrives at Ecko's cabin. She watches her sister go through her belongings, watches her destroy her things as she searches for clues. Then Samara's standing outside, watching as the flames just begin to peek out from under the front door.

Skip forward a bit more, and now the movie is all caught up to the present. She's watching what happens in real-time now, as Samara does the same to the cabin that Charlie and Susan had stayed at, searching it and then setting it on fire before she leaves.

Ecko watches her follow the trail back to her cabin, the fire now roaring out of control and spreading to the trees around it. The wildlife is panicking and fleeing, but she soon realizes that they're not trying to escape the flames. They're running from *Samara* and the evilness of the black fog that she's sending out after them, cruelly chasing them down just for the fun of it.

She sobs when she sees that the animals are running straight into her burning cabin, preferring to throw themselves into the roaring flames, to die in the fire just to get away from the evil behind them. Her disgusting excuse of a sister laughs maniacally as rabbits and deer, foxes and squirrels flee before her.

"How could you?" Ecko whispers, horrified and saddened beyond all comprehension. "Oh, how *could* you?" The screams of those innocent little creatures, willingly throwing themselves to their deaths in the flames, will surely haunt her for the rest of her life.

Samara stops in front of the blazing inferno of what was once Ecko's refuge and relishes its total destruction. She turns away as several police vehicles and firetrucks, with their lights flashing and sirens blaring, pull in behind her. The policemen all jump out and train their guns on her, and she throws her head back and laughs. Ecko can't hear what they're saying, but she knows that they're telling her to put her hands up and to lie face down on the ground.

Samara does what she's told. She lifts her hands up and lays down on the ground. Worlds away from where they are, Ecko frantically shakes her head and screams, "No, no, no! It's a trick! Get out of there!" But they don't hear her; of course, they don't. Samara does though. She raises her head up and grins wickedly. "Oh, *Sister*. I'm *so* glad you could join us."

That's when the officers close in on her and try to cuff her hands behind her back. They freeze, first in confusion and then in fear, when they see the inky black fog flow from her palms. They look to one another for answers as it creeps towards them. As one, the policemen slowly back away, knowing instinctively that whatever this dreadfulness is, it's dangerous, foul and deadly. But it's too late. The Shadow-smoke rises up and pours itself into the mouths of the three closest men. Samara picks herself up and brushes the dirt off her clothes while the non-polluted policemen scream at her to get back down on the ground.

Samara merely spins her pointer fingers in the air to make the 'turn around' gesture, and her three new puppets jerk around to face the rest of the boys in blue. And although they obviously try to fight the compulsion, they nevertheless lift their guns up and open fire on their own partners and teammates. The unsullied policemen and firefighters are too stunned to put up any sort of resistance, and every single one of them die by the hands of those that they'd trusted the most. When Samara's possessed pawns are the only ones left standing, she makes a gun of her finger and thumb and sticks it up under her own chin. With tears and horror in their eyes, and with trembling hands, they lift their own very real guns up and mimic her motions… and then they simultaneously pull the triggers.

Samara grins with wicked delight and gives them a cute little wave goodbye as they fall to the ground. "I hope you enjoyed the show, sister dear," she taunts as she pulls something from her pockets, something that makes her smile widen as she holds it up and inspects it.

Ecko's tears are coming down so fast, so hard that she can barely make out what it is, but she doesn't need to see it anyway. She knows exactly what it is. It was the very first image that the Night Pearl had showed her after switching from the Charlie show to the Samara program. Her demented and very determined twin has taken one of her pill bottles from her cabin's medicine cabinet. And right there, typed in big bold letters is the name of her doctor. Samara has found a very definitive clue that will lead her straight to Ecko's past.

The scene changes one last time. Samara makes good on her promise to return for the old man from the cafe. And when she's done with him, when his screams are finally quiet, she stands before his mirror, grinning at her own grisly reflection. She cleans herself up, washing the blood and gore away. She preens and primps and fluffs up her wild red curls.

Then she leans in close and grins with blood still in the spaces between her teeth. "Can you see me, sweet sister? Oh, I hope you can. I *so* hope you're watching, because it won't be much longer until I know where those two scared little rabbits of yours are hiding. I will find them. And when I'm done, they'll curse the Pale that, no that's not right... the *day*. They'll curse the *day* that they met you."

Then Samara's face disintegrates into that swirling cloud of dust and blows away. The Night Pearl finally shows mercy. The magic recedes and it returns to its inanimate state. It fades back to iridescent black, and her own magic finally, blessedly releases it. Glad to be done with it, she shoves it into her bag without even bothering to wrap it back up.

She quickly rinses her mouth and brushes her teeth to get rid of her puke breath. And then she does exactly what she'd predicted. She burrows into her sleeping bag, curls into a ball, and cries her heart out over the trauma that she had just witnessed. She lays there for hours, shivering and shaking and sobbing. Boodark returns at some point, but he doesn't even bother questioning her. Instead, he simply digs Sir Didymus out of her bag and then prods her until she emerges from her blanket cocoon long enough to accept his offering.

But she doesn't just take the plush from him. Instead, she scoots over and lifts the corner of the blanket, so that he can crawl in too. She pulls them both in close, their little bodies a huge comfort to her wounded heart. Snuggling them close soothes her, and eventually she calms enough so that her mind finally quiets itself. She falls into a desperately needed, dreamless sleep, her exhausted body, troubled mind, and broken heart all in agreement that in order to survive, they must give her this small slice of peace. To-morrow will come soon enough, and they can commence the torture and tormenting onslaught anew when it arrives.

20
BEAUTIFUL BROKEN BOY

Ecko

Ecko awakens to Boodark squirming and squiggling about, struggling for all he's worth to free himself from her clutches and escape the blanket burrito that he's squished into. She grins and hugs tighter, further trapping him in her embrace.

"Let me out!" he gasps. "I need air. And I need to water the trees! *Right now!*"

Her smile disappears, wiped away by the seriousness of the situation. She releases him and lifts the blanket, so that he can shuffle out and fly off to take care of his business. But then she remembers *why* he'd been in the sleeping bag with her. The breath whooshes out of her as the memory of last night hits her like a punch in the gut. All those poor people, those sweet animals... all dead because of Samara. Their blood will forever be on her sister's hands, and on hers, as well.

She acknowledges and shoulders her share of the blame. If she hadn't opened the way, if she'd only been stronger, none of this would have happened and all those people would still be alive. She glances down, convinced that her own hands, mirror images of her twin's, are also coated in the blood of all those innocents. Even though she doesn't see a single trace of crimson, they'll *never* wash clean.

She futilely scrubs them against her pj's as Boodark glides back in and *thwomps* down beside her. Before he has a chance to open his mouth and demand food, she stands up and goes off to take care of her own pressing needs and to change out of her sleepwear.

When she returns, she finds her batty little companion frowning ferociously and muttering to himself. She leaves him to it...she has her own haunted thoughts to contend with. They remain quiet as they go about packing up and cleaning the campsite, both of them lost in their own private thoughts. She sets out a couple of donuts for Boodark's breakfast, but passes on them herself. Her stomach is still sour, and she doesn't want to be sick again.

She sits and waits for him to get done eating, thinking over all that she'd learned. Her mind is still stuck on the nightmares she'd witnessed, as stuck as the Night Pearl hand been to her hands. She can't shake the memories loose, and something keeps nagging at her...other than the overall horror of it all. Her mind keeps returning to that last scene, the one where Samara had gone back for that old man.

It keeps flashing back and focusing on one of the walls in that small cafe, a wall covered in posters and business cards, wanted ads and announcements. She studies the mental image, trying to figure out just what's so important there. What could possibly be so disturbing about this wall, that the image of it keeps coming back, pushing aside and taking precedence over the other, more unpleasant memories.

She just can't figure out why her mind has become so fixated on such unimportant details, such as a wall of mundane announcements. What does she care about the grand opening of the town's new grocery store? Why should she care about Phil Conway's going away party? She doesn't even know Phil.

But then she sees it, the calendar with all its little red X's crossing out the days gone by. The last one crossed out is the 21st. *Of July!* That can't be right. She frowns as she thinks back. She'd discovered her real birthday was on May 18th. That was the day she'd received her magic, the day her mother's spelled tattoo had disappeared from her ankle. It's also when she'd ended up in the hospital, when she'd almost blown up said hospital and nearly killed them all from the magical overload. The very next day, May 19th, was when Samara had pulled her through the mirror and switched places with her.

She thinks back, counting the nights that she's spent here, on Oblerian. She remembers that first terrifying night with Blaxx, when she'd learned about Pitch and Pale. She thinks of the night spent with both Hobglins, tiptoeing through the Scream Patch, and then the night that she'd helped Faoira get her seal skin back and in return, been gifted with the Night Pearl. Then there was that first night with Boodark the Great, and the following night with Boodark the Drunk. They'd spent the next night in the tent, after the rain and their little spat. And then last night. That's seven nights. Exactly one week. It was *not* sixty-three days!

She'd known that her time here wouldn't match up with Earth's. How could it? The Pale and Pitch cycle is roughly thirty-six hours, twenty-three hours of Pale and thirteen of Pitch. Earth has only twenty-four hours in a day/night cycle. Also, in the prerecorded message from her mother, Laelynn had briefly mentioned that time moves differently on Earth. But still…. *nine weeks?*

She quickly does the math in her head. Assuming that the calendar was correct and that the person in charge of marking off the days with red X's hadn't fallen behind, that would mean that there are nine Earth days to a single *one* of this world's Pale's. As shocking as this discovery is, she really should have figured it out sooner. She should have caught on as soon as the Night Pearl showed her how many lovers her sister had entertained, how many lives she'd destroyed, and by how much Samara had learned… because she'd had to take a crash course in learning all about Earth and its inhabitants. And she'd learned it *fast*. In hindsight, she realizes now that Samara couldn't possibly have accomplished all that in a mere seven days, not even with her foul magic at her disposal.

"Oh no," she whispers aloud, in sudden, horrific understanding of exactly what her mind had been trying to point out to her… Charlie. Poor Charlie has been going out of his mind with worry for her, *for two whole months*! She cannot bear it. A fresh wave of urgency crashes over her, threatening to drown her. She has to get out of here! She needs to get back home. *Now.*

"You done eating?" she snaps as she quickly tugs her tennies on and jumps to her feet.

"I've *been* done. I was waiting on *you.*" Then he clears his throat and murmurs, "Ahem. I want to talk to you about something…"

Ecko picks up her backpack and shrugs it on. "Sure. You can talk to me about anything. But can we discuss it as we walk? I really want to make it out of the forest today…uh, before Pitch, I mean. Do you think that's possible?"

Boodark hop/walks along beside her. "It will be close, but yes, I believe so. If no unforeseen cataclysmic events occur, we should arrive at the edge of the Sorrow Marshes by Pale's end. Now, about what I wanted to tell you…"

Her startled gasp interrupts him yet again. "*Oh!* Look Boodark!" She stops walking and squats down for a closer look. Beautiful, brand new blades of grass have sprouted up in a wide patch where yesterday there'd been only barren, lifeless dirt.

"That's what I wanted to tell you!" he cries out in a disgruntled voice. "While I was on my way to…where I was going LastPitch, I got to thinking about how your magic changed the FireFairy Queen. I wondered if that green wisp got a taste of it too. I'm pretty sure that she did. She *seemed* different, although certainly not as drastically as Queen Rowana changed. Then I started thinking about the first time I witnessed your magic, when you got so mad at me and almost lost control of it. I wondered if your magic had touched on anything *then*. I wondered, if I went back to that spot, would I find anything different about it?"

"I had to know, so when I was done with my business, I took a roundabout-way route. I circled back, so I could get a look-see. And I saw it! Oh, you left some magic behind, alright!" He pauses and stares up at her with big, saucer eyes. "Do you remember the tree? You turned away from me, so that you wouldn't accidentally hurt me, and you grabbed onto a dead tree for support."

She winces at the remembered pain that she'd felt, the sickness and sadness of that dying tree. "I remember. But it wasn't dead. It was sick and very near death, but there was still a spark of life inside of it."

Boodark nods. "Well, it's definitely not sick anymore. It's covered in new growth, and the branches are full of new green leaves!" His voice lowers to a reverent whisper. "You healed it…. And now *this.*"

He glances around the clearing for a moment and then turns back to her. "This is the *exact* spot that you were standing when your magic awakened. Your feets were naked at the time. I believe the magic must have flowed from your feets and into the ground."

They both stare down at the new plant life in awe. She can't help but reach out and gently trail a hand over the tender new shoots, and she gasps when the tiny individual blades move. They bend and arch themselves in order to follow her hand! She stills her movements and the shoots sway closer, stretching upwards to curl themselves around her fingers.

Now she's crying...again. But this time it's not because of horror or trauma or guilt. She cries because she can *feel* their thankfulness, their absolute joy at just being alive. The word *AllMother* whispers through her mind and she knows without a single doubt that it was those little sprouts that planted it there.

"They think I'm their mother," she whispers as her heart all but melts into a puddle inside her chest. Her magic comes awake with a sigh of welcome, filling her eyes with a hazy glow, and suddenly she can *see* the tiny life-spark in each and every blade, as her hand begins to tingle and light up with a soft glow.

"Grow," she whispers as she runs her fingers, feather-soft through them. They inch up a bit taller, even as all-new grass babies poke their heads up out of the dirt alongside them. Her tears drip down to water them, and purple buds suddenly emerge and unfurl themselves into the tiniest, most precious blossoms. It is the single most beautiful moment of her life and it almost breaks her heart to walk away and leave them behind. What would become of these sweet, innocent babies in this unforgiving, vampire world, where everything is a predator, but also prey at the same time?

She has no idea if it will work or if it's even possible, but before she tearfully leaves them to their uncertain fates, she places her hands onto the thicket wall that surrounds the Bumbershoot glen and asks it to shield and protect those that she must leave behind. She mentally pushes every ounce of will that she possesses behind the request, amplifying it by projecting mental images of signs saying *KEEP OUT! PROTECT!* And then she shoves herself through, sobbing from the pain of a goodbye that she has no choice but to make.

Boodark watches it all with hope blooming in his heart, just like those flowers that he hasn't seen for over two hundred years, blossoming before his wondering eyes. He truly believes that Ecko is a powerful force of good, come to save his world, even if she doesn't yet realize it. She's a bright, white light in the darkest, blackest Pitch, but her magic is also unpredictable, wild and untamed. *She* is unpredictable, with her broken heart and her wounded soul... with her self-doubt and her inability to believe in herself.

As a brand new Wandelaar, without a mentor's tutelage and guidance, she still hasn't a clue as to what all she can accomplish. She doesn't understand the magnitude of *good* that she could bring about. She has no idea *how* to do any of it. Her magic is raw and untried, and she definitely needs to practice. And she needs to figure it all out as soon as possible. If her father ever gets his hands on her… He makes a vow to himself to do all that he can to help her.

He will push her to become all that she is meant to be… and he won't be doing it for purely selfish reasons now, no matter how it might appear. It's true that he'd originally sought her out because he'd been drawn to her magic. He'd only pursued her, because he planned to use her for his own gain. Does he believe that she's the one, the *only* one that can help him? Yes. Does he believe that she'll be his salvation, that she'll be able to break his curse? Again, yes.

But he also realizes that this situation isn't as simple as he once believed it to be. Things are no longer black and white and all about *him* and *his* problems. There's much more at stake than he could have ever dreamed. Ecko is so much more important than he'd thought, perhaps even crucial to the *whole* of Oblerian. Not just him.

It won't stop him, though. Even knowing that she is perhaps Oblerian's only hope for survival won't stop him from using her to get what he can from her. He needs help, after all. If it were only about him, he might be able to live with the curse, ugly or not. But it's *not* just about him.

But he also can't ignore the fact that *she* needs help too. She's like a babe, an innocent. Her magic is strong, good, and pure, but she doesn't know how to wield it. She knows nothing of this world that she so aptly likens to a vampire. She needs his help as much as he needs hers, and he intends to see that she gets it. He's astonished to realize that he's come to care for her. He almost ...loves her. But he's still terrified to tell her about his Secret. Just the thought of exposing his Secret makes him tremble.

He sighs heavily and his shoulders slump from the weight of his guilt. He needs to tell her. He has to confess it all, and he must do it soon. "Two more Pales," he bargains with himself as he watches her squirm her way through the thicket wall. "You can only stall for two more Pales, Boodark the Coward." He spreads his wings and lifts himself up and over the wall to wait for her on the other side. He hopes she makes it out with less wounds than she'd received when she first went through it. He shakes his head in dismay and mutters, "That girl is clumsier than a pixie baby try-ing out his wings for the first time."

"Ugghh, I am so sick of this!" Ecko wails. She lifts herself up and spits dirt and tiny bits of mulch from her lips. She's been walk-ing for hours, and she's exhausted again. Well, she been walking and face-planting, that is. So, not only is she tired, she's sore and has added a dozen or so extra scrapes and bruises to her already extensive collection of wounds.

Not long after leaving the Bumbershoot clearing, she'd come to a place where there were no more trails to follow, no easy paths to take. The forest had grown denser, the spindly, sickly trees crowding so closely together that it makes passage difficult. The mulch on the ground is so thick here that her feet sink down three inches, and it cleverly disguises numerous trip hazards… and she's certain that she's finding every single one of them.

"I'm so sick of falling on my face and eating dirt. I'm sick of this forest. I hate this place! I hate everything!" She sits up and glares at an oozing scrape on her elbow… just glares down at it like she can't believe the audacity of it letting precious blood escape her body. She's beyond frustrated and she's beginning to feel a sense of hopelessness creeping in. "And why am I so ding dang darn-it tired all the time?" she howls up the canopy of bare, leafless branches above her head.

She continues to sit there on her butt for a moment or two. She's pouting, pure and simple, but she convinces herself that she's merely taking a much-needed break, so that she can catch her breath before she climbs back to her feet and trudges (and trips) onward. Boodark is nowhere to be seen, the little monster.

She'd let him ride on her shoulder because it had been too difficult for him to fly through such close quarters. It was either carry him or wait for him to do that hop/walk shuffle behind her, and that would have taken too long. He has short, stumpy legs that hinder his ability to walk fast. They would be here for the next ten years if he'd had to walk. He *could* have flown over the canopy, but he'd been reluctant to leave her to cover such a large area on her own.

So, she'd let him sit on her shoulder... until he decided that he was going to gas her out and then act like it wasn't *him* smelling up the forest. He'd tried to convince her that it was the decaying mulch that smelled like the Bog of Eternal Stench. And the bad thing was...she'd believed him! Until she'd started falling and planting her face in it, that is. It only took her about seven tumbles before she'd clicked onto the fact that the mulch does *not* smell like a port-a-can pumper truck that had crashed and exploded and the contents had been baking in the Texas heat for three days.

No, it smelled just like mulch is supposed to smell, like dead, decaying vegetation. And she'd known for *sure* it was him when she'd heard a tiny squeak in her ear that could only have come from Boodark's buttocks. She'd just about had a meltdown.

"That stink is *not* the mulch! It… was… *yooou!*" she'd howled as she reached up to grab him. But he was too fast. He'd been waiting for her to figure it out. He shot up off of her shoulder and out of her reach so fast, he might as well have been a bottle rocket. And he *laughed*, practically fell back down out of the air he'd laughed so hard.

"That's disgusting!" she'd shrieked at him "How old are you anyway? Five?"

Wings flapping to keep himself aloft (and out of her reach) he'd held his jiggling belly with one hand and pointed a claw at her from the other as he giggled and howled like a lunatic…a five-year-old lunatic.

"I can't believe it took you so long to figure out! I thought I was going to have to give up on my joke, because I *really* have to go poop! Plus, I was getting pretty tired of clinging to you like a suck-bug on an Octobeast's rump every time you tripped and fell. It's been a wild ride, let me tell you! I thought for sure you'd buck me off, then land on me and squash me like a bug!"

She'd picked up a stick then (probably the one she'd just tripped over) and chucked it at his head. Of course, he ducked it, laughing all the while. But then his face twisted up into a terrible grimace and he clutched at his belly with both hands. "Oh, I gotta *go!*" he'd exclaimed and flew off, clumsily zigzagging away through the trees.

"Serves you right, you little brat!" she'd yelled after him.

"That's the last time I give him a ride," she mutters now as she gets back up once again. "I don't care if his wings fall off and some-one eats his feet right off his legs. He can wiggle his way through this forest on his belly like a worm!" She wipes the blood from her elbow and brushes as much dirt from her clothes as she can. "Onward march!" she grumbles to herself as she continues with her quest of searching for the object responsible for that elusive thrumming sound.

She steadfastly ignores that *other* pulsing beat, the new one that only she seems able to hear. It had taken up cadence just minutes after leaving the Bumbershoot glen. It calls to her like a honeyed voice, tempting her to turn and take a different path. It is a wicked thing, like a heartbeat from a heart as dark as Pitch. It makes her feel ...things. Things she'd never felt before. It scares her, because it tempts her just as strongly as it repels her. So, she does what she does best. She pushes it aside, locking it away in a box inside her mind to deal with later. Or never, which is even better.

Another hour or so goes by and things seem to be getting a bit better. The trees have spread out enough so that she can easily navigate through them once again. There's more light here, dismal though it may be, and the layer of mulch isn't as thick upon the ground. The smell is about a thousand times more pleasant, and she's only tripped once since Boodark left to take care of things.

But she's starting to worry, because he hasn't made it back yet. He's never stayed away for so long, at least not during the day. Pitch is a different story; he stays out late then. But it's *not* Pitch, and she *is* worried, although she's trying to convince herself that it's just taking him longer to get through trees that are packed together as tight as sardines in a can.

She's seriously considering turning back to look for him when she hears crashing and cursing and grumbling behind her. She grins. Her bratty little orc-bat has returned. She sighs with relief and turns her head back to watch him approach. He spots her up ahead and yells, "I just took the biggest poop back there! You shoulda seen the size… *Watch out!*"

She jerks her head forward to watch where she's walking, but she doesn't see what's causing him such distress. She doesn't see the large puddle right in front of her, because it's cleverly camouflaged to look just like the rest of the solid ground around it, the surface sprinkled with dirt and mulch and twigs.

But even though she could see no threat, she knows that there *is* one somewhere, because Boodark is *scared*. She stops walking forward, but not fast enough. Too late, she finds that the ground in front of her is not as solid as it appears. Too late, she realizes that she has, quite literally, walked right into a trap.

Her upraised foot continues on the path that her brain had commanded it to go. Therefore, she steps down and sinks ankle-deep in thick, clingy goo. Long, thin tentacle-like appendages instantly emerge from the puddle of gunk to seize her ankle and wind up her leg. Unfortunately, she's not able to stop her momentum and her body continues forward, while her foot stays firmly stuck in the muck.

Down she goes again, only this time she hasn't just tripped, she's been caught in a well laid trap. Thankfully, she doesn't fall on her face, as is the norm. If she had, she would probably have drowned… in some ooey-gooey crud puddle. She lands on her hands and knees instead, and those strange, goo tentacle-ropes shoot out to further ensnare all four of her limbs. She struggles to break free, but finds that the more she struggles, the tighter they bind her.

"What *is* this?" she cries out with panic in her voice.

"Stop struggling," Boodark commands. "It's a Goo-puddle pit, a trap made from the sap of the Kreeker trees. Be calm and be oh, so still, Ecko. You will only make it worse if you fight it." He hovers beside her right shoulder, so that he's within her sight and so that she can hear his next, quietly spoken words.

"It's the Madar-gens; I can smell them," he commiserates as his shoulders droop, and he hangs his head. "This was bound to happen, sooner or later. I've been avoiding them for years, but I've always known that I couldn't keep crossing through their territory unchecked and unmolested forever. I've always known that this would be the inevitable outcome. They want something from me, you see. And they are just as determined to get it as I am to keep it. I'm just so sorry that they're using *you* to get it. But don't you worry. I'll give them what they demand. I won't let them hurt you."

Her eyes widen in alarm at his tone. "What do you mean? What are you doing? What do they want? Where *are* they?" She tries desperately to turn her torso enough so that she can see exactly what they're up against. The gooey ropes assume that she's trying to break free, so they lock her down even tighter still.

"Come on out, you've got me. I won't run." Boodark loudly calls out and her eyes dart back and forth, searching for the threat.

She hears a slight rustling, sees a flash of movement. The only reason she catches sight of it, so quickly, is because she's down low to the ground, stuck on her hands and knees as she is. It's small and it's hiding, blending into the bushes and scrub, but now that she's seen it, she can't *unsee* it.

"I see you," she informs it, the accusation loud and clear in her voice. And now that she knows what she's looking for, she realizes that it's not alone. They're everywhere. Her eyes run along the low-lying bushes and scrub, picking them out of their hiding spots amongst the undergrowth.

"You may as well stop hiding, I can see all of you just fine!" she yells.

"Not hiiidiiiing," a voice from above her answers in a terrible, hissing whisper. With a startled cry, she jerks her attention up to the tree branches, where even more of the creatures are waiting, watching.

They're the little bird people that she'd seen once before, through Dr Bradburn's 'therapy' mirror back at Regal Falls. Her doctor had liked to make her stare into the mirror to prove to herself that nothing but her own reflection lived in there. But Dr Bradburn had been oh, so wrong about that. All manner of things lived on the other side of the glass, in the OtherWorlds. And Ecko had still been able to see them, no matter how much therapy she received or how many drugs they forced on her. As much as it pained her to do it, she'd had to learn how to lie in order to survive the good doctor with all her good intentions and her college degrees. But oh, how she wishes now, and not for the first time, that Dr Bradburn had been right.

These strange little creatures, the Madar-gens, are bird people, literal bird people. They have bird skull heads with long bony beaks and holes for their nostrils and eyes, but they also possess human-like bodies. In fact, from the neck down they look *exactly* like humans, only on a much smaller scale, with human-like arms and legs, torsos, and hands and feet.

They're all bare-chested, males and females alike. The only garments they wear are tattered skirts and kilts. Standing at about eight inches tall, they're even smaller than Boodark, but they are decidedly more intimidating. Her little orc-bat buddy is ugly and most definitely cringe worthy, there's no denying that fact. But once she'd looked past all that ugly, she'd found that he's not even the least bit threatening.

But *these* things are a walking creep, show straight out of a nightmare. And believe it or not, it's not the look of them that has her shivering in revulsion. She'd actually found them kinda cute, when she first saw that mated pair through the mirror. Gothy and morbid perhaps, but cute, nonetheless. No, it's the *feel* of them that has all the tiny hairs of her body standing on end. In real life, up close and personal, they're not nearly so endearing. They're absolutely frightful, and not at all delightful. And they are 100% hostile.

"Not hiiidiinng," it hisses again. "Waitiiing."

Ecko picks out the one that had spoken and assumes that he's the one in charge, the star of this horror show, the leader of this macabre circus troupe. He's very manly, as manly as he can be, standing at only ten inches tall. He appears strong, with broad shoulders and bulging muscles. A bright yellow light glares out at her from deep within the otherwise empty sockets of his eyes. "Waiting for what?" she demands. "Who are you? What is it that you want?"

He spreads his wings and swoops down from his perch in the trees, drawing her attention to the fact that he does, in fact, have wings. She frowns as she thinks back, trying to remember. The two from the mirror hadn't possessed wings, she's sure of it. She'd watched them walk down a path, hand in hand and they'd definitely been wingless.

Birdman leader lands in front of her, just beyond the goop puddle. He's very unsettling, evoking feelings of dread deep in her heart. She takes a moment to study him further and realizes that his wings don't match! They're similar, but now that he's drawn closer, she can see the differences. They're both black, closely resembling a crow's wings, but the one on the left side is slightly smaller and the feathers are tipped with red.

"Waitiiing for hiiim to sssureeender," he whisper/hisses as he points at her companion.

Defeated and resigned to his fate, Boodark drops down to the ground and pulls his shoulders back. He holds his head up high, proudly, *bravely* as he addresses the leader, "You must promise to let her go when it's done. *Unharmed.*"

Birdman nods, "You haavvve my woooord."

Ecko's almost sick from the uneasiness roiling about in her belly. "What's going on, Boodark? What are you doing?"

He turns to her and again tells her to be calm and then assures her that no harm will come to her. "Why are you avoiding the question?" she demands. "Just tell me. *What do they want?*"

He cringes and turns his eyes away from her as he answers. "My wings. They want my wings."

She's too stunned to reply for a moment, and all she can do is sputter. But then she finds her voice again. "Well, they can't have them." She turns to Birdman. "You can't have his wings. They're his. You can't just go around stealing other people's wings…." Her eyes drop to his mismatched set, and she realizes that's *exactly* what he'd done. She slowly runs her eyes over the rest of the bird people. The ones in the tree branches all have wings, some with matching pairs and some, like him, have two different wings in their set. The ones on the ground and hiding in the shrubbery are wingless.

"What, you can't grow your own wings, so you steal others?" she asks him, but she doesn't wait for him to answer. "That's horrible. You should be ashamed of yourselves! Why can't you just walk, like everyone else that has no wings? I mean, I've always wanted to fly too, but I *can't.* And I would *never* steal someone else's just so that I *could.*"

She turns to Boodark. "I can get myself out of this goop. Don't you let him take your wings. Don't you *dare.*"

But he shakes his head sadly and tells her, "There is no way out of that trap without their help. That's why they chose this particular snare to capture you in. Do not be afraid. Do not be sad. They'll grow back."

He turns and nods at Birdman. "I'm ready."

Ecko grunts as she yanks her hands up, trying to pull them free of the puddle of gunk. She frantically searches inside herself. If she can get to her magic, she might be able to free her hands. If she can get her hands free, maybe she can bubble the leader and do a hostage exchange. She needs to stall them until then.

The winged ones descend to join the ones emerging from their hidey holes, and they all crowd around and begin murmuring a creepy and haunting chant.

"Liieee doownnn," Birdman orders and Ecko immediately starts panicking, thrashing about and screaming.

"Don't you do it, Boodark! I forbid this, do you hear me? I *forbid* you to do this thing!"

He smiles sadly at her and then promptly ignores her cries and does what he'd been ordered to do. He lays down on his belly and closes his eyes tight.

"Wait!" she screams. "Wait! What else do you want? Surely, there's something else we can do for you, something else we can give to you. Name your price; just let him go!"

Her cries are ignored by all and the chanting grows louder as the Birdman takes hold of Boodark's large, leathery wings.

"Look!" she sobs. "His wings are way too big for you, for *any* of you! There's no way you'll be able to make them work on your smaller bodies. Just let him go! *Please!*"

Birdman leans over, the yellow light inside his bony eye sockets shining brightly as his long, hummingbird-like tongue emerges from his beak. The thing is about four inches long, thin and pale and coated in thick, sticky saliva, and he uses it to lick all along the base of Boodark's wings, right where they come out of his back.

Boodark sucks in air with a loud gasp and his claws dig ruts into the ground. Ecko cries harder at the sight, and in the midst of such deep, all-consuming panic, she cannot locate the magic within herself. Desperate for help, she calls to the monsters inside her mind. *He* answers right away.

"*Oh, now you wish to talk? Now we are friends?*" Rage's voice whispers sarcastically in her mind.

"We don't have time for this!" her mental-self screams back. "We have to stop them! We have to save him!"

Rage laughs. "*Too late*" he sighs. "*It's much too late to save him. But… Let me out and we can avenge him. We can make them hurt, just as they are hurting him. And make no mistake… he is hurting. He's quiet, so as to spare your feelings, but he is suffering immensely.*"

She continuously fights against her bonds, not caring that they've grown so tight that she's lost all feeling in her hands and feet. "Please," she internally begs. "Is there nothing we can do to stop this?"

"It has already begun," Rage answers. *"There is no turning back now. Watch. Watch closely at how he suffers, and then tell me true that you do not wish to return pain onto them tenfold. Watch..."* he purrs and then fades away.

Tears stream down her face, because she can do nothing else but witness exactly how horrible the stealing of one's wings truly is.

Smoke is beginning to rise up all along the bottom of Boodark's wings, everywhere that Birdman's tongue had touched him. He hisses in pain and tears leak from the corners of his tightly closed eyes as his skin melts away and splits, opening up a thin, bloody fissure at the place where the wings attach to his back.

A female walks up, tiny, bare breasts swaying, and hands the leader a large coil of vine that's been braided into a thin rope. He takes one end of it and secures it around her friend's wings, just above where the skin has separated. He wraps it around them several times before tying it off, and then yanks on it a couple of times to ensure that it will hold. Ecko howls at the cruelty and carelessness as Boodark cries out from the pain of it.

Birdman pays them no mind and continues on the path he's started down. Satisfied that the knots will hold, he nods at the female, and she flies up and over the nearest branch, stringing the rest of the rope behind her. When she lands back down on the ground, the rope is left draped over the branch. They've just made a crude pulley system and they waste no time in putting it to use. Several strong-looking birdmen grab onto the trailing rope end and when their leader nods, they all begin pulling it taut, so that it yanks Boodark upwards... *by his wings.* They stretch them up and away from his body, until white bone glistens wetly through the gap between his flesh.

Birdman holds his hand up in the 'wait' signal and bends over the silently suffering Boodark once more. He slips his tongue into the gap, all along the exposed bone and cartilage, and it immediately starts hissing and smoking.

Boodark inhales sharply and his whole body goes rigid, then he falls still and quiet as he loses consciousness. The acrid stench of burning flesh and bones wafts over to her, causing her to gag. "Please stop this," she begs.

But no one listens. No one cares. Of course, they don't care if she begs. They have to be completely heartless in order to commit such a terrible crime in the first place, so no amount of begging will change their minds.

A minute or two, that seems as long as a year, passes with Birdman standing over his unconscious victim, closely watching the progress that his acid spit has on the wing bones. When it has eaten all the way through, he nods to the pullers, and they heave back on the rope once more.

At the first tug, Boodark's eyes fly back open and his startled, agonized scream rends the air. He starts thrashing, trying to escape the pain, and Birdman hisses, "Ssssteeady. Be sssteady and ssstill, or sshheee diiiessss."

Boodark's tortured eyes roll around to meet hers and he stops struggling. At the sight of her sobbing for him, he tries to reassure *her.* "It's ok, Ecko... almost done now. It will all be over soon." And then he grunts loudly as the team pulls so hard on the rope that it briefly lifts him an inch or so up off the ground.

She is horrified beyond all thought when she realizes that they are ripping his wings off, tearing them right off of his back. And all the while, he is awake and can feel every excruciating second of it. There's a terrible, slow ripping sound now, so loud that it drowns out every other sound, louder even than her own screams that are ripping from her throat.

The nasty little creatures pull and stretch and tear until his wings are almost completely free, connected only by thin strings of vein-like tendrils. Birdman holds his hand up again and the team immediately stops pulling. They hold them steady and in place, with two inches of exposed tendril-veins stretched between the wings and the bloody mess of Boodark's poor, ravaged back. Then Birdman turns to address his people. "Na-lee, coome fort-tthh, my Daaughterrr."

A female adorned in leaves and braided necklaces, her body painted with black symbols, makes her way through the onlookers. She stops beside Boodark and traces the trail of his tears with her fingertips. "You fly high, loving your wings, even though they are changed things. You fly alone, leaving your family down below, frozen in place. You fly fast and far to escape your guilt, as they sleep the dead sleep. You hurt so, and yet still up in the air you fly, wild and free."

"All I want is to be like you, to fly high and alone, fast and far, wild and free. So, down you must come now, down, down. Back down to the ground, a beautiful broken baby. I will take from you the beauty I have been denied." She lovingly caresses his face. "SShhh. Do not cry, broken boy. It is not so sad. You will fly again."

She leans over and places a kiss on his tear-streaked face and then turns to face Birdman. He dips his fingers into the blood from Boodark's back and paints a tiny, rune-like symbol on her skull head, the vivid crimson contrasting sharply against the white of her skull. She takes a deep breath, turns her back to him, and bows her head. Two males step forward to grab her arms and hold her tightly as Birdman bends down to run his tongue between her shoulder blades and along her spine. She screams and struggles as her own skin splits wide open.

A female approaches and stands behind her, catching the dripping blood in what appears to be the top half of some unfortunate creature's empty shell. When it's full almost to overflowing, she steps back, and Birdman moves up to take her place. He raises up a single, razor-sharp claw clutched in his hands (an obviously *stolen* claw, because in proportion, it's like a butcher knife in the hands of a human man.) He raises it up high as the chanting grows louder, faster.

He turns his attention to Boodark and begins slicing, one by one, through the exposed tendons. He severs them down low, close to his body, so that the long length of the tendrils remains attached to the wings...and they *move.* They squirm and thrash all about like snakes that had their heads chopped off.

The chanting continues to grow in intensity with every single separation. Boodark can stand it no longer, and he mercifully loses consciousness again as the monsters slowly and agonizingly sever all that's left to bind his wings to him.

The chant comes to an abrupt end as Birdman slices through the last remaining tendon. The silence is almost deafening, as they all stare at those wings, watching the veins slither around like decapitated snakes, searching for their missing heads. They seem to be waiting for … something. And then *something* happens. The wings held aloft begin to shimmer. They grow hazy and blurry, almost as if they're disappearing. But they don't disappear; they *change.*

Boodark's poor, leathery bat wings morph into a completely different set of wings. They're no longer huge, bulky things; they've shrunk down and completely changed shape… into a double set of stunningly beautiful cicada-like wings. They look just like someone had taken a pair of emerald-green cicada wings, glued another complete set of lighter, neon green ones over the top of them, and then dipped them both in a shimmering glitter finish.

"Fassst, before they diie!" the bird-girl named Na-lee commands as she turns away, once more presenting her back. The rope pullers lower the new wings slowly, while Birdman directs them to the incision between her shoulder blades. The tendrils have begun slowing their movements, but now they renew their thrashing, stretching and straining towards that bloody hole.

"Braccce heerrr!" he hisses, and the two birdmen on her arms hold her even tighter still. The tendrils plunge themselves straight into that bleeding cavity, and then she's screaming and screaming, as they burrow in like worms in the dirt, pulling the wings in and drawing them down tight against her flesh. Once they've completely burrowed into their new body as deep as they can go, a crowd of women rush forward to quickly sew the edges of the hole closed with tiny needles and shiny, blue thread. Then they pack what appears to be a poultice of mud and moss all around the newly closed, but still raw and seeping wound.

Na-lee sags in a faint and the men lift her up between them and carry her away. The entire crowd of bird people shout in triumph as they pass by. When they've disappeared into the trees, Birdman turns and waves a dismissive hand at Ecko as he hisses, "It isss done. Releassse herrr." The woman holding the shell full of blood walks towards her but stops so suddenly that the contents slosh over the edges. "Her eyesss!" she rasps in a shrill, alarmed voice.

Birdman studies the girl trapped in the muck, trying to determine how much of a threat she would be, once they've let her go. "Haalfff," he hisses. "Pour only haalfff," he commands.

The female creeps forward. It's very obvious that she doesn't want to get any closer to the girl whose eyes have turned into silver pools. She clutches the shell and lifts off the ground to fly a circle around her, pouring the blood into the goo-puddle like it's an offering. The gunky ropes immediately loosen, but not nearly enough for her to get free.

Rage's laugh rings through Ecko's mind. *'A neutralizer, but only at half strength! King Ky-al is scared of us, as he should be.*

He pours in only half of the solution, so that it takes longer to re-lease you, affording them the time to get far away.'

Finished with her chore, the woman quickly flies off into the cover of trees. She does not look back.

Birdman insists, "I have honorrred thhee deal. Do not ssstrug-gle. Theey will releassse you in time." Then he gestures for his bird people to leave the way they had come.

"Wait!" Ecko cries. "What about Boodark? Is he going to be ok?"

Birdman shrugs. "Up to hhiimm," he hisses.

She yanks against her bonds, angry, *so very angry* at the terrible thing these creatures had just done. Rage is livid, not only at them, but at her too. He does *not* want them to be allowed to walk away from this. He fiercely rattles his cage, snarling and slamming himself against the door. *'Let me out! Do it now, before they get away. We can make them suffer like they've never suffered before!'*

She does her best to ignore the pounding and shouting inside her skull. "You can't just leave him like this!" she begs Birdman. "He could die!"

But he just turns and begins walking away. "I care nauugghhtt of hisss fate," he replies and Rage snarls. *'You cannot mean for us to sit back and do nothing!'*

But for now, that is exactly what she must do, unless she intends to let Rage out to go on a killing spree. Because she's certain that's exactly what he intends to do ...slaughter them all. And part of her wants that, wants it desperately. But she cannot, *will not*, become a creature like her sister.

"Curse you." She says it in a quiet, calm voice that belies the storm raging inside her. Although the words are uttered in almost a whisper, they carry across the distance between them. They crash into him, ghost through him like a phantom wind, chilling him to the very core of his being. Birdman freezes in place, and he refuses to turn back to look at her, but he shivers in sudden apprehension as her words knife through him.

"Curse you, Ky-al, King of the Madar-gens of the Black Forest. I *curse* you. You will regret what you have done here. Maybe not today, maybe not even tomorrow. Go on and enjoy what you've stolen...enjoy them well while you have them, because I'll be coming back for you. I *will* find you and I'll take back what you've stolen from him. And know this. If he dies, *so too shall you.*"

He turns back then and stares into eyes that have clouded over and turned completely white. Deep within his heart he understands that he has just sealed his fate, and possibly the fate of his entire clan. He can see his ending, reflected back to him from within her milky eyes.

"Kee-lin, leave tthee bleeed-ssstop," he calls, and a female rushes back out of the tree line, carrying the mossy poultice. She sets it on the ground beside Boodark and bows her head low at Ecko before turning and fleeing back into the safety of the trees.

Birdman nods once and then retreats, walking backwards so that he doesn't have to turn his back to her. She grins a terrible, malicious smile, and had she seen herself right then, she would have been horrified. Because in that moment, she looks more like Samara than herself. Although they're twins and their features are identical, Samara's cruelty and evilness are somehow always portrayed clearly on her face. But she can't see herself, and so the incident passes with her none the wiser of just how much she resembled her sister in those brief moments.

It takes almost half an hour for the last of the muck ropes to let go and melt back into the goo-puddle. She quickly figured out that the blood neutralizer worked faster if she stopped pulling and struggling. The bonds quit trying to fight back when she holds herself completely still. So, for the next twenty or so long, torturous minutes she stays there, trapped on hands and knees, staring intently at her little friend. She strains to see the barely-there rise and fall of his back as he breathes shallowly.

She talks to him while she waits. She wills him to be strong, begs him to hold on. She threatens to withhold granola bars and promises to make him more clothes. She knows that he probably can't hear her, but it makes her feel better to talk to him.

Besides, she doesn't want to give Rage the opportunity to open his big, fat mouth and voice his own displeasure. She's very much aware of it already, as he's steadily snarling in a low, guttural growl. She ignores him. It's best not to even acknowledge that beast.

So, she waits, and she talks until she feels her gooey bonds fall away. She's in motion the very instant the last one's gone. She scrabbles forward, crawling as fast as she can through the muck.

And then she's out, free of the goo-puddle, and she quickly crab crawls to her friend's side.

It's even worse up close. His poor, ravaged back is splayed wide open and tiny blood sucking bugs have crawled onto him and gathered to feast on his torn flesh. She angrily picks them off and tosses them away as she tries to figure out what she's supposed to do now. She can sew it up, she decides, but as she digs in her bag for needle and thread, she recalls him saying that his wings can grow back. If she remembers correctly, he'd said that they grow back in thirty days' time. Would she mess that up if she sewed up his wound? Will they even grow back after being ripped out as they had been? She just doesn't know, but she *does* know that he can't continue bleeding like he is. The wound cannot remain open and exposed.

She quickly Germ-x's her hands and arms, and through her tears, she gently cleans him up and pats the poultice into his back to stop the bleeding. She prays that she's not making a mistake, prays that she's not somehow making it worse. She doesn't know what else to do, and until Boodark wakes up and tells her differently, it's *all* she can do.

Now she must wait until he regains consciousness. She refuses to even entertain the idea that he won't awaken. So, until then, she works on the last bit of her basket-weaving project. Now she knows *exactly* why she'd needed a basket in the first place. It's just the right size to carry a 'sprawled upon his belly' Boodark.

She finishes the basket long before Boodark the Wounded awakens. It suddenly occurs to her, as she sets it aside and reaches for a bottle of water, that she's not covered in goop. Like, not at all.

There's not a single glop of goo on her, not even a smear of it. She turns to look at the goo-puddle and there *is* no goo-puddle, just an empty, hollowed out dip where it had been.

She stands up and walks over to it, careful not to get too close… just in case. The muck has completely disappeared, dissolved or seeped into the ground… or maybe it just magically vanished. There's no way of knowing where it had gone. There's no trace left of it except the empty hole that got left behind.

She shivers and backs away from it, trying to block the memory of how icky it had felt to be trapped in goo. Oh, how she longs for a bath. A nice, steaming hot, four-hour long soak in a tub would go a long way towards helping her forget the cruddy feeling of being stuck in crud.

She returns to her vigil at Boodark's side. He hasn't stirred, but she's decided that they have to be moving on now anyway. She has absolutely no desire to remain here, where such horrors had taken place… where those nasty little things could come back at any moment and try to finish them off.

'*I wish they would,*' Rage snarls.

"Oh, shut up," she answers as she drains her water bottle. She sets the purple basket beside Boodark and as carefully as she can, she lifts him up and places him inside it. He fits perfectly, as if she'd made it just for him… as if she'd somehow known she would need to carry him at some point.

Maybe this is exactly what her dream had been about, and she'd just forgotten it all, except for the compulsion to make the basket.

It's very possible, and stranger things have happened. She reaches into her bag for one of her soft t-shirts, to use as a blanket for him. She's no doctor (or vet?) but she's pretty sure that she needs to keep him warm, so that he doesn't go into shock.

She gets him all tucked in and then shrugs her backpack on. Then she lifts Boodark in his beddy-bye basket, careful not to move too fast and jostle him. She loops the long, purse-like handles over her head, so that he's cradled against her ribs, just below her breasts. This way she can steady him with her hands if her movements become too rough. The thought of causing him further pain breaks her heart.

She never looks back as she holds him close and walks away, gratefully leaving the scene of the crime behind. If she had, she might have seen Ky-al, half hidden in the underbrush, worriedly watching her go.

They'd been of a like mind, Ecko and Ky-al. Much like her thoughts of him and his clan returning to finish them off, thoughts of *her* following his clan and seeking revenge had him remaining behind to stand guard while his people made their way to safety. He should feel relief as he watches her walk away and disappear through the trees. But he doesn't. All he feels is fear and regret. He wishes that he'd never given in to his daughter's demands to own *his* particular wings.

But his Na-lee is spoiled, and no other wings would do. And so, his own daughter's selfishness and his reluctance to disappoint her very well may have cost the entire clan their hard-fought, stolen wings, and possibly even their lives. For that is what he'd seen in the girl's cloudy white eyes as she'd cursed him by his name that he'd not given to her. He'd seen his entire clan standing in a gory, bloody field amid countless, lifeless bodies, wailing over the loss of their hard-gained wings. He fears, in his most secret heart of hearts that he has doomed his people to eternal perdition.

Ecko walks for nearly four more hours before signs of the Sorrow Marshes begin to appear. The ground's growing soggy and her feet squish wetly through two inches of sludge. The trees have spread out and they've grown wider and darker… so dark that they appear almost black. But there's also more green here than she's seen anywhere else.

The ground and the trees are covered in thick patches of moss… thankfully it's the normal kind, not the blue, toxic tofu kind. At least she *thinks* it's normal. She's been keeping her distance the best that she can, just in case it decides to get up and crawl across the ground to try and eat her. She's taking nothing for granted in this place.

She stops when she's gone as far as she can before the *real* swamp begins. If she takes one more step, she'll be wading through black, sludge water for only God knows how long. The marsh stretches as far ahead of her as she can see, and it's absolutely, positively dreadful. She *really* doesn't want to do this. "I *can't* do this," she whimpers. She's terrified of dark, murky waters. It doesn't matter what kind of water it is either, she has issues with them all: lakes, oceans, rivers, ponds, and most definitely swamps. If it doesn't have crystal clear H2O that she can see straight through to the bottom, well then, it's a big, fat resounding nope from her.

"Nope," she mutters. "No, no, no, no." This place is just *no*. She's been dreading reaching its banks ever since Boodark first mentioned that they'd have to cross through it. She had, in fact, immediately loathed the thought of it. The only times she'd ever seen a swamp was in pictures and movies, but she's always known *instinctively* that she would not do well should she ever have to make her way through one… And that was based on *Earth's* standards.

She can't help but think about how much worse *this* world's bogs and marshes will be. Without Boodark to talk to her and keep her mind occupied, she's spent these last few hours thinking about nothing else, but how bad it's going to be. Just how bad will it be? What kind of horrors will she find? She's tried to mentally prepare herself for the upcoming challenge, tried to bolster her courage by reminding herself of all she's already gotten through, everything that she's survived. That doesn't help at all. It just serves to remind her that the things of this world are horrid beyond all imaginings.

And she'd been right. Now that she's here looking at it, she realizes that there really was no way to properly prepare herself. Although there are no monsters in sight (yet) it's just as terrifying as she'd imagined it would be.

'*Such a gloomy, dank, nasty place this is*', she thinks. It dark and dreary, with turbid, scummy waters, and she keeps seeing *things* move from the corners of her eyes...things that hide as soon as she turns to see what they are. A twitch here, a flash there. A faint buzzing sound, as patches of moss tremble in the trees. She shivers as she glares down at the water. Just how deep *is* it, she wonders. What if it's so deep that she can't wade through it? And really, *why* does it have to be so dark and secretive? What's it hiding? Probably dead people and monsters and ghosts and all manner of bugaboos. *Nothing* terrifies her like the thought of being in the water with dead things all around her… unless it's the thought of being in the water with dead things all around her *in the dark.* This is going to be so bad. And *why, for the love of all things holy,* is the air wet?

"I'm not doing it," she matter-of-factly informs the moss that's dangling from the tree beside her. It looks just like the Spanish moss that grows on the Texas Oaks and Cypress trees, but it's full of thin, inch-long, fire-red thorns. They look positively lethal, and she hopes with all her might that she'll be able to avoid them.

"Nope, I'm not doing it," she repeats as she turns and retraces her steps back to land that's dry enough to set up camp. Tomorrow will be soon enough to set out into the Sorrow Marshes. She'll be braver in the morning, after she's had something to eat and gotten a good night's sleep. That's what she tells herself anyway.

She doesn't believe it, but she also knows that there's no way in H-E-double-hockey-sticks that she's going to set out now and chance getting stuck out there in the Pitch. It *has* to be nearing Pitchfall by now, and besides, she really needs to see to Boodark. She wishes he would wake up. Not that she wants him to suffer the pain that consciousness will undoubtedly bring him, but she *needs* him to wake up. She needs to reassure herself that he's going to be ok.

She locates a relatively dry spot and carefully sets his basket down before shrugging off her backpack, grateful to be free of the added weight of them both. She's thinking of lying down right on the dirt and stretching out her back, but the world starts rumbling, warning her to get set up and settled in, or risk having to do so in the black of Pitch.

With a weary sigh, she heaves herself up and gathers enough firewood to cook dinner. The wood's a bit damp, so it takes longer to get the fire going than it normally does, but finally it catches... just as Boodark starts moaning. He murmurs nonsensical gibberish about how secrets are afraid of the dark and who will hold back the Pitch, now that his wings are gone.

She reaches over and strokes his hair away from the side of his face, trying to reassure him the best that she can. "I'm here, Boodark. You're safe now. You're safe."

She continues stroking his hair, gently scratching her nails over his scalp because she knows that he loves the way it feels. A lone tear leaks from his eye and that does it, that just does her in completely and she falls apart.

"I've been so worried! I thought I was gonna lose you! I'm so sorry I couldn't save you. I couldn't stop it. I couldn't free myself in time to stop them from hurting you. I *told* you not to let them do it! I *forbid* it and you did it anyway. And after... I didn't know what to do or how to help you. *And you wouldn't wake up!*" She's yelling and sobbing, her emotions getting the better of her.

"Control yourself, before you kill us both with your wonky magic! And help me out of here," Boodark grumbles. She gently lifts him out of the basket, moving as slowly as she can so that she doesn't jar him and hurt him worse.

"Tell me what to do," she cries as she lays him across her lap, again on his belly. "I have medicine... ointments and bandages and pain relievers, but they're human meds. I was too scared to use them on you. I didn't know how you'd react to them. I was afraid to make things worse. I tried to find one of those trees with the pain-relieving sap, but I think we left them all behind."

Boodark turns his head to search their surroundings. "They do not grow here, and we are *much* too close to the Sorrow Marshes. We should have stopped and made camp sooner, farther back. We do not wish to be exposed to the swamp's influence any longer than necessary." He sighs in resignation as the world goes dark with the Pitch and mutters, "Too late now."

Ecko makes a bed out of the blanket she'd given him and lays him onto it so that she can start dinner. "I'm making you some soup," she says, but her heart sinks when he tells her not to bother, because he's not hungry. He's *always* hungry, even when he's full. He loves to eat, the little glutton. Her heart breaks all over again, because he's in so much pain that he doesn't feel like eating.

"Well, that's just too bad," she insists. "You have to eat or else you won't heal. I'll feed it to you, so that you don't have to move. All you'll have to do is swallow."

He glares at her, but he doesn't argue. She's not sure if he has the strength to put up much of a fight anyway. He suddenly seems so tiny and fragile lying there and she has to fight back a fresh wave of tears. Crying won't fix anything.

"The birdbrains left that moss crud for me to put on your wound. I figured it was safe, because they used it on Na-lee. I didn't sew the wound up, though. I wasn't sure if that would help or hinder." In a quiet, hesitant voice she adds, "Will they grow back?" She gushes on before he can answer. "I know you said they would grow back if they got cut off, but they didn't cut them off. They *ripped* them off. Please, *please* tell me they'll still grow back."

He winces at the memory of it. "As long as they cut the wing tendons and left me some, they will regrow. If they ripped them out completely then no, I will never fly again." His little body goes rigid with tension. "I don't know what they did. I could not hold onto my consciousness. *You* must tell *me*, Ecko. Will I ever fly again?" Then he turns his face away as best as he can in an effort to hide his pain, should she give him bad news.

"They cut them," she hurries to assure him, because she knows how much he dreads hearing her say that he'll forever more be a disgusting ground stomper. He lets out his pent-up breath and his little body relaxes in relief.

"Good. That's good," he breathes, and she can't hold back her rude snort. Nothing about this is good. It could have been worse though, she'll give him that much, but this still isn't 'good'. "Thirty days? I mean Pales?" she asks hopefully. "They'll grow back in just thirty Pales?"

Boodark shifts to the left, trying to get comfortable and she reaches over to help him. "Yes. Maybe. Depends on the damage, how much wing-tendon they left, and whether or not there are any complications. Somewhere between thirty and forty-five Pitch/Pale cycles."

She stirs the soup and says, "That's not so bad. I mean, if you *have* to sacrifice a body part, at least you gave up something that *can* grow back...unlike my feet." She jerks her eyes up to meet his. She stares at him in awe for a moment, then whispers, "Dude, you basically sacrificed your feet for me. Or, at least the equivalent anyway."

He gets all gruff and tough and tries to play it off as nothing. "It's not such a big deal. As I've said, they'll grow back. Plus, I did not give up my only means of traversing the world. I had two means of relocating myself, wings *and* feets." He lifts his feet up into the air and wiggles his toes, and she notices for the first time that he's missing a toe on his left foot.

"Like you, my feets will not grow back, so I am grateful that they only wanted to take the wings. I am grateful that they decided not to rip them out completely, and that they did no permanent damage."

Ecko slowly counts to ten as she pours the steaming hot chicken noodle soup into their bowls, but her hands are shaking so badly that it sloshes out and burns her. She yelps and sets the bowls aside, clasping her hands together to stop their trembling. She desperately tries to steady her breathing...and fails epically. "Grateful? I'm not grateful. I'm *pissed*. They hurt you, and they did it for such selfish reasons. I will *never* understand how anyone could be so cruel and I will *never* be grateful. I'm so mad at myself for not being able to help you. What good is this dumb magic if I can't save the people I love? Hmmm, can you tell me that? It does me *no* good at all!"

She's panting now with the effort that it's taking to keep herself under control and Rage is *not* helping, laughing like a loon inside her brain... encouraging her to just let it all out, let *him* out. That jerk inside her mind is actually singing the Disney movie's 'Frozen' theme song. *Let it go. Let it go. Can't hold it all inside...*She can feel her magic beginning to rise up inside of her.

'Oh, no you don't!' she angrily admonishes herself as she chooses her own lines from the song. *'Conceal. Don't feel. Don't let them see...'* She mentally fires it back at him as she squashes the magic back down. Not this time. If it can't come out and play when she asks it to, then it can't come out at all! And low and behold, it actually listens to her and goes back to sleep. Even Rage is shocked silent.

"We told it to go away and away it goes, Precious," she mumbles in her best Smeagol voice. She takes a deep breath and then another one. And then she takes one more. "I'm sorry, Boodark. It was just really, *really* bad watching them do that to you, knowing that I have the potential inside me to have stopped it all, but that I'm just too dumb to figure out how. Anyway, none of that is your fault. It's mine. All of it's my fault. I should never have put you in the position to have to sacrifice limbs to save me. I should have been more careful. I should have watched where I was walking."

She avoids his eyes as she tastes her soup to see if it's cooled down enough to spoon feed him. She's ashamed of her outburst and she's ashamed of all of her failures and shortcomings. The soup's still too hot, so she busies herself with digging in her bag for drinks. She pours water into a shallow bowl and then adds a Juicebox bendy straw that she'd saved from one of their past MRE meals. A straw will make drinking easier for him. He won't have to move so much to sip from it.

She holds the bowl steady while he drinks, and his eyes never leave hers. When he's had enough, she sets it aside and slowly feeds him his dinner. He stays quiet the entire time, just watching her as he dutifully swallows every spoonful. She wipes his face when he's done and sits back to eat her own rapidly cooling soup.

With a squeaky, almost hopeful voice, he breaks the silence by suddenly asking, "You love me?" He clears his throat and rushes on. "You asked me, 'what good is your magic, if you can't save the ones that you love.' Does that mean that you love me?"

She nods slowly and simply admits, "Yes. I love you."

He smiles a huge, pain filled smile that is somehow as beautiful as it is ugly and whispers, "Then it was worth it." And he closes his eyes and instantly starts snoring.

He doesn't sleep long. Not even thirty minutes pass before he's crying out from the inescapable pain that's followed him, even into his dreams. His eyes pop open and there's such agony reflected in them that it makes her flinch. She's cleaned up the dinner mess and spread her own bed roll right next to his, but she hasn't laid down yet. She's still to wound up. She strokes his little orc-bat face and asks, "What can I do?"

His voice is little more than a raspy whisper. "Unless you have some miracle pain-stealer in your bag, there's not much you can do. I wish I had some Larria nectar. At least then I could drink the pain away. Oh!"

Their eyes meet and she smiles as she reaches for her bag. Sprite works just as good as Larria nectar, or so she's been told. She pours him a bowlful, adds the straw, and then helps him into a better drinking position. Gently lifting his upper body, she props him up with a shirt that she's wadded up into a pillow. He's still lying on his belly, but at an angle, so that he can drink.

He wastes no time and slurps the first bowlful down without even stopping to take a breath. The faster he consumes it, the faster it will put out the fire in his back and numb his pain.

"Aahhh, that's good," he breathes. She pours him some more and he sips it slower this time. "You know you'll have to take the poultice off and clean it, don't you? You'll have to sew it up too, if it's ready. I was going to have you do it in the light of Pale, but it may be best to do it after I drink myself into oblivion... Get it over with while my senses are addled, and the pain is... almost tolerable."

He's right, she *knows* he's right, but she doesn't want to do it. She doesn't even want to look at it, not ever again. Of course, she knows that she must, but she dreads it with her entire being. Now she understands just how her father felt when he had to take the stitches from her neck, after Sigmund the teddy bear tried to eat her. Witnessing a loved one's pain and knowing that there's nothing she can do to fix it, is the worst feeling she's ever felt. Unfortunately, she's no stranger to this sort of helplessness, but it *is* the first time she'll have to stitch someone up. She gulps at the thought of it.

"Drink some more first," she encourages.

"Oh, I plan to!" And he does just that. Twenty minutes later, he grins up at her. "Can we sing?" She assures him that he can sing if he wants to, it certainly wouldn't bother her.

"No!" he shouts. "No Ecko! You're not *listening* to me. Can we sing with your magic singing box?"

Ah, he wants to listen to the music on her iPod. "Of course," she tells him as she gets it out of her bag. "But first, before you're too far gone, tell me what I need to do about your wound. I'm going to wait until you pass out, so I need you to tell me now, while you still can."

He nods enthusiastically and exclaims, "I've had a brilliant idea! You should wait until I'm so intoxicated that I pass out, before you fix me up. Surely, I won't feel a thing then, not even the poke of your needle."

He gulps some more Sprite down and when he continues, his words are just a tiny bit slurred together. "After you remove the moss and wash the wound, you will see four tendons on each side. They should each have formed a little bulb-like blob on the ends where they were cut. The bulbs will be either green or black. Green is good, black is bad. If I am lucky and they're all green, you can go ahead and sew the wound closed, but you have to pull the bulbs out and stitch the skin closed around the tendons. The bulbs *must* poke out so that they can grow. Do you understand?"

She nods miserably and asks, "And what if they're black?"

Boodark loudly slurps the last of his Sprite up and she empties what's left of the can into the bowl. "If they are black, it means they are dying. You will need to cut the dead bulbs off, so that they can grow new ones, green ones. There may also be both, some dead and some alive. You will need to snip all the black ones off, and just leave the wound open until all the bulbs have grown back green."

She feels her face flush and her skin grow cold and clammy at the thought of having to cut anything off of him. She turns the iPod on and selects a happy song before opening another can of Sprite and pouring him more. "Drink up," she tells him, all the while wishing that the soda had the same effect on her, as it does him. She sure could use some liquid courage right about now.

He makes it through half of the second can before his eyes pop open wide and he stares at her with fear on his face. "I have to take a leak," he whispers like it's some big, terrible secret.

And then he starts crying. "What am I gonna do now? I can barely move on my own. How am I supposed to get up and go pee? Oh, curse you, you de-lisss-iouss nectar from the EverLands." He hiccups and glares woefully into his bowl. "I drink you down and you fill my belly until it wants to burst. You *know* that I am wounded and that I cannot move! And still I crave more. Your de-lisss-iousness tempts me. It calls to me, and I *will* drink you up and damn my over-full belly!" Then he bypasses the straw completely and buries his face in the bowl, loudly slurping his 'delicious nectar from the EverLands' directly from the source.

Ecko giggles despite the inevitable unpleasantness that's quickly approaching. She's not sure which will be worse, helping him pee or playing doctor on his back. This whole situation just sucks. So bad. She sighs heavily as she stands up.

"What are you doing? Get your giant paws off of me!" he screeches as she picks him up.

"Stop squirming before you hurt yourself more!" She admonishes him sternly. "You said you have to pee; well, I'm helping you do that."

He sucks in a shocked, horrified breath. "You cannot mean to pull my dinky-doo out of my britches!" he wails. "Just put me back, I will hold it. I don't even have to go that badly. I can hold it, I swear!"

She nearly gags. "I have no intention of touching your uh... dinky-doo. I don't even want to see it. Ever. I'm just going to hold you up, while you do the rest."

He stops crying and starts hiccupping. "Oh, well in that case, can we hurry it along? I'm about to piss all over myself."

She hurries. She lowers herself to her knees so that she can hold him steady on his feet. "Don't look!" he slurs as he fumbles with his clothes. She tells him that even if she wanted to look, she can't see anything through the Pitch. But she still turns her face away when she hears splashing and then his grumbling. "Oh, this is so embarrassing. I hate this. I hate this so much. This is going on my list of unfavorite things!"

And then he toots right in her face, and she mutters, "Yeah, mine too."

Finally, it's over and she settles him back onto his bed and helps him with the straw so he can gulp some more Sprite. She knows that all that moving around had cost him dearly.

"Oh, I love this song. It's called 'How to Dance in Time'. It's Blue October... the same band that sang 'I Hope You're Happy'. You remember that song?" she asks him, desperate for anything that will take both their minds off the unpleasantness that they're experiencing.

He nods drunkenly and she turns the volume up so that hopefully the music will distract him from his pain. He stops groaning and listens intently to the remainder of the song. The chorus plays and the singer tells the story of how he'd broken his woman's heart, even though she means the world to him... of how he begs her to forgive him, and that he knows he should have been a better man to her.

Now Boodark's crying again, his hand stroking the gold band that he wears around his left bicep. It seems like he just can't handle booze and Blue October together. She scrolls through the playlist to find a happy song as he wails about how his Secret has to stay in the dark. She tries to console him by saying that he doesn't have to tell her anything and that he can keep his secrets to himself, if that's what he wants to do.

He blinks at her in confusion for a moment, then with tears streaming down his face he cries, "You don't understand. I can't keep her to myself, that's the problem. I wish I *could!* But she's stuck. They're all stuck. Trapped! And it's all my fault. If only I had listened to my Secret... Why do I *never* listen? I think I killed her, Ecko. I think I killed them all!"

She can do nothing but stroke his hair in comfort as he sobs his heart out. "Who, Boodark? Who do you think you killed?"

He snuggles his face into her hand, his little horns pressing into her skin. In a barely understandable, slurred whisper he murmurs, "My Secret. My mate. My babies... I damned them all. Trapped them for all eternity."

She stares at him in shock for a moment before spluttering, "You're married? *And* you have a family? You said that you didn't have a mate!"

He grunts and drunkenly shakes his head at her. "I said no such thing! Think back. What I said was that I'd have to be crazy to settle down with one female. And I *am* crazy... for *her*. For my Secret. I didn't lie. I just avoided admitting the truth."

And then he's snoring again, his face snuggled into the palm of her hand... out just like a light and she's left to wonder just what in the world he could have possibly meant by all that. She doesn't spend much time dwelling on it, though. There are more important things for her to worry about at the moment, such as performing an impromptu surgery that she's in no way qualified for.

She turns the music off so that she's not distracted, then she spreads out the tarp and moves him to it, laying him down flat on his belly. As quickly as she can, she sets up a triage area with bandages and tweezers, needle and thread, water bottles and alcohol. She adds more wood to the fire and then she sets up every single flashlight that she owns to shine down on the 'operating table.' She Germ-X's everything, her hands and arms included, and then she simply does what needs to be done.

She refuses to think about it, refuses to think about all the things that could go wrong. She absolutely refuses to think about the fact that if she screws up, like she's wont to do, her little friend might never fly again. Or worse, she could mess up so badly that he could actually die. *Yep, I refuse to think about it,* she thinks as she gets through the most difficult, three-hour task she's ever had to perform.

Thankfully, all the tendon-bulbs are a bright, beautiful green and she manages to pull the slippery little things out far enough so that she can stitch the edges of the wound closed. Boodark wakes for a brief moment as she's tugging on the last one. It seems to be shorter than the others and doesn't want to stretch enough for her to complete the last little bit of sewing. His scream only lasts seconds before the pain overwhelms him and he loses consciousness once more.

But her mind plays it on repeat, and she sobs throughout the last several minutes of patching him back together. As she ties the last knot and snips the thread, a single tear falls and lands with a tiny splash on that last stubborn bulb. It quickly soaks in and disappears, and for one brief moment, the entire bulb appears to be illuminated with a glowing, blue shimmer. But then she blinks, and the glow is gone, if it had ever been there in the first place.

As exhausted as she is, it may very well have been her imagination, or perhaps merely a trick of the light. She shrugs, dismissing the mystery altogether. She's just glad that the operation went smoothly. She's even more glad that it's over.

The best thing about the Pales being so pale is that she can sleep as late into the day as she desires. There's no bright sunlight to shine in her eyes and tell her that she must get up and face the new day. Everyone always assumes that she hates mornings, but that's just not true. She likes mornings just fine... as long as she doesn't have to get up too early, she isn't rushed, and there is plenty of coffee to jumpstart her brain. On this world, with no sun to boss her around, she can take her own sweet time waking up and getting ready… until reality rushes in and reminds her of all the reasons that she needs to rush.

When she'd finally gotten done doctoring Boodark's wound, she'd crawled into her sleeping bag and cried herself into an exhausted, dreamless sleep. She managed a few solid hours of restful slumber before he'd started sleep talking, muttering about Secrets and begging for forgiveness and asking how he's supposed to keep the dark away, now that he was broken.

The last words he mumbled before falling silent once more was, "How high can I fly with broken wings?" The words wounded her heart so deeply that she knew they would haunt her for the rest of her life. How high can I fly with broken wings? Such a shattering sentence, she'd thought, just before she, too, fell back to sleep.

She had every intention of sleeping half the day away, but her eyes pop open at Boodark's low groan of pain. She frantically kicks her way out of her blanket cocoon and rolls over to comfort him. He just stares at her, his huge, green eyes dulled from the pain. She imagines he's feeling pretty terrible right about now. Not only had he been brutalized and traumatically wounded, he surely has a massive hangover now, too. Knowing darn well that he feels awful, she nevertheless asks how he feels.

He frowns ferociously at her. "What do *you* think? I feel like poop on a stick. And speaking of... I have to poop, piss, *and* puke, and not necessarily in that order either. If you don't want me to do all three right here in your blanket, I suggest that you help me to my feet, so I can tootle on over there by that tree."

She grins at his grumpy surliness, but it quickly turns to a grimace at the thought of how unpleasant *this* is going to be. She lifts him up to carry him away from the campsite and he immediately starts hollering at her. "I said lift me up *only*. I can walk! Those dirty birdies took my wings, not my feets."

She ignores him and sets him down close to a tree stump that he could hold onto for support. He glares at her and then snarls, "You gonna stand there and watch too?"

She rolls her eyes, mentally begging for patience. She knows that pain makes even the mildest tempered creatures mean and unpleasant to be around... and mild tempered he is *not*, even when he *had* his wings. She knows that he has to be hurting worse than she could even imagine. And she knows, without a doubt, that this is going to be a long, exhausting day.

"I told you, I have no desire to see your dinky-do. This is as much as I'm helping you with; you're on your own for the rest… just like last night. Last Pitch, I mean. I didn't want to look then, and I sure don't want to look now."

She sees the exact moment that the memory of his late night, drunken 'bathroom' experience comes back to him. His eyes go huge, mortified. They even get a little teary, as if the shame of it is just too much for him to bear. She quickly points off to the left and says, "I'm going right over there to take care of my own business. Yell when you're done, and I'll carry you back."

She walks off, muttering under her breath about how hard-headed and difficult he's being. She puts enough distance between them to assure them each their privacy before she does what she has to do. She's squatted down, midway through her morning pee, when she hears a tapping, thumping sound somewhere off to the left.

Of course, she thinks. *Of course,* something has to happen while her butt's hanging out. She whips her head to the side to locate the source of the sound, but it stops as soon as she does so. She turns away, and after a few seconds, it begins again. So long as she's not looking in its direction, whatever *it* is continues tapping away.

Done with her business, she stands up to right her clothing, but she discreetly scans the trees from the corner of her eyes as she does so. There! The movements of something very small up in one of the trees catches her attention, and she adjusts her eyes to better focus on it. Whatever it is, it's up above her head and out of her reach, and it blends in almost perfectly with the tree.

It immediately goes still and silent, so she keeps her eyes trained on it as she moves closer, so that she doesn't lose sight of it. If she loses it, she might not be able to find it again. At first, she thinks it's some sort of bug, but as she moves closer to the tree, she sees that it has two long legs dangling down, two long *humanoid* legs. It had been holding very still, trying to stay hidden, but when it realizes that it's been found out, it becomes a blur of motion. It's kicking and thrashing, and now she *really* can't tell what it is.

'I'll just have to get closer', she decides as she hoists herself up onto the lowest branch. It's been years since she's climbed a tree, but thankfully, she doesn't have to climb very high now. She moves up three branches and now she can see it perfectly. It's some sort of dark, swamp fairy, a female, and she's stuck to the tree trunk, glued there by a large blob of tarry, black muck.

She's five, maybe six inches tall and a pale grey color with large darker grey spots, like freckles decorating her skin. Her long wild dreadlocks stick out in every direction and they're the color of every life-stage of grass, new greens, old greens, dying greens. Then the pale greens turn to yellows, then to hay, and finally the browns of true dead. All those grass-shaded tresses are wadded up together, matted up into long, tight dreadlocks.

And oh! She has the teeniest, tiniest black mushrooms mixed into her hair, growing right out of her scalp! She's beautiful in her own odd way, bringing to mind some sort of exotic, spotted frog. The word *poison* drifts through her mind and she knows that she must be very careful here, because beauty does not always go hand in hand with 'safe' and 'friendly'. There are millions of beautifully deadly things, just waiting to lure you to your doom with said beauty, just like a poison dart frog. And also, like Jaida. *She* was a perfect example of how one could be both lovely *and* lethal at the same time.

"Oh, you poor little thing," Ecko murmurs as she processes the trouble that the wee thing has landed herself in. Realizing that its attempts to escape are futile, the swamp fairy goes still and glares pure hatred and malice at her instead. She reaches up to test the blob, to see just how stuck she is and to determine what it will take to get her free. The fairy slaps her! She reaches out her tiny, miniscule hand and slaps her finger away when it gets within her reach.

"I'm just trying to help you. Don't you want free of that stuff?" she murmurs in a quiet, soothing tone.

It scrunches up its face into an even fiercer scowl. "Hate you," it says in a low, raspy voice.

Ecko grins. "That's ok," she tells the grumpy little thing. "You can hate me all you want. But think about it. Are you really in a position to refuse help, even if you hate the one giving it to you? Would you rather remain here, trapped forever in this...goop?" She reaches up and tries again, and this time she doesn't get slapped away, but she *does* continue to receive the death glare.

The blob covers the fairy's entire midsection, from her neck to her thighs. It looks just like someone had taken a wad of sticky road tar and used it to pin her there to the tree. Ecko tugs on it to see if she can pull it off, but it may as well have been super glued on. Fine. She'll just have to pry it right off the tree. Then she can carry the surly fairy back to camp and figure out how to get the gunk off of her. She reaches into her pocket for her Swiss army knife and opens it up, explaining all the while, exactly what she's doing, so the little one doesn't panic at the sight of a knife coming at her.

"Hold still," she orders. She must be *very* careful. She doesn't want to nick her or her poor, gunk-coated wings. She gently wedges the blade between the blob and the tree and then shimmies the whole thing off. Then she tucks the knife away and lowers herself back to the ground.

"Release me," the fairy demands as she renews her struggling in earnest.

Ecko reassures her the best she can while also ignoring her ridiculous demands. "If I let you go now, without cleaning that mess off of you, you will just go and get yourself stuck to another tree. I'm not going to hurt you, and I'll let you go the very instant we get you clean."

She lifts her up so that their eyes can meet. "I give you my word," she promises before she heads back to the place where she'd left Boodark. He's no longer there, though.

Instead of waiting for her or calling out for help, the stubborn little brat is hobbling back to camp on his own. Without a word, she carefully scoops him up to carry him the rest of the way.

"I can do it!" he shouts and then winces at the pain he's just caused in his own head. He's so surly that he doesn't even notice that they're no longer alone, and he continues to mumble and grumble until she lays him back on his bed.

Perfect, just perfect, she can't help but think. Only *she* could manage to find the two grumpiest, neediest little hardheads in all the world and then somehow feel as if it's *her* responsibility to fix their problems. As if she doesn't have enough problems of her own, she has to add more to the load. Freaking bleeding hearts and grumpy old farts unite.

21

CLOSING IN ON THE GEEZERS

Samara

With Ecko's pill bottle and those wonderfully helpful tools called computers and the world wide web, Samara learns the location of the asylum that her sister had spent so much time in. Tracking down the doctor named on the bottle, a Elizabeth Bradburn, holds no interest for her, but getting her hands on Ecko's records and all that personal information does. She can only hope that the information will include clues as to who the old geezers are, their names and addresses.

Or perhaps someone there will be able to tell her what she wants to know. Surely the old ones had visited her sister, while she'd been locked away. Surely someone would remember them. *Someone* has to know something. And if they don't, she'll just have to go to whatever addresses *are* listed in the files.

Perhaps going to Ecko's childhood home would result in some clue as to where the old ones live… if there's even a home left. She has very good reason to believe that her sister's childhood home had been destroyed.

If she could just manage to learn the names of those two old fools, she would have no problem hunting them down. Isn't the internet a wonderous thing? But she needs a starting point, just one small clue as to who they are. Something deep inside of her, some intuitive instinct insists that she's only hours away from learning everything she desires to know.

Someone in that bedlamite care center holds the answers. It's just a matter of getting the right person to speak, that's all. Now all she has to do is get herself to a place called Texas, the land of barbeque and salsa, sweltering heat and smoking hot cowboys in tall hats, tight jeans, and leather boots.

Samara man-hunts until she finds one that's as close to her standards as she can possibly get. She's not sure if these Earth men are sorely lacking, or if Krispin had just been overly endowed and inordinately superb. As her first lover, her *only* lover before she'd come to this world, it's proven impossible to find anyone that measures up to him. He'd been gloriously insatiable, unbreakable and inexhaustible. He never got enough of her and the wicked things they'd done together. The men here break too easily. But she'll have to make do and settle for less, she supposes. She has no time to be picky anyway. She'll just have to be careful this time.

Don't break this one, Samara, she admonishes herself as her eyes search for one that will be useful to her needs. That shouldn't be too difficult. She not after a bed partner, she's searching for someone that can assist her in her travels.

At last, she spots a likely candidate, a man that's pleasing to the eye but more importantly, he appears intelligent, worldly, and successful. "Congratulations, sir. You're the lucky winner," she murmurs under her breath as she moves in to claim him as her new personal assistant. He's walking along at a brisk pace, and she steps in front of him, just as he glances down to check his watch. Just as she intends, he slams right into her and knocks her to the ground.

"Oh my God! I am *so* sorry!" he cries out as he drops his briefcase and his phone to make a grab for her. "Are you ok? Are you hurt?" He reaches down to help her back to her feet. As she slips her delicate hand into his, she discreetly sends a bit of Shadow out to infect him… just enough to control him and keep the looky-loos from noticing anything strange, while they looky-loo at them.

"I am unharmed," she assures him, but then cries out at a fabricated ankle injury. "Oh! I think I may have twisted my ankle. Please good sir, would you help me to that seat, just over there?" she asks as she points to a vacant bench outside of a clothes store.

He lifts her up into his arms to carry her and she calls out, "Your belongings! Don't leave them behind!"

A bystander picks his things up and passes them to him, then claps him on the shoulder before moving on and going about his own business. By the time her new man carries her over and lowers her to the bench, the nosy people that had stopped to watch the action have all lost interest and moved on with their own affairs.

'*Yes,*' she thinks. '*Nothing more to see here.*' And then she lets the man know that his life will, for the time being, have to be put on hold in order to see to *hers*. His new job will be taking up all his time and energy, and it will also entail some unexpected, spur-of-the-moment travels.

"As to that, I will need you to gain us passage on one of those noisy air flyers. We have business in Texas that needs to be attended to immediately." She stands up, her injury miraculously healed, and she loops her arm through his.

"Get to it, Robert. May I call you Robert? Of course, I may. Well, get on with it. Take us to wherever you need to, so that you may get our affairs in order. I'll just tag along, so that I can learn how it's all done. Maybe I won't need you next time. Wouldn't that be lovely?"

Robert leads her to one of those tall buildings… what are they called… sky touchers, or something like that. "What are we doing here? This is not an air flyer land site."

But she doesn't wait for him to explain what he's up to. She simply reaches in and raids his mind, taking whatever information she wants and discarding the rest. "Oh, I see. This is your place of work, where you typically have *your* assistant see to all of your affairs and book your business trips. I didn't realize when I chose you that you would also need your own subordinates. Very well. Let's get up there and get this done. I wish to arrive at this new destination that I'm bound for as quickly as possible. Now that I have a starting point at this Regal Falls Psychiatric Ward… this head shrinking facility, I find that I am most excited to be back on the hunt."

Robert presses a button on the wall, and they wait for the elevator to reach their floor. When the bell dings, the door slides open to reveal an overly crowded up-down box, and Samara merely waves a Shadow-clouded hand at the tightly packed-in humans.

"Get out," she commands, and they push and shove and trip over one another in their haste to do so. They step in and her man presses the buttons to make the doors close and to make the up-down box go up. The two of them are quiet on the ride up, companionably listening to the provided music until the door reopens and spits them out onto the fifty-sixth floor. Robert quickly leads her down a short hallway that opens up into a reception area.

The frumpy, middle-aged female at the desk (who's probably very good at her job, because she certainly hadn't gotten the position because of her looks) sets the pastry she's been devouring back into the doughnut box and smiles in relief when she sees her boss.

"Oh! Mr. Greyston! I'm so relieved that you're ok! When you missed your luncheon date with Mark and then your appointment with Mrs. Stine, I feared the worst. Thank goodness you're alright!"

When he speaks, his voice comes out in a flat, emotionless monotone, like a robot. "I need you to book us an immediate flight to Texas, nonstop, one way. The sooner we can get there, the better."

The woman's brow creases with her confusion. "Sir?"

"Straight away, Stephanie," he insists as he heads to his office to gather his things. As an afterthought, he calls back over his shoulder, informing her to cancel all of his upcoming meetings.

"For how long?" The woman jumps to her feet and rushes after them. "You know that you're positively *booked* up with meeting after meeting for this entire week! How many of them will I need to cancel? What's going on Mr. Greyston?"

He begins gathering the items that he'll need to bring with them on their trip… his laptop and cellphone charger, antacids for the sick that he feels in his belly. "All of them. Cancel them all. Indefinitely."

Samara can't help but giggle at the fishy look on Stephanie's face, the googly eyes and the wide opened mouth.

"What's going on?" she asks again. "Who *is* this woman? What about your wife? You can't do this to her! Her birthday is tomorrow, for Pete's sake!"

Robert meets her eyes unflinchingly. "Cancel it."

The secretary is too stunned to speak at this point, which also means that she is too stunned to do her job of getting them onto an air flyer. Which means that she is wasting Samara's time. And *that* means that Samara is not happy. And that is *never* a good thing.

"You heard him, sugar tits," she calls out. "Cancel it all. But first, if you do not take your flabby, pastry-eating ass back to that desk and get me onto an air flyer, I will take you to that eatery that you seem to love so much and fry you in the lard vats. And then I will eat you, bite after bite after bite. I bet you'd be oh, so sweet from all that sugar that you consume."

The woman looks her straight in the eyes and whatever she sees there must convince her that Samara is not exaggerating, not in the slightest. She yelps as she spins around and rushes back to her desk, where she hastily begins clacking away on her computer's keyboard. Samara drags a chair over and sits in the doorway, so that she can watch every move that Stephanie makes while she waits.

Ten minutes pass in silence before the secretary lurches to her feet and brings a small stack of papers to Robert, who's spent the entire wait staring at a slightly discolored, barely-there blemish in the paint on his office walls. Stephanie flattens herself against the door jam, just as flat as she can make her plump self, as she squeezes past Samara on her way to him.

"The earliest flight is tomorrow morning at 5:32 a.m. Nonstop and one way, as you requested. I've sent the confirmations to your email." Stephanie never takes her eyes off of Samara as she gives him the details, watching her like a frightened mouse that's just waiting for a predator to pounce.

Before they have a chance to conclude their business, a smartly dressed man with a wicked grin walks in and interrupts them. "What happened to you, man? Why'd you miss lunch? I waited for almost an hour!"

Then he turns back around and takes a closer look at the woman that's seated in one of the client's chairs. His smile widens as he ogles her, his eyes lingering on all of her many attributes.

"Who *is* this luscious little beauty, and why are you always the lucky one?" He winks at Samara and tells her, "Just so you know, Robert's already married. I, on the other hand, am free and clear of any lasting relationships. You just say the word, Beautiful, and I'll be at your disposal, willing *and eager* to help you with whatever pleases you."

Samara grins back at him, that sexy smirk on his face sparking a slow-burn fire in her belly. Oh goody! She's found *exactly* how she'll while away the Pitch-hours, until it's time to board the air flyer.

Stephanie, the old nag, takes it upon herself to snitch them out and divulge all of their plans to the newcomer. Now that she's no longer alone with them, she's obviously feeling braver. Stupid cow.

"I have no idea what's going on here, Mark. They just marched in here and demanded that I book them an immediate flight… to *Texas*, of all places. Mr. Greyston ordered me to cancel all of his appointments. *All* of them! I'm telling you, she's bewitched him. Please, help me! I don't know what to think of all this. I don't know what to d*o!*"

Mark frowns down at Robert who's still staring at the same spot… he hasn't reacted in any way to what's going on around him.

"Is this true?" Mark asks.

When Robert nods his affirmation, Stephanie throws her hands up into the air and wails, "See?"

Mark waves his hand, shushing her. "What's going on, man? You can't leave! Not right now. There's too much at stake for you to be rushing off on some clandestine tryst with some random tart you met on the streets. What about Janice? What about your *wife*? Remember her? You went to all that trouble to plan her surprise party, you're telling me you're canceling it? *Now?*"

He turns to look her over once more and adds, "Don't get me wrong. She *is* tempting… very tempting, but come on, man! You're going to throw everything away for her? Is that what this is? You're willing to throw your marriage away? Your unborn son?" He leans in closer and lowers his voice. "You're willing to lose all your father-in-law's money? For a bit of ass? What's gotten into you, man?"

Samara giggles, drawing all three sets of eyes back to her. She lifts up her hand and blows a flirtatious, provocative kiss at Mark, her air kiss backed by a tiny puff of her Shadows. It hits him and she delves straightaway into his mind, and what she finds in there makes her burst out in delighted laughter. "Oh Mark, dear, *best friend* Mark who always wants nothing but the best for our Robert."

He stands up straighter and brushes off the sick feeling that's just slid over his soul. He suddenly has a very bad feeling, like he's trying to stare down a poisonous snake in a contest to see which one of them would blink first… but snakes don't blink.

"That's right. I *am* his best friend, and of *course* I want what's best for him. That's why I don't think he should follow through with whatever plans he's made with *you*. He has too much to lose. I'm sure you're a fabulous lay, but sex, even mind-blowing sex isn't worth all that he'll lose. You may as well leave. Right now. There's no way I'm letting him go through with it. You can see yourself out.”

Stephanie pulls her shoulders back and gives one firm, smug nod as she harrumphs in satisfaction.

“Oh, let the fun *begin*!” Samara snickers as she gets up and heads for the door. Instead of walking through it to 'show herself out', she quietly closes it, turns, and leans back against it.

“What are you doing? Leave this instant, before I call security!” Stephanie demands.

“Sit your dumplin' butt down and shut your mouth. Don't move and don't speak. I don't want to hear another sound from you, unless I give you direct permission to open that pie hole back up.” The woman immediately plops her butt down onto a chair, her eyes going huge as Samara begins to slowly unbutton her blouse.

“Mark has some things to confess, before we get down to more pleasant, physical activities. Don't you, *best friend* Mark?”

He swallows hard and then stutters, “I…I…I don't know what you mean.” His attention never wavers from her slow-moving hands, but he's obviously beginning to feel apprehensive about this whole situation.

“Oh, *do* go on! Don't get shy now,” she cajoles as she pulls her top open to reveal the black lace beneath it. “Just tell him. Tell him how you've been helping yourself to what he thought was exclusively his. Tell him how you've been bedding his wife, more often even than *he* does.”

"Tell him how you've had her in every room of *his* house, up against every single wall. How you lie in his bed, wearing his robe, after you've had your fill of fucking what's his. Of how you pull your fingers free of her body after you've made her scream and wipe them clean on his pillow." Samara unsnaps the buttons on her jeans, wiggling them down over her hips and sliding them down her legs until she can step out of them and kick them aside.

Mark and Stephanie raptly watch every move she makes while Robert stares and stares and stares at that blip in the paint, his fists clenched, his entire body trembling with suppressed emotion.

"Turn around," Samara croons. "Turn around and look at him. *Look* at him while you tell him that the child that grows in his wife's belly is, without a doubt yours, not his."

Mark has no choice but to turn and look at the man he'd cuckolded, the man whose heart had just been ripped to shreds… because of him. "Ah man, I'm sorry. I don't know what else to say."

Samara finally releases Robert's mind just enough so that he can move and speak once more. His eyes instantly flood with tears, overflowing them and spilling down his cheeks.

"Well, now I know," he whispers. "You can have it. The money, the houses and cars, the wife and kid, the shitty in-laws. It's all yours, *if* Samara decides to let you live long enough to claim it all, that is. Who knows what she has in store for you. I'll just sit back and watch the show. I'll be just as surprised as you are by how this all ends for you."

And that's just what he does. He leans back in his chair, and he watches the real-life pornographic snuff film play out... for the next six hours and twelve minutes... until Mark takes his last, gurgling breath.

Samara rolls off of him, her chest heaving, naked body glistening with sweat. The small splatters of blood contrast shockingly crimson against her milk-white breasts. Once she's gotten her breath back under control, she turns her attention to her captive, but extremely horrified, audience. Robert's off in crazy land, rocking back and forth and muttering, "Cancel it. Cancel it." The huge puddle of piss below Stephanie's chair indicates that the woman's bladder had let go at least once.

"Oh, I am so sorry Stephanie, I forgot you were there! How rude of me. I should have offered to share! I'm sure you've just been dying for a little piece of *that!*" Samara waves a hand down at Mark and fake gasps in shock. "Oh! Too late now, I suppose. Unless... nah, we'd better just let him rest in pieces."

She frowns when the woman continues to sit there without a word, trembling and vibrating like one of those fake cocks in a sex-toy mercantile... vibra-dators they're called.

"Ah, what's wrong Stephanie? Oh! Silly me, I forgot!" She waves her hand to retract her Shadows, and the woman immediately sucks in a breath and then lets it back out in one piercing scream after another. Just over and over again, until the sound of it grates on the other woman's nerves.

"Oh, for fuck's sake!" Samara hisses. "Why are you screaming? It's as annoying as it is redundant. You're not even hurt! Keep it up and we can change that."

Stephanie stops shrieking, but she can't seem to make herself go silent. Pathetic whimpers pour ceaselessly from her throat, as if she's a terrified, wounded dog. Samara rolls her eyes as she gets to her feet.

"Ugh, just look at the mess that Mark made! I'm going to need a bath. Is there a bathing room that I can use to clean myself up?"

Robert stands up mechanically, like he's a puppet and Samara is the puppeteer with her hand jammed up his ass. He attempts to lead her out of his office, all the while muttering, "Cancel it, cancel it," but Samara stops him as she glances down at herself again.

"I can't go walking about like this, can I? Stephanie, be a chum and loan your frock to a girl in need. I don't want to put my own clothes back on until I've washed myself. I don't want to dirty them up, now do I?"

When she makes no move, Samara adds, "You don't want me to give you the Shadows again, do you?" *That* gets her moving, her fat fingers frantically tugging away at the buttons. She pulls the dress off and holds it out, even as she tries to cross her arms over her chest.

"You're wearing a petticoat, why are you acting as if you're naked? Whatever, I really don't care." Samara slips the garment on, complaining all the while that the dress is as big as a circus tent. And it's wet at the ass and stinks of piss too.

"Oh well," she mutters. "Beggars and choosers and all that nonsense. Carry my clothes for me Robert, and lead on! Oh yeah," she calls back over her shoulder. "Don't go anywhere, Stephanie. And don't you try anything, or I promise that you'll regret it. I'll make the last minutes of your life so horrifically unpleasant that you'll wish you'd been lucky enough to die as easily as dear best friend Mark had."

When they return forty-five minutes later with Samara clean and dressed once more in her own clothing, they find Stephanie still seated in the same place they'd left her. That's the first clue. The fact that the dumb secretary is doing her best to look every-where *but* at them is the second. Samara sighs in annoyance. Humans are all so predictable.

"What did you do?" she asks, her voice laced with impatience.

"Me?" Stephanie squeaks as she points to herself.

"Yes, idiot. You. Who else would I be speaking to? What did you do? I know you did something. Confess."

The woman's' eyes go straight to the phone on the desk and then dart quickly away again. Samara sighs again, this time with exaggerated disappointment.

"You called the police, didn't you?"

Her eyes widen and she frantically starts shaking her head. "No! I wouldn't do that! You told me not to try anything and so I didn't. I just sat here and waited and…"

Samara turns and slowly closes the door. "How long ago?" she calmly asks. "How long ago did you call them?" When she turns back to face the terrified woman, her eyes are blacked out, just like the demons on that tv show, Supernatural.

"Fifteen minutes! Just fifteen minutes ago! You still have time to get away. Please don't hurt me!" she wails before breaking down in a fit of unintelligible blubbering.

"Robert! Snap out of it and stop saying 'cancel it' before I cancel *you!*" Samara warns. "How much time do we have until we need to be at the place where the air flyers sleep?"

He automatically glances at his watch to check the time. "It's just after 2 a.m. now, and we'll need to be there perhaps an hour in advance. I'd say two hours. Any more than that would be pushing it. But the police will be here long before that."

She nods in agreement. "You're right. Better make this quick." Then she spins around and slams her fist into Stephanie's nose. "*That's* for calling me a whore earlier."

The secretary howls and throws her hand up to her suddenly gushing nose. "But I didn't! I *didn't* call you that! Not ever!"

Samara steps back and grins down at her. "Not out loud you didn't. But you most certainly did so in your mind. I know. I was in there. Now, what should I do to you in turn for disobeying me?"

The woman cries and begs and pleads, which is usually the best part, but Samara is lost inside her own mind at the moment. "What's this?" she murmurs under her breath, as a purely mental instructional scene plays out, showing her the way.

She turns her attention back to the wailing Stephanie, her eyes lit with wonder and delight as she whispers, "I can bleed them!

Why haven't I thought of that before now? Oh, what fun!" Then she holds her hands up and prepares to let her Shadows out to play.

"Experiment time!" she calls out. "Hold still now, Stephanie. I'm no expert, but I'm pretty sure this is going to hurt."

But Stephanie does *not* hold still. In full panic mode, she jumps from her chair and begins snatching things off the desk, tossing them at the sadist that's spent the last several hours tormenting her and her boss. Not to mention poor Mark... Realizing that none of her launched missiles are hitting their mark, and that they're doing absolutely nothing to help her situation, she rushes around the desk, putting as much distance between the two of them as she possibly can.

But that does no more good than throwing staplers and ink pens had. The Shadows go after her... *fast.* They shoot out of her palms like never before, fast and concentrated into thin ropes... just like that red Spidder-man on the magic movie box, the one that shoots webs out of his hands.

Only... what she produces is inky black Shadow-ropes, incorporeal, but extremely deadly. That's what she uses them for now... ropes. She sends them straight for those twin trails of crimson fluid that are leaking from Stephanie's nose, flowing down over her lips and dripping off her chin in steady streams. The Shadows go *into* that blood, mix into it and grab hold of it.

Then Samara yanks the Shadow-ropes back towards herself. The blood has no choice but to come too, gripped tight by the Shadows. They're so tightly interwoven, that they've become a new thing, a beautiful, horrifying new creation. Blood infused Shadow ropes... like ghost umbilical cords attached to their Shadow mother.

And just like an overprotective and controlling mother, she reigns her Shadows back in, one hand over the other, steadily drawing more and more of Stephanie's precious lifeblood from her... through her nostrils. As Samara reels the Shadows in, all that blood gets wrung out of them... just like what happens to a rag in a clothes wringer. The moisture gets squeezed out as the Shadows disappear back into her, pouring from her hands in a crimson flood as if from a broken spout.

Two minutes, that's all it takes to bleed the woman completely dry. There's not a drop left in her body when she thuds heavily onto the floor. And surprisingly, there's very little mess... other than the blood on Stephanie's face from the initial blow to her nose, and the huge puddle that takes up most of the office floor, that is. (A puddle in which the unfortunate Mark is lying in.) Somehow, Samara's managed to keep herself clean, her blood drenched hands are the only things that she has to tidy up.

Careful not to step in the puddle, she moves over to the deader than dead woman, rips her petticoat off, and then uses it as a rag for her hands. "Robert, come over here. I want you to pick her up and set her in your chair, all nice and neat-like."

Once the woman is settled in and set up just so, they head out, stopping at the door to glance back and observe the scene. Samara grins. The Earth officials will have fun trying to figure out what happened in here... who, by the way, will be here in a matter of minutes. Time to move their asses out of there. Time to get themselves onto an air flyer that will carry them to Texas. Time to make good on her promise to her dear sister. Time to hunt down and put an end, once and for all, to the last two people that Ecko cares about.

Lenny

"What's in Texas, you sweet, psychotic thing?" Lenny murmurs to himself. He'd watched Samara out there on the streets as she searched the faces of all the people passing her, just going about their own business. When he saw her walk out in front of the man in his $20,000 Ermenegildo Zegna suit, he'd known that she'd found her next victim.

He couldn't believe just how smoothly his part in the incident had gone over, as he'd helpfully rushed in to pick up the man's dropped items and then helped him get everything situated, so that he could carry it all along with the added burden of the woman in his arms. It was the perfect opportunity to plant the bug onto the hapless man's collar, as he'd clapped him companionably on the shoulder and then quickly moved on to hide amongst the crowd.

He followed behind when they get up and moved on, far enough back so that he wouldn't be discovered, but not far enough that he had a chance of losing sight of them. Until they disappeared into the man's place of business, that is. That's where the high-tech listening device became imperative. Even though he no longer has eyes on them, he's nevertheless able to eavesdrop on everything that transpires between the two of them.

He listens as the man, Robert Greyston apparently, instructs his secretary to book them a flight to Texas. A little while later, the woman comes back into the audio with the flight details, and Lenny quickly goes online and reserves two seats on that same 5:32 a.m. flight, one for himself and the other for Mr. Chadwick, his chauffeur/assistant/bodyguard/and right-hand man. He quickly scribbles a note, a list of items to purchase for his upcoming trip to Texas, then passes it to Mr. Chadwick along with some instructions.

"Buy yourself whatever you think you'll need too, Mr. Chadwick. We're going to Texas for a bit of fun in the sun."

The older gentleman nods. "Very good, Sir. Should I call the men and cancel your meeting tonight?"

Lenny grunts and thumps his hand against his seat in frustration. "I forgot all about that!" He thinks it over and after a moment of careful consideration, comes to a decision. "No, Mr. Chadwick. You just take care of our trip preparations. I'll call the boys and let them know I won't be around for the next couple of days. Victor will just have to oversee the business for a bit longer… but not for too much longer."

"I need to wrap this up, the sooner the better. I'll have to make my move soon, perhaps in Texas. But this is such a delicate situation. Samara's a bomb, just waiting to detonate. She must be handled properly, with the utmost care and patience. If we disturb her, if we jostle her in the slightest way, she's liable to blow us both to Hell."

Mr. Chadwick slips his coat on and steps out of the car. "Victor is more than capable of handling the business without you… short term, that is. That's why you chose him. It's also why you pay him the big bucks. As for this Samara situation, please don't jostle her, sir."

The two men part ways and go about their individual tasks. After the phone calls have all been made and the instructions for the next two days are passed along to the appropriate channels, Lenny settles himself into the back seat of his Benz to wait.

Two hours later, his man returns with several shopping bags and two small suitcases. Lenny, tired of listening to the sex and torture going on in his ear, passes him the ear bud receiver.

"Here. You take over for a while, so I can get some sleep. Oh, and pack everything into the suitcases for me. That luggage is suitable for carry on, isn't it? We can't wait around on the baggage claim."

The chauffeur assures him that all is well and in order.

"Right, then. Wake me if anything important should happen… something other than fucking and fighting, and murder and mayhem."

22

DOOM ON YOU. AND ON ME TOO

Ecko

"I don't care, Boodark. I said we're staying here for the day and that's final! You need time to recover, I'm exhausted from being up all night, and now this." Ecko jabs her finger at the little swamp fairy who's covered in thick, black tar. "Pout if you must but do it quietly so that *I* can do what needs to be done. Just *look* at her! You can see that she needs our help."

Boodark grunts… again. "Well, she won't be grateful. The moment you get her clean she's going to bite you. *Then* you will understand why I told you to just squish her like a slugbug."

Ecko rubs at her aching head as she pokes around in the ashes of last night's fire, searching for coals in which to rekindle it. She adds more wood and then sets up a pot of water to heat over it. She

539

glances over to where the fairy is angrily glaring at them both, as she awaits whatever fate has in store for her.

"Is that true?" Ecko asks. "Are you going to bite me, even though I'm trying to help you?"

The fairy shakes her head no, but all she says is, "He lies."

Ecko turns away from them both to hide her grin. They've been going at it since Boodark first spotted her clutched in her hand. Well, to be honest, it's mostly just been her bratty little orc friend going at it.

He'd taken one look at the little fairy and immediately hung his head in disappointed resignation, even as he very audibly sighed out his displeasure. He'd woefully shaken his head as he complained to himself. "A Darkling. Gah, I can't leave her alone for one second. The big dummy goes out to poop and comes back with a filthy Darkling, a swamp rat, a bottom feeder of the fae world. And knowing her, she probably wants to keep it too!" Oh, he had plenty more to say, and occasionally the 'Darkling' would snarl back her own cursory insults.

Ecko ignores them both as she prepares a clean-up station. *Better than a triage station,* she tells herself. At least there won't be any blood involved this time. She sets out her first aid kit, with its Q-tips and cotton balls and tweezers. She worries that warm water won't be enough to soften the gunk, but she doesn't know if any of her 'human' cleansers will be safe to use on delicate fairy skin. She interrupts Grumpy and Grumpier's bickering to ask if they know what it is that they're dealing with and if they have any idea what will work to remove it.

Boodark shrugs his ignorance, but the fairy nods. "It Still-Crane scat."

Her demented little friend bursts out laughing, and she in turn hisses at him like an enraged cat. "Ha, ha, ha! You got stuck in *bird poop?*"

She raises her tiny nose up. "Sephyr not get *stuck*. Nallan and clan-mates, cowards all, sneak up. Shoot scat from spit-reeds. Out-numbered, Sephyr was."

Boodark laughs so hard that he hurts himself and he groans at the pain. Ecko, on the other hand, is horrified and absolutely disgusted when she realizes that she's been touching poop. She gags at the thought of it, and then she feels even worse for the poor little thing… all covered in bird poo.

"Oh *man*, that's just nasty," she whispers as she scrubs her hands against her pants. "Well, if it's just poop, soaking in warm water should get it off. Right? Please, please say yes."

Again, the little fairy nods, then she adds, "Yes, but faster with blister-thorn juice." A quick mental flashback of the Spanish moss full of those lethal-looking, fire-engine red thorns pops into her mind. She describes them and asks if those are the right ones, even though she knows darn good and well that they are. Of *course*, they are.

She'd made up her mind to stay as far away from them as she could, so naturally they are the very thing that's needed in this situation. And of course, no one but her can go retrieve them. She heaves a long-suffering sigh and grumbles, "Tell me everything I need to know. Are they poisonous? How many do I need to get? *How* do I get them? And what will happen when I get stuck by them, because I *will* get stuck. We all know it."

Boodark snorts his agreement, "They are not poisonous, but try not to let them stab you anyway. They are extra spicy, and they'll burn like fire if they prick through your skin."

The swamp fairy raises her hand up. "This many," she says and Ecko sees that she has six fingers on each hand.

"Six it is." She stands up and glares at Boodark. "You be nice!" she orders, and he sticks out his tongue at her. "I mean it, Boodark. Be nice. I'll be right back."

It takes no more than five minutes, and miracle of miracles, she makes it back without sticking herself a single time. She walks back into camp to find the two opponents glaring at one another across the battlefield. Good grief, what has she gotten herself into this time?

She sacrifices one of her precious water bottles, cutting it down to make a shallow 'bathtub' for the Darkling to soak in. As much as she values the eight (seven now) plastic bottles that humans blithely toss away *by the millions each and every day*, she absolutely refuses to use one of her eating bowls for poop removal. She *refuses*. She ladles the water in and has the fairy test it to be sure that it's not so hot that it would burn her skin. Once the Darkling is all settled into the tub, she holds out a tiny hand and demands, "One only."

When she passes her one of the blister-thorns, the swamp fairy immediately chews the sharp tip off of it. "I thought y'all said it would burn like fire!" she exclaims.

The Darkling fairy nods and grins up at her as she licks her lips. "Taste good!" Then she turns the thorn upside down. Cherry-red liquid pours out of it and splashes down into the water-bottle tub. The water instantly turns red and begins to boil, so that it now resembles a tiny, bloody jacuzzi. The thorn has lost all trace of color and is now a crystal-clear shell. Apparently, the thorns themselves aren't red, it's the liquid inside that looks like Hell's version of tabasco sauce. The fairy lifts the empty thorn to her mouth and takes a large, crunching bite. It sounds like glass tinkling and breaking as she chews it up and swallows it.

"I guess I don't have to worry about what to feed *you* for breakfast," Ecko mutters before turning to ask Boodark what he wants to eat. He decides on the last four powdered donuts. They've gone stale, but he doesn't seem to mind a bit as he shovels them in one after another.

She takes one look at their rapidly dwindling food supply and decides that she'll have to skip breakfast, and probably lunch too. She knows that she'll have to use her water filtration gear today, because she only has one partial bottle of water left. But ... drink swamp water? Ugh. *So* nasty. She's very aware of the fact that it'll be perfectly drinkable by the time she gets done cleaning it, but just the thought of putting swamp water, even former swamp water, into her mouth erps her out so bad. All that mud and poop and dead things all liquified and mixed together into some kind of funky cocktail. So. Freaking. Disgusting. But it's either clean it and drink it or die from dehydration.

"I choose life," she firmly tells herself. "I will *always* choose life. So, suck it up, buttercup." Thanking God, yet again, that she'd been so *extra* when buying the gear for her 'camping trip', she gathers up the four plastic bags that had been stuffed inside the miniature, emergency bug-out bag and some rubber bands to seal them with. They'll make the chore of carrying water from the source (swamp, *gag*) back to the campsite so much easier and less time consuming. She'll still have to make several trips in order to gather the amount of water that she needs, but it will be better than if she'd been forced to tote it one tiny potful at a time.

Her stomach rumbles as she sets out, leaving the fairy-girl soaking and her grumpy boy sulking. Perhaps she can find some food along the way to help supplement her supplies. She has a feeling that the time for drastically lowering her standards and to stop being so picky is fast approaching. Very soon she'll have to start living by Boodark's motto … "If it doesn't eat me first, then I can eat *it*, even if I only live to do so once." But she's still not eating fairies, and she will literally starve to death before she eats a Vika Vakooja. She will always choose life, *unless* she must decide between adding roach beetles to her menu or death. Death will trump that every single time. Period.

The trip to the edge of the swamp and back proves uneventful and she makes it back to camp with four bags of swamp water to boil and pour through the portable filtration system. While the first potful is boiling, she helps the fairy out of the 'tub'. The water is still red, but now it's a dirty, murky maroon color. It's also stopped boiling and has grown cold. She quickly dumps the gross water and refills it with fresh. As she settles the Darkling back in and hands her another blister-thorn, she tries for small talk. "Tell me about yourself."

Fairy eyes promptly narrow into suspicious slits and Boodark sputters. "PPffftttt, she's not gonna tell you anything."

The fairy pours her tabasco sauce marinade into the tub and the jacuzzi jets immediately get her spicy, Cajun-style boil going. "Why?" she demands, her voice brimming with wariness.

Gah! It's like asking Boodark what his name was all over again.

"Well," she patiently begins as she pokes more wood into the fire. "I've never met a Darkling before. In fact, I'd never even seen a fairy, until I met Queen Rowana and her Hive of FireFairies. I come from a world that has no magic, no Fae, no wee folk… although there *must* have been at some point, because there are stories and pictures and legends all about your world. I've always loved the Fae, and I learned as much as I could over the years. When I was a little girl, I had a book filled with pictures of all sorts of magical beings. Other than my best friend, Didymus, I loved that book above all else. It didn't have any pictures of fairies like *you* though. I would love to learn more about you and your world."

The miniature woman frowns in thought as she splashes crimson water over herself. After a moment, she gives a barely perceptible nod and reluctantly agrees. "Very well." She gestures vaguely in Boodark's direction and adds, "Cantankerous one correct. Sephyr Darkling, but not *only* Darkling. *He* lump us all together when, say true, we are many... much divergent. Ten, ten, ten and two Darkling clans make Sorrow Marshes home, all much different clans. I Sephyr, of clan Irukandji... Mushroom clan."

Her speech is so broken that it takes Ecko a minute to figure out what she's saying, but she eventually gets the gist of it. Apparently thirty-two (Ten, ten, ten and two) different Darkling clans live in the Sorrow Marshes. *This* little fairy's name is Sephyr and she's from the Irukandji Mushroom clan.

Boodark snorts to get their attention, and then plants himself right in the middle of their conversation... like a weed. "What she's not telling you, is what will happen when she bites you...if she bites you. I have made it clear to her that should she even attempt it, I will bite her back. And my bite would cause more damage to her than anything she could do to you. My bite would cut her in half!" He snaps his teeth at her to emphasize and reinforce his threat.

Ecko shakes her head and tsk's at him. "Sephyr has said that she won't bite me, and I trust her. But" she turns to look back at the Mushroom fairy "he does have me curious."

The wee one holds her tiny hands out for Ecko to lift her from the tub. "Water cold. Need new." So, she lifts her out and refreshes the bath. Sephyr's soon settled back in with clean, hot water, armed with her blister-thorn. Ecko takes a q-tip and says, "Turn around. The gunk on your wings looks like it might be soft enough to wipe away now."

Sephyr scowls and hisses at her. "No like turn back on unknowns."

"Are you serious?" she asks incredulously. "How can you still not trust me? I have done all this, just to help you. I could have squashed you a thousand times by now, if I wished you harm."

The Darkling takes a moment to think about it and then grudgingly turns her back to present her wings. "You speak true, but Sephyr still no like!"

As gentle as a feather stroke, Ecko starts meticulously wiping the dragonfly-type wings clean with the swabs. "You said before, that you hate me. Do you hate all people or is it just me?" she asks. She genuinely wants to know. Dip the swab into the bath water, wipe away a tiny section of gunk, re-dip and rinse the swab. Repeat. Over and over and over. It's tedious and time consuming, but she can't rush, lest she damage the fragile wings.

"All," Sephyr replies. "You most!"

Her hand stalls for a moment as she mentally sputters. "But why? You don't even know me! How can you hate me, if you don't even know me?"

The Darkling turns her head to look over her shoulder as she answers. "Sephyr watch. Sephyr hear. All Fae talk of new magic that female with hair like flame bring. Where *you* go, change follow. Sephyr no *want* change come Sorrow Marshes. Sephyr's only home. No want lose it. No want change."

Ecko has nothing to say to that. What *could* she say to that? She can certainly understand not wanting her way of life to be disrupted. "Well, I didn't *mean* to change anything" she grumbles.

Sephyr simply states, "And yet change follow you, same as Pitch follows Pale, whether wish it or no. Blood Lake no longer hold prisoner. Naiad free. Cause much anger. Spread much fear. New, green life in Black Forest. FireFairy clan *big* change. Winds whisper in Sephyr ear that FireQueen swear allegiance...To ground stomper!"

The surly little orc-bat growls. "Ecko's allies and enemies are of no concern to the likes of *you*! Best you mind your own affairs. Now, quit stalling. She wishes to know exactly what your bite will do, should you prove to be as feeble minded as you appear and actually attempt it." He points a claw at the little shroom fairy and insists, "Tell her now, or I will."

Sephyr bares her teeth in a snarl in his direction, but then she shrugs. "Say true, I care not." She pretends to be unconcerned that he intends to reveal things that she wants to keep to herself, but Ecko can see how her whole body tenses. Her guard is up, and it's glaringly obvious that she's mentally preparing herself for either fight or flight. Perhaps even both.

"Fine, I will," he insists. "But first I must explain about the Sorrow Marshes and the influence it has on trespassers. The most important thing to remember is...It wants nothing more than to make you a part of it. It wants you here, and it will do all that it can to keep you... forever."

"It will try to break you, take away all of your hopes and dreams and replace them with lies and doubts and tears. As you lose your hope, you will also lose your way, and eventually you'll lose all desire to leave. You will wander, lost through the mists for many

Pales, forced to eat what the swamp provides, lest you starve. And with every bite of nourishment, every sip of dark, fetid water, every breath of moist, stagnant air, it will claim your soul, bit by bit. So thoroughly lost in your own tortured mind, you will eventually just sit down to cry."

"When you stop moving, the last dregs of your hope will flee, and *that's* when the swamp will know that it has won. You will never get back up. The bog will overtake you...grow on you and you *onto* it. It will root you down into its bed and tuck you in with a blanket of moss. You will eventually become like stone, petrified and unable to move... Just one more victim claimed by the Sorrow Marshes."

Ecko shivers as a chill runs through her when he adds, "Those that are lost to the Marshes become what's known as Gloom Dooms."

All this time, Ecko had been picturing that terrible, traumatizing scene from The Never-Ending Story where the swamp of sadness took poor Artax. She doesn't know which would be worse, sinking and drowning in the depths of the swamp, or slowing petrifying while the swamp grows onto you, *into* you... claiming you as one of its own. Both are horrifying in their own right. "I knew this was going to be so bad! I hate swamps!" she whines, shivering all the while as she tries to dispel the mental pictures of Gloom Dooms that her imagination is creating.

Boodark squirms, trying to get comfortable. She quickly moves to help him into a better position, covering him with his blanket when he complains that he's cold. She touches his brow, worried about fever and infection, but he's cool to the touch. Cooler than he usually is, in fact. She pushes the worry aside and moves on to bottling the now clean and ready-to-drink water. She sets more swamp water to boiling and then she goes back to wiping muck from Sephyr's chest. The little fairy puts her nose into the air as she turns her words to Boodark. "Marsh no take all," she argues. "*Sephyr* free to fly, say true? Marsh only claim weak ones. *You* no last one Pale."

Boodark laughs at her. "It allows you to flitter about, because you were born there… It has *already* claimed you."

Sephyr goes very still as she narrows her eyes into slits. "No true," she rasps.

Ecko tries not to grin, because she can tell by his voice and the sudden sparkle in his eyes, that he's intentionally baiting her, and she's swallowing it, hook, line, and sinker. "Of course, it's true. Do you wish to leave your precious swamp?"

"Never!" she whisper/yells at him.

"Well, there you have it," he says as his mouth stretches wide with a huge yawn. "So, who then is the weak one, hmm? At least I am free to come and go, and have seen more of this world than just your nasty, old bog. Maybe I should call you Weakling from here on out, instead of Darkling."

Her tiny face flushes as she screeches out her anger, cursing him to the depths of the mire. But then the two females stop what they're doing to stare incredulously at one another when they hear loud snores coming from his direction.

Simultaneously they turn to look at *him*, and sure enough, they see that he's fallen fast asleep, tongue lolled out and dangling into the dirt.

"*Much* cretin," Sephyr states with such disgust that it makes Ecko laugh. "He grows on you," is all she says, because really, what more *could* she say?

"Perhaps," the Darkling mumbles, "perhaps grow on you... like FleshEater Fungus!"

She grins as she helps Sephyr out of her lukewarm bath. "I think one more soak and we'll be able to get that last stubborn bit off. What do you think?"

She glances down at herself and grunts, "Yes, once more." Her eyes lift back up to meet Ecko's. "You speaked true? Truly release Sephyr?"

"Yes, I spoke true. I try my best to always tell the truth. In fact, if you really wish it, you can leave right now. Or you can stay, and I will continue to help you. You're not a captive."

She settles the little one back in one last time, and then she cuts the tip of a Q-tip off and hands it to her. It's just the right size to become a bath puff for a fairy to scrub with. "I'm making one more trip to collect water. I hope you're still here when I return, but if you decide to go, I am glad to have met you, Sephyr of the Irukandji clans."

"She snuck off! I can't believe she snuck off without even a thank you for all you did!" Boodark's pissed. He's finally awake...

long after she had returned from gathering the water. She's even had time to boil and filter it all. Now she's busy making dinner. In fact, she's pretty sure it was the smell of food that had done the trick in waking him. His cute little bat nose had started twitching, even before he opened his eyes.

"Most Fae won't say thank you. They find it offensive, like a curse word," she informs him. Boodark huffs in agitation. "I know that! I know more about it than you ever will! I am pixy-kind, you know. I just meant that I can't believe the little coward snuck off without even trying to repay you. I'm sorry's and thank you's may be taboo to the Fae, but so is owing a debt. And she definitely owes you one."

She casually dismisses his ire. It doesn't bother her; she hadn't helped Sephyr to be repaid. She just can't stand to see anything, or anyone, stuck in a nasty, sticky situation... pun totally intended. The only thing that really bothers her is the fact that the little Darkling felt like she *had* to sneak away, and that they hadn't parted ways as friends.

"Well, at least she didn't bite me, as you were so sure she would." She reaches over and sets Boodark into an upright position, so that she can feed him his dinner. Once again, she divides the two MRE meals, chili bowl and ravioli dinner, into equal portions, so they can each enjoy both of them. She feeds him his dinner first, and while she spoons it into his always-eager mouth, she asks, "So, what *would* have happened if she had bit me? I never did find out."

He holds up a claw and mumbles, "Nrung, nrung, nruungg. Oh! Oh, that's *good.* Eat first, talk later. Nruunngg."

She doesn't even try to hold back her grin. He's such a piggy little thing. She sure wishes he would hurry though, so that she can be a piggy thing too. She's pretty sure that her belly is trying to devour itself and watching him eat is pure torture. But finally, he's done with all but the lemon bar dessert, and she quickly puts it into his hand. He can feed that to himself.

And then she's digging into her own food, shoveling it in and making just as many grunting, pig noises as he had. She wonders, had she ever tasted anything so divine in all her life? She devours it all so quickly that she's done with her entire meal before Boodark can finish his dessert.

But that could just be because he's too busy staring at her in shock and has completely forgotten all about eating. When he realizes that he still holds half of the treat, he holds it out to her. "Take it. You're even hungrier than I am. I didn't think that was even possible!"

But she declines with a shake of her head. "No, I'm good now. You finish your dessert." Then she lays back with her head propped on his blanket. "I am so tired; I don't understand it. I mean, it seems like every day I'm getting more and more worn out. I'm starting to think that maybe it really is this world… sucking up all my energy, vampiring the life out of me. All I know is that I'll be crawling into my blanket cocoon and going to sleep the very minute that Pitch arrives, so we better get done with whatever needs to be done, before that time comes. But I'm going to lay here and rest for just one minute, just long enough for you to tell me about Darkling bites."

She rolls onto her side, so that she can look at him while he talks. "Well, like Sephyr told you, not all Darklings are the same, so their bites too will differ. But *her* particular bite contains the poison of the Crippler Caps, which is the mushroom fairy's main food source. They eat so many of them that the poison builds up in their bodies, in their blood and in their spit. They even secrete it out of their skin when it builds up too much inside of them."

"They *have* to let it out when the levels get that high, whether by biting or bloodletting or sweating. Bleeding hurts, and sweat baths are unpleasant, so they make it a practice to *bite* it out whenever they can. *That* is why I assumed she would bite you. That, and the Darklings are a sneaky, tricksy lot that can't be trusted."

He grunts in pain as he rolls onto his side to face her as well, before he continues. "The poison from her bite would have done just what the name 'Crippler Cap' implies. It would have incapacitated you in every way. In your body, your mind, even in your soul. You would get terrible headaches and body pains, and you would spew filth... out of *both* ends. You would sweat all the water out of your body and your skin would become so sensitive that it would become painful just to wear it upon your bones."

"But that isn't the worst part. The bite of the Irukandji causes a disturbance in your brain... it rearranges things up there. You would soon become sad and depressed, and you would feel an overwhelming sense of impending doom. Thoughts of ending your life would plague your mind. *That* is why I became so concerned when I saw that you so blithely carried a member of the Irukandji-kind in your hand."

"When I spoke about the swamp and its influence, it was to prepare you for what is coming, but also to let you know that all things in that swamp work to help the Sorrow Marshes obtain its main goal. The creatures that dwell within are the slaves that feed it and keep it alive. From the Fae to the creatures and bugs, the trees and the plants and the moss… they all live in servitude, whether they know that it is so or not. Even the slime and the mud and the muck must serve their master."

She's thinks about it, mentally replaying all that she's just learned. "You've said that the swamp wants to keep all who enter into its territory, make them become a part of it forever. You said that all the things that live there help it to obtain its goals."

He nods at her. "It's all true."

"Well, what *is* its goal? What does it really want?"

"More. Like every other powerful and corrupt thing of this world, it wants more. More power, more territory in its domain, more slaves to feed it. It wishes to grow, to expand so far that it covers the entire world in mire…. It wants absolute rule over *all*."

Her eyes widen and she whisper-quotes, "Power corrupts, and absolute power corrupts absolutely."

He nods back at her. "Exactly,' he agrees.

The Pale rumble decides to make its appearance and begin its countdown. "Finally," she murmurs and then sits up with a moan and a groan at how tired and sore her body is. While she cleans up the mess from dinner, she thinks about the whole swamp situation. Something's bothering her. "I just don't understand," she confesses. "I don't understand how a swamp can do all that you say it does. How can a *place* want anything? How does it have the mental capacity to do the things you've said? Places don't have wants, other than to simply exist, perhaps. And even that is questionable, because I'm not sure that wanting to exist counts. A want is basically a wish, and places cannot make wishes."

A terrible thought pops into her head then. She turns huge, terrified eyes to her companion as her brain pokes and worries the bad idea like a tongue tends to worry a sore tooth. "It's haunted, isn't it? *Isn't it?* What, it's not freaking scary enough, it has to have ghosts and spooks too?"

Boodark rolls back to his belly, wincing from the pain that shoots through him. Once he's settled and has made it through the worst of the pain, he answers. "No spooks that I'm aware of, but I couldn't say yay or nay, not for sure anyway. I tend to stay as far from the Sorrow Marshes as I can."

She wholeheartedly agrees with that and wishes (again) that there was a way to go around, but both Boodark and Sephyr had already assured her there would be no avoiding the swamp. It stretches for *miles.* So she's back to those bothersome thoughts about *how* a swamp can be a sentient thing and how it can wish and want and strive to become bigger. "*How* does it have awareness and consciousness? To have any sort of mental capacity, it would first need a brain. *Swamps don't have brains!*"

Boodark takes a sip of his water before he replies. "*That* is more difficult to explain. To understand that, first you must understand that The Sorrow Marshes is not *just* a place; it's a spirit, as ancient as the stars. So, it *is* a living, *sentient* thing... of sorts. Some say that this spirit angered the AllMother so greatly, that she bound it here when this world was a new, young thing. She trapped it in the depths of a small but bottomless lake, and then covered it over with dirt and stone to seal the way shut and to block out the light. And here she left it, content in her belief that it could not escape its watery prison."

"The spirit's fury was a fearsome thing, and in one fit of rage after another, it bashed itself upon the ground-seal that blocked the only way out... Much like Jaida had done inside your bubble prison. Try as it may, it could not free itself, and its rages shook the entire world for years to come. But the spirit is a patient thing, timeless and powerful. Over time, its rage became like a poison, and it began to corrupt the physical world around it."

"It turned the once crystal-clear waters black, thick and foul, even as it perverted the small creatures which shared its imprisonment. It polluted them, warped them, turned them into strange, misshapen things that thrive in the dark. Hundreds of years passed, until finally a crack appeared in the ground-seal, a crack so small that it could not be seen with the eyes. But the spirit *felt* it, for it knew its prison well. And it was just enough to allow trace amounts of his foul poison to seep up onto the surface. Mud and muck bubbled up out of it and eventually... after hundreds of years, it covered the area above his jail, and his deformed and gro-tesque pets slithered and crawled up through the ooze, until they were no longer trapped below."

"Though *it* could not leave its prison, it soon discovered that it *could* send out tiny, imperceptible spores of itself, smaller than specks of dust, to infect and influence those that drew near. And so, the swamp was born. It thrived and grew larger with every vic-tim that the spirit claimed, and *all* came to dread and beware the Sorrow Marshes."

Boodark meets her eyes and ends his tale with, "So you see, it's not haunted with spooks... It *is* the Haunting."

She is thoroughly disturbed by that, and those words will stay with for a long time to come. *'It is the Haunting.'*

Finished with all her chores and done with discussing terrify-ing things that she cannot control nor change, she mentally pre-pares to do that dreaded thing that she's been putting off all day. But it must be done. So, she takes out her medical kit and pours a bowl of water from the pot that she's kept warm over the fire's coals.

"I need to check on your wound," she tells him and then helps to get him better settled. She cleans her hands, and as gently as she can, peels the bandage off his leathery skin. His sharp intake of breath as the air hits his raw, angry flesh matches hers, as she gets her first glance at how it looks after she'd sewn it back together. "Oh Boodark, I don't know. It looks bad."

He grunts and says that it can't possibly look any worse than it feels. "You sewed it shut? The bulbs were all green?"

She nods, but then realizes that she's behind him and therefore he can't see her head shake. "Yes," she assures him. "I stitched it up. The bulbs were all a beautiful, healthy green. But now…" She pauses as she studies the little pear-shaped nubs poking out of his skin like strange, macabre flower buds.

"What? But now *what?*" he demands.

"Welll, they just don't seem *as* green today, as they did last night. Maybe it's just the difference in lighting, though. The wound looks swollen and… leaky. I just don't know if what I'm seeing is normal. I don't know anything about wings or weird green alien bulbs, and I don't know anything about orc-bat anatomy!"

She can feel herself starting to panic, her voice rising to match her emotions, and she has to look away and calm herself.

"I have told you many times that I am not a bat, nor am I a orc," he insists, "I would have eaten you by now if I was orcish-kind! Let me see what it looks like through your viewer."

It takes her a moment to process what he's requesting. "Oh! You want me to take a picture. That's brilliant!" She takes several, from different angles so that he can get a real good look. He grunts as she scrolls through them. "The swelling and the seeping are normal, for now. By next Pale's end, it should be better. The bulbs are worrisome though, especially that bottom one, there on the right.

It's smaller, and maybe... not as green as the rest?" It comes out in a question, and she quickly agrees with him.

"I had trouble with that one. Its cord/vein thingy was shorter than the others. I had a hard time getting it to stretch far enough so that I could put the stitches in around it."

She puts her camera away and then carefully washes his back with clean, warm water. She can't risk using any of her 'human' cleansers and topical medications. For now, it doesn't appear infected, and aside from how swollen it is, it seems to be doing what it's supposed to be doing. Boodark doesn't seem overly worried about it anyway. So, she cleans it and gently pats it dry. "Should I cover it back up, or leave it as it is, so the air can get to it?"

He tells her to leave it unbandaged for now and that she could cover it back up when the Pale arrives.

"Ok then. I guess that's all I can do tonight. Let's get our trip to the bathroom out of the way, before it gets dark." She lifts him up and he makes a squinched up face at her. "Walk fast, I've been holding it forever. I didn't want either one of us to have to go through this anymore than necessary."

She is thoroughly disgusted with herself. She should have asked if he had to go. Her busy day is no excuse either. He's already miserable enough, he shouldn't have the added discomfort of having to 'hold it'. Some friend/nurse *she's* turning out to be. But in her defense, she has no experience in either of those departments. She'd never been a nurse *or* a friend before.

"Don't do that again," she fusses. "Don't make yourself more miserable by holding it. I don't mind helping you, not even if you have to go twenty times a day. And I don't care how embarrassing it is...for both of us. It is necessary, it can't be avoided, everyone does it, and so you just need to get over it!"

She sets him down and rolls her eyes when he meekly mutters, "Yes, ma'am." She leaves him to it and walks away to find her own 'bathroom'. "Don't bring *anything* back with you this time!" he shouts at her retreating back. Brat.

When they wake the next Pale/morning, Ecko rushes through all of her chores. She wants to get in, and therefore back *out*, of the Sorrow Marshes before the next Pitch arrives. She has no desire to spend a night in the swamp. None, whatsoever. In fact, she has no desire to step even a single foot into the swamp, but she has no other choice.

She rushes through feeding an uncharacteristically quiet and subdued Boodark his breakfast, cleans and bandages his (unchanged) wound, and then packs up and cleans the campsite in record time. Now she's standing at the edge of the swamp, where the ground changes from solid land to boggy mire. She hadn't thought it possible, but she's filled with even more aversion now than she had been when she'd taken her first look at it. The more she'd learned, the worse she felt about the entire situation.

"You're uh, really going in there, are you?" she asks in her best Hoggle voice.

"Yes, I'm afraid I have to," she answers in her own Ecko voice. She hugs Boodark, snug in his beddy-bye basket, protectively against her chest. She'd probably feel a tiny bit better if she could talk to him, instead of herself, but he's already fallen back asleep. His snores drift up to break the silence. And silent it *is*, as if the entire swamp is holding its collective breath, waiting to see if she'll take the step or turn and flee.

"It *is* the Haunting," she whispers, and she shivers as she takes that first squelching step into the mud. The unpleasantness of the muck filling her shoes, the *ick* seeping into her socks is almost enough to change her mind, but she forces herself to take another step, then another and another, until she's a dozen paces in.

"This isn't so bad," she says aloud. (Don't judge. Talking to herself comforts her in times of great need and extreme fear, and right now she is *terrified*.) "At least the mud's only ankle deep," she murmurs in an attempt to make herself feel better. Then her heart drops into her stomach as she takes her next step...and sinks up to her knees.

She squeaks in fright and throws her arms out for balance. Holding perfectly still for a full minute, she allows her heart rate to settle into a more sensible rhythm before inching her feet forward. She'll have to be more careful and feel her way forward.

What she needs is a nice, long Gandalf stick to poke into the muddy water to see just how deep it is… *before* she steps forward. She looks all around her, but there are no wizard staffs lying about for her convenience. But she's determined to find one. Sooner, rather than later.

For now though, she carefully tests each step before she commits to it. She watches the water in front of her, hoping against all hope, that she doesn't come across any snakes. Something tells her that the old Earth saying about snakes being more scared of her, than she is of them, won't be the case *here*.

But there's not much else to look at right now, anyway. Other than the black, somehow *slimy* looking trees dripping with moss, there really isn't much plant life at all. She can hear what sounds like the buzzing of wings in the distance, whether from bugs or fairies, she can't tell. She *hates* bugs. And as intriguing as she finds the Fae, she really hopes to avoid them too. They're unpredictable and dangerous, and she has more than enough danger in her life just trying to keep from sinking into the mire and becoming a permanent fixture of the Sorrow Marshes.

Each step she takes is a little bit deeper than the last, and she wants to turn back so badly. At this moment, she can't recall anything she'd ever wanted more. She repeats Charlie's name like a litany to force herself to keep moving. So far, it's been enough, but it's a complete game changer when there's another abrupt drop that brings the water level to her waist. The feeling of the water soaking through her pants, the mud oozing into her privates… sliding down into the crack of her butt does it.

"Nope. I'm out," she declares as she turns around to head back, *only to find just as much swamp behind her, as there had been in front of her.* She'd only taken thirty-two steps. (She knows. She counted, ok?) And they'd been small, cautious baby steps, too. She hadn't gone far enough for the dry, solid world that she'd left behind to have disappeared yet; it should still be within view. But it's not. All around her is nothing but dark murky water, mud, and knobby trees with their slime covered roots… that are perfect homes for things that slither.

Thinking, hoping, *praying* (dear God *please* let it be so) that perhaps she'd gotten turned around somehow, she twists back around to check the direction (she thinks) she'd been traveling. But there's only endless, fathomless marsh, eerily still and quiet. Are the trees closer now than they had been?

She swallows back a cry as she becomes convinced that she's no longer alone. She can suddenly feel the heavy weight of someone (something?) watching her, the stickiness, the *itchiness* of it on her skin. Her breath quickens and her heart thuds as she searches for the spectator, but there's nothing. There's nothing but the trees… the suddenly ominous, impossibly tall trees, with their leafless branches, heavy with gobs of tangled moss. The slick, black bark seems more like a skin, leathery and glistening and pulsing, almost like it's covering living flesh. The silence has become too loud, until her eardrums feel like they might burst from the pressure of the void. She turns in circles, desperately trying to make sense of what she's seeing, while doing her very best to ignore what she's feeling.

The trees *are* closer, she's sure of it. She feels as if she's been thrust into a game of Red Rover with the foliage, but she'd never liked that game, and she's not having any fun… *at all.* When she turns around to check on the trees inching up behind her, the ones that had just been in front of her stealthily creep in closer, and then freeze in place once more when she spins back towards them. No matter where she turns, there are trees at her back… and they're slowly crowding in to surround her.

"Red rover, red rover, please make the trees stand still. I don't want them to come over," she whimpers as she twists back and forth in a perpetual, distressed circle.

"Don't panic!" she shouts at herself, because she is, in fact, panicking. Her heart slams to a stop as something tugs at her hair, and sharp boney fingers tap her shoulders. She cries out as she spins around, only to discover that the game has ended, for the trees have reached her. They've won, and as they reach out for her, their branches creaking as they stretch down to pull her into their embrace, she whispers, "I'm so sorry."

But what she's sorry for, she really couldn't say. Sorry for failing, perhaps. Sorry for failing everyone: her family, Charlie and Susan, Boodark, her mother and all *her* people, the FireFairies and Sephyr of the Irukandji clans, the entire planet Earth and Irredarr and even this nasty vampire world. As horrible as this land is, there are still innocents doing all they can just to survive... and they deserve to be saved. She's failed them all...

'It *is* the Haunting' Boodark's words ghost through her mind. She suddenly realizes that it's this place that's making her feel tired and desolate and defeated. She's up to her waist in a haunted swamp; no, a swamp that *is* the Haunting. It's the Sorrow Marshes that's watching her every move... and it wants nothing more than to keep her here, by whatever means necessary.

The sudden stirring of the water, just a foot in front of her, draws her attention away from her erratic, wayward thoughts. It bubbles and gurgles as *something* displaces the muck. Some small slithering thing swimming by? She whimpers with indecision. Remain still and hope that whatever it is decides that it doesn't want her and continues on its icky little way, or flee, screaming like a raving lunatic, like she really wants to do.

While she stands still, undecided, the whispers slink back in and fill her mind again, telling her that she's not enough, that she'll *never* be good enough and so she should just give up. Give up and stay here, where she's wanted. Where she is loved. Where she will never have to worry about failing anyone ever again. But Boodark's words of warning, suddenly louder than the whispers in her head, remind her that if she gives up and stops moving, she will be stuck here forever.

"No!" she shouts and shakes herself out of her indecisive, immobile state. At the sound of her voice, the world around her instantly grows darker, as if a cloud has drifted over the sun to blot out the light. But there *is* no sun here, no clouds, only a bleak grey sky.

She whirls around at the barely-there sound of something slipping into the water *right behind* her. The muck churns and bubbles, and it's something *big* that's joined her in the water. She bites her knuckles to hold back her cries as she watches the tiny waves lap in the wake of something swimming below the surface… straight for her. But then it passes her by, so close that the hard, scaly hide brushes up against her leg.

There's no holding back her screams as it briefly wraps itself around her ankle, as if assuring her that it *could* have, if it had wanted to… If it only had the time to stay and play. But it turns her loose with one last, almost loving stroke, just like a cat that rubs itself against the one that it claims as its own, scent-marking it. The feel of the unseen creature's hold on her lingers, even after she watches the slipstream that it leaves behind in its haste to get away.

"Something wicked this way comes." The words appear in her mind, and she doesn't know if the creature planted them there, or if it's just her sixth sense finally raising its dumb head out of the proverbial mud. But *something* is coming, of that, she's sure. Some big bad something that frightens things that are bigger and badder than she is, and makes them flee. It's creeping in, just as the trees that encircle her and hold her prisoner had... but infinitely worse.

The wind begins to shriek and moan through the bog, a terrifying prelude to the Bad Thing that's approaching. The trees thrash in the wind, the naked branches lashing out their anger against her face. *It* moves in closer and closer, until she can no longer endure the sheer terror of it. She bolts, having no idea which way to go. All she knows is that she must flee.

She slips between two trees, screaming and slapping at the reaching, clutching branches as they try to snatch her back. She dips and ducks below them, even as the thick layer of mud below her feet becomes as thick as quicksand. It sucks at her feet, giving aid to the trees in their determination to hold her down, until *it* reaches her.

She fights against it, pulling her legs through the sucking muck with all her strength. She whimpers as she loses first one and then the other shoe, but she leaves them behind without ever slowing… she can't spare the time to search for them. It's almost upon her, she can feel its cold breath tickling the fine hairs on the back of her neck. Her heart threatens to burst and she's so afraid that even her tears refuse to come out of hiding.

Instead of slapping the branches away, she now uses them to pull herself along, grasping them tightly and ripping her hands to shreds in her desperation to escape the terrible unknown looming behind her. The mud has become so thick now that it's like wading through setting concrete. She drags herself on and on through the thick sludge, her legs on fire, her arms leaden from the strain of pulling herself through the suction of the mud… mud that clings and grips tight as liquid iron. She struggles on for hours, days, years even until she suddenly realizes that the mud level is slowly dropping.

It's no longer at her waistline, but at her thighs instead. She sobs, dry eyed at the relief she feels when it's knee level and the way forward is made easier. She stares down her body, watching as each step brings the level just a bit lower, until it reaches her shins and then finally when it's back to just ankle deep.

The only remaining struggle now is staying on her feet, but she just can't do it. Her jelly legs will no longer hold her weight and she falls to her knees and hangs her head in exhaustion. The breath painfully tears in and out of her chest, and all she wants to do is lie down, just for a moment. Just until she can breathe again. Just until every breath she sucks in no longer feels like it'll cause her head to explode or shred her lungs into bloody confetti.

She hears a slight rustling sound and wearily lifts her head. She's almost made it. Twenty yards ahead of her is the most welcoming sight of dry land and lush green grass she's ever seen. With an eager cry, she drags herself forward, crawling and clawing her way forward, until she reaches that sweet, beautiful green patch.

That last little bit is the hardest yet, as if the swamp is making one last desperate attempt to claim her. With a squelching *plop*, she finally manages to free herself. Digging her fingers into the soft, cool soil, she hauls herself as far away from the muck as she can. Then, using the last bit of strength she possesses, she removes the basket strap from around her neck, so that she doesn't squash her tiny, (incredibly) still snoring friend beneath her when she sprawls flat on her belly in the silky soft grass. And then she just lays there, panting and sweating and thanking God that she'd somehow escaped whatever wicked thing had been coming for her.

As much as she longs to lay there and take the most deserved nap of her life, she knows that she needs to get away from the swamp. She needs to get *far* away, put as much distance between her and *it* before Pitch falls. With herculean effort, she raises her head to search her new surroundings, and her eyes immediately lock onto the beautiful, *magical* scene before her.

A table elegantly laid with flowing white lace and scattered with soft pale flowers beckons in the distance. There's a canopy above it, made from tangled vines, dripping with delicate blossoms and tiny, twinkling lights. It's like something straight out of a fairy tale… and it's *familiar*, as if it had been plucked right out of her very own fairy tale dreams. So captivated, so *enchanted*, so utterly convinced that it's meant just for her, it never even occurs to her that a table set up at the edge of a swamp is laughingly, disturbingly out of place.

Forgetting all about her exhaustion and dismissing her aches and pains, she gets back up on her feet. She suddenly finds herself standing under the canopy, staring up at the fairy lights in dreamlike wonder, without ever having taken a step forward. She feels light, euphoric, as she leans in to smell a trailing blossom.

"Ecko"

She hears Boodark call her name, and she glances down to see him already seated at the table. She laughs and claps her hands in sheer delight, as enthralled as a small child that's been given a balloon.

The table is charmingly set for a party of ten, the soft glow from the candles kiss the scattered rose petals and dance upon the crystal champagne glasses. Nestled in moss and leafy floral arrangements are trays of vegetables, dripping with heaps of melting butter, baskets of fruits and bowls of berries, and plates piled high with fluffy, soft cookies and scones.

"Ecko"

There are trays of crackers, spread with soft cheeses, and elegant, crystal dishes of clotted cream and honey and sweet jellies. Unable to resist, she delves in, sampling everything that catches her fancy, a sweet buttery carrot, yellow grape-like berries that she has no name for, but will never forget the taste of, a light delicate cookie dipped in melted chocolate. She works her way around the table, a nibble here, a taste there.

"Ecko!"

She stops next to Boodark and piles his plate with treats that she knows he'll adore. She smiles as she reaches out and strokes his hair. Someone's braided it and tucked little green leaves into the locks.

"Ecko!" Boodark calls her name again.

"Hhmmm?" she sleepily hums. But movement from across the table catches her eyes and distracts her, and she lifts her head to watch delicate, iridescent bubbles floating up around the chair decorated for the guest of honor... *Her!*

Giggling with delight, she forgets all about her little friend as she skips over to it. Lush, green ivy entwined with little string lights wind up the legs and drape down over the back. It's all ribbons and roses and twinkling lights, and she feels like a fairy princess as she sits down. When she looks out over the wondrous picnic, her heart fills with an unparalleled joy, a happiness that she's never known before this moment in time.

Seated all around her is everyone she's ever loved: her father and Rachael and Karen. Charlie and Susan, as well as Boodark and Sir Didymus. And her elusive mother, Laelynn, whom she'd never really known, but had loved throughout her entire life anyway. Even sweet Maggie has a chair at her table of beloveds.

She smiles at each of them and then she realizes that they're waiting. Waiting for her to give them leave to begin the feast. She raises her glass in a toast, "Eat! Drink! Be merry!" They smile and cheer as they all drink to that, then they eagerly turn their attention to the food set before them. Her dad takes a huge bite out of a pale blue banana. Charlie cuts into something that looks like a sweet potato, but it's violet-purple and almost too pretty to eat. He forks a bit into his mouth, closing his eyes briefly as he savors the taste. By his side, as always, Susan daintily nibbles on a scone, spread with clotted cream.

"Here, sweet daughter. Try this one." She turns her head to watch her mother offer up a pink melon the size of an ostrich egg. She taps it sharply against the table and cracks it open, as if it truly were an egg. A red pomegranate-like fruit pours out onto Ecko's plate and as she reaches for it, her mother says "You'll *love* it. Trust me. I *am* your mother, and mothers always know best!"

Ecko picks it up and brings it to her lips. She takes a big, healthy bite... she trusts her mother. Mother loves her and knows what's best for her. And mother *was* right. It is the sweetest, juiciest, most delectable thing she's ever tasted. She giggles her delight, as the clusters of juicy pulp burst in her mouth and dribbles down her chin. Her mother nods in approval before she turns to her own meal.

Ecko watches her family as she takes bite after bite of that fruit, *and it never grows smaller*. She eventually sets it aside and jumps from her seat when she notices, with great dismay, that poor Boodark cannot reach his plate. His arms are much too short.

"Oh, you poor, sweet dear!" she cries as she rushes over to lift him into her arms. "Come. Sit with me and I will feed you." She settles back into her chair and pops a blue grape into his mouth. She rocks him back and forth as she lovingly strokes his hair. "Such a beautiful dolly," she whispers as he smiles up at her. This is good. This is right. *Finally*, all is right in her world. She is at peace.

Dolly? Oh, this is *wrong*. So wrong. Suddenly, Ecko's no longer seeing the picnic from the viewpoint of her chair, but from *above* it. It's as if her spirit has left her body and now hovers above them all, a silent spectral observer. Her family seems *off* somehow. They eat and laugh and make merry, but they do so with stiff, jerky movements. They look mechanical almost, as if they're robots or puppets on strings perhaps.

"Ecko!"

She watches her dad peel another banana, and it's like watching him peel the skin off of flesh, as blood pours out of it and drips down his hand. He doesn't seem to notice as he takes a big bite and turns to smile at her marionette-self, still seated in the guest of honor chair and somehow still functioning, even though her spirit no longer resides inside her body.

"Ecko!"

Charlie selects another purple sweet potato from the basket, but it turns black as he sets it onto his plate. She cries out his name in a horrified warning as he slices off a piece, and thick, black ooze pours out of it. There's so much of it… an impossible amount! It overflows his plate and stains the lace tablecloth. He smiles at her puppet self as he lifts the bite-sized morsel of *wrongness* into his mouth.

"Oh, Susan," she whimpers when she sees just what it is that *she's* been eating… green, moldy hunks of something that she's spreading her clotted cream on. But it's not cream. It's a bowl full of clotted and rancid blood pudding, teaming with small, squiggling worms.

"Stop," she tells them, but her voice comes out like a squeak, a tiny mouse squeak that can't be heard over their sudden, merry laughter.

"Stop, please stop!" she screams. "Make it stop!"

This time her family hears her cries, and they all turn as one to look up at her hovering spirit. They smile gruesome smiles, with gore in their teeth.

"Ecko!"

She shudders and turns towards the voice. She watches herself stroke her little friend's hair and she is *all wrong.* Her face seems frozen, with blank eyes and a wide plastic smile. There is nothing pleasant about that smile, in fact it's the most frightening thing she's ever seen in her entire life. It fills her heart with ice, and freezes the blood in her veins.

"Coraline's *Other* mother," she whispers as she desperately tries to get back to her body. She has to wake up, has to wake them all up. But she can't move, can't come back down. She's a balloon full of helium, held aloft on a string. She cries out as she watches herself lift the fruit from her plate and begin eating once more. She cringes as her mechanical, marionette mouth bites into it, and the juice that's not juice, but blood, runs down her face.

"Ecko, please!"

Her puppet self smiles reassuringly down at her little orc-bat friend. "It's ok, pretty dolly. Everything is fine… fine…. fiiinneee…. fffiiiiiiiiiiiiiiinnnnnnnneeeeeee………"

Everything slows down around her, like toys when their batteries start to die. Even the words spilling from her mouth slow down, down, down, until they at last come to a final resting place. Pretty dolly? She *hates* dolls; she's *always* hated dolls. She would never set anything upon her lap, smile down at it, and call it a pretty little dolly.

Her marionette self suddenly throws her head back and locks eyes with her spirit self. Her mouth opens wide, so wide, *impossibly* wide and she screams, one long blood curdling scream after another.

"Yes! Wake up Ecko! Wake up and see true!"

And just like that, the balloon holding her spirit aloft pops, and she's snapped back into her body. But she immediately wishes she could leave it again. Leave it all behind, and just float away and never look back. The words, '*Come back to us, come back into the Dreaming. Stay with us!*' whisper desperately through her mind.

The Dreaming had been ghastly and dreadful, but this… oh, this is so much worse, because it is the real, true story. This is the reality.

She sits, not in a guest of honor's chair at a beautifully laid table, but at a large flat rock surrounded by a circle of knobby tree knees and stumps (chairs). Her legs and buttock are submerged in foul, stagnant water, the surface thick with a skin of bright green scum. It's not Boodark sitting on her lap, grinning up at her; it's a foxlike creature, long dead with matted moldy fur and worms in its eyes. It bares its teeth at her in a perpetual, gruesome snarl. Crying out in alarm and utter revulsion, she pushes the half-rotten corpse off her lap and wipes her filthy hands on her even filthier shirt.

Teetering on the verge of full-blown panic, her eyes dart back and forth, desperately searching for something familiar, something comforting, something to prove that she's still trapped inside the Dreaming. Nothing is familiar, nothing is comforting. She notices for the first time, the 'food' set out on the rock (table).

In front of each tree stump (chair) is some new and revolting horror. A black turnip with several bites taken from it, revealing the mushy, liquifying rot inside. A cluster of deadly looking mushrooms, many of which are missing their tops. A bloody root with a single large chunk missing, so that the blood inside runs free and thick and foul. A mass of thin, stringy roots that look like spaghetti, rescind that… they're worms, squirming into and around one another. A blob of congealed blood jelly. A pile of…. teeth?

And then she sees the fruit set right in front of her. Oh, it's bad. It's *so* bad. Just like what she'd seen in her Dreaming state, it's like some sort of pomegranate mutant, made up of thousands of juicy bubble clusters. Rich and red and swollen, almost to bursting with juice (blood?) the clusters *pulse* as if they each contain a heartbeat.

She looks closer and throws her hand over her mouth as she gags. Inside each little bubble is a tiny white seed, writhing and squirming like mosquito larvae, or *sperm*. And then one of those bubbles *does* burst. The juice (blood) pours out, spilling the seed-worm out with it. It wriggles its way through its birth fluids and across the rock (table), until it bumps up against the black turnip. She watches it burrow and disappear inside, in search of a safe dark place, the *perfect* place, to embed itself and grow…very much resembling sperm in appearance and purpose.

With absolute horror, she counts just how many Ecko-sized bites are missing from the sperm-worm fruit. Her stomach rolls once, giving her just enough warning for her to turn aside and wretch, adding to the foulness of the stinking mud beside her. She vomits gallons of red juice (blood) and thick, stringy ropes of saliva. She can feel the sperm-worm seeds crawling up her throat like foul, rancid maggots, watches them wriggle out of the vomit and swim away through the sludge water.

She throws up for a very long time, until her stomach is purged and there's nothing left inside of her, foul or otherwise. She scoots herself backwards, away from the mess she's made. She scoots away, until she can no longer smell all the horrors in front of her, the death, rot and decay, and her own sick. She scoots away, until her back thumps up against a tree stump and she can go no further.

"Are you, *you* again?" She looks down and with a glad cry of relief, sees her little orc-bat friend lying there, his beddy-bye basket half-submerged in the mud. His face is pinched, eyes dull with pain, but filled with hope at the same time.

"Boodark!" she cries out as she picks him up and hugs him to her chest, filthy beddy-bye basket and all. She holds him and loves him and just gives thanks that she hadn't lost him while she'd had her break from reality.

Her eyes pop open as she suddenly realizes that the Pitch is rumbling its warning. "Oh! We have to find somewhere safe to spend the night! I can't believe I've been wandering around the swamp with my mind trapped in the Dreaming all day. I'm so sorry. I had every intention of being far away from here when Pitch fell. How long do you think we have left?"

She gasps at the pain that getting to her feet causes and takes a minute to stretch her back, trying to alleviate the biggest discomforts. She feels terrible, absolutely *wretched.* Every single inch of her body screams in agony and she feels like she hasn't slept in a week.

"Two," Boodark grunts.

"Two?" she asks, confused by his answer. "What do you mean two? Minutes?"

He closes his eyes and explains "No." (Big, soul weary sigh) "Two Pales. You wandered the Sorrow Marshes all of LastPale, all throughout the Pitch, and then this entire Pale. I couldn't wake you, couldn't get through to you. I thought you were lost to the Sorrows forever."

Huge, fat tears leak from the corners of his eyes.

Wait, what? "Two *days*?" she whispers. "Two whole days and… and a Pitch? I wandered the swamp....*in the black of night*?"

He nods weakly and she feels like she may be in shock. "Remember. Nothing?" he asks in a halting, breathless voice.

She frowns as she thinks back, *way* back, before the gruesome picnic. "I remember the trees coming to life and trying to get me. I remember fear, *immense* fear, and running, getting stuck in thick mud. And something... something *Wicked*."

She shudders and then purposefully steers her mind away from all but finding a safe place to ride out the approaching darkness of the night. After arming herself with flashlights (thank you, sweet baby Jesus, her backpack is still strapped to her back, because it could very easily have been lost during her earlier 'confusion') and securing the straps of Boodark's basket around her neck, she starts walking, her muscles protesting every step that she takes.

There's no point in trying to determine what direction she'd come from or even which way she should now go. She just turns in the general direction of that mysterious thrumming sound that she's in perpetual search of, and heads for a clear-ish path through the trees, stumps, and all the new vegetation that she's just now noticing. Tall grasses and reeds and strange orange pods. Oh, and look...there's a Gandalf stick.

She picks it up on her way past and uses it to test the depth of the water. About twenty minutes into her search, she spies a lone tree atop a tiny hill of land. Only a five-foot diameter around the tree and just barely elevated above the waterline, it's more of a bump than a hill, but it's (mostly) dry. She sighs in disappointment, but immediately takes it back and sends up a prayer of thankfulness, instead. At least she found *something*, and she is no longer foggy headed and lost. It could be worse. It could *always* be worse.

She climbs up the tiny hill to the spindly tree and hangs Boodark's basket on a sturdy branch. Biting her lip to hold back her cries of pain, she peels her backpack off. It is *not* a relief. Now that the weight has been lifted, the pain can no longer be ignored. It screams like a child having a tantrum, demanding to be seen, heard, and catered to.

But she cannot indulge it, not just yet. Boodark needs her; he's been neglected for far too long already. So, she ignores the throbbing, screaming pain in her back, her leaden arms, the fire in her legs, and her swollen, bruised feet. She really, *really* wants to sit down and cry like a child, but instead she unrolls and spreads her tarp out on the tiny section of land and secures it in place by tying it to the tree.

"Alright Boodark. Bathroom first, then we need to get some fluids and food into you." She lifts him out of the basket and gasps in dismay at the feel of his cold, clammy skin.

"I don't think I can do it, Ecko. I have no strength left in me," he murmurs, his eyes closing against the shame of showing weakness.

"Don't you have to go?" she asks. Then she frowns. "Have you held it this *whole time*?"

He weakly shakes his head. "No. You stood very still… for a long time on three separate occasions. The second time it happened, I had enough strength to crawl my way out and take care of… things. But I almost didn't make it back in time. You started running before I could make it back into my basket. I barely had enough strength to hold onto you, until you stopped again. Sorry about your shirt."

She glances down at herself and grimaces, but not at the sight of the holes that his claws had ripped into the fabric. No, it's the amount of filth that she's currently wearing that's got her cringing. But first thing's first.

"Well, if you can't take down your pants by yourself, I'll just have to do it for you. I won't look at… anything." He sighs miserably, but that's all he can do. Unless he wants to mess himself and sit in it, accepting her help is the only alternative.

"Let's get it done then," he whispers with shame in his voice.

She carries him to the other side of the tree and they 'get it over with' in a surprisingly short amount of time and with way less fuss than either one of them had thought possible. When it's done and over with, she lays him onto his blankets and tucks him snuggly into them.

"Stop feeling bad. You're not weak, you're wounded. And if I'm right, you're sick now too. Besides, I probably went all over myself… several times. There's no way I held it for what, roughly forty-five hours or so?"

"Yeah, I can't even hold it for eight hours. I definitely, at the very least, peed all over myself. Tell you what…what happens in the swamp, stays in the swamp. We will never speak of it again. But now I *really* need to hurry up and get out of these clothes!"

She pours him a bowl of water and holds the straw for him. While he drinks deeply, she drains the rest of the bottle without even coming up for air.

"Now it's my turn and I…." The world suddenly goes dark, but she's already prepared. She clicks the keychain light on and then rummages in her bag for more flashlights. She sets three of them up around their little camp and then grabs a new bottle of water and one of her clean socks.

"Now it's your turn to not look. I'm going around to the other side of the tree to pee, but I'm not staying that far away while I clean up. I want to be right here beside you, just in case… just in case of anything. Be right back."

She disappears to the bathroom area of their miniature island and takes care of her business. She can't bear the filth a single second longer and she strips off her disgusting clothes right then and there and tosses them out into the Pitch. She would gladly go naked, before she *ever* puts them on again.

Holding her hands over her private parts, she calls out, "Don't look!" and eases her way back around to the camp side of the tree. Standing just beyond the tarp, she gives herself the best sponge bath she can manage. Scrubbing at her body, she finds that not only are her hands torn up from her mad flight from the trees (something *Wicked!*), but she's also covered from head to toe in scrapes and bruises. Blisters and friction burns have formed where the straps of the basket and her backpack had dug into her skin. Every bit of her either stings, or burns, or aches, or throbs…relentlessly.

She still feels dirty and gritty when she's done with her make-shift bath, but it's all she can do against layers upon layers of dried filth, armed as she is with only one precious bottle of water. She can't afford to waste any more clean water on bathing, so she pulls her pj's on and lets Boodark know that she's finished.

"Ok, I'm decent. You can look now." She gently eases herself down to the tarp and tugs on a pair of her thick, wool socks. She feels chilled all of a sudden and that reminds her that Boodark feels several degrees cooler than he should. She decides that some soup will do him good, and so she quickly sets up one of the little stoves and canned heat. As the soup's heating, she swallows down three extra strength, rapid release Tylenol capsules.

The two of them are quiet as she spoons the soup into his mouth. They're both so exhausted, that it takes all the concentration they each can muster up to get through it.

"Not. Eating?" Boodark asks with great effort.

She gags at the thought of eating *anything* after the meal that she'd consumed earlier at her '*We're all mad down here*' tea party. "No. I'm not hungry," she mumbles.

When he's finished with his meager meal, she tells him that she needs to check his wound, clean and rebandage it, and then they could get some much-needed sleep, but he shakes his head at her. "No," he grunts. "Wait...until...Pale."

"Sleep...now," he mumbles with his eyes already closed.

She's not sure that's such a great idea, but she doesn't argue. "I guess it's waited this long, and all I can really do is clean it anyway.

But I'm checking it in the morning. I don't care if you argue about it or not."

Then she stretches out the remainder of her paracord rope and lashes everything to the tree. *Everything.* Her backpack and Boodark's beddy-bye basket, and even herself. This way, she won't roll (or get dragged) into the swamp. She won't allow the Sorrow Marshes to take a single thing more from her.

She sits up, with her back pressed against the tree, paracord looped around her waist, securing her to the immobile force at her back. Then she very carefully lifts Boodark up, cradles him in her arms, and covers them both in a mound of warm blankets.

"Rest Boodark. I'll keep you safe," she whispers.

It's a long, *long* night and Ecko is gladder then she can ever express when it's finally over and the light switch gets flipped back to the 'on' position. She'd been afraid to go to sleep, afraid of all the what if's, and so she'd resisted for as long as she could. But her body had begged for rest, and her mind had *insisted* on it, and eventually she'd had no choice but to give in to their demands.

As exhausted as she was (and still is) she still only managed a few solid hours of sleep. She could use about three more weeks of uninterrupted rest. But she doesn't have three weeks, and she certainly can't remain here, tied to a tree and perched atop a tiny lump of land… *in the middle of a swamp.*

Yeah, time to get up ('No!' her mind shouts) and get moving ('No!' her body screams) and finally find her way out ('No! Stay here' The Sorrow Marshes whisper) and never, ever look back. So, ignoring all the protests, she peels back the blankets to wake Boodark up, so they can get the day started.

Her heart stops and screams fill her mind when she sees that his eyes are open, blank, staring up at nothing. Before the screams can erupt from her mouth, Boodark blinks, and so she bursts into tears instead.

"Boodark! What is it? What's wrong? What do I do?" She sobs as she watches the almost imperceptible rise and fall of his chest.

He focuses his dull, lackluster eyes on her for a brief moment and whispers, "I falter."

Just two little words, but they blow huge, *massive* holes into her heart. "No. No, you will *not* falter. I won't let you." She lifts him up out of the nest of blankets. He's cold. He's oh, so very cold and lethargic. His limbs flop and his head lulls back so that she has to support it like an infant's. She lays him face down across her legs, and as gently as she can, she peels the bandage from his back.

"Oh, Boodark. Oh, I don't know. I think…it's bad. It's really bad. And that one, that one that was different and difficult, it's turned *blue*." She washes the angry, swollen flesh and she knows that it must hurt, but he never makes a sound. "What does blue mean Boodark? Green is good, black is bad. But what about blue?"

He doesn't answer her, and his silence pierces her heart. She's not sure that he *can* answer. She quickly rebandages him to keep as much swamp filth off of the wound as possible. After she forces some water into him and drinks some herself, she wraps him in every extra shirt she has before tucking him into his basket. Then, she sets out, moving as fast as she can through the shallow water. She *has* to get him out of the swamp...today. And she needs to find someone that can help. She refuses to lose him. She will *not* let him falter.

Three hours go by and Ecko feels like she's not getting any-where, like she's just been walking in circles. She wants to sit down. She desperately longs to take a break. But every time she peeps into the blankets at Boodark, he looks up at her with glazed eyes, dull with pain. And so, she pushes on, steadily moving forward. It's all she can do.

Eventually, she begins to hear something...some sort of clack-ing sound off in the distance. *Clack, clack!* She can't tell which di-rection it's coming from, or even how far away it is. Sounds carry and echo in weird ways in the swamp. And anyway, she can't make up her mind if she should pursue it or avoid it.

She can't imagine that it will be anything good or helpful, not in *this* place. So, she follows *her* sound, the thrumming that she feels more than hears, just as she has been all along. She follows it and ignores the clattering...until the clattering is all she can hear. *Her* sound is suddenly, disturbingly absent. Just gone, as if what-ever it is that's been calling to her all this time has disappeared. (Even that other sound, that so bad, but oh so deliciously tempting beat...the one that she'd been ignoring, is gone also.)

And the clacking is *loud* now. Like, really, *really* loud and it sounds like it's coming from all around her... *Clack, Clack, Clack!* coming *at* her from all directions. She turns in circles, trying to pinpoint it, but it's no use. The swamp twists and distorts sound… all the better to disorient intruders.

She walks on, ever vigilant, as it gets louder and louder *CLACK, CLACK, CLACK, CLACK!* Then she sees it, just up ahead. It's one of those bone men, and it seems to be stuck up in a tree. No, it's hanging by its neck from a branch, just dangling there like a morbid, macabre Halloween decoration. And it's clacking and chomping its teeth at her, as if it's starving and she's breakfast. The closer she gets, the faster it chomps, *ClackClackClackClack!* and now it's reaching its one good arm towards her, its fingers trying to clutch her, but grasping only air.

She refuses to think about where that other arm is right now, as she wades through the water, even more carefully than she had been. No way is she going anywhere close enough to be grabbed, but she almost *wants* to. Get near it, that is. She feels a deep pity for it, and she wishes there was something she could do for it…. At the very least, she could let it down, but then it would come after her. She can't run and she can't fight. And Boodark's her main priority, anyway.

So, she turns her face away and determinedly ignores it as she passes by.

A short, terrified scream erupts from her mouth as the bone man's missing hand grabs her ankle. Then she realizes it's only a tree branch, submerged and hidden in the water. "Stupid," she mutters as she continues on her way. She wants to get so far away that she will no longer be able to hear those clickity clackity teeth.

But now she has no guideline in which way to move, no internal sound-map to point her in the direction she needs to go.

Before this moment, she'd resented the pull that those two opposing beats had on her soul, but now that they're gone, she wants them back. And where are all those little drawn in the dirt arrows, the stick and twig markers set up to boss her around and tell her which direction to turn? Where are they when she actually needs them? Whoever had been sending the messages had apparently given up on her, because she hasn't seen a single message since before the Madar-gens incident.

She feels more alone now than she ever had before. More alone than when she'd lost her family, because there had been so many other people around, whether she'd wanted them there or not. And then there'd been Charlie, her angel guardian, and he'd brought a bit of the sun and warmth back into her life. More alone than when she'd first arrived here on this vampire world. She'd been too shocked and scared to feel alone then.

And soon after, she'd started hearing/feeling the thrumming inside of her and the arrows had started appearing, so *someone* had been there, watching her. For good or for bad, she couldn't say, but they'd been out there, somewhere.

Then Boodark had come along to fill in the cold, empty void of loneliness. But now he's hurt and he's sick, and he's depending solely on her to make him well again.

Her thrumming sound has gone quiet. Even the message-leaving watcher has abandoned her. Alone. She is alone, and it's an emptiness that she's never known. Throughout all her life, she thought she knew it well, but come to find out, she'd never really understood it at all. At last, she understands. Orson Welles once said, 'We are born alone, and we will die alone.' And that is the loneliest, most desolate and sorrowful truth she's ever faced.

EPILOGUE

Samara

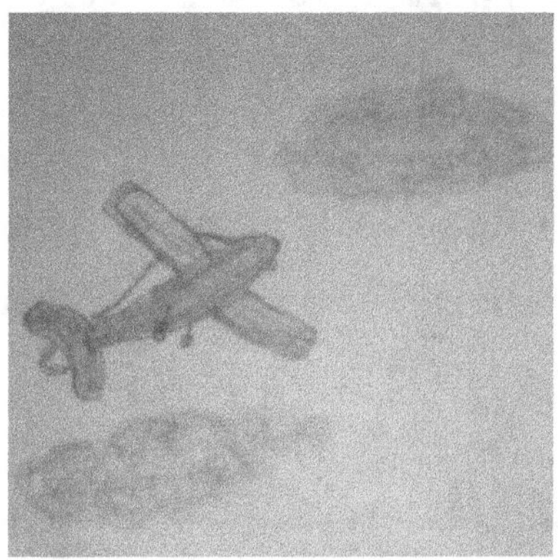

The manmade, air-flying beast charges down the runway, gaining speed with every passing second, rolling faster and faster and faster so that when it raises its snout up into the air, it has enough momentum for its huge steel ass to follow. Everything between the two, from nose to tail, begins to rumble and shake. Samara slams her eyes shut and clutches the armrests as the great metal beast lifts off the ground and makes its way upwards, higher and higher. The belly of the beast, where the passengers are held, rattles and rumbles and shakes in protest, as if it has ingested something unpleasant that doesn't agree with it. She's convinced that she, along with every other passenger, is about to be expelled. Violently.

She grunts as the beast finally reaches its designated altitude and levels out. The shaking subsides, but that does little to convince her that all is well. She trusts only one creature in existence, and that's herself. She loathes the necessity of putting her life in the incapable hands of others. Especially humans. Samara is the only one that cares enough about Samara to ensure Samara's survival. And humans are idiots. Period.

Her entire life, she's dreamed of flying. She's longed to soar across the skies, to fly so high that the world below becomes a small, insignificant thing. *This* is not how she envisioned it. Not at all. This isn't flying. She grits her teeth as the air flyer shudders and jerks from turbulence. No, this isn't flying. *This* is something else entirely. This is downright unpleasant and almost scar….

"Now don't you worry. There's nothing to be scared of, pretty little lady."

Her eyes snap open and she glares pure hostility at the nearly decrepit old man that had dared to interrupt her inner musings. He smiles reassuringly as he reaches a gnarled, wrinkled hand out to pat hers. Ugh. She hates old geezers. She lets her Shadows rise up to fill her eyes, turning them black as demon pitch. Her lips pull back away from her teeth in a snarl as she hisses at him like an enraged, feral cat. His face pales, losing every trace of color as he jerks his hand back.

"There, there, silly little man. There's nothing to be scared of," she mocks with a malicious grin as she quickly raids his mind for his secrets and hidden fears. She doesn't have to search long. Her

Shadows delve right into a time of battle, of raining blood, and thick, squelching mud. And screams… so many screams.

It was a time of war, back when he'd been a young man in his prime. Oh, what perfect little nuggets of horror he'd witnessed in the sweltering heat of the Vietnam forests! Earthlings, weak and dumb though they may be, can be every bit as ruthless and sadistic as she, even if most of them are sorely lacking in imagination.

"Isn't that right," she croons. "There's absolutely nothing to be afraid of. Is there, *Max the Ax?*" The man pales even further at her use of the nickname that he'd believed, that he'd hoped and prayed, would stay buried deep in his troubled past. He swallows hard as he fumbles with his seatbelt, and she can't help but giggle as he lurches to his feet and scurries down the aisle to search for another seat, a safer seat. He didn't even wait for the seatbelt light to go out!

Silly Max. *No* seat is safe from her. Mr. Robert Greyston can attest to that! Her hapless travel companion steadily rocks back and forth, muttering under his breath some nonsense about canceling himself. She ignores his useless rambling as she delves deeper into Max's pain.

"There's no escaping me, Max," she whispers, her voice reverberating throughout the old man's mind as she continues to root through his most traumatic experiences. She forces him to watch along, memory after dreadful memory, making him relive each and every atrocity until his mind is nothing but a cesspool of remembered horrors. Still, she trudges on, dropping each new tidbit into the pot of fear stew that's brewing in his mind. Each relived nightmare becomes an added ingredient, dropping down into the pot, one after another, until it becomes a thick, chunky, goulash that's oh, so bitter to the taste. They plop into the rot-broth, the backsplash rising up to lick at the sides of his mind.

Samara gleefully stirs the pot; stirs, stirs, stirs as the old man's tears sprinkle in like seasoning, adding flavor to the simmering fear stew that's brewing in his head. Her Shadows amp up his emotions, churning and agitating it until at last, it boils over and his mind breaks. He no longer sees his current surroundings. He sees lush, green forests, rain, blood, and gore. He smells the foul stench of it, tastes it upon his lips. He huddles in his seat, his mind convinced that he's hunkered down in a dirt pit with the what's left of his platoon…two other war-beaten soldiers, squatting down and shivering in a mud hole, hiding from their enemies.

She's still giggling to herself when, ten minutes later, the seat-belt light does go out and the passengers get up and begin to move about. Bored with Max and his silly war games, she turns her attention to them instead. She sends little wisps of her Shadows into anyone that walks past her, entertaining herself as she raids their minds and spies on all their most secret thoughts.

That's when she sees *her*, a woman who looks so much like herself that it could be… Is that…? Is that *Ecko*? Has her twin managed to find a way back? And she's *here*? Now? Oh, what fun!

But alas, this is not her dear, sweet sister, after all. This woman's hair is not quite as fiery red, the curls not nearly wild enough. Her eyes are blue, not vibrant green and flecked with silver, as if the stars are dancing in their depths. Her nose is all wrong too. It's too broad, and the tip doesn't tilt upwards like it should. Everything else though, it's just like the woman that stares back at her from the mirror every morning as she carefully applies her own makeup. It's no wonder she'd though it was Ecko.

Well, this woman may not be her sister, but she will nevertheless pay for her sister's crimes. Oh, how she'll pay. If only they had more time... They'll be landing in Texas all too soon. She better hurry. She loathes being rushed, but this time it just can't be helped. Surely, this woman is a gift, sent just for her. It would be a shame to let this opportunity pass by without having a bit of fun. Let the games begin!

She retrieves her Shadows from the other passengers, quickly reining them back in so that she can send them into her doppelganger instead. She wants to know every secret, unveil every single fear that she harbors. She'll learn every detail of this woman's life … before she takes it away from her.

The Shadows surround the woman, whose only crime is that she too closely resembles her bothersome twin. They swirl around her, slithering across her skin, feeling her, tasting her, getting to know her on the outside before they delve inside for the good stuff... the intimate details. *Amber, her name is Amber,* the Shadows whisper as they take control of the woman's mind and limbs.

"Well Amber, sit back down and buckle up. This is going to be a most unpleasant ride... for *you*," Samara laughs. The Shadows obey their mistress, forcing the woman to lower herself back into her seat as she picks through the general information of who Amber is. "Twenty-seven years old, youth counselor at a summer camp, teacher's aide, wilderness guide… blah, blah, blah. Boring! You might as well *be* Ecko, Miss Goody Goody, my booty don't stink Amber. Come on, give me something to work with," she mutters as the Shadows delve deeper. ""Hmm, now this could be interesting."

Amber, she discovers, had gone on a teacher's training trip and is now on her return flight back to her home and her boyfriend Alan… who is *not* he man she'd spent last night with. Apparently, she's not the good girl that she tries so hard to make everyone believe she is. She's had a long string of lovers, of one-night stands and dirty little trysts that she's kept secret for years.

Samara rifles through these memories, noting that all the men were prime examples of the human male species. Handsome men with well-built, muscular bodies that the little slut loved to run her hands over. She stops memory surfing to watch a particularly steamy session, watching as Amber takes all of that male hardness into her gloved hands, wrapping her leather-clad fingers around it before…wait. "Why are you wearing gloves, Amber? Why are you *always* wearing gloves?"

She rushes back through the memories, man after man after man. Amber wears the gloves with *all* of them. Butt-ass naked, rolling around under the covers, pushed up against walls, in back seats, watching herself in a mirror's reflection while she's on her hands and knees with her ass up in the air, lying on a thick carpet in front of a warm, crackling fire in a fireplace, or leaning back with her ass on the edge of a swimming pool, a man's blonde head buried between her thighs…she's never without those gloves.

But it's not just the sexual encounters. She always, *always* wears them. She's wearing them now, even. Samara ransacks the poor woman's brain, speeding through memory after memory in search of answers. "Why? Why do you wear the gloves?" she murmurs. "Come on, give me something I can play with."

She sifts through the memories, traveling backwards through time, watching as Amber grows younger and younger, the gloves still present, just in smaller sizes and brighter, youthful colors... happy colors, meant as a distraction to hide the underlying ugly truth. Oh, it's an ugly truth. Of this, she is certain. She can feel every emotion that Amber feels as she tugs those gloves on, day after day... for *years*. Fear, pain, anger, and shame. So much shame.

"What are you so ashamed of?" Samara whispers. "What did you *do*?" The Shadows continue their work, scrolling through the memories like they're flipping through television channels, rejecting movie after movie... until at last, they find the one that she's searching for.

"There you are," Samara sighs as she settles herself more comfortably in her uncomfortable seat and hits 'play' on the memory movie in Amber's mind. It's too bad that they don't serve popcorn on these air-flyers. Oh well, peanuts and pretzels will have to do.

Amber whimpers as whatever demon has hold of her raids her mind, forcing her to relive things that she tries so hard to keep buried. "No, no, no, no...not that one. Please, I don't want to remember!" But the demons that have possessed her have no mercy. They *want* her pain. They crave her shame. She turns her head to stare sightlessly out the window as the tears trickle down her cheeks. She does not see the sky or the clouds lazily drifting by. She sees the events of *that* day, the day that shaped her entire life.

Samara watches as a fresh-faced, sixteen-year-old Amber receives her very first kiss from her very first boyfriend. She watches as the love-struck girl gets stars in her eyes as he shares his strawberry ice-cream shake with her. She feels how her tiny, rose-bud nipples tighten and the heat pools deep in her belly. She watches as the school bell rings and they say their goodbyes, tagging along as the infatuated young woman skips home, her tender, hopeful heart pounding with its first taste of love, her body on fire with lust for the very first time. Young Amber hums to herself as she goes about her evening chores, and she wears a silly grin as she does her homework. Her eyes are dreamy and far away as she eats dinner with her strict, staid mother. She sways to a beat that only she can hear as she clears the table and quickly washes the dishes.

"Goodnight, Mother," she calls in a singsong voice as she places a kiss on her mother's wrinkled cheek and then dashes up the stairs to her bedroom. She does not notice how Mothers' shrewd eyes follow every move she makes.

Young Amber gets ready for bed and slips under the covers, sighing dreamily as she whispers her love's name. But sleep refuses to come. She tosses and turns, turns and tosses. She cannot quiet her mind long enough to fall asleep. Her body is not her own tonight, and she doesn't understand it. She can't stop thinking about the boy's lips pressed to hers. She can still taste the sweetness of strawberries as his tongue slipped into her mouth, stroking against her own. She does not know what compels her to do so, but she slips her hand into her panties where there's some sort of wet, scorching fire. She closes her eyes and gasps as her fingers press into that wet heat…

Thwack! She cries out as a belt strikes her hand and across her hips. Her eyes snap open. Mother stands beside her bed, belt held at the ready and trembling with fury. "I knew it!" her mother snarls. "I knew you'd been rutting with some filthy boy. Whore! I could smell the sin on ya! Git yer hands outta them panties! Git out 'ta bed!"

But she doesn't give her a chance to comply. Mother grabs her by the hair and drags her out of bed, dropping her to the floor. "Please Mother! Please stop!"

But Mother doesn't stop. She drags the sobbing girl out into the hallway and down the stairs, stopping only when she reaches the cellar door. "Tell me, girl, and do not lie. Who was it?" she demands.

"It was just a boy at school, Mother. It was nothing! We just shared some ice cream and then he kissed me. That's all! It wasn't wicked!"

"You didn't lay with him? You didn't spread your legs for him? He didn't push himself inside you?"

"What?" Amber gasps. "No! Of course not! I swear, Mother! It was just a kiss."

Mother slaps her face hard enough that her teeth snap together and her head rocks back. "Fool!" she shouts. "That's how it starts, with just a kiss!"

"Please Mother, I won't do it again. I'll be good, I promise! Please don't put me in the dark!"

But into the dark, she goes. Mother opens the cellar door and shoves her in. "Sit in the dark and repent whilst I prepare you a bath. We must warsh away this wickedness. We must burn it out with fire, beat it from your bones with pain.

Amber cries out, "Please don't, Mother. I didn't know. I promise I didn't know!"

Mother reaches out and cups her reddened cheek in the palm of her hand. "Don't worry, dear. Mother will cleanse you. Mother will save you from your own wickedness. Trust Mother," she croons as she closes the door, sealing the terrified girl in the darkness.

Several hours later, Mother returns for her. She forces her into a bath filled with boiling-hot water, then scrubs every inch of her skin with a heavy-duty scrub brush and harsh, lye soap while she howls in misery. When Mother is satisfied, at last, that the sin has been washed clean, she allows her to crawl out of the tub. Her skin is fiery red, burned and blistered and raw. She stands on a towel, dripping wet and shivering, and even the cool air on her skin is agony. She hangs her head in defeat as Mother takes a pair of shearing scissors from the pocket of her apron, points to the toilet, and barks, "Sit!"

She obeys immediately, her tears falling anew. "There, there, child," Mother croons as she snips off the first lock of hair. "It wasn't your fault." *Snip, snip.* "I know that. You didn't know any better." *Snip, snip.* "It's those filthy, whoremongering boys! They're all the same. They'll try to poke their disgusting rods into every pretty girl they meet." *Snip, snip, snip.*

Amber closes her eyes tight to block out the sight of her beautiful curls falling all around her as Mother continues. "We'll put a stop to that! We just have ta make you ugly, that's all. It won't stop them all, mind you. They'll stick their peckers in any hole offered to them, so *you* have to be the strong one… the righteous one. Lord knows, men are weak and dumb creatures. They live to fill their own bellies with food and whiskey and womenfolk's bellies with their seed. *You mustn't let them.*"

The last lock falls onto Amber's lap and she curls her fist around it. "There now, child. It is done. You've been cleansed. We've done what we can to repel the no good, womanizing louts, to keep their lusts at bay. All that remains is your punishment for the part that *you* played with that foolish boy. I've decided on twenty strikes to your buttocks with the belt. I'm being merciful… *this time*, for I truly believe that you didn't know any better. But…"

Mother's hand darts out faster than a striking snake, hidden in the grass. She grabs her chin with a cruel, bruising grip and jerks her head back, so she has no choice but to meet her eyes. "That business in 'ta bed… *that* wickedness was all you. I don't want to do it. I dislike hurting you, but I must teach you. I am your Mother. It is my duty to squash that sinful wantonness out, to drive it away. It will take time and a fierce determination to see it through. But I have faith. I *must* have faith. You are my daughter, and I will do whatever I must to save you from your own depravity. Do you understand?"

She tries to nod, but Mother grips her face harder. "Say it," she commands.

"Yes, Mother, I understand."

"Good. Now get yourself dressed. Then go out back and pick a switch, a good, sturdy one, long as your arm, wide 'round as your thumb. You'll get thirty lashes across't your palms tonight. We'll figure out tomorrow's punishment when tomorrow gets here."

Wordlessly, Amber eases into her clothes, trying not to cry out as the cloth rubs against the oozing, weeping patches of raw skin. She turns to go, and Mother calls out to her retreating back, "Remember girl, I do what I must because I love you. Love is a heavy burden, but I bear it... for you."

"Yes, Mother."

Samara watches the next memory, then the next and the next. Amber's crazy mother had it in her head that she could beat and torture the basic, human desires right out of her own daughter. She believed that if she could inflict enough pain into Amber's hands, then her hands would learn to do nothing to offend thine eyes. There were ways and ways and ways to inflict pain on her hands and feet, and it could all remain their own dirty little secret.

No one would be the wiser, because there would be little to no marks to show the abuse.

What followed that fateful day was two years of 'cleansing'. Sadistic torture is what it really was. If there's one thing that Samara understands, *truly* understands and appreciates, it's torture, and that woman was every bit as sadistic as she herself is… and she was bat shit crazy, to boot. Amber's punishments included lashes across the palms and needles plunged into them, where the tiny, pinprick holes that were left behind remained virtually invisible. Her wrists were bound so tightly that the circulation was cut off… for hours and hours at a time. On multiple occasions, her fingerprints were singed off with a hot iron, and the bones of her hands were squeezed tight in vises. They were plunged into buckets of freezing ice water for so long that the girl begged God to let them fall off, just to end the agony. Her fingers were stretched and smashed, bent at odd angles, and shocked with waves of electricity. Tiny, thin slivers of wood was shoved under her nails and into the nailbeds.

The abuses eventually escalated. Her hands had been covered in tiny, bloodless papercuts, then squirted with lemon juice. They'd been dipped in honey and set into ant piles. She'd been forced to remove wasps' nests with her bare hands so that they got stung repeatedly during the process. The list of 'cleansing' methods went on and on, and they had steadily intensified to the point where there was physical proof of the abuses being left behind.

Her mother had eventually grown worried that she'd be discovered, and she'd gifted Amber with her first pair of gloves to hide the evidence. She'd only been looking out for herself, but Amber had taken to those gloves as if they were her saving grace. She refused to take them off… unless her mother insisted, of course.

She wore them every second between her 'cleanses". She ate with them, and she slept with them. She even bathed with them. Her mother had done her job better than even she could have guessed. She'd taught her daughter to hate the feel of her hands on her body. She could no longer tolerate the feel of her own fingers on her skin. In fact, she could no longer stand the feel of *anything* under her fingertips.

Samara smiles. She knows just what to do. At last, she has a plan on how to handle Amber, the woman who looks too much like her sister… and she'll punish the meddling Max the Ax as well. *Perfect.*

Amber unbuckles her seatbelt and moves up the aisle, lurching and stumbling as the Shadows that control her limbs make her clumsy and unsteady. She whimpers as she lowers herself into a vacant seat beside a trembling, muttering old man.

Samara quickly raids his mind again, this old man who dared to suggest that *she* was afraid… of *anything*. She sends her Shadows straight into the heart of the memory that haunts him the most. It takes a matter of seconds to find it. His mind is already turned towards it, the bloodiest day of war for him, in a land so far from his home. He's recalling the atrocities that he witnessed, he's reliving the horrors that he, himself committed… over and over again.

Max the Ax huddles in his seat, pressing his face into the window. He has no need to look, no need to set his eyes upon the newcomer beside him. He can feel the evil just beyond his shoulder, glaring at him with deadly intent. It radiates off her like a stench of sickness and rot, riding upon the moist, sweltering heat waves of this God-forsaken land called Vietnam. He cannot look, because he knows the truth of his impending death will be reflected in the eyes of the one come to kill him. The enemy has found him.

The Shadows force Amber to raise her fearful eyes to the man, but she no longer sees him. She sees her mother. Her eyes fixate on those stern, pinched lips, the disapproving scowl... and those cruel, gleaming eyes that proved she enjoyed hurting her own daughter, no matter what she said about doing it to 'save her from herself'. Those eyes are filled with promises of upcoming punishment and unspeakable pain.

"Take off your gloves," Mother commands.

Amber begins to cry as she tugs the leather from her fingers. "I've been good, mother," she whimpers. "You don't need to cleanse me anymore. I have been so good."

But Mother shakes her head. "You're lying, you filthy, rotten, diseased whore! I know what you've been doing. I know all about those men. You spread your thighs for every swinging dick that points in your direction. It's ok though. Mother will fix it. Mother is going to cleanse you like you've never been cleansed before. Trust Mother. *Now take off those gloves!*"

Samara grins and squirms in her seat as she watches Amber retrieve her cosmetic bag and remove a disposable razor. She's almost giddy with excitement as the other woman removes the blade and begins to slowly, meticulously cut, slicing a thin, deep gash in a perfect circle around her left wrist.

A flight attendant named Katy passes by and notices the strange behavior of the Shadow-possessed passengers… and then she sees the woman slice a ring around her own wrist. She's too stunned to make a move, too shocked to even call out for help as the woman gently lays the bloodied razorblade onto her tray table, shoves her fingers under the loose flap of skin, and calmly begins to peel the skin off of her own hand as if she was merely removing a glove. The gush of blood as the skin-glove pulls away from bone spurs her into action.

"Stop!" she cries out as she unthinkingly makes a grab for Amber's hand… and encounters nothing but bare, gleaming white bone that's slick with crimson blood and warm, squishy exposed muscles.

Max the Ax turns at the sound of the flight attendant's voice, but what he sees is a man from his past, a man gone insane by the horrors that they'd seen and endured, and the atrocities that they had committed. Blood Bucket Bill, he was called, and he had *earned* that name. He was a man with a very unpleasant penchant for carrying out astonishingly cruel acts of violence against the enemy… and in the end, to his own teammates.

"Let go!" Amber insists as Katy the flight attendant restrains her ungloved hand. "Mother says I need to remove my gloves for my cleansing. You're going to make her *so* angry, and then she'll have to cleanse *you* too! *Let. Go!*"

But Katy does not let go. She's petrified in place, staring in horror at the skinless hand that she's got a hold of. So, being the obedient daughter that her mother wishes her to be, Amber picks up what's left of the razor, the broken, pink plastic handle, and she plunges it straight into the interfering woman's left eye. *That* makes her let go, and as the other flight attendant rushes to her aid, Amber quickly uses the bloody bones of her skinless hand to first cut and then remove her other skin-glove. "I'm ready for my cleansing, Mother."

But Mother is not satisfied with that, not at all. "I'm afraid that just won't do, Amber dear. You're rotten on the *inside*. I tried my best to cleanse you, but the corruption runs deeper than I realized. It's festering in your heart, consuming your soul. *That* is what needs to be cleansed. I see that now. I need to get to the source of the wickedness. I need to gut it out. Take it all off. Take everything off and we'll get you better, child. Mother will make you all better."

Amber immediately pulls her shirt up over her head and then takes up the razorblade once more. "Yes Mother, cleanse my heart," she whispers as she makes the first cut on her breast.

Max the Ax watches as the enemy/Amber stabs Blood Bucket Bill/Katy the flight attendant in the eye. Blood explodes from the ruptured globe and ravaged socket. The other flight attendant rushes in to help her, but Max does not see her either. Instead, he sees Slim, the last man standing from their squad, dragging Blood Bucket Bill away to administer first aid. Max the Ax is left all alone to face a fate that he knows he can longer run from. The enemy has found him. The enemy has got him in their sights, and he realizes he can fight no longer.

His heart pounds, the sound of it reverberating in his eardrums as a painful tightness grips his chest. His vision goes grey at the edges as the world swims in and out of focus. The pain in his chest builds and builds until he can no longer draw breath. He clutches his chest, his eyes wide and full of imagined horrors as they fix on his enemy. The evil that he senses lurking inside that deceptively beguiling woman finally does him in. He sucks in one last anguished cry, the pain of it slicing through him like razor-blades. Then his eyes roll back, and he slumps forward in his seat, his head thunking onto the back of the chair in front of him. That last lungful of air gets expelled back out as a low, agonized moan of fear and pain, and he does not draw in another. The war is over for him, at long last.

Two brave men rush forward to put a stop to Samara's fun. One man grabs Amber's wrists to stop her self-mutilation while the other spins a roll of duct tape around her. He first immobilizes her by taping her arms against her chest. Then he winds the tape around her torso and the back of the seat, effectively pinning her in place so that she can no longer hurt herself... or anyone else.

Samara is angered by the interference, but she realizes that she'll have to let the nosy, fun-sucking men off the hook because the seatbelt light has lit back up and the pilot makes the announcement that they are approaching their destination. He tells everyone to remain calm and assures them all that they'll be landing safely in just a few moments. He tells everyone to remain in their seats when they come to a stop, so that the paramedics can come in and remove all injured parties first.

Thirty minutes later, Samara disembarks along with the rest of the passengers. They're all being detained for questioning, but she has no time for that… nor does she have the patience for all that nonsense. Playing with Amber had only amplified her need to find Ecko's loved ones. She has a burning desire to exact her revenge on her sister, and now that she's so close to achieving her goal, she finds that she's grown impatient. She should have done this months ago, but Earth offers so many pleasant distractions… But no more. It's time to see this thing through.

She cloaks herself and her companion in Shadows so that she can walk unseen past the security unit. Then she Shadow-wraps the two men that have been following her, so that they too can pass. Foolish men. They think they're so stealthy that they managed to sneak past the officers. They have no clue that she helped them. They have no clue that she's on to them and has been since they first started spying on her. They are a distraction, but so far, they've been a interesting one. She's not quite ready to put a stop to it. She'll let it play out for a bit longer… at least until she grows bored with them.

Samara exits the airport and grins as the fierce, humid Texas heat slaps her in the face. Even the weather is hostile here, and she immediately feels right at home. She briefly wonders if Amber will survive the blood loss. She wonders if her mind will ever repair itself if she does manage to live through her ordeal. But then she forgets all about Amber as she climbs into a taxicab and speeds towards her destination. She's got a hot date with a fancy-pantsy doctor. She can't miss that.

EPILOGUE

E c k o

Miserable to the depths of her soul, Ecko wades through the knee-deep sludge, her head bent low with fatigue and her heart heavy with unspeakable sorrows. Boodark's been crying for the past two hours, silent tears in a never-ceasing trickle, without a single word of explanation. Indeed, without a single word, period. He's stopped talking. No matter how much she pleads and begs, her loud-mouth chatterbox little friend remains silent, his words all dried up and withered away. The last words he'd said plays on a loop inside her mind. "I falter." And he is. He *is* faltering. She's losing him. If she doesn't get him out of this abhorrently vile swamp and find help, he will surely perish.

So, on and on she trudges through the thick, clinging mud that wars against every step that she takes. She has made it, finally, to the heart of the Sorrow Marshes. She does not need to be told that this is where most lose their way, their hope, and their lives. The very air is heavy with sadness and hopelessness, and broken, withered dreams dance like ghosts through the trees. There are no signs of life here, nothing to indicate life has ever been here. No buzzing of insect wings, no croaking of frogs, no splashing of creatures diving into the water to escape her trespass into their domain. No more tall, rustling grasses, nor reeds, nor pads for frogs to perch upon. The only live things in sight are the trees (Debatable. They have no leaves, no new growth) and the mosses that cling to them and hang down from their bare, spindly branches. It's gloomy here. Sad. Empty. Unwelcoming. Her heart aches with loneliness and burden.

When she stumbles onto a large stone slab, she decides to set up there just long enough to see if Boodark will eat something...at least get him to drink some water. He refuses to open his mouth for the soup, but she manages to get a tiny trickle of water into him. Not enough, not nearly enough. She lays back on the stone, just for a minute, and looks up, desperate to see something, *anything* other than marsh and mud and trees. She wants to see the sky, even if it *is* grey and bleak as the mud. But the trees have grown so tall that she can no longer see the sky. They blot out the light and drench the world in such dismal depression that even Eeyore would pack his bag and find a cheerier place in the Hundred Acre Wood to build his little stick home.

She sighs miserably and rolls onto her side to stare out at her dreary, depressing surroundings. She's so tired. Maybe she can take a nap… just a small one. Just long enough to catch a second wind. Maybe they could just stay here, set up camp, get some *real* rest and then get a fresh start in the morning. Maybe….

A loud '*Creeeaaakkk*' sound and a slow, almost imperceptible movement from the corner of her eye puts a stop to thoughts of resting and makes her sit up. A tree stump, covered in a thick layer of dark green moss is *moving,* twisting itself in her direction. *The trees really are coming to life,* she thinks as her heart speeds up with apprehension. But when a pair of bright blue eyes suddenly pop open, she can see that it's a *person,* blackened with mold and filth and covered in patches of lichen and slimy, green algae. A GloomDoom, it *has* to be. Boodark told her that the swamp was full of them. And *this* one's staring right at *her*! So clearly can she make out the shape of him that she wonders how she hadn't been able to see it before. The roots below him aren't growing *down* into the swamp as tree roots do, but up *out* of the water. They latch onto him and anchor him down, rendering him immobile…. Just another stump in a world full of tree stumps. Now she's wondering just how many of the 'stumps' that she'd passed right by without a second glance had been people… people lost to the Sorrow Marshes.

She stares at the closest one… (*Please* be a tree stump!) So close that she can reach out and touch it, *if* she had the slightest desire to, that is. Which she *doesn't*. It very well could be a person under all those tangled roots, contorted into some painfully twisted position. She leans in, peering intently…. Brown eyes full of tiny black root/veins pop open. A mouth stretches wide in a silent, horrified scream, a blanket of moss covering its tongue and sprouting from the cracks between its teeth.

"Time to go Boodark," she announces as she hastily straps her bag back on and settles his basket back in place. Whether the GloomDooms had intended it or not, they'd probably just saved her from their very same fate, because in the moments before they started waking up, she'd wanted nothing more than to just sit there on that rock and give up, at least for the rest of the day. They'd set her mind right back where it needs to be... in terrified, 'get the heck out of here' mode. Because fear is now the only thing stronger than her sorrow. Boodark isn't the only one faltering. She is beginning to lose her hope, succumbing to the whims of the spirit that dwells beneath the Sorrow Marshes. Fear is the only thing strong enough to drive her now. Fear for Boodark, fear of failing and the two of them becoming permanent residents of the Sorrow Marshes force her to put one foot in front of the other. But they're slow, grudging steps as she continuously checks on Boodark's condition. She knows, in her heart of hearts, that she won't make it out of the swamp if he falters.

She's crying too and has been for a while now. She can't stop it. The tears steadily pour from her eyes and drip down her face. The GloomDooms wake and turn towards her as she plods by, their stiff wooden joints creaking from having lain dormant for so long. She doesn't even look at them anymore. She no longer cares if they sleep or if they wake. She's not sure she would care even if they got up and started following her. She doesn't so much as flinch when she suddenly plunges into mud so deep that it brushes against the bottom of Boodark's basket. What does it matter that it's become so thick that it's like trying to walk through a deep pool of cold molasses? Why should she care how long it takes to complete each step? She's not sure she cares about anything at all.

The way forward is so *hard,* but she refuses to stop, refuses to stand still, even for a moment. She no longer remembers or even cares *why* she must keep going, she just subconsciously knows that she must. And although her steps only move her forward an inch at a time, and inch forward is still forward. It's still moving. She has not stopped, and she has not *yet* given up all vestiges of hope. Not quite yet.

She pushes the shirt swaddling aside to peek in and check on Boodark. She *hates* that unfocused gaze that just stares up at her, stares *through* her without seeing. She loathes his quiet, his stillness, and his tears that just won't stop coming. It's *wrong.* He should be flying beside her right now, laughing at her ignorance and hurling insults, calling her a big dummy. He should be asking if they can stop to eat again, pestering her about what they'll eat when they finally do stop.... *if* she will ever take pity on him and stop trying to starve him. He should be driving her crazy with his endless inquiries about Earth food and foodorators and flowers and elastic and plastic. Not to mention his insatiable curiosity about movies and television. No, this cannot be the end of all that. This cannot be the end of Boodark the Great, Boodark the Fearsome, Boodark the Annoying. Boodark.... her piggy little orc-bat friend.

She strokes his hair, sobbing and pleading, both of their faces so wet with tears it seems like there are faucets inside their eyes and someone's left the water running. She doesn't know what to do and she goes into full-on, hysterical panic mode when his eyes suddenly roll back into his head, nothing but the whites visible. And then he's convulsing, his body tensed and jerking with seizures. She snatches him up out of the basket... he's choking! He's choking on his own swollen tongue! She thrusts her finger into his mouth and dislodges it, pulling it out of his throat to clear his airways. She ignores the teeth that cut her finger to the bone as she holds his tongue down so that he doesn't bite it. She sobs from the torment of watching her friend die in her arms. Because that's what's happening, isn't it? He's faltering right before her eyes and she's just standing there allowing it to happen. She rages inside at being useless and powerless to help him. He won't stop convulsing, his poor body tensed with one spasm after another.

"What do I do? What do I *do!*" she whisper/yells. She's helpless and desperate and she feels absolutely *crazed* inside. Her magic flares to sudden, intense life and her hands tingle for one brief moment as the world around her plunges into a Pitch of her own making... a Pitch that she can see clearly in. It's not true Pitch, it's merely the magic affecting her eyes, making it look as if the world's gone dark.

She blinks at the trees around her, trying to figure out what her magic is up to this time. She has about half a second before the 'weird' kicks in to wonder what her eyes look like with this new facet of her magic. And then she couldn't care less about what they look like; all she cares about is what they're *doing.* She throws her arms out for balance as her eyes begin to oscillate. It feels like her pupils are quivering, vibrating on high speed. Everything is dancing, shivering in place. The trees, the GloomDooms, each strand of moss… they tremble and quiver as if the entire world is some sort of snow globe and God is shaking it to wildly rattle the contents.

She glances back down to the little bundle in her arms and he's the only thing that's not trembling and vibrating. He's gone oh, so still and silent. Is he…? Is he…???

And *now* she starts screaming. She's screaming and screaming and just *screaming.* She throws her head back, and all that pent-up anguish and fear and rage bursts out of her mouth and pours up into the air in a black cloud of desperation. It's as dark as anything that Samara has ever produced. It fills the sky and it spreads, threatening to engulf the entire world with her grief… and for a moment she's glad. For this one single moment in time, she welcomes the destruction that the churning, roiling black cloud promises. For a moment, she wishes that it was all over. Oblivion promises a soft, comforting peace. She nods once with complete acceptance of her upcoming destiny, a fate of *her* own making. She pulls Boodark in closer, cradling him against her chest. "Let it come," she whispers as she closes her eyes and smiles. "Let it come."

Dear Reader,

I feel the overwhelming need to apologize. I never meant to leave you hanging, as I've had to do. When I wrote Ecko in the Dark, I never intended to leave Ecko wandering, lost in the Sorrow Marshes. I never meant to leave the fate of her orc-bat buddy, Boo-dark the Wounded, unknown and unresolved. As for Samara… well, *she* is out of control, and even I can't tame her.

This second book in the Mirror Walker series originally contained 320,000+ words. That's double the length of what it is now. I had to split it into two separate books. The good news is, because I had to split it, book #3 is already completed! So be assured… Ecko won't be lost in the swamp for much longer.

If you've stuck with us this far, you know that we still have a long way to go, but things *will* get better. They may get worse before then, but Pale always follows the Pitch. The dark can't last forever.

So, this is my apology letter. I know things seem hopeless right now. I am sincerely sorry for the way that I have left things. But it's also a promise, too. Ecko won't be lost in the dark forever. If you can bear with us, we will find the light. Together.

I promise.